Popularity
Rules

ABBY McDONALD

arrow books

Published by Arrow Books in 2009

2 4 6 8 10 9 7 5 3 1

First published in Great Britain in 2008 by
Arrow Books
Random House, 20 Vauxhall Bridge Road,
London SW1V 2SA

www.rbooks.co.uk

Addresses for companies within The Random House Group Limited
can be found at: www.randomhouse.co.uk/offices.htm

The Random House Group Limited Reg. No. 954009

A CIP catalogue record for this book
is available from the British Library

ISBN 9780099533894

The Random House Group Limited supports The Forest Stewardship
Council (FSC), the leading international forest certification organisation. All our
titles that are printed on Greenpeace approved FSC certified paper carry the FSC
logo. Our paper procurement policy can be found at
www.rbooks.co.uk/environment

Typeset by SX Comping DTP, Rayleigh, Essex
Printed and bound in Great Britain by
CPI Cox & Wyman, Reading, RG1 8EX

For my mother, Ann – for everything.

Prologue

Nobody knew exactly where *The Popularity Rules* first came from. Some said it was a gift from the bitter pen of an ex-beauty-queen mother; others swore it was the work of a group of jaded New York socialites. Whatever the origins, it surfaced at Camp Kellerton, Maine, one muggy August afternoon when a homesick camper begged off swimming. Crawling into her bunk to cry (for crying is the main pastime of plump and lonely sixteen-year-old girls) she discovered a battered journal tucked into a nook behind her bed.

Reading the faded calligraphy under her covers by torchlight that night, the forlorn girl was remade. Back home in Larch Springs, Indiana, she dropped twenty pounds, dyed her hair and (with the mere mention of the words 'drugs' and 'gang feud') convinced her parents to switch her to another high school across town.

Pretty and confident, the new girl made a group of lasting friends, was elected to the student council and won early acceptance from her first-choice college in California.

The summer after graduation, that camper returned to Kellerton as a counsellor, and on the first night – after pledge songs had been reluctantly sung and the reality of communal showers was sinking in – she gathered the eight sullen teenagers of Cabin Freedom and passed out photocopies of the rulebook that had changed her life. Eight girls a session, three sessions per summer. As the years passed, high schoolers

1

became college grads and twenty-something women clambered their way up the career ladder, yet still those pages remained a staple of life at Camp Kellerton.

The Popularity Rules. How a girl can get whatever she wants.

All's fair in love, war and popularity.

Whatever they told you is a lie: grades, good behaviour and hard work mean nothing. Popularity is the only prize that counts.

The popular kids get an easy ride their whole lives. Not because they're special or smart, but because they know how to lie and cheat and manipulate their way to the top. Popularity isn't friendship, it's power and status you can use to win everything you want. Why settle for cast-offs? Become popular, and everything else follows: the homecoming crown or the corner office, it makes no difference. If you want to get anywhere in life, you've got to play dirty.

> The meek don't inherit a thing.
> Nice girls win nothing but regret.
> Virtue is wholly overrated.

> If you don't do it, some other girl will.

Chapter One

Never fall in love with a rock star. That's what Katherine Elliot's mentor had said on her first day at *Think Louder* magazine: never fall in love with a rock star and carry pepper spray at all times. Alan was gone now, of course, and Kat was no longer the same wide-eyed girl whose hand shook transcribing notes from her first big interview, but she did her best to impart that wisdom to all the other new hires.

If only they would listen.

'Are you OK?' Kat wanted to use the toilets before the main act arrived on-stage, but a weeping blonde blocked her way to the cubicles.

'Wha . . . what?' The girl raised her head long enough to fix Kat with a pathetic stare, blue eyes smudged black.

'Jessica, isn't it?' Kat recognised her latest intern under the wispy fringe and moved closer. 'What's wrong?'

Jessica sniffled. 'You wouldn't understand.'

'Try me.' Kat might not share the intern's penchant for hot-pink mini-dresses, but she knew a thing or two about broken hearts.

'It's . . . it's over!' Jessica broke down again. 'He said he, he needed some space. And, like, we were better off apart. And . . . !' Burying her head in her hands, Jessica resumed her sobs, this time louder than ever.

No, they never listened.

As Jessica shook with lovelorn sorrow, Kat looked around

for support, but they were still alone in the dark tiled bathroom with nothing but the low hum of the air-conditioning as interruption. 'Let me guess,' she murmured, stroking the girl's shoulders in comforting circles. 'He's in a band, and things are really happening for them, but he's *so* committed to his music, it just wouldn't be fair on you to stay together.'

'How did you know?' Jessica blinked at her in surprise.

Kat tried not to laugh. 'Just a hunch.' She passed a handful of tissues, wondering if things ever changed. Twenty-eight was too young to feel this jaded, but in a world populated by barely legal ingénues in leggings and 'vintage' nineties denim, Kat was practically ancient. 'Clean yourself up and go enjoy the show, and don't waste any more time crying over him,' she advised. 'There are hundreds of guys like that in London. I bet he'll even come crawling back once his major label deal falls through.'

'Right, he will, he totally will.' Jessica brightened.

'That's not a good thing!' Kat exclaimed, but the intern wasn't listening.

'Devon's probably just scared.' She turned to the mirror and set about repairing her eye make-up. 'You know, with the intensity of it. He did say he'd never felt this way before.'

'Right . . .' Kat was still spinning from the girl's sudden mood change. 'Wait, did you say Devon?'

Jessica glanced down, faux-coy. 'Devon Darsel. You can't tell anyone; we've been keeping things quiet.'

'I bet you have.' Kat's sympathy quickly dissolved. Devon was notorious on the scene: the pale-faced lead singer of a hotly tipped rock act, he was the kind of tortured artist who could make even the most bitter journalists start gushing things like 'Shakespearean eloquence' and 'air of dissolute tragedy'. He also had a penchant for the *Think Louder* interns. Kat shook her head, watching Jessica hopefully apply another layer

5

of electric-blue mascara. She was getting off lightly; the last junior writer to enjoy Devon's affections had fled back to Birmingham with nothing but a broken heart and a suspicious burning sensation to show for her grand love affair.

'Thanks Kate,' Jessica beamed, surveying her reflection one final time. 'You're the best.'

'It's Kat,' she corrected, but the girl had already sashayed back into the bar, no doubt in search of another boy to break her heart. 'And you're welcome . . .'

As career planning went, serial seduction wasn't bad; it was certainly cheaper than plying writers with cocaine like most of the other edgy Brit-rock bands. But as Kat reluctantly wandered back into the main room of a too-cool East London bar, she had to admit that Devon didn't need to stoop to those kinds of tactics. No, The Alarm were actually going to make it, unlike the opening act that night. It was an invite-only industry showcase, so the room was thick with air-kisses and skinny jeans, and everyone was ignoring the poor performer stranded on-stage with her electronic keyboard and a single spotlight.

Taking pity on her, Kat found a corner of relative calm and began to make notes until a PR girl swooped into view.

'Hiya!' Oblivious to Kat's reluctance, the girl leaned in and bestowed the ubiquitous air-kiss, almost falling out of her white vest in the process. 'Oh my God, you're not drinking!' she exclaimed, eyes wide. 'Let me fix that.'

'Don't worry, I never drink on the job.' Kat shrugged. The glossed pout dropped open.

'Never?' she echoed, her mind clearly boggling as she tried to comprehend a work-night without hilarious tequila black-outs and vaguely consensual hook-ups.

'Never.' Kat repeated with a small smile.

'Oh.' A frown, then recovery. 'So, like, enjoy the show! I know you're going to love these guys. They manage to capture the harsh nature of inner-city deprivation and urban struggle with incredible insight.' That last sentence was recited with such a flat edge that it had to have been ripped from the press release. 'Anyways, it was great to see you – we must catch up sometime!' The girl stretched her lips into another gleaming smile and then was gone, leaving Kat in a cloud of such insincerity, she felt her teeth itch from the aspartame.

Soho or Shoreditch, it made no difference: the scene was always the same. Hipsters, scenesters, general '–ers' of the week – the trends changed with dizzying speed, but the core of uber-cool chameleons remained, parading around the VIP section like it was a personal catwalk. At first, Kat had found them an amusement, but years of being ignored by the same faces at every show had left her uneasy and a little resentful. She didn't have to put up with it, she knew, but whenever she was tempted to quit music journalism for an industry where people had principles, convictions even, all Kat had to do to restore faith in her chosen profession was cue up her favourite song in the world.

On the bus, in the office, even hiding in the corner of a car-crash event like this, there was one song that could restore her sanity, her belief in music as something more than a fleeting background soundtrack or pretext for a shallow, drunken party like the rest of the piranhas here tonight. Abandoning her notebook and the chatter around her, Kat slipped her headphones in place and for a few moments, escaped.

Soaring chords, heartfelt lyrics and a melody she could feel shivering behind her ribcage; it swelled, surged, broke like nothing she'd heard before, or since. The reclusive singer, Eliza Monroe, had released only one album in the last decade, and her tiny, self-run label ignored every one of Kat's impassioned pleas for an interview, but somehow that just added to the mystery. It was the one track Kat could never capture in a few well-crafted phrases, the piece of magic she had yet to convey printed on the page.

But God, she loved to try.

The keyboard girl had long since fled the stage when Kat spied her friends through the haze of artful bed-heads and violently straightened fringes.

'I'm late, I know!' Whitney flung her oversized leather bag down on the narrow banquette and gave Kat a warm hug. 'The grant meeting ran on for ever and by the time we got the notes finalised . . . Never mind.' Peeling off her suit jacket, she happily surveyed the room. 'God, I love these things. Thanks for getting me on the list. Have I missed anything?'

'Not at all.' Kat didn't understand Whitney's fascination with the scene, but having her as a plus-one was better than sitting in the corner alone all night. 'Hi, Nate.' Kat made room for one of the online editors from work.

He collapsed beside her with a groan, idly scratching his two-day stubble. 'There better be a fucking open bar!'

'Keep dreaming,' Kat teased. 'There was some promo vodka doing the rounds, but that lasted oh, five whole minutes.'

'You're kidding.' Like half the other men in the room, Nate was sporting a plaid shirt and thick, black-framed spectacles. Kat assumed they were aiming for a hip, Buddy Holly-esque look, but personally she thought they were more akin to a collection of geeky Canadian woodsmen. 'Don't they know alcohol necessarily equates to good reviews?'

'Maybe they want the act to be judged on talent alone,' Whitney suggested, pulling her red curly hair back into a ponytail. Kat and Nate burst into laugher. She gave a rueful grin. 'Perhaps not.'

'You know, it's good we've got Whitney around,' Nate slung his arm around her shoulder, creasing her spotless white shirt, 'to remind us how cynical we're getting.'

'She's still so wide-eyed and enthusiastic,' Kat agreed.

Whitney raised an eyebrow. 'Says the woman who can't find joy in anything.'

Nate snorted. 'She's got you there!'

Kat shrugged. 'That's me. Ageing, bitter, in need of caffeine . . .' She nudged Whitney.

'All right! I'll get this round if somebody else goes to the bar.'

Nate pretended not to have heard.

'I will,' Kat offered with a sigh, levering herself out of the booth. 'I have to hunt down a girl about a thing. Usuals?'

'Please.'

Spotting her target across the room, Kat swiftly cut through the crowd and accosted a tall, reed-thin woman draped with jet black jewellery that matched her Bettie Page haircut.

'Lacey, what happened with the Duval interview?'

The woman broke off conversation with her tiny blonde friends and blinked at Kat.

'You told me Monday at four and they called at lunch today with her waiting on the line,' Kat explained. 'I looked like a complete idiot.'

'Oh.' Lacey flushed. 'Sorry.'

'It worked out OK in the end, but I don't have time for your mistakes. I could have been out on another job.'

The group exchanged looks. Lacey tried to steer her away, 'Why don't you give me a call next week and—'

'It can't be hard to get a simple date and time straight.' Kat stood her ground, remembering her panic when the call had come through. She'd fumbled her way through the interview with a mouthful of tuna salad and no prep notes at all. Surely it couldn't be asking too much for everyone else to do their jobs with a vague sense of competence?

'Look, I can't do anything now, but if you just call—'

'You'll be lucky to get her in *Think Louder* at all,' Kat noted. 'She's not high-profile, or buzzed any more. And the last album's sales were awful.'

Lacey narrowed her eyes, and Kat remembered too late that she'd been working publicity on that release as well. 'I'm sorry,' Lacey finally admitted, looking at Kat with new resentment. 'Look, I'll sort you time with Mindwarp next week to make it up, OK?'

'Fine.' Kat was already turning to leave. 'Just make sure to get the details on this one right!'

The bar was a dense tangle of limbs, as always, but she managed to find a familiar face at the far end.

'I'll let you in if you give me notes on that last act,' Jackson bargained, already sweaty in a blazer and hopefully ironic Robbie Williams T-shirt. He freelanced for some of the daily free-sheets: distilling hours of events into a few alliterative sentences to be discarded on Tube seats and pavements.

'Deal.' Kat squeezed into place beside his short, stocky frame and flipped through her notes. 'It was electro-funk, "*As if Maroon 5 and David Gray bred a stillborn mutant.*"'

'Ouch.'

Kat allowed herself a smile. 'The next lot won't be much better – white boy hip hop. And I have to interview them afterwards.'

Jackson snorted on his beer. 'You're kidding me. Rob's

letting you near that lot without protection? For them, I mean.'

'I know, I didn't think so either.' Kat frowned, still wondering how she'd fill half an hour of conversation with a gang of rappers. To say it wasn't her area of expertise would be an understatement; she doubted there would be much feminist analysis to be had from songs like 'Mo' Money in Da Southside Hood'. 'But it's a last-minute thing for this issue. He pulled our centre spread at the last minute.'

'What's going on with *Think Louder*, anyway?' Jackson wrinkled his brow. 'The last couple of issues have felt different.'

'They have?' Kat paused. Her magazine was a relic in the industry, she knew: the lone hold-out in an era of flashy commercial titles, and the only place Kat could turn in an extended exploration of domestic abuse in classic folk and not get laughed out of the office. 'I thought we'd just settled down again.'

'Maybe it's nothing.' Jackson waved her concerns away. Kat began the epic task of getting the barman's attention as a group hustled loudly into the space beside them.

'Jackson, my man. What's up?'

Kat waited on the edge of the crowd while a complex series of macho back-slapping and fist-bumping ensued. The men were a strange mix of nerdy music critics and over-styled media types, but there was a lone woman glittering in their midst with enough poise to make Kat wish, for the first time, she was wearing something smarter than her usual work uniform of jeans and a band T-shirt.

'Kate,' the girl finally cooed, fluttering her fingers in an approximation of a wave.

'Jessica.' Kat felt a bite of resentment at the girl's cooler-than-thou routine. Thirty minutes ago she'd been sobbing in Kat's arms, and now she was acting as if they'd barely met?

11

'So what's this I hear about you and Devon Darsel?' One of the men, whippet-thin with black jeans and a pointy little face, nudged Jessica.

She blushed. 'Oh, nothing really. We hung out after his last show.' Carefully, she swirled the cherry in her Martini, never hinting at her earlier heartache. Kat rolled her eyes and turned back to the bar.

'So is it true, about his thing for bondage?' Whippet Man snorted. Kat would have thrust a limb somewhere soft, but Jessica just giggled and swirled her drink some more.

'I don't kiss and tell.' She tilted her head and smiled at him while Kat hovered, somebody's shoulders pressing into her back.

'Aww, c'mon. We've all heard the tales.'

'Yeah, tell us the gory details.' The men closed in on Jessica. They tried to stay cool, but Kat could see their faces light up with an eager glow, awaiting news of their icon. This was, after all, about as close as they'd ever get to Devon's wayward rock 'n' roll lifestyle.

'My lips are sealed,' Jessica proclaimed, beaming at the attention. 'He was a total gentleman.'

That was too much. 'You know, if you don't want to wind up weeping in the women's bathroom, maybe you should stay away from wanker rock stars like Devon.'

Whoosh. Suddenly everyone's head snapped around, and Kat found herself on the receiving end of half a dozen disapproving stares.

'What?' She shrugged defensively. 'It's true. That was never going to end well.'

Jessica narrowed her eyes at Kat, but her lower lip began to tremble.

'It's OK, Jess.' The men closed rank around her protectively. 'Don't worry.'

12

'Let's go.' Whippet Man shot Kat a dirty look from under his trucker hat. 'I heard XS are having their after-party at Soho House – you can all be my guests.'

'I only meant that—' But even Jackson was looking at her like she'd started kicking a small puppy, so Kat just admitted defeat and murmured, 'Excuse me.'

She paid for the drinks and slipped away, a sting of rejection in her step. Bad enough that music writing was such a boys' club, where she was doomed to feel like a perpetual outsider simply by virtue of her breasts, but when Jessica just waltzed in and acted like they were all back in the school playground again . . .

Kat swallowed back her anger. It couldn't be helped. She'd grown up with role models: Liz Phair, moody and complicated on the cover of *Rolling Stone*; Courtney Love (back when she was a rock goddess and not a pharmaceutical case study), and her mother, now a renowned professor of feminist history. Girls like Jessica may have been only five years younger, but they'd only ever seen perfect, polished pop singers out on stage, or indie rock 'chicks' adored more for their thigh-high boots than their musicianship. Was it any wonder they were such drama queens?

'There you are!' Whitney relieved Kat of her glass of white wine just as a sharp-suited executive began to introduce the big act. 'Here, I think it's starting.'

'. . . And so, I'm thrilled to introduce the hottest new urban act on the planet. The fresh, the great . . . G-Link!' Throwing out his arms, the exec finally stepped aside. The tiny stage darkened, anticipation grew, Handel's *Messiah* boomed out in the crowded space until finally the spotlight went up to reveal a trio of skinny white boys, layered under an avalanche of puffy sports gear and shiny silverware, baseball caps casting shadows over their pimply faces.

'Yo yo yo!' They cried, twisting their fingers into arthritic gang signs. 'Check it, make some noise. Woooo-eeee!'

Kat slumped back in the booth. It was going to be one of those nights.

It was only when the barrage of bling, beats and basic misogyny had been playing for thirty minutes that Kat finally gave up her hope it was actually a satirical statement and not, well, sincere. But as the Michelin men swaggered off-stage – low-slung jeans miraculously still clinging to their adolescent arses – she had to admit the truth: they were for real. And, most likely, set for multi-platinum, worldwide success.

'I have to go now,' she apologised to Whitney. 'My deadline is ridiculous.'

'Don't worry.' Whitney looked past Kat to the assorted crowd. 'I'm going to stay around for a while. But I'll see you tomorrow? Everyone's coming.'

'Of course!' Kat promised, collecting her things. 'I can't wait to see the new place.'

As she made her way backstage, Kat ran through the performance again and wondered how she was supposed to interview those boys with a straight face. The printers were waiting for her copy, so she'd have to bluff something together, maybe hope that they would—

And then Kat caught a glimpse of a woman, fifteen feet away in the crowded room. Honeyed, shiny hair spilling over a pair of familiar blue eyes that widened in recognition. They both froze.

'Kat?'

She couldn't hear a sound over the thumping beats, but saw the woman's lips move to make the word nonetheless.

Kat's blood turned to ice. The years fell away, and suddenly she was sixteen again, sullen in a scratchy woollen blazer and green plaid kilt. She blinked, but the apparition stayed there, glowing a dull golden even under the harsh fluorescent lights. And then, finally, her paralysis broke. Kat ducked back into the crowd and lost herself in the mess of drunken laughter.

She didn't look back.

'How long must we forgive in the name of hot beats?'
Jessica Hopper

G-LINK interview transcript

(START TAPE)

KAT: I'm going to record this, OK?

VOICE ONE: Sure thang, girly.

VOICE TWO: Can I get a mineral water over here?

VOICE THREE (assistant): I'll go. Anyone want anything else?

VOICE FOUR: I could get me some of yo fine ass!

(LAUGHTER)

KAT: Can you just introduce yourselves?

VOICE ONE: I'm Daryl P, this is ma main man Flava, and Triple A next to you in the corner.

KAT: No, I mean, your real names. For the record.

VOICE TWO: I'm sorry. I'm Samuel Goldstein, that's Daryl Birchford and Triple A is otherwise known as Anthony Adams-Allworth.

KAT: And how did you get the nicknames?

SAMUEL: These be our street IDs.

DARYL: Yeah, need to have tha props for shout-out stylings.

(PAUSE)

KAT: (AUDIBLE SIGH) Right.

DARYL: And that over there be my muscle, P-Dog.

KAT: Oh. Does he always stay during interviews?

DARYL: Where I go, he goes. Ever since Flytown tries to bust my ass, I gots to have my muscle.

KAT: Flytown?

DARYL: We was cruisin', jus' chillin', you know? And BAM! Outta nowhere they comes and tries to take us down. Croydon massive gettin' nasty.

SAMUEL: Fo real, them mo'fo's askin fo' it. Beyotches.

(MUFFLED LAUGHTER)

KAT: (COUGHS) Umm, sorry.

SAMUEL: Yo bitch, where's my water at?

KAT: So . . . Daryl, why don't you tell me how G-Link got started? Where did you meet?

DARYL: On tha streets, fo' real!

KAT: Which streets?

DARYL: Middle S-to-the-E-X, sexy baby!

KAT: Middlesex?

SAMUEL: Hell yeah! We bunked off and hooked up, right to the top!

DARYL: Ma man!

KAT: OK . . . Tell me more.

SAMUEL: Simple, me an' Daryl, we be at school. Link up, drop some beats, check tha rhymes. All good.

KAT: And which school was that?

DARYL: (MUFFLED)

KAT: Sorry, I didn't get that.

DARYL: Harrow.

KAT: Oh. Isn't that where Prince Harry went?

SAMUEL: Whatevs. And then Triple A comes through and we all like, word. Now it's straight to the top, right bitch?

(PAUSE)

KAT: Please don't call me that.

SAMUEL: Say what?

KAT: Bitch. I prefer not to be spoken to like that.

DARYL: Don't you go getting all PC on our asses. Niggaz jus' tryin' to represent.

KAT: But you're not.

DARYL: Huh?

KAT: Niggaz. You're representing rich, English white boys.

SAMUEL: Whatever, beyotch.

DARYL: Dyke gettin' nasty!

(PAUSE)

KAT: Moving on. What's the new record about?

SAMUEL: It's about the street, man. Abouts the babes and the bling and the BAM-BA-BAM BAM!

DARYL: Sho' nuff nigga!

KAT: OK, I'll be more specific. The single, 'Hell Yeah' – what's the story behind that?

SAMUEL: (RAPPING) Bitch be all what?/ like 'please oh baby'/ Get me on top jus' y'all try 'n' stop me/ Turnin' her around/ Wave that ass in the air/ Bitch be yellin' no but I'm sayin' hell yeah!

DARYL: Hell yeah, hell yeah!

SAMUEL: Bitch be yellin' no but I'ma sayin' hell yeah!

DARYL: Yeah!

SAMUEL: Alright! Take it maxed out baby!

(PAUSE)

18

KAT: So the song's about rape, then.
SAMUEL: Nah! She be lovin' it.
DARYL: Bitch need some thug lovin', aight.

(SOUND OF MOVEMENT)

DARYL: Hey, where's you goin'?
KAT: I've got enough material.
SAMUEL: Baby, stay a lil while. G-Link wanna play.
KAT: No thanks.

(MOVEMENT – A STRUGGLE)

KAT: Get your fucking hands off me, idiot.

(LAUGHTER)

ANTHONY: Hell yeah.
DARYL: All right, beyotch. That's one fine ass you gots.
KAT: Sexual assault. Nice. You realise this is all being taped, right?
DARYL: Fer real? P-Dog! Get the fucking recorder!

(A SMASHING SOUND FOLLOWED BY LAUGHTER)

SAMUEL: Whatcha gonna do now, bitch?
DARYL: Now get over here and work it.

(SOUND OF AN AEROSOL SPRAY FOLLOWED BY ASSORTED SCREAMS)

ANTHONY: What the fuck?!

DARYL: My eyes! P-Dog, where are you?
SAMUEL: It stings, it stings!
DARYL: Mummy!

(END TAPE)

Ditch the superiority complex.

You probably think you're way above the cool kids, that you're smarter to stay out of the petty social games they all play. I bet you tell even yourself you wouldn't want to be popular even if you could be, like they're the ones wasting their time with flirting and fashion.

Wrong.

Are you happy out on the edge of the crowd – excluded from everything? Do you like sitting on your own, eavesdropping on gossip from parties you were never invited to? Didn't think so. You want to believe you're so much better than them, but in the end, you're the one who winds up miserable and alone.

Chapter Two

'Anton? Anton, can you get out of there?' Kat hammered uselessly at her bathroom door. The shower had been running for half an hour, but now silence had descended and there was no sign of life. 'Anton, please. Some of us have lives too, you know!'

God, she hated her flatmate.

'What you yelling about now?'

Kat spun around. Anton was leaning against his bedroom door, naked save a pair of tight, greying briefs. He scratched at his crotch.

'Put some clothes on.' Kat shuddered at the dark clumps of hair springing out of his pasty chest. 'And tell whoever's in the bathroom that hot water is not an infinite resource.'

'Tell her yourself,' Anton shrugged, hand still lingering by his balls. 'But you might want to be nicer. Kasia's . . . kind of sensitive.' His pinched face spread into a smirk, one dark cowlick draping over his forehead.

Kat despaired. 'Picking up teenage girls on depression chatrooms isn't some kind of achievement! You know, you—'

She was interrupted as the bathroom door swung open, steam drifting out around a painfully skinny girl. Wrapped in Kat's towel, she clung to the fabric with bony hands, a procession of pale scars spiralling up her arms.

'Hi,' she breathed, blinking back and forth between Kat and Anton. 'Sorry I took so long.' She scurried past Anton into his bedroom, revealing a scroll of black ink on the back of her neck.

'There,' Anton smiled at Kat, the kind of smile that made her want to scrub her skin away. 'All yours.'

Slamming the bathroom door on him, Kat prayed for a few last drops of hot water. She tried to think of living with that man as research – like forcing herself to read the *Daily Mail* – but ever since he'd made the blinding discovery that mental instability made a woman more likely to sleep with him, he'd been impossible to bear. Apparently, the internet was swarming with pale, self-harming girls with a taste for light S&M and complete arseholes; Kat couldn't leave her room on the weekends without finding some poor thing cutting her dry slice of toast into nine equal squares or, most often, just weeping softly over *The Bell Jar*. She littered the living room with Samaritans flyers and copies of *Female Chauvinist Pigs* but it made no difference. Anton was scum, and she was trapped by the marginally affordable rent.

Oh, the bargains she made . . .

By the time she emerged from half an hour in the steam, the flat was empty. Empty and blissfully silent. Kat wandered absently back to her large, cluttered room, wondering again if it was worth moving. Living alone was still an impossibility on *Think Louder*'s meagre wage, but surely she could find a decent human being to share breathing space with – one who did the dishes before the crust began to mould, who didn't watch porn all afternoon in the living room, who maybe even possibly had a soul. Right. All that within reach of a public transport line to work? She could dream.

Casting a brief look at the stack of bills and anonymous receipts cluttering her dresser, Kat quickly dressed in the nearest pair of clean jeans. She'd set aside today for some serious financial planning, but even Suze Orman's encouraging smile couldn't tempt her near that doom, so with a quick tug of her fingers through tangled hair, she grabbed her laptop bag and headed for the bus stop.

If only she'd discovered a burning passion for management consultancy like all her Oxford classmates, Kat mused, ignoring the pack of squat, feral boys behind her attempting to dismantle the swings in the community playground. Or at the very least, a burning passion for a management consultant's lifestyle sufficient to smother any creative leanings; then, perhaps, she might not spend approximately forty-three thousand minutes on, or waiting for, buses every year. Of course, she would have become a loathsome, City-suited consumerist bitch, but that was the price you paid. Even Whitney's devotion to the environment was supported somewhat by the large amounts of grant money she was tossed every time a new report about melting ice-caps or rural drought was released.

Love, as her mother insisted on repeating, was sacrifice, and so Kat settled for Zone Six ex-council blocks, Anton's sleaze and professional fulfilment. And reading all her journals and books in Borders, rather than buying them herself. Without fail, Saturday found her snuggled in a velvet-covered armchair on the top floor, while irritated shoppers eyed her prime window spot and hovered, hoping to drive her away. Amateurs. Kat could make a syrupy coffee last half the afternoon.

She always set this time aside to brainstorm, but today her subject came easily. Kat began to smile as she considered her latest project: a cutting new article about the rock star-groupie dynamic as a manifestation of sexual inadequacy fears. And her main case study? Devon Darsel.

The words took shape on her screen, her encounters with Jessica and Anton's latest conquest still fresh in her mind. The imbalance of power, the undertones of exploitation obviously hiding deep personal insecurities – this kind of material was her forte, but three thousand words later, even an extravagant slice of cake and the lush strains of a Broken Social Scene soundtrack weren't enough to distract Kat from the restlessness in her veins.

As her eyes drifted over the same paragraph yet again, she saw a pair of teenage girls squashed together on the couch only feet away, their heads bent together over a magazine in a riot of dark and pale curls. Dressed in denim, summer vest tops and armfuls of plastic jewellery, their voices spilled over each other in a rush of youth and enthusiasm.

'Shhh! I do not!'

'You so do, and I'm going to tell him!'

Watching them, Kat finally allowed herself to think of the blonde woman at the bar, and those blue eyes, widened in surprise.

Lauren Amelia Anderville.

There had been a time when the two of them had been so close. Inseparable. For years they had been each other's only warmth in that cold, red-brick boarding school, while Kat's mother was off accumulating academic glories and Lauren's father dominated various European investment banks. The American misfit and the English mini-feminist: they were an unlikely pairing, but together, they worked. A warped mirror-image of each other with uncontrollable brown hair and sullen, blue-eyed stares, they'd stood together against the girly cliques and macho bullies, sneaking lunch breaks away down in the woods and hiding out by the reservoir with old Brit-pop cassettes and copies of *The Handmaid's Tale*. They'd been equally hated and equally alone, but together, school became almost bearable.

And then they'd turned sixteen, and everything had changed.

Kat felt a tightness in her chest just remembering it. It was silly, to still feel the pang after all these years. After all, people changed, friendships drifted away; it was a basic human truth, and Lauren had just been Kat's first, painful lesson in the way the world worked. She never discovered what prompted the change. Blonde hair, contact lenses and brand new clothes – as makeovers went, there was nothing original about it, but when Lauren had walked into the dull, grey-walled dormitory after the summer holiday, Kat could hardly believe her eyes. And the transformation wasn't just on the outside. Inseparable became semi-detached; friends-for-ever became friends-until-she-upgrades-you. Soon – too soon – they didn't speak at all.

Kat swallowed another sip of Frappuccino and wondered what Lauren was doing in London. The last she'd known, the other girl had headed back home after sixth form with her parents, to their sprawling estate in North Carolina, and a life of shining blonde perfection as the debutante she'd sworn she'd never be. Kat had followed her own path to university, vowing never again to trust somebody who sold out to mindless social hierarchies and spent five minutes blotting lipstick. And for the past decade, she hadn't.

Shaking away old memories, Kat turned to her laptop and the article at hand. For once, Devon would get what he deserved – in print, at least. She may not be able to put a dent in his sleazy hipster ways, but if the girls of London had fair warning . . . Well, she held out hope that not all of them were Jessicas, tripping eagerly along the path of drama and self-destruction. Somewhere in this city there must be girls who cared more about dignity than a top-ten digital download hit. And this, like most of her writing, was for them.

Five hours later, all of her noble thoughts about passion and sacrifice were paling beside sheer, unbridled envy as Whitney whisked Kat through her new flat.

'And this is the second bedroom, but I'm thinking of using it as an office-slash-yoga room.' Whitney waved at a beautiful, small room with cloud-blue walls and a skylight. Kat bit her lip and tried not to demand how much all of this cost.

'The kitchen came fully fitted, of course, but I'm not sure about the flow, so I might tear it out and knock that wall through.' Leading them past a cluster of people nibbling hors d'oeuvres, Whitney presented the next room. 'What do you think?'

Kat studied the gleaming work surfaces, brushed steel appliances and dark-green tiles and tried not to whimper with longing. Her flat was furnished with the mismatched shelving left by the last occupants, her only extravagance the Ikea folding dining table set. 'I think it's all . . . lovely.'

'Did I hear you say you were thinking of more renovations?' A wan blonde looked past Kat without a flicker of recognition. 'Because I'm looking for a new contractor and it's a nightmare trying to find someone reliable.'

'Don't get me started,' Whitney exclaimed, her plump cheeks flushed pink as she reached to pour herself a glass of wine. 'It was an epic saga finding Yevgeny. I still wake up sometimes panicking about damp-proofing!' She looked back to Kat, 'Oh, sorry, you know Erica, right?'

Kat tried to smile. 'I think we were all at Oxford together.'

'Were we?' Erica blinked with pale, clear eyes. 'I can't say I remember you.' She laughed lightly. 'But you know how it is – so many faces!'

'Of course.' Kat echoed. As she recalled, Erica had sat next to her in tutorials for an entire year. 'What are you doing now?' she added politely, as Whitney disappeared to play hostess to another group of arrivals.

'Oh, I'm in consulting,' Erica answered, her gaze drifting past Kat to the hallway. 'I own a boutique firm specialising in ethical business practices.'

'You mean not all businesses are ethical?' Kat joked, but Erica just looked at her vaguely. There was a pause, and Kat prepared to roll out her own response about music journalism and the magazine, but Erica didn't ask.

'Sweetie!' A petite brunette woman barrelled towards them, somehow covering Erica in air-kisses despite the fact that her face only reached the other woman's shoulder.

'Lou!' The vague expression suddenly became animated. 'How was Nairobi? Did you visit the Jamia Mosque like I said?'

Kat drifted towards the food as the two women began to exchange their tales of international travel and fabulous local cuisine. Whitney's crowd were the complete opposite to the rock-scene hipsters, but Kat sometimes felt just as out of place; only instead of lacking a ridiculous mismatched hipster wardrobe and a DJ/film-making side-project, here she was the only one without air-miles and a mortgage.

She loaded her plate with tiny puff pastry casings and an array of salads and meandered through the flat again, searching for a familiar face. She'd met some of these people, she was sure – at one of Whitney's dinners or drinks parties – but gathered in small cliques, armed with wine glasses and laughter, they all seemed anonymous. Soon, she bored of scanning titles on Whitney's neat bookcases and arrived back in the kitchen, lingering on the edge of Erica's group.

'So tell me about your work, Kat.' When they finally finished discussing the delights of Kenyan cuisine, the petite woman turned to her. 'Whitney mentioned you were in journalism.'

'That's right.' Kat tried to remember her name. Louise, that was it. Married to Ahmed, the lanky investment banker over by the bookcase. 'I write about music.'

'Lucky you.' Lousia's smile was perky and bright. 'I love classical.'

Kat played with her fork. 'I stick to rock music, mostly, some indie.'

'How exciting!'

Ahmed appeared behind his wife, interrupting. 'But the whole industry's in turmoil, so my media brokers tell me. Share values plummeting.'

'A lot's changing,' Kat agreed pleasantly. 'But it's great for the performers, that they're not dependent on big corporate labels any more.'

Ahmed chuckled. 'I don't think you'll sound so happy when you check your pension plan.'

Pension? Ha. Kat was reminded of her money planner, still untouched back at the flat. She pressed on. 'But there's a real revolution going on with new technology and ways to get music heard.'

'I'm all for downloading,' Whitney announced, joining them again. 'I think it's far better for the environment.'

There was a murmur of agreement from Erica. 'I hadn't thought of that, but you're right – none of that packaging going to landfill.'

'Just imagine if more entertainment was available in non-physical product.'

'Exactly. It could really make a difference, not just in the disposal, but a cut in production.'

'All the factories, the shipping . . .'

'Maybe someone should commission a study?'

Kat silently ate another puff. She'd felt like an old woman at the show last night, but now it was as if she were a teenager, restless in the midst of lives that bore no resemblance to her own. What thrilled them? she wondered, letting her gaze drift around the room. What quickened their pulse and brought them a stab of fierce pride? Was it a well-received sustainability report? The arrival of their organic produce box? Did Erica get the same hot joy from planning her new bathroom renovations as Kat felt seeing her words in print? Or was the order and neat stability enough in itself for her to feel as if life were as she planned?

'. . . Don't you think, Kat?'

She blinked, settling back in the conversation. Three guesses what was being discussed. 'Not so much,' she ventured, tired of staying politely silent.

Louise widened her eyes. 'What do you mean?'

Kat saw Whitney bite her lip, but didn't hesitate. 'Personally, I don't really believe in the environmental drive. I mean, of course global warming is a problem, but this endless rush to offset carbon and use cloth bags?' She gave a small snort. 'It's ridiculous. Think about it: a drop in consumer energy use will never even equal a percentage point of the developing world's growth, so why even bother? Just a way for people to try and claw back an illusion of control about their lives and the future.' With a shrug, she crunched down on a celery stick.

There was a pause.

'Kat's always been the provocative one,' Whitney

awkwardly announced, and Kat immediately felt bad for making a scene. 'Forever picking a fight, isn't that right?'

Louise gave a polite laugh.

'Valid point, I suppose.' Ahmed nodded carefully. Kat wasn't too concerned about his validation, but she held back another retort.

'How about dessert?' Whitney clapped her hands together, as Kat calculated how much longer she should stay before making her excuses. 'I have some wonderful roast peaches, from a farm down in Surrey. I bought them at the farmers' market just the other day.'

Bitches never win.

⊗⊗⊗

Take a lesson from history: strong, opinionated women always get screwed over in the end. The world is packed with vile and useless people, but if you keep picking fights with them, you'll be the one who suffers. If you make people feel bad about themselves, they'll be waiting to stab you in the back. Men can't stand being cut down to size, so find a way to deal with assholes and idiots that doesn't mark you out as a bitch.

Once you're popular, you can show your ruthless side, but until then, act like a Texan beauty queen and be Miss Congeniality at all times.

Chapter Three

'Way to go, Kat. You outdid yourself on that G-Link piece.' Nate tipped his fingers in a mock-salute as he greeted her on Monday.

'How does it look? I haven't seen it yet.' Catching her breath, Kat pulled off her jacket and shoved aside the pile of letters and printouts on her desk. Anton had been having loud sex with some unfortunate girl in the living room all morning, so Kat had been a prisoner in her own room until the amateur porn had finished. She was un-showered, un-fed and wholly uninformed.

'Here.' Nate pushed a shiny new copy of *Think Louder* in her direction. Kat collapsed at her desk, grabbed a stale muffin from her bag and eagerly began to flick through. Reviews, news, ads . . . There it was!

She paused, mid-bite. 'Mac kept everything?'

'Yeah, that was kind of . . . surprising,' Nate agreed, idly flipping through his mail.

'No, it's great,' Kat chewed slowly. 'I just thought he would, you know, edit it.' She scanned through the article again, but there it was: word for word as she'd written, the G-Link transcript in all its hilariously awful glory. She'd hoped it would get past their editor's red pen, but Kat had never expected it to run untouched. She brightened. 'Maybe he's finally settled in and is willing to take some risks.'

'Could be.'

'He's nixed a load of my stories lately,' Kat continued, thinking fast. In fact, Mac had been visibly recoiling from anything stronger than puff profiles for months. 'But I'll pitch some of them again. God knows this magazine needs a little edge back.' She glanced over at the corner office. It had been exactly a year since Alan had died, but she still half-expected the old editor to burst out, complaining about too many five-star reviews. 'Where do you think you work?' he would yell, screwing the pages up and lobbing them good-naturedly at the offending author. 'Is this the *NME*?'

But those days were over.

It had been sudden; that was something at least, Kat told herself. A heart attack one night as he watched an old *Have I Got News For You?* episode; the way his wife told it, the sight of Boris Johnson had just been too much for him to take. Kat still couldn't smile at that. She knew that as deaths went, it was one of the better ways to go, but 'better' could never be the right word for the hole it had ripped through her. By the time Alan was buried, there were already five candidates clamouring for his job, and while Kat could have fought for it, she was still reeling. Besides, she was too young and too female to stand a chance, and editing would mean she'd never have time to write another article again. That wasn't the life for her.

Rob Mackenzie was the least offensive of them all – as a deputy, he'd at least served time on the magazine, unlike the *GQ* wannabes who eyed the corner office with such blatant ambition – but it wasn't the same. Long-time writers drifted away, Mac packed the payroll with dirt-cheap graduates and interns, and the sharp, irreverent tone that had set *Think Louder* apart for so long was slipping into the same inane flattery and breathless hype as every other magazine and blog around.

It would never be the same.

Kat busied herself with email and eating until Warren, another writer, slunk by with what looked like a killer hangover.

'Good night?' Nate called.

'Hell yes,' Warren's stride became a swagger. 'Haven't slept for days. The things some girls do when there's a video camera around . . .'

Kat rolled her eyes. 'And yet you still moan about never meeting "nice girls". Did it ever occur to you that you're looking in the wrong place?'

'Like you can talk,' he replied, eyes rimmed with red, no doubt from another night off his head on ecstasy. 'When's the last time you got laid?'

'I'm not the one who thinks naked bodies are hairless and gravity-defying,' she retorted.

'You mean they're not? What the fuck?' He rolled his eyes.

Kat saw the copy of *Maxim* under his arm and despaired. 'How many times do I have to tell you – exposure to porn increases sexual aggression and reduces sympathy to rape victims. There are studies!'

'Was the rape victim a feminazi dyke? 'Cause I can see their point if—'

'People.' Nate cut them off with a groan. 'Give it a rest. It's early, you know?'

Warren held his hands up. 'I didn't start it!'

'Mature,' Kat informed him, and began to deal with the pile of paperwork awaiting her. As usual, there were stacks of submissions from bands all hoping to be catapulted to most-hyped next big thing. Kat scanned half a dozen hyperbolic press releases and pushed them all into her waste basket. Just once, she'd like to get something written with a little honesty:

'Meet Killing Time! The band is a bunch of arrogant, unoriginal arseholes, but our label bosses signed them in an overhyped frenzy, so if this record doesn't shift fifty thousand units, we'll all be laid off by Christmas.' There, that would be a marketing angle she could get behind.

And then there was Oscar.

Kat allowed herself a smile as she slit open the envelope and pulled out a sheet of heavy cream writing paper. The letter was a dying art, he'd proclaimed in his first fan-mail last year; email was the domain of punctuation-free, porn-hungry idiots, and thus he would write properly as the greats of literature intended. Kat had filed him under 'eccentric and possibly unstable', but the elegant missives, scattered with quotes from Dorothy Parker, Mae West and de Beauvoir, had turned into the highlight of her month. They certainly beat the rest of her reader correspondence, an imaginative array of 'UR a dyke!!' to 'lay off the alarm, they're like, so amazing and your just jelous and old and I HATE YOU.'

Today's missive was brief, just a few lines in response to her last feature on sell-out second albums. ' "When dealing with people, remember you are not dealing with creatures of logic, but with creatures bristling with prejudice and motivated by pride and vanity." – Dale Carnegie, American motivational writer (1888–1955),' he wrote. Pride and vanity: that sounded about right, Kat thought, as Jessica drifted into earshot.

'Jessica Star. S-T-A-R. Like the lights, in the sky?' she was sighing into her mobile phone. Her lurid neon-green tunic barely skimmed her crotch, leaving a long expanse of leopard-print leggings before the prerequisite three-inch heeled boots came into view. 'I'm from *Think Louder*. Uh huh. And can I get a plus-one?'

'Jessica?' Kat interrupted loudly.

The intern rolled her eyes. 'What?'

'I need today's clippings.'

'Yeah, all right, in a minute.' She began to turn away.

'No, now.' Kat crossed her arms. 'You know, I shouldn't even have to ask.' Jessica pouted at her, but snapped her phone shut. 'I was sorting the post and doing clippings packs for a year when I started,' Kat added. And she'd done it with dedication and good humour. 'It can't all be guest-lists and after-parties.'

'Fine.' Jessica pursed her glossy fuchsia lips and glared. 'Can I, like, go now?'

'Be my guest.' Kat waved her towards the photocopier and wondered, yet again, when she would find an intern whose sole aim in life wasn't bedding half the brooding musicians in London. 'And when you're done, can you—?'

'Kat!'

Jessica waltzed away with a smirk as the editor's bellow echoed out across the cluttered office. Nate looked at her expectantly, but Kat waited, resentfully flicking through the rest of her mail. She wasn't a pet poodle; if Mac wanted to talk to her, he could ask.

'Kat?' The yell came again from the corner office, other staffers falling silent until only The Alarm's latest stadium anthem could be heard on the stereo. Kat remained in her seat.

'Will someone find that fucking girl and tell her to get the fuck in my office?' Mac blazed out onto the main floor, his thick Scottish accent hoarse.

'Did you want to talk to me?' Kat asked pointedly, finally getting to her feet.

'No, I want to rip off that fucking head of yours and use it for goal practice,' Mac boomed. 'My office, now!'

37

Kat sighed, carefully picking her way across the room. As a monthly title with a small (if devout) readership, *Think Louder* inhabited not a towering glass and chrome fortress, but a ramshackle warehouse in an area of East London yet to be gutted by developers and filled with overpriced boutiques. Kat had a full range of Indian take-out options for the (many) nights she ended up working late, but it made workplace health and safety a distant dream.

'So,' she began, edging into the dark, messy room. Alan had always run an open-door policy, but Mac was liable to scream his head off should she dare step foot inside without due deference. 'What did you want to discuss? The Duval piece should come together, and I've got a lot of ideas for—'

'What the fuck were you playing at?' Mac turned, and Kat saw for the first time that his face was stormy. 'You crucified them, for fuck's sake!'

She paused, confused. 'G-Link? I have the tapes. They smashed the first recorder, but I always keep a second one running. It's there, practically word for word,' Kat added. 'And they can't sue, because it was self-defence. In fact, they're lucky I didn't press assault charges against them.'

'Lucky?' Mac repeated. He threw the magazine down on his desk with obvious rage. 'We'll be bloody lucky if MegaBeat ever let us in spitting distance of any of their acts!'

Kat bridled. 'Well, what was I supposed to do – write a empty puff piece? After *that*?'

Mac collapsed heavily in his chair. 'You could have shown a bit of . . . restraint.'

'Why?' Kat challenged. 'They're a bunch of pseudo-street, pro-rape wankers! And anyway,' she folded herself onto the rickety chair opposite, 'if you had such a problem, why didn't you cut it, or call me?'

Mac's eyes shifted. 'That's not the point. You've made things fucking hard for us.'

'Things were already hard,' Kat said quietly, thinking of their sliding circulation figures. If print media was in its death throes, music magazines were practically in the ground.

'So why in God's name did you fuck it up again?'

'Wait a minute,' Kat protested, indignant now. 'This isn't new – this is what I do; it's what I've always done. I don't fall at a band's feet in mindless worship and I don't hold back when they've got it coming.'

'No, you don't,' Mac agreed with obvious regret. He took a file from the stack beside him and began to leaf through. 'June 2007, Alex Baker complains when you call him 'lecherous and perverted'.

Kat smiled faintly at the memory.

'March 2008,' he continued, 'Dalton James initiates legal proceedings after you allude to drug use.'

'They were dropped,' Kat pointed out quickly. 'Both the photographer and tour manager saw him shoot up.'

Mac quelled her with a glance. 'And last month, the business with those DJs and the underage models.'

'Come on, it comes with the territory, you know that. Alan had a whole freaking wall of complaints.' Literally. He framed them as a point of pride, but Mac had taken the lot down, leaving them surrounded only by peeling old rock posters and a much-changed print schedule.

'And Alan had a bloody personal fortune to run this magazine!' Mac put his hands together and looked at Kat, his face faintly mottled. 'Surely you understand, Katherine, you're not a kid. You just can't pull this kind of shit any more.'

Sitting perfectly still, Kat tried to stay calm. 'So why didn't you stop me?' she asked again. 'I copied you on my email; if there was something wrong, you could have called and had me rewrite.'

Mac looked shifty. 'I was away from my computer.'

'Where?'

'Away.'

'That's right,' Kat finally remembered. 'Prague. A stag do, wasn't it?' Her voice was icy.

'I shouldn't have to play nursemaid,' Mac blustered.

She glared back, unmoved. 'But you should check copy before the issue closes. If there's a problem with the G-Link piece, it's your fault, not mine.' With anger bubbling in her veins, Kat got up to leave. Of all the incompetent, blame-dodging, weak little—

'I'm putting you on probation.'

'What?' She spun back.

'Another cock-up like this and you're gone, you understand?'

Kat struggled to find words. 'You go off and get hammered, and I'm the one to blame?'

Mac's frown hardened into a deep crevice. 'I'm doing you a favour here. I could fire you right now, but I'm giving you a chance to get it together.'

'Thanks, boss.' Kat's voice was thick with sarcasm. 'I'm glad my years of service are worth something.'

'Damn right!' he bellowed. 'They're the only reason I haven't kicked you out that door already!'

Kat caught her next yell before it left her lips. 'Like I said,' she spat, taking every last measure of self-control not to slam the door in his face on her way out. 'I appreciate it.'

Storming out of the building, Kat spent the rest of the day 'working remotely' in Starbucks. If she had to even look at that pathetic excuse for an editor . . . Instead, she drank half her bodyweight in Frappuccinos and revised her groupie story. It was shaping up well: biting, sharp and full of scorn for the legions of rock-god wannabes and their messiah complexes. She made a note to send a copy to her mother when it was done; Professor Susanne Elliot (BA, MA, PhD) would appreciate it, she was sure.

'You had a few calls,' Nate reported when she dragged herself back to the office that evening to pick up some copy-edits. 'Jessica left them on your desk.'

'Thanks.' Kat scanned the indecipherable pink post-it notes. Her super-intern really was going above and beyond. Sighing, she dialled the first number that wasn't smudged beyond all recognition.

'Hello?' She picked at a hang-nail and scanned her emails on-screen. 'You called earlier? This is Kat Elliot.'

'Kat? Finally.' The voice was American, smooth and butter-soft, and right away, Kat knew. 'They wouldn't give me your cell. It's Lauren, Lauren Anderville!'

For a moment, she couldn't speak.

'I don't know if you caught me, but I was at the showcase thing the other night.' Lauren sounded breezy and utterly relaxed, but just the familiar tone of her voice was enough to make Kat's chest ache with a dull pain. 'Anyway, I figured we should catch up now I'm in town. I'm over here for work until Christmas, at least. I'd love to hang out!'

'No, I didn't see you.' After a few agonising seconds, Kat finally recovered. She sank into her chair. 'It's . . . good to hear from you.' The image of Lauren, polished and chic in the bar last night, was branded into her memory. So was the last time she'd seen her – over ten years ago. But she wasn't going to think about that.

'Want to get together?' Lauren pounced. 'Would tonight work?'

'Tonight?' After twelve years of silence? Swallowing back a hysterical laugh, Kat quickly tried to think of an excuse. 'I have a gig I need to review.'

'If you don't have time for dinner, let's do dessert and drinks!' Lauren exclaimed. 'Where's the show?'

'Out near Soho,' Kat found herself answering. The image of Lauren in the bar had been replaced by an image of them together at fifteen, happy and so naive.

'Perfect! I know this awesome dim sum place, Yauatcha; I'll book it for nine.' Lauren chattered away while Kat concentrated on taking small breaths. Inhale, exhale. What was she going to do? She should claim prior plans, or illness, or . . .

'Listen, Lauren,' she began to interrupt, but something stopped her. Some tiny spark of curiosity had been growing ever since that night in the bar, and now, to her surprise, Kat felt it burn. What had Lauren made of herself, the person she'd become? All these years, she'd wondered in passing – hearing an old, familiar song on the radio, seeing a battered copy of their favourite books. And now she had the chance to know.

'See you at nine.' The words spilled out before Kat could take them back, and it was done.

Everyone has an agenda.

You don't believe in Santa or the tooth-fairy, so why still think people are generous and self-sacrificing? Everyone has ambition, even if you're too blind to see it, and everything they do will be for the sake of number one. The charity organiser likes feeling worthy, the soup-kitchen volunteer loves how noble she looks, and don't tell me the politician is in it to improve life for ordinary people – they want the power, pure and simple.

Don't ever accept people for what they say they are. Everybody lies.

Chapter Four

By the time she arrived at the stylish Soho restaurant, Kat was certain she'd made a mistake. Hadn't she spent most of university on a therapist's fading tweed couch just to be able to move on from those last, dark days at boarding school? Abandonment issues, he'd said: the bullying at Park House Prep and Lauren's betrayal were obviously just manifestations of her father issues, transference of her latent grief. Damn Freudian. Her mother had trained her not to accept such a phallus-centric point of view, but the end message had been the same regardless. You can't control other people's actions, only your own responses. In other words, do what you can and move on.

Yet here she was, walking right back towards that painful former self of hers like the past ten years had meant nothing, as if she hadn't grown up at all. A crowd of laughing women in draping, glittered tops pushed past her, breaking Kat's reverie with the sound of their heels tip-tapping on the cobbled street. She tried to steady herself.

Just an hour, she promised. You can survive that. An hour to see what Lauren had made of herself, and then it would be over.

The restaurant was sleek and glamorous, with cubed furniture and spotlights dotting the space with small pools of soft light. It was pretty, of course, but exactly the kind of overpriced, overexposed place she usually avoided. Kat turned over her worn, leather jacket to an unsmiling hostess and steeled herself as she made her way to the long, blue Perspex bar. Lauren was there already, flirting with some businessman, but the moment she laid eyes on Kat, her entire face lit up.

'Look at you!' she exclaimed, making other diners turn at the sound. 'It's been so long!'

Kat reluctantly accepted the hug and double air-kisses, her stomach still tight. 'Jack and Coke,' she quickly told the waiting barman. There was no chance she was going to try and make it through this sober. 'Light on the Coke.' Placing her bag on a stool, Kat adjusted her black vest and finally, when there was no more avoiding to be done, she turned back to Lauren and took in the girl she'd used to know.

Expensive silk dress in teal and maroon, jewel-coloured strappy heels – the changes in school had been superficial, light on the surface, but now Lauren had settled securely into her other self, Kat saw. Lauren's skin was tanned, her eyes looked unnaturally blue, and wide, glossed lips stretched over an impossibly white soap-opera smile.

Some last, distant hope in Kat slowly ebbed away.

'You haven't changed at all.' Lauren beamed. Kat forced a smile and turned back to the barman. He passed her the drink. She took a long gulp.

'Let's go sit down.' Lauren plucked a tasselled leather bag and her glass of champagne from the bar and began to steer Kat towards a table. 'They do a divine dessert menu; I hope you've left room.'

Kat could only follow wordlessly as Lauren sashayed across the floor on towering heels. 'Don't they hurt?' she asked, momentarily distracted. She nodded at the shoes.

'Like a bitch,' Lauren agreed, sliding onto a low, leather bench.

'So why wear them?'

'Studies show that seventy-two per cent of men associate high heels with negative feminine attributes.'

'Oh.'

'Vulnerability, dependency, et cetera,' Lauren continued, opening a menu. 'I had an important meeting with a total asshole earlier,' she explained. 'I needed him to underestimate me.'

'Did it work?' Kat was transfixed by Lauren's poise. There was no sign of nerves, no hint of the history they'd shared.

'Of course.' Lauren sounded surprised she would even question the logic. 'He was so busy trying to ask me to dinner, he didn't check the contract closely enough. He should have thrown out the whole section on intellectual property.' She began interrogating the waitress about dairy, nut and carb content while Kat glanced around. The table next to them was packed with a flock of young women: a fashion spread tableau of glossy hair, glamorous little dresses and jewellery glinting off slim wrists and throats. They drank cocktails from small, elaborate glasses and laughed with just the right level of detached amusement. Women like that had always been a foreign breed to Kat. Women like Lauren.

'Then I guess I'll go crazy and get the berry sorbet – no sauce, no pastry,' Lauren finally decided. 'Kat?'

She eyed the options. 'Chocolate ganache.'

'But what about your headaches?' Lauren frowned.

'I'll be fine,' Kat lied, thrown that Lauren still remembered her migraine triggers, after all this time.

There was a pause.

'It's really great to see you again,' Lauren repeated, carefully folding her white linen napkin over her lap.

Kat nodded, taking another sip of whisky. It left a soothing burn in her chest.

'So . . .' Lauren gave a small, awkward laugh. 'How have you been?'

'You know,' Kat shrugged. 'Good. Great.'

The waitress delivered a single, tiny cake to the table next to them. The cluster of women fell upon it with exaggerated 'mmmm's and 'ahhh's of delight, yet somehow barely made a dent in it with their minuscule forkfuls of crème. Kat wondered why they even bothered with the charade.

She tried to pull herself together and make the pleasantries Lauren no doubt wanted. 'I mean, I don't know where to start. I went to Oxford, but I guess you knew that. It was . . . fun. Mum's there now, actually; she's a Fellow at St Hilda's.'

Lauren kept smiling that even, gleaming grin, 'Oh, that's cool. And you're at *Think Louder*? That's a great magazine.'

'Well, I got into music writing at uni: interviews and features, that sort of thing. I started at *Think Louder* right after graduation, and, well, I've been doing it ever since.' Kat paused again. 'And what about you? What have you been doing?'

Lauren took a slow sip of her drink. 'I went to Yale for undergrad, double majored in psychology and sociology, then I moved to New York for my Masters. Columbia.'

'Oh.'

'I like the pace of things up there, so I stayed. Since then, I've been working mainly in branding.'

'Like cattle?' Kat quipped.

Lauren laughed, a little too hard. 'No, corporate advertising, that kind of thing. Last year I set up my own consultancy focusing on teen campaigns. I tell companies how to appeal to younger demographics, how they can sell products to teenage girls.'

'How . . . astute.' Kat blinked at the stranger in front of her. Lauren sat there, reminding her of all the pain she had caused, but still Kat found herself absorbing every detail. From the solid gold cuff at Lauren's wrist to the pale stretch of skin beside her collarbone where a birthmark had once been, Kat felt compelled to take it all in.

Lauren gave a small shrug, her hair rippling in a glossy wave. Kat's never came close to that kind of perfection, even when Whitney dragged her to the salon for a long-overdue trim. 'It's interesting work,' she continued. 'I landed a couple of British clients, so I thought it would be smart to move over here for a while, use London as a base for the European market. *ChicK*,' she said, naming a teen magazine, 'and Domina jeans.'

'I've never heard of them,' Kat responded politely.

Lauren grinned. 'That's because you're not fifteen.'

'I suppose.'

The waitress arrived with their desserts, giving Kat a welcome reprieve. She sank her fork into the dark, dense pastry with pleasure while Lauren speared a single blueberry and chewed it, slowly.

'And how's your family?' At last, she remembered Lauren's ever-perfect older sister. 'Is Delilah good?'

'Yes.' Lauren let out a small breath, pressing her lips together. 'She's getting married in the fall.'

'Congratulations. Your mum must be thrilled,' Kat added wryly. Her memories of Eleanor Anderville from parents' days and school holidays were downright chilly. She'd been forever imploring Lauren to socialise with the other, more respectable girls, as if Kat was a radical tearaway out to infect Lauren with the horrors of feminism and independent thought.

'Oh, she is.' Lauren finished her champagne in a few swift swallows. Another pause, filled only by the low ring of their forks against porcelain as they picked around their desserts. Kat felt the silence acutely – it reminded her of the awkwardness between them when the teenage Lauren had first transformed. Those awful confused conversations, full of resentment and rejection; Kat felt the painful memories return. She drained her glass, ignoring the burn. This had definitely been a mistake.

Lauren looked across at Kat. 'Want another?' she asked. And then her beam faded slightly, became real and almost sad. 'They have a peach drink that reminds me of those awful concoctions we used to make. The schnapps and syrup, remember?'

Despite herself, Kat's lips spread into a smile. 'God, they were foul. Didn't we use tinned peach juice that one time?'

'And half a cup of sugar.' Lauren's laugh bubbled up. 'I was sick for days, I swear.'

'We both were.' Kat's breath caught. For a moment, Lauren's features had rearranged into something familiar. A flash of mischief in her eyes, the tug of a grin on those cherry-glossed lips – and then it disappeared, and the perfect, grown-up woman stared back again. 'Another drink then,' Kat agreed with a sigh. That girl was gone for ever. 'I'll have a double.'

By the time Kat reached the bottom of her second sugary cocktail, the pain in her chest had melted a little. Surrounded by soft blue light and a warm daze of alcohol, all those past betrayals seemed very far away. Apparently, drinking was the vital activity necessary to ease even the most traumatic teen memories.

'So come on.' She slouched back in the booth, kicking her shoes off under the table. She was sick of small-talk; she wanted details. 'We've covered family, career and university, now for the good stuff. Major heartbreaks, relationships and general romances of the past ten years – go.'

'Hey!' Lauren protested, nibbling on a slice of pear garnish.

'What?' Kat rolled her eyes. 'You said you wanted to catch up. So spill.'

'Well,' Lauren sighed, relaxing her beauty queen posture for a moment. 'There's not much to tell. I've dated, I guess. I date a lot.' Her forehead crinkled. 'And there was this thing, in college, but . . . No significant other. I don't really have the time.'

'None?' Kat couldn't help but feel a little pleased. If Lauren had been engaged to some square-jawed media mogul, that would have really been too much.

'Uh huh.' Lauren swallowed. 'What about you?'

Kat snorted. 'Right. Because I was always perfect girlfriend material.'

'Don't say that,' Lauren protested.

'Why not?' Kat paused. She'd forgotten that she was supposed to be keeping up the facade of perfection, but it was too late now. 'Flings are one thing,' she shrugged, thinking of the men she never wanted to call again, and worse, the ones she did. 'But eventually you realise they're not going to turn into anything. Men in this city . . . All they want is a fan to validate them, not a real woman. It would be so much easier if I were gay – my mother would throw a party, for starters. Rejoice in the ultimate rejection of patriarchy, or something.'

'God, you really haven't changed,' Lauren grinned. 'You wouldn't even deign to crush on any of the boys in school.'

'Do you blame me?' Kat snorted. 'Vicious brats with acne and raging hormones.' She shuddered. 'No thank you.'

'But don't you miss it?' Lauren leaned over and pressed her fingertip into a couple of stray chocolate flakes on Kat's plate. 'The excitement, the giddy rush of it all?'

'You sound like a cheap romance novel,' Kat teased. 'But then, you did always have a things for those.'

Lauren blushed. 'Shut up!'

'That's right,' Kat laughed, suddenly remembering. 'Didn't Miss McClarkson catch you with that Mills and Boon book about the horny cowboys? She made you read aloud the scene with the lasso and saddle grease and—'

'Stop!' Lauren squealed, her face flushed. 'Oh God, that was so bad. I thought I'd die!'

'Hopefully that taught you to read better books,' Kat said wryly.

'You're not still doing that whole "must consume only worthy culture" thing are you?'

'And what's wrong with that?' Kat protested, draining the last gems of pomegranate from her drink and looking around for their waitress. The women at the next table had been replaced with a group of Japanese patrons, enjoying what looked like a never-ending flow of tiny dim-sum dishes.

'Only everything.' Lauren's eyes gleamed in the candlelight. She gave a wistful sigh. 'We had some good times, didn't we?'

And just like that, all Kat's good humour fell away.

She stiffened. 'I suppose we did. Before . . .' She hesitated on those next words, the truth that they'd avoided all night. But who was she to dance around it? Kat looked up, squarely meeting Lauren's eyes. 'Before you dropped me.'

Lauren looked down. 'I didn't—' But Kat didn't even let her finish the sentence.

'We're adults now; you don't need to pretend,' she said evenly. 'I mean, we both know what happened.'

There was another long pause, loaded with history. It seemed impossible to Kat that they'd been laughing together, only a moment ago; now, the pleasant warmth of alcohol in her blood was no match for the sobering memories that trickled back into her mind. The tearful nights alone in the dorm, watching Lauren giggle and shine in the midst of some other crowd. Before then, Kat hadn't known that loneliness could be a physical pain, but spending the rest of her school-days barely uttering a single word to anyone had taught her that solitude was a sharp ache, heavy and permanent.

When Lauren finally spoke again, her voice was soft and hesitant. 'Did you ever wonder why I changed?' Her eyes caught Kat's, dark in the dim light but unmistakably sincere. 'Back at Park House, after that summer.'

Kat felt a chill. 'You wanted to be part of the cool crowd.' Her reply was matter-of-fact. 'You figured being a mindless drone, and hanging around with girls like Lulu and Alison was more important than . . . more important than me.' She looked around again, but they were unnoticed, tucked away in the corner and out of earshot.

Lauren shook her head slowly. 'It wasn't like that.'

Kat raised her eyebrows, feeling her defences slowly shift back into position. She'd let her guard down, lulled by nostalgia and reminiscing, but now she was back in control. 'You don't have to explain it to me now. After all, you never felt the need back then.'

'I want to.' Lauren's expression became pained, suddenly so fervent that Kat didn't interrupt when she pressed on. 'That summer, you know my parents sent me to that camp way up in Maine. Well, they . . . Something happened there; it changed the way I saw the world – the way I saw myself, what I could be.'

Kat stared back, confused.

'There's a secret tradition for my cabin and it still goes on today.' Lauren paused, awkward again, twisting the green

52

gemstone ring on her finger. 'I don't know how to explain this to you. They have this book, this rulebook, and with it, you can get whatever you want. It's called *The Popularity Rules*.'

'*The Popularity Rules*?' Kat repeated, her voice laced with scepticism.

Lauren nodded. 'Once you understand the rules, you can do anything – achieve whatever you want.'

Kat tried to process the strange confession. Lauren's change hadn't been spontaneous, some impulse to fit in that had gone too far like she'd always told herself. No, it had been carefully planned, every step of the way.

'You chose those rules over me.'

The accusation hung between them.

'I was sick of always being an outsider, feeling like every day was a battle. I wanted to be happy.' Lauren let out a soft sigh. 'I guess I wasn't as strong as you.'

Kat sat blankly. She didn't understand this – Lauren's confession, the intensity in her voice. Even the story of some sacred book made no sense.

'We were sworn to secrecy,' Lauren continued. 'It's why I never told you.'

'Until now,' Kat said slowly, still not following. Did Lauren want some kind of absolution?

'Until now.' Reaching past their empty glasses, Lauren took her hand and fixed her eyes on Kat. 'See, I thought . . .' She swallowed. 'I thought I could teach you, the rules I mean.' Her words tumbled into one another. 'You could get any job you liked, make way more money – whatever you want, I promise. And it's perfect timing, because I'm in the country for a while, and you could even crash with me because I have tons of space and—'

'Stop!' Kat snatched her hand away. She could feel people

looking, but she just stared at Lauren, aghast. 'Is this some sort of recruitment drive?'

'No, I—'

'After all this time, you have the nerve . . . !' Kat swallowed back the tears that were suddenly rising in the back of her throat. She should have known this was a mistake.

'But if you just listen!' Lauren insisted. Her expression was plaintive, and so sincere it hurt Kat to see. This still mattered to her, she realised; ten years on, Lauren was still caught up in her rulebook and quest for success. 'You'll understand: the rules can change everything.'

'Listen?' Kat exclaimed. 'Don't you get it? Those rules are poison!' She reached for her bag and struggled to slip out of the tiny space, already hating herself for giving Lauren a chance to talk. 'I'm happy the way things are, and besides, what you did isn't right – it's shallow, stupid selling out.'

'But you haven't even heard what—'

'I don't want to!' Kat stared fiercely at Lauren. How could she think Kat would want any part of this? 'I know what they did to you, so I know enough. I don't want anything to do with them. Or you.'

Lauren's face slipped out of alignment for a split-second. 'You're not thinking straight,' she said, recovering her determined look. She slid back her own chair and rifled in her purse for a few crisp notes. 'We'll talk about it when you've calmed down.'

'We won't.' Kat was certain of that, if nothing else. 'You wanted to catch up, so we've caught. We're finished now.'

'But—' Lauren was still determined, but Kat had been through enough.

'If what you say is true, then those Popularity Rules ruined everything.' Kat leaned close to tell her, careful and cold.

'Don't you understand? I'm fine without them.'

Lauren looked at her. Kat's determination must have shown in her face because Lauren sighed, as if finally accepting defeat. 'Well, it was good to see you. Really.' She pulled a card from her bag. 'Here are my details. The offer stands, if you decide to change your mind.'

Kat was tempted to rip the card to shreds right there, but instead she affected indifference. 'Fine,' she shrugged, pushing it into her pocket and already backing away. 'See you around, I guess.'

It was over.

You are your own worst enemy.

So you think it's everyone else's fault: you're unhappy because he did this or she ruined that. It's so unfair! If they'd only just give you a break then everything would be fine, right?

Whatever.

No matter how much you want to pin the blame on somebody else, your life is the way it is because of you. That's right – you're the one screwing things up, and as long as you keep playing the victim and whining about everyone else, you'll never get what you want. It's time to step up and start thinking about the choices you make, because there's one thing for sure, and that is you're not doing it right.

Chapter Five

Kat didn't know where to begin. That Lauren would call her up after so much time, expecting them to exchange gossip and girl-talk over cocktails; that she would dare try to justify what she'd done all those years ago; that she'd even try to recruit Kat for her social-climbing project, as if they were teenagers again – panicking over where to sit in the dining hall or standing alone by the refreshments table at an end-of-term disco. She spent the rest of the week turning every detail of their encounter over in her mind, but it still made no sense to her at all.

What did make perfect, painful sense was the glittering success Lauren had become, and despite every better instinct, Kat couldn't help but view her own, haphazard life with a new sense of bitterness, and – yes – even failure. Mac was holding true to his threats of probation, sending her out on insulting assignments and demanding she run all her copy past a deputy ed before he even deigned to lay eyes on it, while Jessica, supposedly the lowest on the *Think Louder* ladder, was now ignoring her requests, as if Kat didn't even have the authority to boss around her teenage intern! She couldn't even count on unwinding at home, faced with Anton's rudimentary hygiene and the revolving parade of pretty, damaged girls.

Tonight would be no better. Mac had ordered her out to interview one of the minor skinny Brit-rock bands she loathed so much, but that wasn't enough – no, she was under strict instructions to watch every one of the three unknown opening acts too, in case the next saviours of British music happened to be stuck playing a seven thirty p.m. support slot in a dingy bar. Kat despaired. On the tiny stage, a trio of nerdy-looking boys in white lab-coats and protective visors were calling forth space-age sounds from their keyboards with intense concentration. Aside from a cluster of devoted girls right in front of them, the room was deserted. Kat took a stool at the empty bar and, in her solitude, found her thoughts returning again to Lauren and their meeting.

It hadn't been what she'd expected. Tracing circles on the scratched old bar, Kat tried to make the new memories sit alongside the old. She'd suspected Lauren would be polished and perfect, of course – the other girl had taken on a pageant-style demeanour even back at Park House – but Kat hadn't been prepared for the mask to slip. Those moments when they were tipsily reminiscing, Lauren's face flushed and guileless, the years had fallen away until she was almost her old self again.

Almost.

With a sigh, Kat slumped further onto her elbows and ordered her first whisky of the night, her 'no drinking on the job' rule clearly not fit for times like these. Despite those brief glimpses of the girl she'd once been, Lauren was still the shining beacon of a world Kat couldn't comprehend: a world that seemed to revolve around overpriced accessories, synthetic beauty standards and a career exploiting insecurities in the name of consumerism. In other words, everything that the two teenage girls had stood against, sneaking down to the woods after prep to eat Lauren's imported Hershey bars and plan their glittering futures as human rights activists, brilliant lawyers or authors of insightful feminist tomes.

Once she'd started, Kat was powerless to stop the flood of

teenage angst and awkward memories playing out in glorious, Technicolor splendour. It had been like this all week: every quiet moment, any spare second. She didn't know why it was all still fresh after so many years – perhaps because she'd never let anything hurt her so much since. They said that you never forgot the first time your heart was broken, but by the time a sandy-haired boy in faded corduroy trousers got around to breaking hers at university, Kat's already had the scars.

'Hey, Jules.' The sight of a passing label guy in skinny jeans and a pink keffiyeh reminded Kat why she was even there. 'Are the guys around yet? I'm supposed to have a slot with them at eight.'

'I'm sorry,' he called, barely slowing. 'They're out drinking somewhere. You'll have to wait until after the show.'

Great.

The math-synth-pop group finally finished their set to a smatter of applause and were replaced by a doe-eyed folk singer strumming a ukelele. Kat checked the printed run-down pinned behind the bar and calculated she had at least another two hours of moping mediocrity ahead of her.

'I'll go the distance if you will.'

Kat looked up. The club was filling up a little, and further down the bar now sat a man in dark-wash jeans and a perfectly fitting white T-shirt. He was looking at Kat expectantly.

'I always feel pathetic, drinking alone,' he added, giving her a grin that crinkled the edges of his eyes.

Only the sight of a Tegan and Sara logo fading on his sleeve stopped Kat from turning away immediately. Chances were he was just out to score more cool points by flaunting his taste for Canadian lesbian indie duos, but Kat had always loved that band. It earned him a second glance. He was attractive in that arrogant hipster way, she supposed, his chin smudged with stubble, dark hair curling slightly, pristine new sneakers on his feet, and no doubt an iPod packed full of obscure Justice remixes to soundtrack his independent film project. But she had time to waste, so Kat nodded slightly and waited. It was encouragement enough. The man scooted over onto the stool beside her and summoned the bartender.

'White wine? G&T? Vodka?' he asked. Kat gave him a withering stare.

'JD,' she replied, absently kicking her boots against the bar. Five seconds in and he already had a black mark for condescension. This didn't bode well.

'As the lady demands.' He slid a ten-pound note across the bar and accepted two more drinks. 'Cheers.' Clinking his glass against hers in an exaggerated gesture, he gulped it down.

Kat followed suit, silently taking a short sip.

'So, does the drink buy me a name?' Again, he tried the boyish smile, as if it had been proven irresistible.

She surveyed him thoughtfully. 'Do you think a drink buys you anything?'

He raised his eyebrows, but the caustic comment didn't send him running immediately for a safe, dark corner. 'I'm Ash,' he said, offering his hand to shake. Kat took it, slowly considering the arch of his wrist and long fingers curled gently around hers. She always paid attention to a handshake. Forget about physique, a man's grip told her everything she needed to know, and Ash's was firm and assured.

'Kat,' she answered finally, sending him a cool smile. Her decision was made, even though he didn't know it yet.

'Good to meet you, Kat.' Ash nodded, relaxing beside her. He put his mobile on the bar, moved a coaster to the side: taking clear ownership of the space like it was his living room. 'So, are you drinking from boredom, misery or pleasure?'

Kat paused. 'A little of the first two,' she admitted, but immediately chastised herself. Don't get personal. She'd been through this before. None of it would matter in the morning.

'Hmmm, let's see if we can't switch that around.' Ash's eyes were dark, shining in the dim light against a backdrop of scrawled graffiti and flyers, and Kat couldn't help but remember what Lauren had said about the excitement, the giddy rush of love. The heat gradually warming in Kat's veins wasn't exactly sweet romance, but it was something. Some distraction.

By the time the main act shuffled on-stage the room was cluttered with people and Kat and Ash retreated to a corner table. Once the initial advances were over, they'd fallen easily into a familiar routine, whip-smart retorts parrying back and forth at speeds that would do Bacall and Bogart proud. Kat relaxed into the rhythm: his arm slung around her shoulder, her fingers tracing a soft circle on his thigh. She knew where this would go: the same place it always did. A bed, a couch, the backseat of a car. She supposed she should be too old for these kinds of random liaisons. Whitney always met any confession with a concerned look and questions about her feelings, but Kat almost preferred the simplicity, the straight, swift line from loaded glance to the feel of somebody's body pressing down on her. Expecting anything more only led to disappointment; Kat had learned long ago. Men may rise to her sarcasm and wit for a while, but once the challenge wore thin, they went back looking for devoted girls who didn't protest being left weeks without a call, who didn't demand that they actually turned up when dates were planned.

'So what do you think?' Ash's stubble lightly scratched her cheek, his breath warm with whisky.

Kat took a moment to watch the band she'd barely noticed playing. 'Give them another year and a good producer,' she finally decided, moving slightly to the fierce beat the drummer was thrashing out on his kit.

'What do you mean?' Ash seemed amused by her criticism.

'They're too . . . messy.' She listened to them frantically chasing chords as if all that mattered was the volume and speed of the song. 'They haven't learned to strip it all away yet, to just let the melody or lyric stand for itself.'

He nodded slowly. 'Think they'll make it?'

'To what?' she teased. 'The big-time?' He laughed with her as she shifted position, curling her feet up under her. 'I don't know; it's not a science. I know plenty of bands that were good enough who never made the charts, and plenty of mediocre ones who went platinum. It's never just about the music.'

'Spoken like a true cynic.'

'No,' she corrected him with a smile, as the band crashed to a conclusion and loped off-stage. 'Spoken like someone with a functioning brain.'

'So let me get this straight.' Ash leaned back, his arms spread across the edge of their seats, and regarded her with amusement. 'You could hear the best song in the world, a song so brilliant that it moved you to tears, or to dance, or whatever – and you still wouldn't bet on it being a hit?'

'Not at all,' Kat declared. He was goading her, she knew, but the look in his eyes was playful. 'The world just doesn't work like that. It's about marketing budgets and radio play-listing and a dozen things other than the music.' She shrugged, a little wistful. 'Some of the best songwriters of our generation are working as call operators and, I don't know, bank tellers. And all because they chose to make real music, and not sell out with assembly-line pop rubbish.'

Ash grinned and reached for his drink. 'It's selling out to be successful?'

'I didn't say that,' Kat protested. 'But there's a big difference between creating something authentic, something real, and churning out that mainstream chart stuff.'

'Then a toast, to the unsung heroes of authenticity. You want another?' he said, noting her empty glass.

'Just water for now,' Kat decided.

'Got it.' Ash unfolded himself from the seat. 'I have to make a call, so see you in ten?'

'Sure.'

While Ash strolled over to the bar, Kat took the chance to go in search of Jules. Thanks to her unexpected distraction, she hadn't minded waiting around, but leaving her hanging for so long when they had an interview scheduled was inexcusable – to her.

'Oh, Kat, you're still here.' Jules was looking shifty when she finally located him behind a speaker stack.

'Yes, I'm still here,' she said, with far more patience than he deserved. 'I have time scheduled, remember?'

'Yes, about that . . .' Jules tugged the fringe on his scarf. Kat was briefly tempted to ask him about his opinions on Palestinian separatism, since he was wearing their traditional headdress – wrongly – but focused instead on Jules's evasive expression.

'We set this up days ago,' she reminded him. 'I seem to recall you begging me for the time.'

'Yeah, well a lot's happened since then.' His eyes flicked over to a back corridor where the band was emerging, sweaty and full of swagger. 'The bloggers really loved the new single; they're raving over the EP. Things are good.'

'Which doesn't explain why I'm standing here with you

63

instead of getting my interview done. Jesus, Jules – I'll be ten minutes, tops.'

'I know, but an old friend's dropped by and they want to go out.'

'That's it?'

'Hey, what can I do?' He shrugged nonchalantly, as if it wasn't his job to physically drag them to their appointments. Kat watched in disbelief as he went over to the band and gave them all enthusiastic high-fives and fist-bumps. A rag-tag bunch with messy beards, ripped denim and questionable amounts of chest hair showing, they glowed with rock-star ego as they chatted to the small group of coltish girls surrounding them.

Kat marched over. Normally, she would write it off and leave (swearing never again to reply to Jules's enthusiastic emails), but this was the final insult of a long and exhausting week. She could have been home hours ago, snug under her comforter with hot tea and her *Firefly* DVDs, but instead she'd been enslaved to other people's decisions, as if she couldn't control a damn thing in her life.

'Ten minutes, Jules.' Planting herself at edge of the group, Kat crossed her arms.

Jules looked annoyed, but not enough to drag himself away from his buddies and the doe-eyed brunette girl hanging on his every word. That was OK; Kat could wait.

'You guys were like, so amazing.' A girl with pixie-cut blonde hair and a Home Counties accent thrust herself at the sweaty lead singer. 'Seriously, so good.'

'Thanks, sweetheart.' With a lascivious grin, he draped one arm around her shoulders – resting his hand on her right breast, Kat noted with disdain. 'We appreciate your support.'

The girl broke into giggles, clutching her friend's hand with glee. Their T-shirts were printed black on neon, topped with bright patterned hoodies and armfuls of metal bangles.

'So are we heading out?' another band member asked, pulling on a beat-up leather jacket. 'I'm dying for a smoke.'

'Yeah, D will be out in a sec, hang on.' The lead singer leaned over to whisper something in the pixie girl's ear. She blushed and started giggling again.

'If you're waiting around,' Kat quickly interrupted, seeing her in. 'We could use the time and—'

'I'll sort the cabs.' Jules spoke over her, shooting Kat an irritated look. 'I reckon we should head to Cargo and then Freddie's after-party.'

'Works for me.'

But not for Kat. As the group assembled jackets and bags – the adoring female followers now ensconced in various hairy embraces – she cornered Jules.

'Look, I came out of my way tonight for you.' She hated to sound desperate, but Mac was just looking for an excuse to make life even more unbearable.

Jules looked impatient. 'I told you, schedules change. We've got other commitments tonight and— Great, everyone's here!' He broke off, looking past Kat to a pair of new arrivals. 'Devon, good to see you, man!'

'J-dog, always.'

Kat turned in time to see Devon Darsel amble over, pale-faced and foppish in a trilby hat and painfully tight jeans. Two steps behind him, Jessica strutted along in vicious black heels and a fraying denim mini-skirt. Her white silk vest draped over a black lacy bra, clearly visible, as if revealing half the garment was somehow classier than the usual peek of strap. Kat felt her resentment harden.

'So are we all set?' Jessica slipped her hand through Devon's arm and gave the other girls a proprietary glare.

'Absolutely.' Jules began ushering the group towards the exit. Kat blocked his way.

'And who's this?' Devon paused, running his eyes over her. His Irish accent lilted softly but his eyes were bloodshot and unfocused.

'Oh, that's just Kate.' Jessica gave her a syrupy grin. 'She works with me at the magazine.'

'Jess, you're at *Think Louder*?' Jules's expression brightened, taking in her matte, pink lips and – more importantly – her proximity to Devon. 'That's perfect. You can chat to the band while we're en-route, get some backstage insider stuff.'

Kat was still speechless from Jessica's claim that her intern duties of bad note-taking and half-finished photocopying qualified as 'work'.

'Totally!' Jessica cooed, brushing past Kat. 'Whatever you need.'

The group moved off, exiting the club like a convoy of fashion-victim chosen ones, while Kat was left alone in the middle of the sticky, littered floor.

For a moment she didn't move, just stood there, focusing very hard on not smashing the glasses on a nearby table or hurling a stool across the room. All the hurt and rejection that had slowly been accumulating that week was finally crystallised into a shard of sheer fury, and Kat was shocked by just how powerful it was. She felt on the edge of something – lashing out, or breaking down entirely, her whole body shaking with pent-up emotion.

'Ready to go?' Ash appeared behind Kat, making her jump.

'Absolutely,' she declared, trying to swallow back her anger. Mackenzie, Lauren, this damn interview – it was all a waste, nothing but one hit after another until she could barely breathe.

She didn't resist as Ash laced his fingers through hers and led her up the narrow stairs, pushing out into the cool night air. Suddenly they were surrounded by people: traffic noise, neon and pedestrians filling the pavement around them.

'So what now?' Ash turned, pulling her closer. Now that there was more light, Kat could see his eyes were brown, flecked with gold reflections from the sign above them. 'Do you want—?'

She didn't let him finish. Reaching up, Kat locked her hands around his neck and kissed him, hard. He made a small noise of surprise against her lips but then responded, holding her tight against his body with one arm, the other hand tangling in her hair. Kat tried to stop thinking, tried to ignore anything other than the bite of his teeth against her bottom lip; the harsh rasp of his chin on her cheeks, against her neck. She wanted to disappear.

Her mobile began to ring, vibrating in her pocket between them. Kat ignored it, but Ash detangled himself and fished it out.

'It's fine,' she said, breathless, and reached for him again, but he laughed and pressed the phone into her palm, kissing her lightly on the forehead.

'I'll get us a cab,' he said, and retreated to the kerb.

Kat flipped open the phone. 'What?' she demanded. Something was igniting in her veins – some rush of endorphins and lust she hoped would be enough to keep her going – but reality still threatened to drain it all away.

'Hey, it's Nate. We've got a problem.' He sounded desperate, but Kat didn't have the time to care.

'Not now, please.'

'No, really, you've got to help me. The server crashed. All our online content has disappeared!'

'Why are you telling me this?' she interrupted Nate's panic. 'Where's Mac?'

'I can't reach him! I've tried his mobile, BlackBerry, home number – everything.'

Typical. She rolled her eyes, kicking shards of broken glass along the pavement. Ash was still trying to find a taxi, walking further down the street to avoid a pack of Japanese tourists. 'So wait until morning.'

'And have a ten-hour gap in hit rates? We're setting our ad rates off this week's traffic; they'd fucking crucify me, Kat.'

'Well, what can I do about it?'

'I'm rebuilding the pages from scratch, but I can't find half the articles. Have you got anything I can use?'

'I don't know; we just closed the last issue. I haven't even begun my new stories.' Then Kat remembered. 'Wait, I do have something.'

'What?'

She heard her name being called; Ash was waiting with a free taxi. 'Go to my "in progress" file,' she said, hurrying down the street. 'There's three thousand words on Devon Darsel.'

There was a long silence while Kat tumbled into the car and Ash gave the driver a Shoreditch address. He pulled her close again, running his tongue lightly across her jawbone. She sighed.

'Kat . . . ?'

'What?' She blinked and put the phone to her ear again, lights blurring outside the car window. When he spoke, Nate's voice was hesitant.

'I'm not sure about this . . .'

'What do you mean?'

'You're on probation!'

'So?'

68

Ash was watching her with a smile, his hands snaking under her shirt. Kat shivered as his fingers traced the ridge of her spine.

'Look, do you want to use it or not?'

'It's your call . . .' Nate tailed off.

For one last moment, Kat ignored the man beside her. She thought about Devon, the slow arrogance of his stare and the girls he'd left weeping in bathrooms all over the city. So what if her article was rather . . . provocative? Mac would come around once he saw what an impact it could make. And then there was Jessica. Kat remembered her drama queen act, and her resolve hardened. She was sick of waiting around for these people, hovering on the edge of their crowds. What gave them the right to act like they were better than her, like they were somehow special because they wore the right ridiculous clothes and had tickets for that exclusive after-party? Just once, they should get what they deserved.

'Run it,' she told Nate, defiant. 'I'll deal with the rest.'

There are always consequences.

Chant it like a mantra: there are always consequences. You may not see it coming, and it might not happen right away, but everything you do is guaranteed to come back and bite you on the ass, so you better make damn sure you think things through before you take action. People forget the good moments, but they hold grudges for ever, and you don't want to be out in the world wondering when they'll take their turn to strike.

Some people call it karma, but they're wrong: it's not the universe balancing bad and good, it's just poor planning. You can screw people over all you want as long as you plot way ahead and cover all possible outcomes. Find a helpful geek to teach you some chess moves – you'll need them.

Chapter Six

'Now Katherine, I've tried to be supportive, but don't you think it's time you get yourself together?'

Kat pulled herself upright long enough to hear her mother's words of disappointment echoing down the line before slumping back into her default position. She lay on the couch with remote controls to her left, stale biscuits to her right, and now a phone wedged on her shoulder and the full force of her mother's wrath making light work of the fifty-odd miles separating them.

'It's been nearly a month now,' Susanne continued, 'and you don't seem to be dealing too well.'

'I'm dealing.'

'Wallowing in misery is not dealing, Katherine.'

'And I'm not wallowing, either!' Kat studiously ignored the litter of junk food wrappings, old issues of *Think Louder* and heavy ache in her head that would prove otherwise. So what if she'd barely moved from her bed to the TV to the kitchen all day? Unemployed, miserable and alone: she was more than entitled to her despair.

It wasn't supposed to be like this. When Kat had arrived at work that next morning to find her belongings waiting in a torn cardboard box, she'd been incandescent: fuelled by sheer rage at Devon Darsel for running to his lawyers, Mackenzie for giving her up, even at Lauren for flaunting her success and glossy perfection. *Think Louder* had been her home for years, but within minutes, she was gone. Kat had channelled every pang of anguish into fearless determination. She would show them all.

At least, that had been the plan, but as the weeks passed, Kat's resolve began to falter. Throwing herself into the hunt for a new job, she had searched newspapers and the internet for openings: out of the door first thing every morning, she lingered in cafes and bookstores until she could creep home and fall into an exhausted, dreamless sleep. But now what little savings she had were draining away, and still there was no sign she could win back the life she had fought so hard to build.

To say she wasn't coping would be an understatement.

Up in Oxford, Susanne tutted. 'I just don't understand why it's so hard to find another magazine position. You've got years of experience, and that degree.'

'You don't understand.' Kat slouched deeper under her knitted comforter, tired already. 'This isn't academia. More magazines are folding every year – qualifications and experience don't mean a thing; it's all about who you know.'

'Well, surely you know somebody. What have you been doing all these years?'

'I don't know. My job?' She was being difficult, but Kat was entitled to her misery. Hundreds of articles, all that overtime, years spent living and breathing music journalism, and for what? Only to discover she should have been out snorting coke with the rest of the freeloading media scum, that's what.

At first the rejections hadn't phased her. Just look how long it had taken to work her way up at *Think Louder*. The perfect job was out there; she just had to search harder. But the weeks passed, her few contacts stopped returning her calls, and slowly Kat began to lose hope. There were openings, sure, writing online content for five pounds a review, but she had bills to pay. Bills that would soon be overdue. When even Anton passed her by with pity in his lecherous eyes, she knew things were beyond saving.

'I didn't expect you to just fall apart like this.' Her mother's tone was bemused.

'Thanks, Mum.' Kat picked at the fraying edge of the throw.

'Although I suppose I should have seen this coming. You never did process Alan's death, and it must have replicated all your father issues, with—'

'Alan has nothing to do with my father!'

'Come on,' Susanne tutted. 'An older man you visited every Christmas but never had sex with? Classic father replacement.'

'We're not going into that again.' Kat unravelled another row of stitches.

'You could always ask Michael for a loan to tide you over. God knows he owes us for all that maintenance.' Susanne's voice took on a familiar bitter edge.

'I'm not asking Dad for anything,' Kat sighed. 'Where is he now, anyway?'

'Stanford, I think. Leching on impressionable students, I'm sure.'

Her mother had been one of those impressionable students, many years ago. The way she told it, Professor Michael Purcell had dazzled her with academic intensity, frequent private tutorials, and an extensive library of rare Victorian manuscripts. Kat suspected it was his more his dashing, Harrison Ford-like stature that did the dazzling, since reading clearly wasn't all they did. By the end of her second year Susanne was pregnant, and in an effort to save her beloved from academic disgrace, she quietly withdrew from her studies and dutifully tended house, and child, in an approximation of liberal domestic bliss – until the great professor secured a prestigious fellowship in America and decided that a young bride and baby would only keep him from realising his true intellectual potential.

His absence had always been a matter of fact for Kat, the rare periods when he decided to grace her with his presence far more awkward than the many years in between. Her mother had done everything for her, working soulless secretarial jobs to keep the young Kat in new shoes and My Little Ponies (Barbies, of course, weren't welcome in their home), and so by the time a bequest from a distant aunt made Susanne's own dreams of academic distinction possible, Kat couldn't hold it against her to follow her newly fervent feminist dreams. Park House Preparatory School and the joys of co-ed boarding it was.

'Can we get back to my job?' Kat was keen to stop her mum before another discussion of male egos and the sacrifices of fertile female minds.

'I thought the point was, you don't have one.'

'I'm temping,' Kat reminded her. Technically it was true: she'd signed up to half a dozen agencies right away in the hope of finding something to support herself. Admin work, sub-editing shifts – she wasn't picky, but the pool of cheap student labour all vying for minimum-wage work had left her phone silent. Apparently her skills just weren't transferable enough, there being no demand for an ethnomusicologist specialising in feminist narratives and indie rock.

'Look, I'd better go.' Kat looked down at her greying tracksuit bottoms and realised she was running late. 'I'm meeting Whitney for drinks.'

'Well good luck,' Susanne mustered an enthusiastic tone. 'And if it doesn't work out, then there's always work with the network. Jodi could use some help transcribing testimonies, I'm sure.'

Kat gulped. Her mother's colleague was working on an oral

history archive of human rights abuses. The last time she'd volunteered, Kat had wound up transcribing first-hand accounts of the rape and mutilation of the women of Darfur. Important work, undoubtedly, but hardly the thing to lift her out of this despair and restore her faith in humanity again.

'Sure Mum, thanks. Bye!'

Spurred on by the terrifying vision of her future, Kat went searching for the slip of paper that held her last remaining hope.

'I'd love to help,' Jackson apologised when Kat finally located his scribbled number. 'But we've got a six-month waiting list for internship placements.'

'Oh.' Kat fought an inexplicable rush of tears.

'Nobody's hiring, you know that.'

'I do now.'

Her voice was low but Jackson must have heard something in the tone because he quickly added, 'I can give you the number of a friend at *Music Nation*; I know he's looking for a temporary editorial assistant.'

'I'll try anything,' Kat swore. 'I really appreciate it.' A month ago, she would have despaired at the idea of sorting mail and photocopying again, but at that moment, it sounded like bliss.

'OK. They can cover your costs, which is a plus.'

'Costs?'

'Fifty pounds a week for travel and lunch. It's a six-month internship, so there's a lot of competition, but I could put in a word and—'

'But it's full time!' Kat couldn't believe it. Six months unpaid? What did they expect her to live on?

'Of course.' He was shocked, 'But all entry-level media jobs are now. And maybe afterwards you could get a proper position, sixteen k if you're lucky.'

Kat felt like laughing with despair. This was the state of the industry now, teenagers fighting to do unpaid slave labour? No wonder every *Think Louder* intern had acted like they had a trust fund: they really did!

'I don't understand. When did it get like this?'

'It always has been. You were one of the lucky ones, getting in with Alan like that,' Jackson explained gently. 'We all talked about it at the time. You were our dream. So do you want his details?'

'Yes,' she decided at last, resigned to her fate. 'Please.'

'OK, I can't promise anything though.'

Kat scribbled down the number. 'Thanks, this means a lot.'

'No problem,' Jackson assured her. 'Got to look out for our own, right?'

Kat hung up and stared at her notebook, wondering how she could make it work. She'd have to sign up to another dozen temp agencies, work nights and weekends in some soul-destroying data-entry job, live off pasta like she was fresh out of university again and move even further into the outer boroughs. Maybe it was time to consider the unthinkable and give up on music journalism altogether – find some normal, ordinary job in an office that bored her to death but kept a roof over her head. But if it was impossible to find a temp job, just what was the real job market like?

Kat pressed a palm to her aching forehead and tried not to despair. She couldn't let herself wallow any more. Whitney would have some answers; she always did.

Finally showered and wearing something other than her dressing gown for the first time in days, Kat searched for Whitney's familiar red hair amongst the after-work crowd that jostled in the busy Covent Garden bar. She'd forgotten how packed and rowdy these places could be, and after weeks

76

without human interaction, she wasn't sure if she felt relieved or overwhelmed by the be-suited bankers and cliques of business-casual women clutching glossy handbags and glasses of wine.

'Hi sweetie.' Whitney had nabbed them a prize corner table, arranged with low leather-covered blocks in black and white. She kissed Kat on both cheeks, her beaded earrings dangling against their faces. 'God, I haven't seen you in for ever!'

'How have you been?' Kat hugged her warmly. Whitney had their drinks already waiting, a breeze fluttered in from the open windows and at last, Kat felt something close to human again.

'Hectic!' Unwinding a green silk scarf from her neck, Whitney settled solidly in her seat. 'There was the Stockholm conference, and years of consultation meetings, and I told you about the department reorganisation, right?'

Kat shook her head.

'Oh God, it's a nightmare. I swear these people are trying to drive me insane!' Whitney laughed. 'And what about you? What's the latest on the *Think Louder* affair?'

'Nothing new,' Kat shrugged. With Whitney's busy schedule, they'd only managed quick calls and a couple of emails since the Devon Darsel debacle. 'His lawyers made noise about defamation lawsuits and libel, but none of that will stand. Of course, Mac didn't care – he just buckled right away.' Kat couldn't believe the ease with which she'd been cast aside. If Alan had still been editor . . .

'And what are you doing now?'

Kat sighed. 'Job-hunting.' She gave Whitney a rueful smile. 'Not that it's getting me anywhere. There's nothing going in music journalism except unpaid internships. I don't under-stand it, how they expect us to get by without a wage for three, sometimes six months!'

Whitney looked suitably horrified. 'But you have to eat!'

'Right, and pay rent. Although Anton's been trying to chase me down over that, so I'll probably be on the streets before long.' Kat tried to laugh. 'Anyway, I'm looking outside journalism too. To be honest, I'll take anything.'

Whitney squeezed her shoulder sympathetically. 'Well if you need help with your CV, just let me know. I feel like an expert after all my job-hopping!'

'That would be great.' Kat let out a breath, relieved. 'If you could keep an eye out for openings, I'd be so grateful.'

Whitney blinked. 'In policy consulting?'

'Absolutely,' Kat nodded, even though it pained her to consider the last resort. 'Admin, communications . . . I'm willing to try anything, and you're always telling me how you're crying out for good people.'

'Yes, but—' Whitney paused, frowning slightly. 'You're not really qualified.'

'I know, but neither were you, and look how that worked out.' Kat smiled, remembering Whitney's panic as they tried to prepare her for her interviews. They had spent days poring over DEFRA white papers and trade magazines until she was familiar with everything from biofuels to carbon contracts. 'I reckon my journalism experience can count for something. I'm not looking for a managerial position or anything,' she added quickly. 'Just an ordinary office job.'

'Oh.' Whitney sipped her drink. 'Well, of course I'll ask around, but I don't want you to get your hopes up.'

That was becoming a theme. 'Whatever you do will be wonderful,' Kat swore. 'Thank you. To be honest, it's been really hard,' she admitted. 'I haven't been holding up too well and—'

'Louise! Over here!' Whitney interrupted her, waving across

the room. She turned to Kat just as two other women descended on their table. 'Hope you don't mind, but I invited Louise and Erica along, I thought we could all catch up.'

'No, not at all . . .' Kat lied, her voice quickly buried under their loud greetings.

'Martini for me,' Louise demanded, throwing her navy jacket onto the seat beside Kat. Her dress was cream with thin navy pinstripes, buttoned all the way down the front. 'Two olives. And Whitney will have white wine, won't you?'

'Please.' Whitney reached up and gave them both air-kisses. 'You remember Kat, don't you?'

Erica fluttered a wave in her direction before disappearing towards the bar in a haze of floral print. Louise collapsed on one of the low cubes and eased the straps on her pointed brown heels. 'Oh God, these shoes were a mistake. They were on sale, so I couldn't resist, but my blisters have blisters by now!'

'What have I told you about sales?'

'I know, I know. But it was this little place that does vegetarian shoes, so I couldn't resist, and . . .'

While the two women chatted, Kat retreated into herself. Suddenly, her private conversation had become an episode of *Sex and the City*, complete with cocktails, wardrobe discussions and a variety of hair colouring. This was not Kat's world.

Soon Erica returned with fresh drinks and a vacant smile.

'Fabulous.' Whitney took hers and held it up in a toast, 'To . . . hmm, what shall we drink to?'

'Success,' Louise proposed, pushing back her fringe. 'After all, you've got your promotion coming up, and Erica landed that new account.'

'To success then!' Whitney beamed.

Kat silently touched her glass to theirs. 'You got a promotion?' she asked Whitney. 'You didn't say.'

Whitney looked awkward. 'I didn't want to make a big deal, not with everything you're going through. Kat was fired,' she explained to the others.

'Oh no!' Louise gasped. 'That's terrible.'

Kat tried to smile. 'I'll be fine.'

'Of course you will,' Erica added with a solemn nod, as if she knew everything about it.

'Let's talk about something more positive, hmm?' Whitney sent Kat a sympathetic look. 'Any news or gossip from anyone?'

Louise frowned. 'Nothing new that I know of. You were at Tim's last week, so you know all about Frances . . .'

'God, Frances!' Whitney exclaimed. 'I'd nearly forgotten.'

'I think we all wish we could.' Louise nodded. 'An old friend,' she added, seeing Kat's confused expression. 'She decided to quit everything and go surf in Sri Lanka.'

'Oh,' Kat commented uselessly.

'I mean, I could understand if she had a plan,' Whitney said, eyes wide. 'To start up an eco-tourism business, or work with local NGOs. But what's she going to do – just lie around on a beach all day?'

'I knew she was going to crack.' Erica twirled the straw in her glass. 'Lance got married a few months ago, and we know she never got over him.' They all nodded.

'What about you, Kat?' Louise turned to her with interest. 'Are you involved with anyone right now?'

'No,' she replied, thinking suddenly of Ash. Their night together a month ago was the closest she'd been to a relationship recently, even though she'd left the next morning before he woke up to avoid the pretence of exchanging numbers and 'stay for breakfast' small-talk.

'Kat doesn't date.' Whitney sighed. 'I'm forever trying to set her up, but she just refuses.'

'Find me the right sort of man, and maybe I will,' Kat said lightly, feeling penned in.

'And what's the right sort of man?' Louise looked at her expectantly. Kat shrugged. She knew she was probably supposed to start gossiping about sex and relationships, but she didn't know these women. What business was it of theirs?

'I'm still deciding.' She began to get up. 'Can I just slip out for a sec?'

Kat left them to their chatter and ducked through the crowd to the relative calm of the toilets. She'd hoped a night out with Whitney would lift her spirits, but instead it was cementing her bad mood. She sighed, watching her sullen reflection in the mirror as she rinsed her hands. This wasn't helping at all.

When she returned to the group, Whitney was gesturing wildly in the middle of some anecdote, eyes bright.

'I'm going to take off now,' Kat announced, awkwardly reaching over to pick up her bag.

'So soon? We've hardly talked! Oh, well, we have to do something soon,' Whitney promised, hugging her goodbye. 'Maybe a lunch? I'm booked solid next week, but once June starts, it should ease off.'

'OK,' Kat remembered to smile at the others. 'Louise, Erica – it was nice to see you again.'

'You too!' Louise exclaimed. 'And keep your chin up; I'm sure you'll find the perfect job soon.'

Kat murmured noncommittally and edged away. The moment she stepped out onto the cobbled street outside, she reached in her bag for her phone and notebook and resigned herself to making that final call.

'Hi, Jackson said I should get in touch. About that editorial assistant position . . .'

The truth doesn't matter.

In the real world, facts don't count for a thing – all that matters is your reputation. Just ask the girl everyone says is a slut. I'll bet she hasn't done half the things all those boys claim, but is that truth any good to her? I don't think so. A bad reputation can haunt you for ever, so cut your losses and leave it behind: switch schools, change jobs or even move away. Just make sure you can start from scratch and take control of what they think about you this time.

Repeat after me: you are nothing but what they say you are.

Chapter Seven

Kat wasn't sure which was more humiliating: that she was going after an unpaid work experience placement, or that she had to interview to get it. There was a waiting list for these positions, she'd been informed by the bored-sounding HR woman, but they'd meet with her for an 'informal chat' and see what they could do.

It wasn't the enthusiastic welcome she'd been hoping for, but Kat wasn't in a position to choose. God, it was good to have a reason to get up, she thought, gulping down some semi-suspect juice and scraping the black bits from her toast. It may not be much, but even she could recognise her slow downwards spiral as something dangerous, a creeping lethargy that, if left unchecked, could take over. She'd had dark spells before, in sixth form, and then when Alan had died, and Kat knew how hard it would be to tug herself out once utter hopelessness set in.

But this time would be different, she told herself firmly. This time, she would be just fine. As soon as Anton's latest morose nymph vacated the bathroom (leaving three types of eyeliner and four bottles of prescription drugs), Kat gave herself a final once-over and tried to talk herself up. She *would* get this job. Pulling her damp hair back into a neat plait, she checked that her Fiona Apple T-shirt and jeans were clean and rip-free. There. She'd spent half the night organising her portfolio, so she was more than prepared for whatever they could throw at her.

'I'm still waiting for next month's rent.'

Kat looked up to find Anton's unshaven face reflecting behind her in the mirror.

She turned reluctantly. 'I'm working on it.'

'Yeah, but it's late.' He was wearing tracksuit bottoms at least, so she only had to contend with the sight of his bloodshot eyes and hairy chest, rather than his greying underwear. Oh, small mercies. 'If you can't get it together, I'm going to have to find someone else for the room.'

Kat's jaw clenched. 'I'll manage.'

Anton assessed her with a slow stare. 'You know, if you need some fast cash, I know this guy who runs a website—'

'I said, I'll manage.' Kat cut him off before she could get scarred by any unsavoury mental images.

'Whatever.' He shrugged, giving her one of those lecherous smiles. 'Just have it to me by Monday.'

Kat tried very hard not to slam the bathroom door behind him. It would be all right, she told herself. After this interview, she'd drop by the temp office again and refuse to leave until they found her something. With another cash advance on her credit card and what was left in her account, she could maybe come up with enough to keep Anton quiet for a few weeks. And then it would all be back to normal. Kat repeated the words over in her mind, refusing to panic. It would all be back to normal.

It was only as she sat in the reception area of *Music Nation's* offices – clutching her portfolio and subtly attempting to pick an overlooked stain from the knee of her jeans – that it occurred to Kat she might well have been wrong. About everything.

Unlike *Think Louder*, with its ramshackle office and simple design, this magazine was based in a trendy Shoreditch ware-house, complete with neon decor, free vending machines and a publication list that ranged from *Horse Monthly* to *Tween Beat*. Watching the flow of workers as they strode through the security barriers balancing coffee cups, bakery bags and over-sized handbags on svelte frames, Kat felt that bubble of panic return. She didn't belong.

At *Think Louder,* the interns' fashion and make-up had been a running joke for the scruffy staff, but here, such attention to trend-setting detail was the norm. Yes, there were the occasional band T-shirts and jeans amongst the striking work-casual outfits, but the shirts were artfully ripped to reveal tanned flesh, studded with diamanté and worn a size too small, while the denim was tight and skinny. Much like the staff.

Kat tried to ignore her unease, turning instead to the table of magazines in front of her. Avoiding the multitude of celebrity gossip headlines, she found herself reaching for the new issue of *ChicK*. Hadn't Lauren mentioned they were a client? The cover boasted typical teen girl fare: 'Mate or Date? How to tell he wants more!' and '62 Summer Style Steals!' Not that Kat cared, she corrected herself quickly, dropping the magazine again. She didn't care what Lauren was doing, not at all.

Kat gripped her portfolio tighter and sent a silent prayer to whatever deity might possibly be listening. She wasn't picky: she addressed them all with her heartfelt plea.

Just let her get this job. Please. Let her get this job.

'Katherine Elliot?' A girl in black drainpipe jeans and a teetering pair of red patent heels was looking at her expectantly.

'Call me Kat.'

'Great, I'll just take you up.' Kat followed her obediently into the elevator, trying not to stare at the fifties pin-up girl silhouette emblazoned across her guide's chest.

'Do you work here, or . . . ?'

'Staff writer.' The girl smiled prettily from under sweeping dark curls.

'Oh.' But she couldn't be more than a teenager!

The girl looked at her curiously. 'Are you here for the deputy editor position?'

'No . . .' Kat felt herself begin to blush, reminded again of just how far she'd fallen. She'd already been rejected for that job. 'I'm interviewing for the internship.'

'Oh.' Now it was her companion's turn to be quiet, pressing her lips together in an awkward expression and averting her gaze until the lift doors slid back and Kat was led out into the office.

Open-plan, light and airy, the room was filled with busy chatter and the loud, angular sounds of The Alarm. Kat absorbed the familiar chatter, already wanting this job so badly her pulse began to race in time with the music's fierce thrum. This was where she belonged: deadlines, angry sub-editors, broken coffee machines and all. She fed off the frantic energy, the speed – just walking through this place made her feel more alive than she had done all month.

Kat followed her guide past a group clustered around the flatscreen TV, watching a honey-limbed singer strut in perfect time to her drummer's angry flails.

'Why the hell did they pick this for lead single?'

'I know,' sighed a dishevelled man, kicking his ancient sneakers up on the desk. 'Back to the eighties post-punk revival. Again.'

Kat longed to join the group, but already the dark-haired

girl was gesturing her towards a row of chairs outside what was obviously the editor's office.

'Thanks,' Kat remembered to smile back at her. After all, they'd be co-workers soon.

'Sure,' she shrugged and sauntered off, back to the real, paid job that Kat could only dream about.

As Kat perched on the edge of her seat and clutched her portfolio, she reminded herself to stay positive. Just because she was starting at the bottom again, it didn't mean she couldn't get where she wanted. She would write freelance pieces on the side – because really, how much time would photocopying take? – and soon they'd see how indispensable she was. She could get it all back. She *would* get it back.

'We'll be in touch.' The door opened and a young woman emerged.

She tossed her tousled blonde hair and cooed, 'It's been like, so great to meet you all! And tell Jacinta I'll see her in Cornwall for bank holiday.'

Kat felt like doing a victory dance right there in the middle of the floor. The girl looked like she was barely out of school, let alone literate! In that instant, her remaining nerves melted away. She was a million times more qualified than this child, plus she could actually attend gigs without requiring a fake ID. Rising to her feet, Kat strode into the room with a grin.

'And you have no administrative or secretarial experience?'

'Well, not exactly, but I've years of experience in consumer music publishing, and my portfolio here shows my range of work.' Kat tapped the black leather file that lay untouched on the glass-topped table in front of her. The men opposite looked at it wearily.

'Right.' With a sigh, Theo the features editor began to leaf through it, barely glancing at the collection of articles that represented the best work Kat had ever done. She recognised him from gigs and after-parties; in fact, she was almost certain she'd lent him her dictaphone one afternoon during a Kings of Leon press junket, but there wasn't even a flicker of familiarity on his face.

'Filing, transcription, typing speeds . . . ?' The HR head beside him pulled his outrageously fashionable glasses lower on his nose and scrutinised her application form.

Kat felt herself blush. 'I'm a very quick learner, and like I said, I'm experienced in—'

'A consumer music magazine environment. Yes, we know,' Theo finished for her. 'Do you blog? Vidlog? Any experience at all with Web 2.0 platforms?'

'No,' Kat answered in a small voice. Who needed stupid applications cluttering up their computer when pen and paper more than sufficed?

Theo sighed again. 'Look, I'll be honest. I know who you are; you're an excellent writer.'

'Thank you.' Kat relaxed instantly. God, for a moment she'd actually been worried.

'I mean, the G-Link piece you ran?' Theo snorted. 'Inspired.'

'Really great,' the HR man added. His dark hair was cut in some kind of modern mullet that baffled Kat on every level, but she gave a modest smile and wondered if she could negotiate to get some kind of wage instead of just travel costs. After all, she was definitely overqualified.

'Insightful, brutal,' Theo continued. 'It's a real shame I can't hire you.'

'Really, it was nothi— What?'

'I can't give you the job.' He slid her file back across the desk but Kat could only look at it in shock.

'But why?' she exclaimed. She didn't understand, after everything he'd said!

Theo shot a sideways glance at the HR guy before looking back at Kat. 'You don't mind if I'm blunt, do you?'

'I—'

'You're a liability.' Theo didn't wait for her reply. 'Your work, it's all so . . . aggressive. Controversial. I know this is an admin role, and you're more than qualified for it, but you won't be happy with that.' He looked disapprovingly at her. 'You'll try and write, and really, I can't take that risk.'

'I won't!' Kat exclaimed desperately. They couldn't do this to her. It was her last chance! 'I'll do exactly what I'm told, and—'

'Now,' Theo held his hand up to silence her, 'it's OK. What you do is fine, the whole feminist thing.' He practically wrinkled his lip in distaste at the word. 'But not for us. And even if you changed your style completely . . . Well, let's just say you have a reputation.'

Kat's breath caught in her throat. 'I do?'

'Sure. That whole Devon Darsel thing, for a start. It didn't do you any favours.'

Kat felt that familiar chill descend through her. 'Devon,' she repeated slowly.

Theo rolled his eyes at her as if she was stupid. 'We're a business, Kat; we depend on access to the biggest stars. I just can't risk you running your mouth off like that. Look, I'm sorry,' he added hurriedly, and Kat realised with horror that her distress must have shown. 'That feminazi thing might be fine over at *Think Louder*, but honestly, our target demographics are thirty-year-old men. Do you really think they want to read about how misogynistic and oppressing they are?'

'I can change,' Kat protested weakly, shocked. 'I can try—'

'I'm sure you can,' Theo smiled back indulgently. 'But not here.'

No. No, they couldn't . . .

'You don't understand,' Kat cried, her control finally slipping. 'I really need this job!'

The men recoiled at her show of emotion. Of course they would. 'Don't make this worse.' Theo briskly began to gather his papers together. 'I gave you the interview as a favour to Jackson, but it's not going to work.'

Kat nodded, her last hopes draining away. She followed him to the door, numb. 'Thanks for your time,' she recited quietly. 'I appreciate it.'

'Not at all,' Theo shrugged. 'We, ah, it was good to talk to you.'

Kat wandered back across the office floor and tried her best to ignore the scenes of professional bliss at every turn. It wasn't until she was on the pavement outside again that she realised her portfolio was still lying abandoned on the conference table.

They didn't want her.

The thought echoed in her mind as Kat wandered back towards the Tube as if on autopilot. They didn't want her. *Think Louder*, *Music Nation*, every damn magazine in the city. They didn't want her. Who she was, what she did: it just wasn't enough for them.

She didn't know how, but Kat managed to keep herself together for the rest of her journey home, swallowing back tears and pressing bitter half-moon nail-prints into her palms until the front door swung shut behind her. The flat was dingy and dim, just as she had left it: a jumble of flyers and ominous printed envelopes on the floor by the door, the faint whiff of damp in the air, and the bulb in the hallway flickering, despite Anton's half-hearted pledge to get it fixed. Kat slumped to the floor, too weary to make it one more step.

She'd tried everything. She'd searched and struggled and even begged, but she was still unemployed and alone. And the worst part was, she'd been here before: back in school, after that break-up, job-hunting fresh out of university – it may be a different floor, different tears, but it was still the same terrible rejection all over again.

When would it be over?

Kat didn't know how much longer she could do this – how many times she could offer herself up to the world and get nothing but insincere 'no thank you's, and bored 'not for us's. Perhaps it would be different if her writing wasn't so much a part of her identity; if people were only rejecting what she did, not who she was. But to Kat, shaking now with loud, messy sobs, it was all the same.

She'd never thought it would be so hard. As a child, the only thing that had got her through those long, aching years was the certain knowledge that it would get better. Life would be easier. That was what her mother always told her; that was what kept her strong as she stumbled through a succession of lonely days with Walkman headphones over her ears and that tight pain threatening to consume her chest – the comforting mantra that when she finished school, when she got to university, when she finally made it out into the world, she would be happy. She would be successful. And she would never be left weeping on the floor again.

But it had been a lie.

The bullies and petty bitching never stopped; they just hid their spite with passive-aggressive undermining and new ways of excluding her. Kat wasn't looking for a seat in the dining room or waiting to get picked for a netball team any more, but she was still left hovering on the edge of a crowd, watching prettier, more popular people take everything she had worked so hard for. Those dreams that had kept her going as a child were just illusions, she realised with exhausted resignation; she had grown up, but the world never changed.

Pins and needles were beginning to itch in her legs, so Kat shifted position, her gaze falling on the jumble of post beside her. Unpayable bills, no doubt. She sighed, pushing them aside and revealing the new issue of *Think Louder*, shiny under its protective cellophane wrapper. Her throat clenched with new sadness. Of course, today was the day of truth – the day she'd always proudly leafed through her articles, reading back those words she'd worked so hard over. But there would be nothing of hers in this edition.

Numbly, Kat stripped off the wrapper and discarded the free cover-mount CD. The cretinous, leering faces of G-LINK stared back. Kat could hardly muster surprise. Mackenzie was offering up the whole integrity of the magazine to scrape and simper to those MegaBeat label suits, as if firing her wasn't enough! Suddenly fearing what was to come, Kat paused, the magazine heavy in her hands. She was going to need fortification for this.

Her shelves in the stained linoleum kitchen were predictably bare of anything interesting or indulgent, nothing but value packs of own-brand pasta and a few dented tins of tomatoes, but behind a can of minestrone soup Kat spied a half-full pack of Madeleine cakes. Armed with soft almond sponge, she took the magazine and collapsed on the scratchy couch, flipping through the rest of the issue with a heavy heart. They'd pulled her articles, of course, and now there was nothing to break up the parade of male bylines and bloke-centric content, except . . .

Kat stared at the double-page spread in disbelief, her snack turning to dry crumbs in her mouth.

'Getting Drunk With Jessica Star*' the title read, above a photograph of her former intern sprawled on top of half the members of some generic London indie band. The article was nothing but transcription of their wasted ramblings, with Jessica gasping and murmuring assent at frequent intervals. 'Our crazy new column from London's hottest scene star!' the magazine promised. 'Check out the uncensored pics online!'

It took Kat at least three minutes to muster a coherent thought. Jessica? *Jessica*?! The girl who had once asked Kat to explain the meaning of the word 'surreal' had not only been promoted in her place, but been given a column, picture byline and a pay cheque? Kat let the magazine fall to the floor again and despaired. How could this be right? She was turned away from every job in town while Jessica was simpering from the pages of her precious magazine!

'It's not fair,' she muttered with dismay, hurling a cushion across the room. Of course it wasn't fair. This was the real world. Actual ability had nothing to do with success; hadn't she been paying any attention for the last five years? Everywhere she looked, gurning idiots with double-barrelled last names and an eating disorder effortlessly glided up the food chain while she slaved twice as hard for every break. God, she was stupid. What kind of bubble had she been living in, thinking she would get ahead with nothing but hard work and integrity?

Maybe Lauren was right. Kat exhaled bitterly, remembering what she'd said that night in the restaurant. Maybe there was a secret code, an unknown playbook that made sense of this oxymoronic world. Lauren had figured it out, hadn't she? Sure, she'd sold out and become a shallow, consumerist clone in the

93

process, but she'd found a way to become successful, confident, in control of her life.

Control? That was something Kat could only dream of. She could barely control the temperamental dishwasher, let alone her own career.

As she stayed slumped there on the couch, the things Lauren had said came back to her, a little louder every time. She could have whatever she wanted.

What if that was true?

The Popularity Rules. After everything she'd been through, Kat didn't even recoil as the words tumbled over in her mind. She took a breath, letting herself imagine – just for a moment – she wasn't crying alone in a shitty flat on the far outskirts of London. Imagine the life she could build, the security she'd have, if only those rules were real . . .

No, it was just a myth, she told herself. As if some rulebook could just change everything! But the memory of Lauren's breezy confidence dampened her protests. Lauren, who had the kind of effortless success Kat longed for. Lauren, who had been the same as Kat all those years ago until she'd chosen to play their game – and win.

For the first time in her life, Kat wondered if Lauren had chosen right.

Could she really bring herself to ask for help? Kat turned the idea over and considered it from every angle. What options did she even have left? Crashing on her mother's couch and accepting failure? An empty life without writing, without her magazine, without even the pretence of a social life? She could keep trying, of course. Keep sending out applications, chasing down leads, but God, even Kat wasn't so naive as to think it would be any different this time. And what was the worst these rules could even be? So she'd get a hipster haircut and learn not to recoil in horror from day-glo romper suits – she could manage that, surely? Just because Lauren had become a shell of a person, that didn't mean Kat would lose her mind and follow suit.

The justifications were quiet, and to Kat – still furious at the sight of Jessica's smug grin – they were painfully seductive.

She could just sit around, waiting for more rejection. Or she could fight back.

The business card was lying in a pile of scrap paper and receipts on her messy desk, but it still took Kat another half hour before she picked up her phone and steeled herself. This was to save her career.

'Lauren Anderville.' The voice was so familiar, and for a moment Kat struggled to find a sound.

'I . . . It's me. Kat.' She swallowed, the words sticking in her throat.

'Hi!' Lauren sounded surprised, but she wasn't the only one.

'It's about the Popularity Rules . . .'

'Yes?'

Kat wavered one final time and then resigned herself to her fate.

'I'm in.'

Don't ever tell.

The Popularity Rules are secret for a reason. Once you know the tricks and techniques in this book, you become immune to them. If everyone found out, nothing would work any more. Sure, you'll be tempted to tell your old friends, or boast once you get successful, but any slip is absolutely forbidden. Do you really want to be the one to destroy years of hard work and secrecy? You've been lucky enough to get this chance to change your life, so take it seriously and respect the code of silence.

Don't screw it up for everyone else.

Chapter Eight

Kat was deposited on Lauren's doorstep that evening, bearing three overstuffed bin-liners and an assortment of boxes. Lauren had been tied up in meetings, but sent a driver to ferry Kat out of the grafittied ex-council block and into the quiet, leafy backstreets of Notting Hill. She didn't mind the superior gesture. Trevor, the ageing driver, had lifted her hi-fi equipment as if it weighed nothing and politely asked Anton to put some clothes on when he finally emerged, half-naked from his dark pit of a room.

'Where are you going?' he'd asked, blankly staring at empty shelves and Kat's heap of belongings.

'To stay with a . . . friend.' Kat's vocal cords almost rebelled on that last word, but she didn't have a choice. 'I can't pay rent, remember?'

'But I can give you longer, if you need.' His face softened slightly in sympathy, but to Kat, that was worse than any sneer.

'Bye, Anton,' she said firmly, hoisting her black sack of clothes and following Trevor out into the stairwell. 'I doubt I'll see you around.'

Lauren had insisted: Kat was staying with her. They would have far more time to work on the Popularity Rules, plus Kat needed to be centrally located for all the networking and parties she would be attending. Spending two hours on the night bus just to get home wasn't an efficient use of her time or energy. Kat quietly acquiesced. They both knew she didn't have a choice.

'Hey, come on up!' Lauren greeted her at the door, barefoot in jeans and a crisp white shirt. It had been a month, but she was exactly as Kat remembered her. Blonde, perky and completely alien. 'You get everything packed OK? Sorry I couldn't help, I've been video conferencing with Japan.'

'Uh huh.' Kat followed her up a flight of pale wooden stairs. This was a mistake. Just the sight of Lauren made her want to turn and bolt immediately, but Kat clenched her jaw and ventured into the flat. You don't have any options left, she reminded herself like a mantra. Tolerating Lauren was just the price she had to pay.

'So, you think you can handle this for a couple of months?' Lauren grinned as she excitedly presented the flat, twirling like a game-show model showing off the latest washing machine prize. To Kat, the gesture felt unbearably smug, but she bit back her retort and slowly absorbed her new surroundings. Open-plan, the main living space stretched right to the back of the building, with huge bay windows at both ends and a ceiling full of warm spotlights. In between was a testament to chic, designer minimalism. Bare floorboards, spotless white couches – the granite-topped galley kitchen beat even Whitney's for gadgetry and style. It was perfect.

Kat swallowed back her creeping sense of failure. 'I suppose.'

Lauren let her arms fall to her sides. 'You can see it better in daylight; there's a raised deck out the back and the skylights really open the place up.'

'Oh. Lovely.' Kat thought of her own 'outside space', as Anton had optimistically called it: a two-foot-wide ledge to the fire-escape ladder, overlooking an industrial workshop. But she didn't live there any more.

'Did you just move in?' Kat slowly made a circuit of the immaculate room. She didn't realise scenes like this existed outside upmarket furniture catalogues or *Homes and Gardens* photo-spreads. Where was the clutter, the undeniable debris of actually living like a real person? There were no photographs or papers on any surface, no dishes in the stainless steel sink, not even a bowl by the door for the keys and Oyster cards and spare change that always filled Kat's pockets.

'No, I've been here a couple of months now,' Lauren answered, directing Trevor down a hallway with Kat's baggage. She oversaw the unloading of the meagre haul and then showed him out with a warm grin and instructions to send her best to his wife. Kat was still waiting, disorientated, when she reappeared, speaking as if they'd never left off. 'I prefer taking furnished rentals; it saves me so much hassle with shipping, you know?'

Kat nodded silently. International shipping hassles? Oh sure, she knew them well.

'Anyway, you're just down here.' Lauren's ponytail swished as she led Kat off the main space to a large bedroom with a cherry wood vanity and gauzy white drapes, Kat's pathetic collection of bin-bags already overflowing beside the wardrobe. 'We can stash the rest of your stuff in my storage, down in the basement.'

'Fine,' Kat answered absently. The walls were painted a calming shade of sky-blue, a matching silk throw adorning the queen-sized bed.

Lauren watched Kat, eyes bright. 'So . . . Your new home. Not a bad place to start your Popularity Rules training, right?'

'It's fine,' Kat repeated. She didn't want to be rude – after all, Lauren was saving her from near-homelessness – but she couldn't bring herself to gush gratefully the way she knew she should. She traced the embroidery on the bedspread back and forth, back and forth. 'It's only for the summer, anyway.'

'Oh. Well.' Lauren waited. 'You want some food?'

Kat tried to remember the last time she'd eaten. A chicken salad sandwich before her *Music Nation* interview, she thought it was. She nodded reluctantly.

'I'll be in the kitchen.'

Alone at last, Kat looked around, still numb. Back at home, surrounded by her old possessions and familiar routine, she could pretend things hadn't changed. Here, the truth was unavoidable. A month ago she'd had a life that made sense, and now she was sitting in a strange flat while her ex-best friend sang merrily along to some teen-pop hit down the hallway.

Everything she used to know was gone.

Suddenly overwhelmed by another wave of loneliness, Kat felt tears begin to bubble up in her throat. She swallowed them back. Enough weeping, enough wallowing; she was here to make things different. Carefully wiping her eyes dry with her sweatshirt sleeves, Kat wandered back down the hallway and into the living area.

'What are you in the mood for?' Lauren asked, assembling antipasti on a huge, white plate. She turned the radio down. 'I stopped by M and S, so you can take your pick.'

Kat approached the gleaming, American-style fridge. The shelves were stacked with ready-prepared salads, low-calorie dressing and single-serving gourmet meal packs laid out in neat rows. She picked one at random. 'Do you . . . ?'

'Oh, no, I'm good with this.' Lauren gestured to the plate of thin breadsticks and wafer-like Parma ham.

'Right.' Kat awkwardly manoeuvred past her and found the microwave. She'd forgotten: Lauren didn't eat real food. 'Sorry. You're probably going out anyway.'

'Actually, I cancelled.' Lauren sounded breezy but Kat caught the hopeful look in her expression. 'I figured we could stay in. You know, talk.'

Kat carefully selected a slice of salami and tried to think of something to say.

'I even got some DVDs,' Lauren added, nibbling an olive. '*My So-Called Life* – remember how we used to love that show?' she grinned. 'You drooled so much over Jared Leto. Every time I see him now with all that eyeliner and those starlets, I wonder what you'd make of him. Who knew he'd peak with the boiler-room and all that brooding flannel?'

Kat looked at her blankly across the expanse of dark marble countertop. The gossip, the chatter – Lauren couldn't be serious. Did she honestly expect them to just fall into some fake kind of friendship, as if nothing had happened? Kat may have very little left in her life right now, but she did still have her dignity.

Lauren must have taken her silence as encouragement, because she reached for another wisp of ham and continued, 'It's great you're here. My calendar is always so crazy, I never take time just to hang out at home with the TV and ice-cream and—'

'I'm not here for a slumber party.' Kat tried not to snap at her, but her tone was harsh nonetheless. Teen betrayal and twelve years of silence didn't disappear the moment she walked through that door. Lauren's smile slipped.

'I know, I just thought . . .'

'That we'd sit around braiding each other's hair and painting our nails?' Despite her tiredness, Kat still felt a burn of anger at Lauren's denial. 'We're not sixteen any more, Lauren, and I'm not here because I want to "hang out".'

Lauren's eyes flicked away, and when she looked at Kat again, her expression was unreadable. 'Fine. I was just trying to be nice, you know – ease you into this.'

'Thanks,' Kat replied, pulling down a plate and cutlery from the cabinet. 'But I don't want nice. I want my old life back. That's why I'm here, so let's keep this a business arrangement, all right?'

Lauren shrugged with exaggerated nonchalance, lips pressed together thinly. 'Fine. Business it is.'

There was a long silence, interrupted only by the clash of metal on china as Kat busied herself with food containers and fetching a drink. Finally she took a seat at the corner of the long, glass-topped dining table. There were fresh tulips arranged in a blue square vase and unused candles standing in antique silver candlesticks, and it felt like cheating to be eating a microwaved meal and not a four-course culinary master-piece. Lauren was still standing by the counter, pointedly ignoring her.

Kat picked at the Moroccan lamb couscous for a minute, but it was impossible to relax with Lauren hovering by the counter behind her. 'Why don't you sit down and we can get started?' she finally suggested.

Lauren gave another shrug. 'Are you sure you want to talk while you eat?'

Kat wanted to roll her eyes at the passive-aggressive tone, but she needed to remember Lauren was doing her a favour – however much Kat hated begging for help. She swallowed and tried to sound civil. 'Call it a business meal. I still don't know what these Popularity Rules even are.' She waited while Lauren brought over the snacks and settled on the opposite side of the table. 'How about you start by telling me what the plan is? I'm assuming there's a plan.' There had better be one, otherwise Kat was taking her bin-liners and catching the next bus up to Oxford.

'Of course there's a plan.' Lauren relaxed in her seat, elegantly crossing her legs.

Kat waited.

'But first, you have to promise not to repeat anything I'm about to tell you,' Lauren frowned. 'I'm breaking my oath by teaching you the rules, so you have to swear you won't say a word. Not to anyone.'

Kat raised her eyebrows, amused. 'What am I supposed to do, cross my heart?'

Lauren sighed. 'You could take this seriously, for a start.'

'All right, I swear. Top secret, pain of death, blah blah.' Kat took another mouthful of couscous. It wasn't as if she had anyone to tell. 'So . . . ?' She waited expectantly for the words of wisdom, the secret handshake that would apparently change her life for ever.

Lauren looked at her squarely. 'The Popularity Rules are based on the simple, psychological truth that nobody ever recovers from high school.'

There was silence.

'That's it?' Kat asked, still expecting a grand revelation.

'That's all you need.' Lauren crunched on a breadstick. 'No matter how much we think we change, we always carry around in the back of our minds the person we used to be. Class nerd, sports team captain, drama queen – we're programmed as adolescents to defer to the popular kids, and we keep doing it for the rest of our lives.'

'Seriously?' Kat blinked.

'Sure.' Lauren beamed at her, smug. 'I mean, I could waffle

on about sociological conditioning and Pavlovian response mechanisms, but that's what it comes down to in the end.'

Kat tried to understand what she was saying. 'But how is this going to help me? You know what I was like in school: I was miserable.'

'Right, and that's part of the problem now. You haven't changed at all.' Lauren looked faintly amused. 'You're still a textbook outsider. It would be funny if it weren't so tragic.'

'Tragic. Lovely.' Kat stabbed at a piece of apricot on her plate.

Lauren sighed. 'Don't get all huffy. I'm helping you, remember?'

Kat tried to control her irritation. She took a long sip of water from the heavy glass goblet and placed her hands on the cool table-top. 'So, we all got programmed. Now what?'

'Now we all respond to the world in pretty much the same way as we did then,' Lauren explained. 'We react to cues about who is powerful or desirable or cool; those of us who dominated social circles back in school use those skills to keep doing it, and the rest of us automatically defer and give them whatever they want.'

Kat tried to find fault with her logic. 'But people succeed without being popular. They work hard, they earn respect, they— What?' Lauren was trying not to laugh.

'I'm sorry, it's just you're so . . . idealistic!'

Kat crossed her arms and glared. Only Lauren could make that sound like an insult.

'Come on, deep down you know I'm right. Everything is social – media, for sure, but even creative industries, or academia or science. It's just the cues and criteria for popularity that change.' Lauren smiled, confident in her case.

104

'Show me any group of people in the world and I'll show you a group ruled by popularity.'

'Maasai warrior tribes?' Kat challenged.

'Absolutely,' Lauren laughed. 'Only with them it's simpler, because they measure value by cattle and the size of their families, not how many MySpace friends you have or what kind of denim you're wearing.'

Kat protested, 'But aren't you just talking about basic social status stuff? They count cattle; we bow down to rich people and supermodels.' She shrugged. 'It's hardly revolutionary.'

'You're not getting it.' Lauren pushed her full plate aside and stared at Kat intently. 'Popularity is different. It doesn't necessarily come from things or predictable facts. Money and beauty are currency, sure, but they don't buy you everything. It all comes down to high school.' She tapped her manicured fingertips on the glass to emphasise every word. 'In the end, we're just playing out the same dramas of our high-school selves, over and over.'

'Sounds like fun.' Kat was tired already.

'It's not supposed to be fun.' Lauren's smile was quiet and thin. 'But if you figure out how to manufacture those popularity cues, how to create status and manipulate everyone to follow you . . . Well, then you can overcome your own conditioning and get everything you want. That's what the Popularity Rules will do.'

Kat finished her meal in silent contemplation. Even as recently as yesterday, she would have been arguing with Lauren, trying to disprove her cynical theory of human behaviour. 'People grow up,' she would have cried. 'We move on!' But Kat had spent hours that afternoon slumped on the floor thinking just the same thing. The world didn't change. Everyone was still stuck in a nebulous social hierarchy, paying service to the in-crowd and pushing outsiders like her aside. Wasn't that why she was here – so she could learn how to be one of those special few and never be rejected again?

She exhaled reluctantly. 'So where do I begin?'

Lauren got up, clearing their plates. 'I have it all mapped out. We'll start tomorrow.'

'Why not now?' Kat followed her to the kitchen area.

'Because you're tired and emotional,' Lauren answered briskly, 'and I need you in peak condition.'

'You make it sound like a marathon.' Kat muttered, only half-joking.

Lauren turned on her. 'This isn't a game, Kat. It's serious and it's hard work. We've got years of programming to overcome, not to mention strategies, goals and your not exactly shining attitude.'

Kat refused to be chastened. 'So let's be serious for a minute. What do you get out of this?' The question had been haunting her ever since Lauren had made the offer. Kat was getting free rent and personal Popularity Rules coaching, against every precious oath Lauren had sworn. But what was in it for her?

Lauren paused. 'Call it a war of ideas,' she said finally, watching Kat with an unreadable expression. 'You've spent the last decade thinking I'm some kind of terrible person for choosing the Popularity Rules, and fine, I've accepted that. But now it's your turn. Who knows?' She gave a twisted smile. 'You might end up agreeing with me.'

'I doubt it,' Kat replied with disdain, looking at Lauren and seeing nothing but the immaculate blonde shell of the girl she'd once known. 'I would never be such a heartless bitch.'

'Maybe not,' Lauren answered, infuriatingly calm. 'But perhaps you'll understand.'

Kat turned away, not even bothering to respond as she

stalked back to her bedroom, her Converses making muffled thumps on the floor. She'd sworn not to go back to that old betrayal, but there Lauren went, dredging up the carcass of their friendship as if it was something to be proven right over.

'Don't stay up too late,' Lauren called after her, as Kat closed the door and collapsed, weary on her bed. 'I don't want you looking a wreck in the morning!'

It's all or nothing.

⸻⸰⸻

The Popularity Rules aren't optional. You can't just browse through the rules like you're shopping for trends or picking out classes from a catalog – every single stage matters, so either you commit to taking them all on, or just go back to sitting at the loser table.

Everything about you has got to change, so prepare yourself for a complete life overhaul. Think of it as a three-step program to cure yourself of pathetic social failure: first comes how you look, then how you think, and finally, how to control other people. Say goodbye to your boring, lonely life; you won't miss it one bit.

Chapter Nine

Kat slept like the dead. She tried to tell herself it was down to exhaustion from all her emotional trauma and insecurity, but when she drifted awake the next morning at eleven a.m. to sunlight streaming through the pale drapes and the soft scent of lilacs from the vase on the bedside table, she had to admit: expensive mattresses and Egyptian cotton bedding may not be the status-driven rip-offs she'd always thought.

Yawning, Kat slipped out of bed. Her navy dressing gown was crumpled in one of those bin-liners, she knew, but instead, Kat found herself reaching for the green silk robe Lauren had helpfully left hanging on the back of the door. It fell around her skin, light and unbelievably soft, and Kat wondered again if there might not be some . . . fringe benefits to this Faustian pact of hers. She'd expected Lauren to come bursting in at dawn and drag her off to contort her body into agonising yoga poses, or make a sacrificial offering to the gods of grace and charm, but perhaps she was easing Kat into this. Or maybe she'd been distracted plotting a minor military invasion.

Either way, Kat still felt a tremor of apprehension as she padded out into the main living area, the polished floorboards cool against her bare feet. By now, Anton would usually be sprawled in front of the television, filling the flat with the loud cheers of overexcited football hooligans, but now Kat could hear only blissful silence. Silence, and somebody talking in German.

Maybe she'd been right about that invasion.

'Das kommt darauf an.'

Kat followed Lauren's voice to a large nook off the living area. She'd overlooked it the day before, but now she could see it was a home office space, with another glass-topped table, flatscreen Mac and stacks of paperwork neatly arranged. Lauren was already dressed in a vibrant poppy-print sundress, sitting in a black leather executive's chair and arguing with somebody on speakerphone. She saw Kat and hit a button.

'Morning.' She smiled brightly. 'How are you doing?'

'Um, fine.'

'Sleep good?'

'It was OK.' Kat paused. The man on the other end of the line was still ranting in guttural German. 'You know, I can go . . .'

'No need; I'm all finished here.' Lauren hit the button again and wound up the call. At least, that's what Kat assumed she was doing. Her own language skills had reached their zenith with GCSE French.

'So, what's the plan for today?' Kat trailed after Lauren to the kitchen, wondering how she could be so crisp and organised so early. Well, it was early for Kat. Then Lauren headed straight for the elaborate silver contraption taking up half the counter and it all became clear: caffeine.

'We're meeting a friend of mine for brunch,' Lauren replied, over the shaking and spluttering of the vast machine. 'And then we're beginning the first phase of the rules: total external transformation. We're going shopping.'

'Shopping?' Kat repeated grimly. 'But I don't have—'

'I'm loaning what you need while we do the rules,' Lauren cut her off. 'A new wardrobe is non-negotiable.' She must have mistaken Kat's horror at the words 'new wardrobe' as an objection to the credit arrangement, because she added, 'I'll keep track of everything we spend, don't worry. You'll pay me back.'

Kat nodded slowly. She hadn't really thought about the funding of this great, misguided Popularity Rules project, but surprisingly, she didn't mind the thought that Lauren would be footing the bill, at least for now. Lauren owed her, and by the looks of the flat, she could afford it.

'You'd better get moving,' Lauren added, taking the tiny espresso cup from the bowels of her machine and gulping it back in one shot. 'We leave in half an hour.'

Forty minutes later, Lauren had vetoed every one of Kat's jeans-and-T-shirt outfits. 'Don't you have anything remotely fashionable?' she cried in despair.

'I thought that was the point of the shopping!' Practically every item of clothing Kat owned was littered on the once-spotless floor, her soothing haven of a room now resembling a minor disaster zone.

'Yes, but they actually have to let us *in* the store first.' Finally, Lauren disappeared back to her own wardrobe, returning to thrust a basic black dress at Kat. 'This could fit you,' she said optimistically.

Kat doubted it. The last decade of physical torture and occasional starvation had left Lauren's assets far higher, tighter and slimmer than Kat's, but she was too impatient to argue. Taking the dress with a sigh, she slammed the door shut between them and pulled the soft fabric over her faded bra. The wrap-style dress fitted, just about, even if it did skim and cling a little closer than Kat preferred. 'And no sneakers!' Lauren yelled as Kat tugged the dress closed around her.

111

'Having comfortable feet is the most important thing,' Kat repeated her mother's shopping mantra.

'No sneakers!'

'Here will be fine,' Lauren told the taxi driver, slipping out of the car on a busy stretch of Oxford Street. Kat looked around dubiously. The Disney Store and HMV hardly seemed like Lauren's scene.

Lauren caught her expression. 'This way, come on.'

Kat followed obediently as she cut through a narrow gap between the shops and emerged in a long, sun-drenched courtyard lined with potted plants, chic-looking stores and restaurants. The busy rush of traffic outside quietened; the hordes with their Primark plastic sacks were replaced with polished shoppers dangling glossy paper bags. Footsteps away from the main street, they were suddenly in a different world.

She followed Lauren until they reached a cafe with a dark-green awning.

'Kat, meet Gabriella Casarez,' Lauren led her to a table on the square where a petite woman in a yellow T-shirt awaited them, her dark hair cut choppy and artfully flicked out around a heart-shaped face. 'She's a stylist friend of mine, currently revolutionising *ChicK*. Gabi, this is your new project.'

Kat hung back as Gabi bobbed up from the table and kissed her exuberantly on both cheeks. 'I'm guessing this is a sign of your faith in me!' Gabi playfully scolded Lauren in a thick Brooklyn drawl, as Kat caught a glimpse of a trail of tattooed butterflies peeping over the edge of her neckline. She wasn't sure what she'd been expecting from Lauren's trusted stylist – fearsome French chic perhaps, or an achingly hip Hoxton man – but it certainly wasn't tattoos and a bright Warhol-style Britney shirt.

'Sure, I have faith.' Lauren settled in a shaded chair and imperceptibly gestured for a waiter. 'If anyone can save her, you can.'

'Hmmm.' Stepping back, Gabi assessed an increasingly self-conscious Kat, her lightning-quick look zipping from Kat's hair (damp from the shower) to her feet (clad in plain black flip-flops). 'How long have we got?'

'Can you manage a week?'

'A week!' A laugh bubbled from Gabi's fuchsia lips. 'Wait, you're serious?'

Despite her earlier despair over Kat's fashion deficiency, Lauren now gave a careless smile, crossing her legs elegantly and slipping on a pair of tortoiseshell-framed sunglasses. 'She'll be a quick learner, right Kat?'

Kat nodded reluctantly. Even with a friend around, Lauren was all business. Kat should have been careful what she wished for.

Or maybe this *was* Lauren in relaxed mode.

'A week it is.' Gabi shrugged. She caught Kat's expression as they took their seats. 'Don't worry, I'm not that bad,' she reassured her. 'You might even have some fun.'

Fun. Right. Biting back an impassioned monologue on submission to social standards of beauty, Kat turned her attentions instead to the menu. She was going to need fuel for all this conforming, but instead of a comforting range of food options, she was faced with . . .

'Salad?' Kat exclaimed, her voice heavy with woe. 'Bran flakes? But what about the bacon?'

'Don't whine,' Lauren sighed, ordering an egg-white omelette and dry toast from their young bronzed god of a Spanish waiter. 'You need healthy food for energy; shopping is an endurance sport.'

'I'll alert the Olympic committee.' Kat begrudgingly chose a fruit platter as Lauren and Gabi began to discuss her imminent transformation as if she wasn't even there, scribbling notes and making illegible lists.

'We'll need statement hair, of course, and maybe even a trademark accessory.'

'A crop is out; maybe a bob, no bangs?'

'You know, I was thinking Halston, Hollywood Hills, Rachel Zoë to begin with, but now I think a sharper palette would work.'

'Right, because of the pale skin. Some Dita, some Leigh; those structured Lim pieces would work, and if we find the right lip tones, it could be pretty dramatic.'

Kat didn't even recognise half the names they were rallying back and forth. She listened silently to their plans until she was struck by a terrible thought.

'Wait, is this the part where you take off my glasses and tie my hair back and suddenly I'm the most sought-after girl in school?'

Gabi snorted into her juice. She grabbed a napkin and dabbed at her streaming nose. 'I like this one!'

'You know what I mean.' New clothes were one thing, but the way they were talking, Kat would soon be unrecognisable. As somebody who'd always sworn Ally Sheedy looked better before that Molly Ringwald got her hands on her in *The Breakfast Club*, Kat wasn't exactly itching to follow that same sell-out path.

'I know exactly what you mean.' Lauren moved her notebook aside as their food arrived. 'And I don't know what you're objecting to; the cliché stands for a reason. It worked perfectly for me, remember?'

'Vividly.' Kat couldn't keep the ice from her reply as she

recalled Lauren's miraculous switch from sane, normal teenager to a blonde, pushed-up, blown-out version of her former self.

'And the answer is yes,' Lauren continued unconcerned, nudging an offending square of butter to the far edge of her plate. 'It's time to get you out of those terrible clothes and make you realise that you have to dress for success.'

'What, you mean, "ten ways to wear my summer wardrobe"?' Kat couldn't help but make another dig as she surveyed her plate: three strawberries, a wedge of pineapple and a small pot of yogurt did not a meal make.

'No, I mean you need to create a new first impression.'

'What's wrong with my old one?'

'OK.' Lauren turned to the woman who had been watching them argue with wide-eyed interest. 'Gabi, you know nothing about Kat except those articles I sent you and what you've heard from general gossip, right?'

'Right.'

'So tell her.'

Gabi looked uneasy. 'Really?'

'Everything.'

'Umm, well . . .' she hesitated.

'I can take it,' Kat assured her. What was the worst she could say?

Gabi took a breath. 'The general opinion is that you're . . . an argumentative, objectionable, feminist bitch.'

There was silence at the table. A group of teenage girls strolled past, huge sunglasses perched precariously on top of messy, bed-head styled blonde hair. '. . . That's, like, *so* unfair! I can't believe they would even *do* something so harsh . . .'

'I know! I told Mummy it was *totally* out of order, but she . . .'

115

They drifted on, tassels swinging in unison from their voluminous handbags, and Kat finally spoke up.

'But I knew that!' she exclaimed, relieved. 'You say it like it's a bad thing.'

'And it's the very reason you're in trouble right now.' Lauren looked appalled. 'That reputation ruined you. You're unemployable.'

Kat stopped, remembering the *Music Nation* interview.

'You don't give anyone a reason to think differently,' Gabi added apologetically. 'Look at you, at what you're wearing.'

'This is Lauren's dress!'

'Yes, but look at how you're wearing it: no make-up, no accessories, plain hair . . .' Kat glanced down as Gabi rattled off her first impression. 'You've managed to take a timeless designer piece and make it totally dour and utilitarian!'

'Isn't dour is the new cheerful?'

Gabi laughed. 'It's not accessible. Unless you change how you look, you're pretty much screwed. You'll never get rid of that bitch reputation.'

If she hadn't suffered through the last month of rejection, Kat would probably have brushed off their comments. But now, after everything, the words seemed to slip past her usual defences. She deflated a little in her chair. They were right. The very things she'd always prided herself on – refusing to fit in, rejecting the stereotypical music journalist image – were the things that held her back now. Even the editors at *Music Nation* had made their minds up about her before she'd said a single word.

'I don't understand why you've kept this up so long,' Lauren continued, her tone matter-of-fact. 'I mean, you're not dumb; you must know people have images they associate with various roles. When they hear 'cutting-edge rock critic' they think of scenesters and alternative fashion. That's not you.'

'Two seconds in, and you've already lost the battle of credibility,' Gabi agreed, making another scribbled note in her pink leather notebook.

'OK!' Kat protested, cutting off their no doubt endless list of criticism. 'So I'll just get an ugly hipster haircut and a pair of those awful wet-look leggings and an oversized red belt.' She steeled herself for the indignity ahead. 'No need for all the drama.'

Lauren and Gabi exchanged a loaded look.

'It's not quite so simple,' Lauren began.

Kat swallowed another piece of fruit. 'Why am I not surprised?'

Gabi laughed at her exasperation. 'Why stop there? You could just get people to jump to the right conclusions about you, or you could go further and learn the theory behind it all.'

Kat paused. 'There's a theory?'

'Of course! If you do it right, this can be a powerful weapon,' Lauren agreed, as if this were common knowledge. 'You've got to learn about image psychology; how to use your appearance to lull people into a sense of belonging and respect. It's a basic popularity rule.' She paused as her phone began to vibrate discreetly on the table. Lauren glanced at the screen. 'I've got to take this. Gabi, you fill her in.'

'Wait,' Kat interrupted, looking back and forth between them. 'The Popularity Rules? I thought you said they were secret.' She was surprised to feel a stab of annoyance. Lauren had made such a big deal over confiding in her; was she really just going around telling everyone?

'Relax.' Lauren looked amused. 'Gabi is one of the original students from summer camp. She was in my cabin when I taught the girls as a counsellor.'

117

'Only I was smart enough to ignore all the world domination bullshit,' Gabi told Kat with a grin. 'Unlike some people . . .'

Lauren fixed her with a cool stare and then retreated inside the cafe to take the call, while Kat looked at Gabi with new interest. Until now, she'd just assumed that the Popularity Rules had necessarily led to Lauren becoming such a ruthless automaton. But Gabi had followed them too, and here she was: seemingly friendly, normal and well-adjusted. Kat needed time to think about this, but Gabi propped both elbows on the table and gave her a determined look.

'Listen up. You may think clothes are just something we wear, but they're way more than that.'

'A tool of the capitalist system of conformity?' Kat quipped. She reached across to steal some of Lauren's toast, and that glorious offending pat of butter. There, actual carbohydrates!

Gabi grinned and continued, 'That too. People are total pack animals. The easiest way to get them on your side is to blend in and make them think you're one of them.'

'What, a disguise?' Kat asked dubiously.

'Exactly.'

'But I thought this was about making me successful, not pretending to be someone else.'

Gabi shook her head. 'This isn't about who you are, it's about who they think you are. If you want to win the media scene over, you have to disguise yourself well enough to infiltrate their groups, lull them into a false sense of security, then strike!'

'Strike?' Kat was taken aback by her relish. Gabi caught herself.

'OK, so maybe I've been spending too much time with Lauren, but the point is the same: you want to be able to blend

118

into any group, anywhere, and make them accept you – look up to you, even. You'll never have to feel like an outsider again.'

'Oh.' Kat paused. Even she could see the allure of not being left on the fringes any more – all those times she'd watched the media cliques whirl by. 'But can an outfit really do all that?'

'Sure it can!' Gabi looked amazed.

'It's that high-school thing again,' Lauren added, slipping back into her seat. She saw Kat munching on the buttered toast and shook her head slightly, but didn't stop talking. 'The jock uniform, the cliquey girl uniform: we label ourselves with clothes and accessories in order to signify where in the social hierarchy we belong.'

Gabi nodded. 'Seriously, deep down everybody is still using the same cues they did when they were teens. I mean, I haven't recovered from that whole cut-off pants thing.'

'And side ponytails!' Lauren sighed. 'Remember how everyone wore them in senior year?'

'I was still thanking God for those pop princesses and the era of bare stomachs,' Gabi gave a sly grin. 'Tanned teen flesh everywhere I looked for years.'

'So you see?' Lauren turned back to Kat. 'Everyone still thinks that way, as if there's a trend they have to fit into, and anyone who doesn't is out of bounds.'

Kat began to nod, remembering how Jessica came into work with an ironic university shirt and within a week, the office was a sea of Harvard gear.

'Come on.' Lauren tucked some bills under her coffee cup and stood. 'We've been sitting around long enough. It's time for a little field work.'

Everybody likes pretty things.

❈❈❈

So it's totally shallow and unfair for beautiful people to get everything they want, but that's the way the world works. Go look in the mirror: what are you telling the world about you – that you're too poor to afford the hot trend? That you're not controlled enough to fit in those size fours? Face it: the way you look is the most important thing about you now. We only care about what's on the outside, and kind thoughts and a good heart won't get you anywhere.

Get over the injustice already and use it to your advantage. Anybody can be halfway pretty with some effort and money, so get an after-school job, buy *Vogue* and *Cosmo* and use make-up, styling, diets and surgery until you look awesome. Watch the in-crowds until you know what they're wearing, and make sure everything about you screams 'popular'.

Remember, size fourteen is not fat. Go watch Marilyn Monroe in *Some Like it Hot* and learn to dress better.

Chapter Ten

The three of them strolled back out onto the main street, Lauren leading them purposefully through the crowds until Kat found herself swept through a pair of heavy doors and into the vast, hallowed halls of Selfridges.

'There,' Lauren sighed happily. 'Now we're getting somewhere.'

'Yup, hell,' Kat muttered, almost under her breath. Gleaming surfaces and glittering display cases were twinkling at her in every direction, chandeliers loomed overhead, spotlights shone on the polished marble floors, and all around her, people surged in an acquisition-fuelled consumer frenzy.

She felt a headache coming on.

Gabi linked an arm through Kat's, no doubt to keep her from bolting back into the natural light of day. 'The way somebody looks says two things about them,' she began, pulling her deeper into the Accessories section. 'First, the things they want you to think about them, and second, who they actually are. Their aspirations, insecurities, everything. Even you.' She took in Kat's outfit again. 'You're just making a different kind of statement: that you don't care about image.'

'Maybe I don't.' Kat had to jump sideways to dodge a parade of Middle Eastern women marching down the aisle in full-length hijabs.

'So straight off the bat I can tell you're nonconformist, and damn smug about it too.'

'Hey!'

'Come on,' Gabi grinned. 'You look down on us fashionistas as shallow consumerists, blah blah. I get it. No hard feelings. Anyway, your turn: look around, pick someone.'

'Ummm, her.' Kat pointed to Lauren, who was browsing a display of zebra-print handbags with worrying sincerity. Yes, zebra.

'Ha, OK.' Gabi pretended to study Lauren, 'The vibrant print on her dress is eye-catching, so she's obviously comfortable with attention, and the simplicity of the outfit is a hint at confidence and control-freakery.'

'I can hear you,' Lauren called over without looking up.

Gabi laughed and turned back to Kat. 'But seriously – see how she's wearing a simple bracelet and the espadrille sandals? She hasn't layered herself with jackets or flashy accessories to show style or status. Clean, classic, expensive.'

'So what?' Kat frowned. All she could see was proof that Lauren was a creature from a different world, utterly at home among the designer brands and snooty salesgirls. Kat didn't know women like that, didn't even come close to encountering them in her natural habitats of grungy backstage dressing rooms and packed Tube carriages. 'I don't get how noticing any of that helps me.'

'You can use that information.' Lauren rejoined them. 'It all helps you build a profile of their personality. With me, the outfit lets you know I'm confident and secure in myself – you would have to be just as chic and classy for me to ever consider you an equal. I don't have any obvious insecurities, so you'd better be looking for another target to manipulate.'

'And so modest, too.'

They strolled through the labyrinthine concession stands, Lauren with one eye on the expensive wares while Gabi was already scanning the crowd for their next fashion victim. 'Now, look at her,' she nodded over at a woman in her early thirties browsing a stand of sunglasses nearby. 'Shaped jacket with huge metal buttons, high-waisted jeans and that awful zebra-print bag. What does that tell you?'

'I don't know.' Kat tried to look at her with fresh eyes. 'She's a stupid fashion victim?'

'Almost!' Gabi laughed. 'OK, see, right away you can tell that she cares about trends and is trying to be on the cutting edge. Fashion matters to her, so you can probably win her over with some easy flattery about her style.'

'Oh.' Kat looked at the woman, still browsing on the other side of the narrow display. Could she hear them?

'I'd say she works in a creative industry, on a low salary, but socialises with people way wealthier than her,' Gabi continued, her voice low. 'She wants to fit in despite the difference. She's actually pretty desperate.'

'How can you tell all of that?' Kat asked in a hushed tone. It was as if Gabi was reading a language she didn't understand.

'It's simple when you know how,' she reassured Kat, pointing out the different parts of the outfit. 'Start with the jacket: it's next season's shape, but it's cut kind of cheap, so it's not designer. And those jeans don't flatter her at all, so she cares more about looking fashionable than looking, you know, *good*.'

Their whispers obviously weren't quiet enough because the woman glared at them. Kat felt a rush of embarrassment.

'And that bag's a disaster,' Lauren added, loudly. The woman made a noise of protest as if she was about to confront them, but at the sight of Lauren's steely gaze she evidently changed her mind, slipping wordlessly into the crowd. 'It's typical,' Lauren sighed. 'She totes around that hideous thing just because it's designer and she wants us all to know what it cost.'

'But I thought you said she was on a low wage.' Kat was confused.

'Right,' Gabi explained gently, 'so the fact she cares enough to spend six hundred pounds on a mess like that shows how much she wants to fit in with her rich friends.'

'She spent that much – for a bag?!' Kat exclaimed. *Vive la révolution* indeed.

'Like I said, pathetic and insecure.' Lauren paused. 'Which would make her a perfect target, by the way.'

Kat tried to process all the new information. 'It can't be that simple, can it?' she asked, a little wistfully. 'We are who we are, and wear what we want and that's it?'

'That's not the way the world works, honey.' Gabi shot her a sympathetic look, but Lauren wasn't so patient.

'This is vital material, Kat. The Popularity Rules say you have to select each outfit depending on the occasion, the social scene and how you want to be perceived. The more work your clothes do, the less you have to try to fit in – it's all there in the very first impression.'

She pulled Kat to a halt at the start of the high street clothing concessions, a vast hall of rails, mannequins and pushy teenagers. Blouses, jewellery and little sequinned dresses seemed to be draped off every surface to attract the passing magpie shoppers. 'Right, time for you to put all this theory into practice.'

Kat blinked.

'You've got, say, half an hour to pull some outfits together.' Lauren checked her BlackBerry for the time. 'We'll meet upstairs; I'll call you.' She gave a brisk nod, and then to Kat's surprise, turned to leave. Wait, they weren't going to guide her through this?

Gabi caught Kat's expression. 'Don't panic,' she called as she followed Lauren away. 'Think rock scene, hipster, statement accessories!'

They disappeared into the crowd, and Kat was left alone to contemplate her task.

A whole new image. This couldn't be too hard, surely?

Halfway through her allotted time, Kat wasn't feeling quite so confident. She'd wandered around the hall twice now in an aimless daze, Lauren and Gabi's instructions blurring in her mind as she considered the huge array of fashions on offer.

Comfort and practicality – those had always been her watchwords. A good pair of jeans, a T-shirt and maybe a plain cardigan or her old leather jacket and that was it: outfit complete. But now, Kat had a dozen new things to think about: did a red dress convey more confidence than a purple one? Was gold jewellery more aspirational than silver? Did high heels show strength or insecurity? What about if they were boots, not sandals?

Aware that her time was quickly running out, Kat panicked. Lauren would lecture her for not taking this seriously if she returned empty-handed, and Kat didn't want Gabi thinking she was a lost cause on her very first day. She looked around. Over in the Topshop section, a young woman was browsing the racks; she must have been twenty, or thereabouts, wearing a vintage-looking plaid dress, complicated rope sandals and several draped necklaces. Her blunt-cut fringe and bright lipstick reminded Kat of the way Jessica looked, prancing about the office in a completely unsuitable outfit.

Now it was Kat's turn to be completely unsuitable.

Discreetly shadowing the woman, Kat watched what she

was looking at – and then quickly grabbed it in her own size. Vintage-style skirts, vest tops, filmy chiffon blouses: Kat soon amassed armfuls of clothes and accessories, so by the time her mobile rang, she had a respectable haul.

'Ready to meet?' Lauren asked.

'Uh huh!' Kat struggled to hold the phone to her ear. 'I don't think I can carry anything else.'

'Really? That's great.' Lauren sounded surprised. 'We're on the second floor. Just follow the signs to "personal shopping".'

By the time Kat found the others, her arms were aching. She'd dropped a heap of jeans on the escalator, trailed a flimsy wisp of a top through the designer hall and ignored more haughty glares than she usually faced getting backstage at a major label show. In short, she was not warming to the shopping experience.

Until Gabi put a plate of tiny cream cakes in her hand.

'Wait, what is this place?' Kat asked. She dropped her haul and looked around. Instead of sweaty, curtained cubicles and lines of bored customers, the small room was totally private, lined with elegant mirrors, soft lighting and plush pastel couches. Gabi was lounging with a glass of something bubbly while Lauren flicked through a freestanding rail of clothes.

'Private dressing room, for preferred clients,' Lauren answered, more than a little smug. She clapped her hands together and took some of the clothes from the heap where Kat had left them. 'Now, let's see what you've found.'

The first outfit – a mini-skirted smock over a white blouse with layers of charm necklaces – drew swift head-shakes.

'Storybook slut,' Gabi decided. Kat took one look at the

amount of thigh on show and had to agree with the sentiment, if not the language.

The second, with skin-tight jeans, boots and a drapey sequinned top, inspired yawns and shrugs.

'Bor-ring, seen it everywhere!' Lauren barely looked up from a magazine.

'I thought I was supposed to blend in,' Kat protested. She hated the heavy scrape of the sequins and felt like her flesh was being squeezed to oblivion in the jeans, but this was what everyone wore to those after-parties and shows. Wasn't that what they wanted her to look like?

'Next!' Lauren merely ordered, turning to a new page. Kat retreated behind the heavy brocade curtain with a sigh and reached for another indignation.

It was only when she was standing in front of them in her fifth ensemble (a wet-look leggings/layered vest outfit she remembered seeing on some PR girl at a rock show) that Gabi and Lauren exchanged worried looks.

'Did you really think about the visual cues you want to communicate?' Gabi began gently.

Lauren wasn't so soft: she folded her arms and glared at Kat with obvious disapproval. 'Have you been listening to a single word we've said today?'

Kat stared at her reflection and tugged awkwardly at the vests. 'I tried,' she answered in a small voice. She hated the feeling of inadequacy that had set in. The other two women were sitting there expectantly while she delivered only disappointment. It wasn't her fault! She'd spent her life filling her mind with useful, intellectual material, instead of poring over *Vogue* and *Grazia* so she could tell the vital difference between an empire waist and a smock.

'This is all the kind of stuff Jessica Star wears,' she added, with a small twist of resentment on the name of her rival. 'And the women I see around shows . . .' Kat trailed off, sinking down on one of the circular stools in defeat.

'Let me guess: blonde hair, heavy on the eyeliner and trust funds?'

Kat nodded.

'That's OK, it's a rookie mistake.' Gabi leaned over and patted her shoulder reassuringly. 'You're on the right track.'

Kat didn't see the silent exchange between Gabi and Lauren, but she knew there must have been one, because when Lauren spoke up again, she used a softer, more supportive tone.

'Those girls may be part of the crowd, but are they the ones calling the shots?'

Kat shrugged, exhausted. 'They're women – what do you think?'

'Right.' Lauren's expression began to sparkle again. 'Which is why you have to bring some status into the outfits. The looks you put together are fine, if you're a disposable intern – nothing but eye-candy – but you want to be taken seriously too. You want respect.'

That made sense. The cliquey girls may act as if they were the most important people in the room, but they were relegated to sound-bite jobs and trophy positions: not what Kat wanted, or deserved. 'So how do I get it?'

'With these.' Lauren got up and wheeled the rail of clothes into the middle of the room. Kat had thought it left over from a previous client, full of bold, designer pieces, but Lauren and Gabi began sorting through the garments with obvious glee.

'It was so much fun shopping for you,' Gabi told her, eyes bright. 'I haven't dressed anyone like this in ages, and there are so many awesome looks around.'

'You've got to get the balance right,' Lauren added,

thrusting a dress at her. 'Edgy and modern, but with one thing that screams "authority".'

'A statement necklace,' Gabi agreed. 'Or some amazing shoes.'

Kat obediently took their selections to the curtained corner, relieved that creative control was now out of her hands. In fact, she had to applaud Lauren's tactics, she decided, as she pulled off the hideous leggings: by giving Kat free rein at the start of this restyle – and completely exhausting her with failure – Lauren had pre-empted any protests or resistance for this, the real makeover.

'Ready yet?' Lauren called impatiently, as Kat struggled to pull the complicated straps straight.

'Nearly, I—'

Lauren yanked back the curtain and shook her head at the sight. 'It's called nude underwear, Kat, and it's your very best friend.'

'Hey!' Kat pulled the dress up over her (admittedly greying) bra.

'What do you think for a shoe?' Lauren turned back to Gabi. 'Something low-key, aggressive?'

'I know!' Gabi delved into a pile of boxes. 'And I have the perfect bracelet . . .'

There was a light tap at the door, and then a polished-looking woman with soft grey hair walked in, her pink tweed jacket topped by a slim row of pearls. 'Everything all right in here, ladies?'

'Just great, thanks.' Lauren beamed. 'No, Gabi, pass me the Gucci.'

'Oh, very nice.' The woman looked at Kat. 'A very daring look.' She moved closer and began picking the tangled straps apart. Lauren knelt at Kat's feet and started pushing her toes into a pair of flat, buckled boots. Gabi advanced, tugging Kat's bra out of sight and adding a long, swinging swan pendant in hammered metal.

It felt as if she was being swarmed by a pack of eager fashion drones.

'Stop it!' Kat lunged backwards. Three shocked faces stared back. 'I mean,' she recovered, 'could I just have some room?'

Lauren swung around to the Selfridges woman. 'I think it would be best to have some privacy; you know how people can get,' she added with a meaningful look.

'Of course,' the woman nodded. She backed out slowly, giving Kat an extra-patient smile. Kat bristled. It wasn't her fault she had a normal sense of personal space!

'There, now what do you think of that?' Gabi took Kat's shoulders and turned her towards the mirror. She opened her mouth to reply, but Lauren answered first. Of course, it wasn't as if Kat's opinion mattered in all of this.

'Perfect.' Lauren nodded.

'I know.' Gabi grinned. 'Kat?'

Kat tried to see herself through their eyes. To her, it was just a complicated dress, with vaguely military-looking straps crossing her shoulders. The boots were nice, she supposed – no heels, at least – but whatever miraculous shift in image projection and status cues they wanted her to see, Kat was coming up blank. 'Umm, sure.' She finally replied. 'I mean, it's . . . nice.'

Lauren exchanged a very uncharacteristic high-five with Gabi and then turned back to the rail. Kat idly picked up the tag hanging from the side of the dress. She caught a glimpse of a three-digit number and promptly hated herself, just a little.

'They're not exactly the great equaliser, are they? The

Popularity Rules, I mean.' Kat was struck by a thought as she gazed at her reflection. 'You make out as if they help the downtrodden outsiders, but really they only help the girls who can afford to buy all of this.' Kat gestured around the room. 'The girls who have enough money to spend the summer at some ritzy camp and get inducted in the first place, who can get a stylish haircut and buy designer clothes and pretend they're just like all the other rich kids who make up the popular cliques.'

She ran out of breath, letting her arms fall to her sides. She sounded ungrateful, she knew. After all, magazines and the media would have her believe that millions of women wanted nothing more than to stand in a private dressing room in one of the wealthiest cities in the world, while personal stylists draped them in hundreds of pounds' worth of clothes. But Kat wasn't other women. And that seemed to be the problem. 'I'm just saying, it doesn't seem very fair.'

Lauren looked outraged. 'You want fair? It's a secret guide, not a progressive social system!'

'And anyway, you're wrong.' Gabi quickly moved between them. 'Not about the rich bitch cliques, but about the rules. There are plenty of normal kids who go through that camp, who get their places through scholarships and outreach programmes. I did. And you don't need any of *this* to do the Popularity Rules.'

'You don't?' Kat was still dubious.

'Not at all!' Gabi laughed. 'It's just about the theory and projecting the right look. Teenagers don't need bandeau dresses and heels! You can use vintage clothes, thrift store, even chain stores if you do it right.'

'So what are we doing here?'

Gabi cracked a grin. 'Because *she*—' she jerked her head in

Lauren's direction, '—is footing the bill. And you're not a teenager any more.'

'You're nearly thirty,' Lauren added.

'Am not!' Kat whipped around and glared at her.

Lauren smiled at her distress. 'Yes, you are. You've been in denial for years with your student job and ratty T-shirts and tiny, crap apartment, but you've grown up now. You need to start acting like an adult.' She moved to Kat's other side, so that Kat was flanked in front of the mirror. Trapped.

Lauren gave her a quiet smile.

'It's time you started winning.'

It's not rocket science; it's harder.

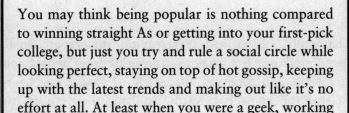

You may think being popular is nothing compared to winning straight As or getting into your first-pick college, but just you try and rule a social circle while looking perfect, staying on top of hot gossip, keeping up with the latest trends and making out like it's no effort at all. At least when you were a geek, working hard was allowed – to stay popular, it's all got to seem like a breeze.

Sure, it takes less effort to just be one of the crowd, but if you're going to be the one running things, you can't slack off. Discipline, self-control – you haven't shown much of these so far, but get with the program. Sometimes it takes the most work for the most frivolous things.

Chapter Eleven

Thankfully, Lauren had a presentation to prepare, so Kat spent Sunday in her pyjamas, recovering from her shopping marathon and studying the stack of magazines Lauren insisted she know backwards. Studying their covers from across the room while she finished reading her thick historical biography, that was.

Monday, however, wasn't quite so forgiving.

'Kat? Kat, are you awake yet?'

'Mneuh.' Rolling under her covers, Kat ignored the insistent tapping on her bedroom door. Of course she wasn't awake; it was early. Nobody sane would ever dream of being up so early. Now, if she just pretended the pesky noise didn't exist . . .

'Because we— Oh great.'

Kat heard the brisk sound of Lauren's heels clicking into the room. So much for privacy. Circling, the footsteps paused by the window and then approached the bed. A moment later, Kat's soft, warm, comforting duvet was yanked away.

'Whatd'youwant?' Kat mumbled, squinting up at Lauren. Pale light was spilling through the drapes from another glorious summer's morning, but Kat was more concerned with the position of the clock hands on her bedside table. She gasped. 'Six o'clock – in the *morning*?'

'We're leaving in ten minutes,' Lauren informed her.

'You're insane.' Kat flopped back. Without Gabi to act as a buffer between them, Kat's prickly sense of resentment

134

returned. She really didn't like this woman. 'Officially, certifiably, mad.'

Lauren gave a small smile. 'If you're awake enough to use five-syllable words, you're awake enough to come to the gym.'

The gym. Such simple words, such dread they inspired. She looked up properly for the first time, and was horrified to see Lauren dressed in a sports vest and pair of leggings, wearing an expression that said she would not be denied.

'No!' Kat shrank back, thinking quickly for an excuse. 'I can't! I . . . have no clothes to exercise in!'

'I thought as much, so I bought you these.' Lauren picked up a shiny bag and dropped it in front of her. 'Go on, we'll be late.'

She stood over Kat, arms crossed and utterly determined. Kat turned and buried her head in her pillows, but Lauren just stood, looming above her. The minutes ticked by, until it became clear that the only person alive more stubborn than Kat was there in that very room. At last, Kat broke.

'Fine!' Slowly pulling herself into a sitting position, Kat rubbed the sleep from her eyes. 'I'll be ready in a minute.'

'You have three.' Lauren smiled victoriously and left her alone with the Lycra.

Oh, the Lycra.

Kat stumbled over to the dresser for underwear. It was becoming very clear that Lauren's good humour was directly related to Kat's total obedience, and could disappear in a flash should she dare to resist whatever torturous regime her new mentor had in mind. As much as a smug, all-knowing Lauren filled Kat with frustration, she had a feeling that the pissed-off, drill-sergeant version would be even less fun.

'Perfect,' Lauren beamed when Kat emerged. 'Look, we match!'

So they did. Kat took in their reflections in the mirror by the door, Lauren all glowing and blonde, dressed in purple with hot pink piping, and then there was her: navy-blue and lime-green outfit and a deep frown line cutting across her face.

They always had gone together.

'Body fascists . . . social pressures . . .' Kat gasped as she stumbled to keep up with the treadmill, 'patriarchal . . . means of . . . domin— Oh!' To her relief, the evil machine finally counted down the last few seconds of the program and slowed to a halt. She bent double, gulping for air and clutching her abdomen. She hadn't felt a stitch like this since the dreaded school cross-country runs. Why would anyone choose to spend their morning in this agony?

'Sorry?' Lauren looked over, barely breaking stride as she jogged along in perfect time to the Beyoncé track that boomed out across the gym. They were in the middle of a vast concourse of polished wood, mirrors and Lycra-clad exercise devotees starting their day with pain and glucose drinks. The sign on the door may have used the words 'health club', but Kat was quite sure it was mistaken. This was, in fact, hell.

'I said,' Kat straightened, her heart rate slowing enough for her to hear something other than the frantic thunder of her own pulse, 'this is a conspiracy. Men trying to keep women down by—'

'Oppressive beauty standards blah blah blah.' Lauren took a sip of water from the bottle clipped to her station. She shot Kat a familiar grin. 'It's pointless lecturing me; I'm immune, remember? I was, like, thirteen when I learned to tune out the moment you mention patriarchal bonds.'

Kat waited until she didn't feel she was about to die before speaking again. 'But what's the point of me doing all this? And if you say "to get in shape" I will walk straight out of here,' she added fiercely, despite the fact she wasn't sure if she *could* walk. 'I will not diet, do you hear me?'

Lauren rolled her eyes. 'Calm down, I'm not stupid. And your figure's just fine.'

'Thanks,' Kat shot back sarcastically. 'Your validation means the world to me.'

Instead of replying, Lauren simply reached over and set Kat's machine to start again, not even breaking stride. 'It's not about weight or appearance, although the Popularity Rules do say— No, never mind.' Lauren quickly stopped that dangerous train of discussion. 'For you, it's about being healthy.'

'I am healthy!' Kat protested, through gasps of exertion.

Lauren raised an eyebrow. 'I'm guessing you've spent the last month of unemployment stumbling from your bed to the couch and back again.'

Kat didn't answer.

'Exactly: that's not healthy. Once we get you out on the scene, you'll be racing around, going to two, three different parties or events every night. What are you going to do, miss prime networking opportunities because you need to take a nap?'

Kat guessed that the question was rhetorical.

'No, your whole lifestyle needs to change,' Lauren didn't even take a breath as she slowed her machine to a halt. 'You've got to have some discipline if we're ever going to change things: not just research and strategy, but exercise, better nutrition, maybe even some yoga to balance your energies better.'

Kat scowled. Yes, this was officially hell.

'Of course,' Lauren looked over at her, a definite challenge in her eyes, 'if you don't think it's worth it, you can always quit.'

There it was: the wonderful little word that had been taunting Kat for the last three days and two miles. Quit. She could do it, so easily, just catch the next bus up to her mum's in Oxford, be done with all these rules, and treadmills, and constant reminders of her own failure – for ever.

And Lauren. She would be done with Lauren.

'No.' Kat replied through gritted teeth. 'No, I'm still in this.' Quitting was a luxury, for people who had contacts and back-up plans. Who could pay their rent. Who could bring themselves to abandon everything they'd worked for.

'Great. Then I think we should start you with some cycling.' Lauren stopped Kat's treadmill and began to steer her towards the bank of stationary bikes. 'Then a mixed program for flexibility and strength.'

'Start? But I've finished!' Kat gripped Lauren's arms in horror, struggling to remain standing as her thighs went numb and blood rushed to her head. She may not be quitting the Popularity Rules, but she had to draw the line somewhere. This was her health and survival at stake! 'I came, I exercised. I nearly died on that thing!'

'Just think of it as training,' Lauren comforted her. 'For when you have to run away from all those big, bad patriarchs wanting to drag you back to the kitchen.'

Kat would have kicked her had she any strength remaining in her legs. 'Please,' she begged instead, 'let's go now. I'm done.'

'Sorry, hon.' Lauren looked at her with sympathy, even as she was binding Kat's feet down to the pedals. 'That was just your warm-up.'

After a combination workout that would put most athletes to shame, Kat was too dizzy and exhausted to protest as Lauren sped them back to the flat, pushed her towards the shower, directed her to a pre-selected outfit from their new purchases, and then propelled her out of the door again. It was only when Kat was sitting, light-headed, in the back of a taxi, that she even thought to wonder what new Popularity Rules programme was in store for her today.

'Uh, Lauren? This outfit doesn't exactly scream "hipster music journalist".' Kat looked down, confused. For all the lectures about image association and visual cues, Lauren was leading her forth on her first real day wearing a surprisingly conservative blouse and pencil skirt. Only the pair of turquoise high heels (already nudging a blister to life on Kat's left heel) hinted at any bold colour or creative flair.

'It doesn't.' Lauren looked pleased that Kat had even noticed. 'But it does say "confident, competent assistant".'

Assistant. The word hung between them in the back of the cab as they swerved through early-morning traffic. Kat baulked.

'No. No way. You never said anything about me being your slave!'

'Relax,' Lauren seemed amused. 'It's not for real. No offence, but you're completely unqualified to be my PA.'

Kat wasn't comforted by that fact.

'No, this is part of the programme,' Lauren continued, pulling out her sleek leather notepad and her copy of *The Popularity Rules*. 'Observation and learning.' She paused, frowning. 'Usually we take weeks on this section; training the campers how to watch us in action, picking up all the tools they'll need for their own work back home. But we don't have weeks for you.'

Kat didn't see what that had to do with being Lauren's lackey, but she reached for the battered red book all the same.

It was the first time she'd held *The Popularity Rules* for herself, and she slowly turned the faded pages, gazing at the neat, handwritten notes as Lauren laid out their schedule.

'We need to overlap some stages, so setting you up as my assistant will give you the chance to watch me in action, at the same time as your basic transformation and research. You might have to do some menial tasks . . .' Kat's mouth dropped open in protest at that, 'but it's all good experience. And, as you'll find out soon enough, having someone running around after you helps establish power and authority.'

'I thought those were part of your natural aura.'

'They are. But this denim firm we're at today has a total asshole doing their marketing. It'll be useful having you there. An extra pair of eyes.' She handed a portfolio of files to Kat. 'Here are the details on Domina Jeans, and my other main client, *ChicK*.'

Kat took a cursory glance at the pages, and then stopped: there were background checks, credit records, even surveillance photos. 'Wait, why do these look more like intelligence files than brand presentations?'

'The importance of thorough research,' Lauren answered with a worrying gleam. 'Don't worry, we'll get to that later. For now, your job is to watch and learn.'

So watch and learn Kat did.

The Domina Jeans collective was housed in a large, Scandinavian-style office near Piccadilly, within striking distance of a Starbucks and equipped with a state-of-the-art copier. Which was lucky, because that seemed to be the sum total of Kat's assistantly duties for the next four days. Never mind observing any of Lauren's people management skills, she was too busy gasping her way through morning workouts, fetching coffee, printing documents, and imagining a dozen painful deaths for Lauren every time she ordered Kat around without so much as a 'please' or 'thank you'. Kat understood that it was all an act to shore up her authority with the Eurotrash, overtanned marketing guy, but nonetheless, it took every ounce of self-control not to pour Lauren's coffee down her spotless pale-blue dress when she publicly scolded Kat for daring to bring it back with regular milk, not soya.

'Get it right next time or we'll have to have another review,' Lauren told her crisply, not even raising her eyes from the documents in front of her. Kat flushed, backing away. She didn't know, or care, what the conference room full of hip creative executives thought of her, but she still hated being made to look like a useless idiot.

Retreating to her temporary perch of a desk in the sole dark corner of the office, Kat eased her feet out of another pair of heels and discreetly rubbed her painful arches. Her feet, head and pride all ached. This was not working out the way she'd hoped.

It wasn't as if she'd thought Lauren would simply wave a magic wand and transform her overnight into the most sought-after, well-paid music journalist in London. Well, she may have dreamed of something so miraculous, but Kat wasn't completely foolish (no matter what the clean-shaven men of Domina Jeans might now think). She'd known that it would take real work and planning to undo the years of isolation, exclusion and general invisibility she had settled for, but running down the street to fetch bottled Evian because the office only had Volvic and the visiting CEO wouldn't dream of drinking anything different? Not on her agenda.

The more she thought about it, the more Kat wondered if the Popularity Rules would get her any closer to her goal, or if they were just a painful, exhausting distraction from the reality of her pathetic life.

When she dared suggest as much to Lauren, the reaction was disbelief.

'Of course it's hard work, Kat.' Lauren looked at her with obvious disappointment as they wearily climbed the stairs to the flat, just after ten p.m. The work day didn't end at six, Kat was discovering – not when there were colleagues to chat with in an upscale bar, or potential clients to woo over dinner, or distant industry insiders to 'spontaneously' run into for cocktails and gossip. Kat found the extra-curricular activities just as draining as her daytime duties, only instead of dashing around after Lauren's every whim, she had to smile and laugh and attempt not to alienate Lauren's entire client list.

'Using the Popularity Rules to win over adult social circles, industry elites, and all without years of experience or training . . . These aren't just cliquey schoolgirls you have to fool; they're far more savvy than that.'

'I know, and I'm willing to suffer for it.' Kat followed her into the flat, kicked off her shoes and threw herself, exhausted on the couch. Even Lauren looked relieved as she sank down in an armchair. It had been a long day. 'But I still don't see how what I'm doing will help with my goals – the music industry, journalism, all of that.'

'You're doing your research, aren't you?' Lauren frowned. 'Those magazines and DVDs aren't for fun; they're about establishing a cultural connection to your peers.' Kat thought of the stacks of pop culture detritus untouched in her room. She stayed silent. 'And your external transformation is coming along,' Lauren continued, as if checking off a mental list. 'We've done clothing, make-up, and you're set to see Giles tomorrow for hair. We're right on schedule. This is all according to plan.'

Kat sighed. 'I guess I thought, well, that I would be *doing* things, not just going shopping and sitting around with back copies of *Entertainment Weekly*.'

'Some people would think that was heaven,' Lauren noted with a teasing smile.

Kat managed a faint laugh. 'And some people might think tracking your client's online browsing history was a gross invasion of privacy.'

They both grinned, and for a moment Lauren wasn't just the authoritarian sell-out determined prove herself right, she was the friend Kat used to know. Then Lauren peered at Kat, frowning. 'Didn't I tell you to do something about those eyebrows? If you don't pluck them yourself, I'll have to book you in for a wax.'

'Fine!' Kat sighed, hauling herself up and limping towards her bedroom. Lauren was no friend; she was just a necessary ally. 'Book me in for whatever you want!'

Make your own mask.

Honesty, openness – you've probably been raised to think these are good things. Hell, your clueless parents probably coached you to 'just be yourself!' too, as if the world will shower you with shiny trophies for simply existing. As you've figured out by now, it doesn't. Confiding in people only gives them ways to hurt you. Sharing who you really are and what you think just sets you up for attack.

The only way to win is self-control. Sure, it's practically sociopathic, but acting on impulse could ruin all your strategy. Start thinking about yourself from the outside in: decide what face you're going to show everyone, and then stick to it. It doesn't matter how you feel; nobody should see the truth – only the act you put on to achieve what you need. You can seem like you don't give a damn, or you can look vulnerable and weak, but it should all be a performance, just part of your plan.

Chapter Twelve

It only took her until the next morning to rue those words, when Kat found herself sitting with her head yanked back in a hairdresser's sink and industrial quantities of bleach scalding her scalp.

'I thought you said blonde wasn't part of my core personal brand!' she yelped, as the renowned – and sadistic – Giles massaged the lotion even deeper into her burning skin.

'Which is why we're going for auburn,' Lauren answered. She was sitting in the chair next to Kat, having soothing herbal conditioner massaged into her own hair, while Gabi flicked through magazines on the stool nearby, frequently consulting with Giles. Neither of them seemed to be concerned about the flames of agony licking at Kat's head. 'You can only get the real vivid hues if you bleach out the colour first. You know, it's not supposed to hurt,' she mused. 'You must have a sensitive scalp.'

'You think?!' Kat clenched her jaw. Her head was soon swathed in some kind of wrap and she was parked beneath a spherical heater, like an old woman in rollers. This must be what everyone meant when they wittered on about beauty being pain. She did not agree. Pain was an evolutionary tool designed to keep you alive, not something to wilfully ignore in pursuit of a particularly fetching shade of hair dye. And what kind of 'vivid' red demanded that they strip all colour from her own, poor brown hair?

'It'll be worth it, I swear,' Gabi said, not for the first time. 'Just look at what a good hairstyle did for Agyness Deyn, or Leigh Lezark.' She named two women Kat recognised more for trading on their looks than any useful skills or talents, but she supposed that was the point.

'It's a Popularity Rules shortcut,' Lauren agreed, snatching Kat's book out of her hands and replacing it with a copy of *Heat* magazine. 'If the hair's brave and bold, they'll assume you are too.'

But Kat didn't feel particularly brave or bold when, two hours later, Giles uncovered his handiwork with a flourish. Instead of her normal, somewhat tangled locks, she had a sleek film of bright red hair swinging from a precise side-parting to about four inches below her jawline. It swooped low across her forehead, the edge razor-sharp right the way to each fearsome tip, and the colour . . .

God, the colour!

Not ginger, or strawberry blonde, or even a respectable auburn shade like they'd promised. No, Kat's hair was a gleaming, dark metallic scarlet – a shade never found in nature, let alone atop an unsuspecting woman's head.

She let out a whimper.

'Fabulous!' Gabi cried, clapping her hands together and kissing Giles exuberantly on both cheeks.

'Love it,' Lauren declared. For a moment, Kat's horrified expression was ignored as they set about congratulating each other and themselves for such amazing vision and style. Finally, Lauren met her eyes in the mirror. Her proud smile slipped.

'It's a shock, I know,' she began carefully, as Kat tried to hold back the tears inexplicably pricking the edges of her eyes.

'Oh, sweetie, it's OK!' Gabi rushed to her side.

'But . . . look at me!' Kat cried. She didn't know where to start. The style that she'd never in a million years be able to replicate, not even armed with every appliance and product in the Western hemisphere? The colour, which made her think of sweets packed with artificial flavours, and Ronald McDonald?

Or how about the worst thing of all: the fact that she didn't even recognise herself when she looked in the tall, bulb-lined mirror. Some other woman was staring back at her. Some other woman with truly ridiculous hair.

Lauren squeezed her arm in an approximation of support. 'Look at it this way: at least there's no going back now. You're in this – committed to change. To being a success.'

'And haven't you been saying we place too much value in external appearances?' Gabi slowly led her away from the mirror, Lauren silently handed Kat her bag, and somehow, Kat found herself propelled back onto the bright, sunny street. 'You'll get used to it. Eventually.'

She didn't.

For the rest of the day, Kat felt like a stranger in her own skin, ignoring double-takes at the Domina Jeans office, avoiding stares on the street, and turning away from her own, alien reflection. Lauren was right, she thought grimly, lying awake the next morning and staring at the ceiling; she couldn't go back now. Not without a bucket of black dye and some gardening shears.

'You'll be at ChicK by eleven?' Lauren knocked lightly and then poked her head around the door. Apparently, she spent her Fridays overseeing the temple of teen consumerism, and thus so would Kat. 'I've got a staff meeting, but then we can slip out for lunch. I emailed you directions, and contact numbers in case you can't get hold of me.'

'You told me last night,' Kat sighed. She should be happy – her post-haircut trauma meant that Lauren was letting her skip the usual early gym torture session – but after a week of prodding, pushing and dyeing, Kat felt as though happiness was a distant dream.

'It's a different environment from the Domina offices,' Lauren warned, this time in a bright blue exercise outfit. 'You'll need to go edgier, fashion-wise: something young and hip, but still professional.' She began to leaf through the wardrobe, pulling out new designer pieces.

'I can dress myself!' Kat protested, sick of having every little decision pre-empted. 'I can even tie my own shoelaces.'

Lauren refused to rise to the bait. 'That's great, but you won't need to.' She dangled a pair of high-heeled Mary Janes in the air. 'These have buckles, see?'

'Enough!' Kat hurled a pillow at her. 'Don't you have, like, a demonic spinning class to get to?'

'You're right, I do.' Lauren's eyes widened. 'Thanks!'

She hurried out, the front door slamming shut soon after, and finally Kat was left alone.

Alone, how glorious. It was hard to believe that even a week ago, Kat had been slumped in Anton's empty flat all day, starved of human company. Now, she barely had a moment to herself. If trailing uselessly after Lauren at work wasn't bad enough, Lauren and Gabi thought nothing of invading Kat's space during lunchtimes and evenings too – ransacking her wardrobe to dispose of every last threadbare T-shirt and forcing her to sit through make-up tutorials.

Yet despite the hundred-odd hours they'd spent together, Lauren was still a complete stranger to Kat.

As she wandered towards her bathroom and turned the shower to its strongest setting, Kat wondered how it was possible to be with somebody for so much time and yet still know so little. All week she'd been waiting for the facade of perfection to slip, but it seemed bulletproof: Lauren was officially the most controlled, outwardly poised person Kat had ever met. From traffic jams to late contracts, nothing seemed to ruffle her. Even when idiot clients cracked question-able jokes, or strangers tried to hit on her in restaurants, that warm smile never disappeared – it only upgraded to charming and perky when the situation demanded. Kat was exhausted just watching her.

Was that the kind of woman she was supposed to be? An emotion-free automaton that never so much as blinked in the face of mindless stupidity? Struck with a sudden curiosity, Kat towelled herself dry, pulled on a thick, fluffy robe and padded silently down the hallway to Lauren's bedroom.

She shouldn't be snooping, she knew. It was rude and sneaky, an invasion of privacy, but still, Kat's slight sense of guilt wasn't enough to stop her pushing the door open and stepping inside. She needed to know more.

Chic and minimal, the room was decorated in the same white as the rest of the flat, utterly clean and clutter-free. The only colours came from the items carefully arranged on display around the room: a teal silk dress hung outside the wardrobe, a pair of beautiful jade leather pumps adorning a corner chest. But to Kat's disappointment, there were no clues of any kind to tell her something more about Lauren – no letters or photographs, no vacation mementos. Even the bookcases were carefully stacked with generic volumes of vintage poetry, Shakespeare, Eggers and Franzen.

Kat traced the perfection with her fingertips, coming to a stop by the antique corner cabinet. She opened the doors, expecting a rail packed with shoes, or purses, but instead she found a hint of the girl Lauren used to be. Stacked neatly in one corner was a pile of DVDs: *Singin' In the Rain, Funny Face, On the Town* and the rest. Musicals. Beside them, three dresses were carefully hung: heavy vintage cuts with full, swirling skirts and nipped-in waists. Nineteen forties, Kat guessed, or maybe earlier. They were displayed almost reverently, the matching shoes or clutch placed beside them, awaiting that tea dance with Gene Kelly, or midday park stroll with Fred Astaire.

Kat smiled slowly, a rush of nostalgia coming over her. As an awkward teen, Lauren's love of musicals had been a deep, fervent thing. Kat had tried to explain that the seven brothers had technically kidnapped their seven brides, and that Henry Higgins's treatment of poor Eliza amounted to nothing less than psychological torture, but Lauren would not be swayed. Whenever the senior girls tired of their MTV hunk-fest and relinquished the student common room, Lauren would take up residence, lost in a world of wide-brimmed hats, endless cheer and spontaneous bursts of song. And Kat would sit humming right along with her.

Maybe Lauren hadn't changed completely after all.

After a quick breakfast Kat returned to the bathroom mirror, and all the trials that awaited there. Initially, she had taken pride in her cluelessness when it came to the finer points of skincare and hairstyling, but now it felt like a weighty handicap – somehow Kat had half the amount of hair, but it still took her at least twenty minutes to straighten it to a sufficiently artful sheen. Then there was the dewy-effect foundation, dark-lined eyes . . .

This was why women hadn't rebelled against the system that oppressed them, she thought bitterly, attempting to get her fringe to flick out the way it had done in the salon – they just didn't have the time.

When her mobile rang, Kat paused, eyeliner wand halfway to her face. It was her mother, she just knew it was. Somehow, the universe had sent out a broadcast that Kat was engaging in un-Elliot activities, and Susanne was on the line to find out what.

'Katherine, I've been ringing for days.'

She was right.

'I know, Mum, I'm sorry.' Bracing herself, Kat finished her eye make-up with the phone lodged between her ear and her shoulder. She may as well deal with two unpleasant tasks at once. 'I've been . . . busy.'

'You have? That's wonderful. I knew you'd find something. What is it?'

Here came the difficult part.

'I'm helping out a friend.' Kat paused. 'Lucy, from Oxford; remember her?' Lucy was a good name – sweet, reliable, the kind of woman who would come to her rescue and keep a cupboard full of Earl Grey tea. 'She needed somebody to do some freelance editing. Anyway, I'm crashing on her couch for now.'

'You could have told me. I sent some books to your old flat.'

'It's OK. Anton will pass them on.' The lies sounded metallic and false to her, but perhaps the distance would mask them.

'So you've sorted everything out?' Kat could hear rustling in the background. She pictured Susanne in her dark study, liberally adorning first-year essays with her red pen. 'Are you sure you don't want me to put that call in to Jodi too, just to be safe?'

'No, I'm fine now.' Kat turned away from her decidedly un-fine reflection. 'How have you been?'

'Oh, all right, I suppose. Planning for the conference is getting stressful, but that's always the same, I suppose, and at least this time . . .'

Her mother's complaints about the finer points of organisational bureaucracy took Kat through her blusher, lip stain and a spritz of a clinical-looking body mist that Lauren swore would emphasise her natural pheromones. All the while, Susanne discussed the programme for her upcoming conference, unaware of her daughter's temporary defection to the dark side.

'. . . and I'm really looking forward to Greta's paper; she's exploring women in the media, and how they perpetuate damaging gender stereotypes.'

Kat jerked, knocking a pot of loose powder over the whole counter. 'Shit!' she muttered, trying to sweep the mess of shimmering particles into the sink.

'Katherine?'

'I'm fine, Mum.' Fine, except for her temporary rejection of everything her mother believed in, that was. Luckily, Susanne was oblivious.

'Why don't you tell me what you've been doing? How are you feeling?'

Now that was a tricky question.

Kat swallowed. 'I'm actually running kind of late right now.'

'I'm glad to hear you're back on your feet. I was worried, you know.'

'I know,' Kat gulped. Susanne's concern over unemployment and minor depression would be nothing compared to her worry if she found out about Kat's current situation.

'Well, I suppose I'll prepare for my next tutorial. Take care!'

'You too.' Kat hung up, leaving the phone in the bathroom

152

and closing the door as if to distance herself from the conversation.

The lying was unfortunate but necessary, she reminded herself. After all, it was Lauren's teenage transformation that had inspired Susanne's critically acclaimed book on adolescent betrayals of female identity. And if her mother could see her now . . .

Kat felt a flicker of guilt rise in her again as she reached for the bright plaid pencil skirt and tank tops Lauren had laid out for her to wear. Fashion, make-up, painful high heels and figure-hugging outfits designed to showcase her body, not her mind – Susanne had spent her life raising Kat to reject these things, to stand against the mainstream, sexist conformity of society and cut her own path, with integrity, with principles. With honour.

Her hand wavered. All week long she'd been wearing a costume, trying to remember her lines, but now Kat wanted nothing more than to relax back into some semblance of her former self. Gabi and Lauren had ruthlessly purged her motley collection of jeans and T-shirts, but she still had a few garments stashed away. Just because Lauren kept her true self locked away in that cabinet, it didn't mean Kat had to as well.

The guilt melted into rebellion, and just like that, Kat reached for her old jeans.

Appearances are the ultimate deception.

∞∞∞

Now you're changing everything about yourself, you need to start changing what you think about everyone else, too. Don't underestimate anyone. You've probably got into the habit of writing off anyone who seems shallow and dumb, like somebody who uses glitter eyeshadow is automatically a waste of space. But think about it: you look like that too now. So, if you're putting on an act to blend in, trying to manipulate them, what makes you think they aren't as well?

Take time to figure everyone out. If they really are as clueless as they seem, you'll be able to run rings around them, but if they're playing the game too, then you've just saved yourself some major humiliation.

Chapter Thirteen

Kat was prepared for the *ChicK* offices to be a shiny, brash temple of gender encoding, but wandering down the main hallway she was still hit with a sense of numb disorientation, as if she'd wandered into a scientific experiment to create the ultimate teenage girl. Posters of Disney pin-ups or pop stars adorned the walls, and every desk was cluttered with a jumble of CDs, make-up and various teen knick-knacks. The staff seemed young and energetic: chatting on phones or plugged into headphones at their bright flatscreen computers, and as Kat drifted, feeling supremely out of place, she spied one woman watching episodes of an American teen show on a large TV, making occasional notes, while another slowly leafed through the latest *US Weekly*.

Ah, to shape young minds, one awesome lip-gloss colour at a time.

She paused by a vast wall of shelving, stacked with what looked like every magazine ever published. Were those back issues of *Sassy* and *J-17*?

'You must be Kat.' A young woman approached her, bright in a polka-dot blouse and city shorts. 'Hey, it's so great to meet you!'

'Hi,' ventured Kat. The girl's tone was suspiciously perky. She glanced around. 'I'm looking for Lauren . . .'

'She told me to find you. She's like, in a meeting now?' The girl beamed, her inflection making every other sentence seem like a question. 'I'm Anna. I'm an intern here.' She paused, her gaze drifting down Kat's casual outfit for a moment before recognition registered on her face. 'Oh right! Lauren said you might be faking a "before" photo for our makeover!' Anna giggled. 'I totally forgot. Anyway, the fashion closet is that way. Let me know if you need anything!'

'No, I'm fine, thanks.' Kat managed to stop herself from scowling as she backed away and followed the girl's directions deeper into the labyrinth of offices. Lauren had been expecting her to screw up! She'd primed the *ChicK* staff to expect Kat as a scruffy loser, as if she'd known Kat would try and switch back to her old wardrobe the moment she was left alone.

Kat was surprised to feel a begrudging sense of admiration for her tutor. It was vastly irritating, but nothing got past Lauren; she had a contingency plan for all eventualities. Including Kat's stubborn rebellion.

'Hey sweets!'

Kat found Gabi in a red dress and thick, black-rimmed glasses, sitting on the floor in the midst of what could only be described as sheer chaos. Clothing and accessories were strewn two feet deep around her, hanging from every available surface, draped out of bags and boxes. Kat had once passed an H&M the day the Marc Jacobs collection arrived, but this was even worse.

Struggling to her feet, Gabi grabbed Kat's hands. 'But what happened? You were doing awesome!'

Kat rolled her eyes, self-conscious now. 'It's just a pair of jeans!'

'And a ratty shirt, and those boots!' Gabi wailed, picking at a handful of Kat's T-shirt. 'Has Lauren seen you yet?'

'No,' Kat sighed. She paused, looking at Gabi hopefully. 'So

. . . maybe this could be our little secret?' The fewer lectures, the better.

Gabi mimed locking her lips and tossing away the key.

'You're allowed a few relapses,' she told her, wading into the debris and plucking out an armful of garments. 'For me, it was my glasses. It took me months to get used to wearing contacts when I first started; changing all my clothes was OK, but stabbing my eyes every morning with those tiny plastic lenses . . .' She shuddered. 'Thank God glasses got hip again. Anyway, these should work for you.'

'Thanks.' Kat retreated behind a screened corner to change, quickly re-emerging to view the damage in one of the free-standing mirrors Gabi was using as a hanger. Tight black denim pencil skirt, oh-so ironic 'Fresh Prince of Bel Air' T-shirt, and all finished off by armfuls of gold, chain-link jewellery.

Foiled again.

'Don't look like that; it's not the end of the world.' Gabi began to hum an unfamiliar tune as she settled back to cataloguing the chaos. 'It's only fashion!'

Kat wasn't so sure.

'This idea that all we need is a makeover and suddenly everything will be perfect . . . It's wrong. I'm sick of all those stupid teen movies and magazines; it's such a cliché.' She swept aside a stack of trilby hats and perched on the edge of a chair, pulling on her mandated pair of heels with a sharp, bitter motion. 'What's so bad about comfortable clothes, and having body hair, and, I don't know – being normal? It's like we'll never be enough, as we are.'

Gabi looked up, serious for a moment. 'But do you even think about why the cliché works? I mean, why we keep watching it, over and over?'

Kat shrugged. She didn't think about reasons, not when

there were solutions to be found. 'Because we're brainwashed into zombie-like consumerism?'

'Nope. It's the possibility.' Gabi paused, clutching a tangle of belts. 'We love the idea of transformation, so we can make ourselves something more than just ordinary. It's why you're doing this, isn't it?' she asked. 'You don't want to settle for what you are; you want to be more. You want to win.'

There it was again: that reference to winning. It was like watching Lauren talk about the Popularity Rules all over again, Kat realised. At the mention of change and transformation, Gabi took on a reverent glow. But Kat wasn't a swooning disciple just yet.

'I can win without heels and lip-gloss,' she pointed out.

'Really?' Gabi looked at her thoughtfully. 'I guess you have more faith in society than me.'

Kat snorted. 'I doubt that.'

Gabi grinned. 'Me too. But you're writing off the lip-gloss too soon, I think. Sometimes it takes looking different to really start changing, and then there are times a makeover is mandatory to even get in the door,' she added, resuming her sorting. 'I mean, before that summer in Maine, I was just that geeky kid from a bad neighbourhood who looked at other girls too long. My life sucked.'

Kat studied her curiously. She couldn't believe that the tiny, tattooed style genius had ever been anything but fearless.

'But you're still the same person, underneath it all, aren't you?'

Gabi shook her head. 'You don't understand, the Popularity Rules, what Lauren taught us – they gave me the tools to change everything. I got brave, I got smart. You think I could have ever made it to fashion school on my own, or managed to come out, or even wound up here in London?'

Kat stayed silent, fiddling with her bracelets. Gabi's fervour was unnerving – not because she was a blind ideological nut, but because it made too much sense.

'I'd better go find Lauren.' Kat leapt up. 'She probably needs me to get coffee or something.'

Gabi grinned. 'Go fetch.' She tossed Kat one of the belts. 'Drape the T-shirt over it . . . Yeah, like that.'

'Thanks.' Kat sent her a warm smile and then retreated once more into the labyrinth of workstations. Only she didn't have anything so welcoming as a mythic Greek beast awaiting her.

After she'd wandered the hallways for a while, another helpful, perky intern directed her to an office next to the kitchen. Lauren wasn't there, but a tall, dark-haired woman was by the desk, elegantly leaning over some large mock-up pages.

Kat tapped lightly on the door. The woman looked up, her hair falling in a chic bob.

'Hi.' She gave a thin smile. 'Can I help?'

'I'm . . . an associate of Lauren Anderville's.' Kat still couldn't bring herself to say 'assistant'.

The woman's smile broadened. 'Come on in; I'm looking for her myself. I'm Nina Myles.'

'The editor.' Kat recognised her name. Lauren had given her one of those ridiculously fat files on the *ChicK* project, but Kat had only glanced through it. She didn't need to know somebody's marital history and online user-names just to fetch photocopies.

'That's right.' Nina looked back at the pages on the desk. 'I was waiting for Lauren's feedback on these designs. Why don't you take a look?'

'I don't know.' Kat stayed in the doorway. 'I haven't really seen—'

'But that's perfect.' Nina ushered her in the narrow office.

Kat couldn't believe it belonged to Lauren: it was dim and gloomy, and she could hear every movement in the kitchen next door. 'You can give me some fresh eyes!'

'Well, OK.' Kat moved closer, looking at the layouts. She didn't know anything about magazine design, but she remembered what Lauren had been reciting practically all week: tell people what they want to hear. By the way Nina adjusted one set of designs, fussing with a tiny smudge and making sure it was perfectly straight, it was clear which she preferred.

'That one,' Kat announced, pointing at Nina's choice. She must have been right, because Nina's face lit up.

'You think?'

'Definitely,' Kat nodded quickly. 'It's eye-catching, and . . . bright.'

Nina smiled at her again. 'Fresh eyes, I told you.' She glanced at her watch. 'Oh, I completely forgot – editorial meeting! Grab those, will you?'

'But Lauren . . . ?'

'Is probably already in the conference room.' Nina sailed away, leaving Kat to follow her, trying hard not to crease the large pages. She tripped along on the loathsome heels, rounding a corner and coming to a halt in the doorway of a sunny room. About ten staffers were sitting around a long, glass table, and at the head was Lauren. Looking murderously at Kat.

Of course, Lauren would never do something as uncontrolled as look murderous in public. To a casual observer, she was the picture of ease: relaxed posture, folded hands. Kat knew better.

'Just put them on the table,' Nina waved, sashaying to the other end of the table and taking a seat. 'This is, Kat, right?' Nina didn't wait before telling everyone, 'She's working with Lauren. She's been *so* helpful.' The staff shifted, nervous. Kat looked from Lauren down to Nina and back again. She gulped. It was clear there was an epic power struggle under way, and she had inadvertently stumbled right into the middle of it.

'I looked for you,' Kat whispered apologetically, slinking to a seat beside Lauren.

'Mmm hmm.' Lauren casually scribbled some notes. Kat felt a lurch of guilt. She may be a complete novice when it came to projections of power, but she guessed that having your assistant trot obediently after someone else wasn't exactly high on the list of how to exert authority.

'Sorry.'

'No problem!' Lauren's tone was bright, her smile gleaming. Kat didn't believe her for a second.

'Let's get started, shall we?' Clapping her hands together, Nina rose to her feet. 'We've got a lot to get through, so, Graham, why don't you tell us where you are with our September celeb, and—'

'Actually, Nina,' Lauren interrupted, her voice warm, 'I have a call scheduled, so why don't we skip right to it? I think we were going to see some redesign ideas.'

There was a pause. Kat glanced sideways at Lauren, who was leaning back in her chair as if she owned the place. The table was clear, save a notepad, but Kat knew that glint in her eye: a gauntlet had just been thrown down.

'Actually, I've decided to work with our existing design for now.' Nina carefully folded her hands and smiled fakely at Lauren. 'We revamped just a few months ago, and the testing has been very positive.'

'I'll be interested to see those numbers,' Lauren replied, unmoved. 'But we really do need to see those designs, for comparison.'

'Of course.' Nina shot her an insincere grin. 'They're right here.' She passed them along to the woman on her left, who passed them on down the line. She didn't, Kat noticed, move to hand them to Lauren herself. 'And I totally agree about the comparison. In fact, I was showing the designs to your associate just before the meeting, and she agrees with me.'

'She does?' Lauren raised her eyebrows.

Kat froze. It had been a set-up? Nina had asked her opinion just to throw it back in Lauren's face, and she'd been foolish enough to fall for it! Holding in a groan, Kat slouched lower in her chair. She couldn't even bring herself to look at Lauren.

But Lauren was unmoved. 'Well, it's always nice to get a broad range of opinions,' she said, 'although it's not like you to lose sight of our core demographics.'

'I—'

'No, that's fine. It's settled, if that's your decision.'

Kat blinked. She couldn't believe Lauren was giving up so easily, but just as Nina allowed herself a victorious look, Lauren sighed, as if regretful. 'Although, it is a shame,' she murmured, making notes in her file. 'I was hoping to have some new material to show the board, before they made their decision . . .' She shrugged lightly. 'But I guess not.'

Kat watched Nina's face slip. 'Decision?' she asked, struggling to keep her composure. 'I didn't know the board were actually looking to make changes. I thought this was just a general overview.'

'You're right,' Lauren beamed. 'Forget I even said anything. I think we're done here for now?' She closed her file and made as if to get up. 'Victor's waiting for my notes.'

'I suppose we could get some feedback on these new designs,' Nina added, as if it was an afterthought.

Lauren raised her eyebrows. 'Only if you think so.'

Nina's jaw tensed. 'OK, absolutely.'

'Great.' Lauren beamed again. 'Good meeting, everyone.' She swept out of the room. Kat fumbled to follow.

'I'm sorry,' she apologised again when they were out of earshot, walking back towards the lifts. 'I didn't realise she was setting me up.' Kat felt another flush of shame before finally admitting, 'I should have read that file.'

Lauren stopped and looked at her for a long moment. 'It's OK,' she sighed. 'No harm done.'

'Are you sure?'

Lauren nodded. 'That was just grandstanding. Nina knows she's cornered.'

'Oh, OK.' Kat felt a strange sense of relief. It shouldn't matter to her – this didn't have anything to do with her real life – but still, she felt bad about letting Lauren down.

'Was that true?' she asked, as they waited for the lift. 'Are the publishers going to sell, or fold it altogether?'

Lauren turned to her. 'Did I say that?'

'Well no, but . . .'

A careful smile spread across Lauren's face. 'Ninety per cent of this game is bullshit, Kat. It doesn't matter if I can shut this place down, only that Nina believes I can.' She shrugged. 'Some people only change if they think they don't have any other choice.'

Kat frowned. 'But what if she finds out you don't have that kind of authority?'

'That doesn't matter, because I never said I did.' Lauren noticed Kat's confusion and continued, 'If people believe you have power, they fall over themselves to give you more – that's just the way things work.' She smiled, wide and victorious. 'Ninety per cent bullshit, I'm telling you. Now, let's get lunch.'

Kat silently stepped into the elevator and wondered how much of that applied to her.

Build your army.

The first stages of any strategy are simple: figure out what you want, and who can help you get it. We're not talking about vague things like 'happiness' or 'world peace' – you need specific goals to plan for. Once you have your wish list, you can start researching the people who are standing in your way: they're your enemies, so hold off going near them until you have a ton of dirt and are truly unbeatable.

What you need right now are allies to help get you started. Sure, you're in this to begin with because you're not popular, but even someone like you will know some classmates, or distant cousins, or maybe even people you've never met before who can help you out. Either way, you'll need them to feed you information, party invites and insider gossip so you can start to put your plan together.

Chapter Fourteen

Not surprisingly, Nina had a sudden change of heart about the redesigns – and Lauren. When they returned to the office after lunch, Lauren had miraculously been reassigned to a new, sun-drenched office, while Nina cooed with enthusiasm whenever their paths crossed. Kat's next challenge, however, was not so easily overcome. Her time for sitting back and learning was over. Now, according to the Popularity Rules, she needed a strategy, and to get that, she needed allies.

'Three names, that's all you've got?' Lauren swung her towel over the front of the stationary bike and hopped up onto the seat. 'You've had ages to think of people!'

'I've had four days,' Kat corrected, climbing onto the bike next to her and giving a few experimental turns of the pedals. They were into her second week with the Popularity Rules, and since she hadn't yet made any more humiliating mistakes, they were celebrating with the dubious honour of a spinning class. Kat would have preferred some Chinese takeaway, or the right to wear her old jeans again, but Lauren had raved about the endorphins as if pedalling to nowhere was some kind of religious experience.

'You wanted to know who I can count on for help, so there they are: Whitney, Nate, and my mum.' Kat glanced around. The fierce look of the pert, toned women stretching out in every row made her wonder if she really was set for half an hour of invigorating fun. More likely, death.

Lauren shook her head, gripping her handlebars as the warm-up music began to play. 'I should have known it would be bad.' She sighed in disappointment, but Kat just focused on pumping her legs in time with the beat. This wasn't too awful, right? Almost like taking a nice bicycle ride on a summer's day – except instead of the joys of nature, she was trapped in a gleaming gym room, faced with a mirror and led by an instructor yelling orders over a terrible Ministry of Sound album.

Then, just when Kat was feeling somewhat reassured, the pace began to increase.

'Ten years out in the world,' Lauren sighed again, seemingly unconcerned by the new gruelling rhythm. 'And all you have to show for it is one friend, a co-worker and your mom. Jesus, I've seen geeky outcast teenagers with more social leverage than you!'

'Can you give it a rest?' Kat asked, already straining at the pedals. Her thighs were definitely not used to being abused like this.

'I'm not going to sugar-coat it for you,' Lauren warned. 'You've got to learn to face facts if we're going to get anywhere.'

'I am facing the facts!' Kat exclaimed, gasping for air. Just how insensitive could Lauren be? She could handle criticism or physical torture, but not the two at once!

'Are you sure you're not overlooking anyone?' Lauren tried again. The song came to an end, but there was still no relief: the instructor simply barked to keep working until the next thumping dance anthem began. 'No ex-roommate who now works for a major label? No cousin who got engaged to the editor of *The Times*?'

Kat broke. 'I know it's your greatest joy in life to remind me just how unpopular and disliked I am,' (pant) 'but I get it, I really do.' (pant) 'You don't have to keep telling me over and over again!' She groaned, collapsing forwards on the handlebars as the speed of the routine finally dropped again.

There was a pause, filled only by the obnoxious dance beat pumping from the speakers and the faint wheeze of Kat's breathing.

'I'm sorry.'

When Kat mustered the strength to sit up, she found Lauren looking at her with a subdued expression. Kat managed to shrug, as if she didn't care.

'No, I am.' Lauren looked down, adjusting her sweatband. 'I forget sometimes that not everyone's as . . . analytical as me, that's all.'

She seemed so wistful for a moment that Kat began to feel uncomfortable.

'It's not a big deal,' she lied, forcing herself to start pedalling again. 'I'd just prefer something more constructive. We are supposed to be making things better, not going over my failings again and again.'

'Right.' Lauren quickly agreed. 'So have you made your list of goals yet?'

Kat pedalled harder.

'Kat!'

'You know what I want,' she protested, channelling all her frustration into the evil weapons of torment strapped to her feet. 'A job, a place to live, something approaching a pension plan.'

'Uh huh.' Kat was gratified to see a faint glow of sweat start to appear on Lauren's ever-perfect face. 'I think we can manage that.'

167

'Even with my woeful lack of social capital?' God help her, she was even absorbing Lauren's motivational boot-camp language too.

Lauren nodded. 'Right,' she agreed, breathing faster. 'Just . . . makes it more challenging.'

'And we like challenges,' Kat reminded herself. For instance, her current challenge to keep breathing. She wasn't sure how much longer she could keep this up: her muscles ached, she was gasping for air, and—

'Oh!' Kat exclaimed, as a strange lightness began to flood her body. Slowly, the pain eased and her limbs became elastic, moving on their own as her heart pumped faster and she felt a kind of dizzy elation. It was almost . . . it was almost like sex. She looked around, and found the grim-faced women all beaming with similar contentment. No wonder Lauren worked out six days a week!

Lauren laughed, noticing her expression. 'Not bad, huh?'

'Why didn't I know about this?'

'Trade secret.' Lauren grinned, still pedalling furiously. 'And don't worry about your list. We'll just have to make it work with what we've got.'

What they had was her old co-worker, Nate. He must have been run off his feet with the latest issue, because for days, Kat's breezy, casual message to meet for a catch-up was left unanswered. Finally, Lauren insisted they get proactive, and so Friday found them hovering on the busy pavement outside his lunch spot of choice, an upmarket burger cafe.

'I don't see why we can't go in now.' Kat was discovering that her three-inch-heeled boots may have been designed for several purposes, but standing wasn't one of them. 'He's sitting right there.'

'Yes, but then he gets to choose whether or not to talk to you,' Lauren explained, tapping away at her mobile console. 'Far better to wait until he's eating, then he has to forfeit his food to get away, which we both know is way less likely.'

'Oh.' Kat turned to Lauren, impressed. 'Sneaky.'

'I try,' she smiled. Immediately, Kat remembered that Lauren's duplicity was no good thing. Lying and treachery were not admirable qualities.

She stiffened. 'Fine. We'll wait.'

Lauren had probably restructured the entire financial system by the time the bored waiter delivered Nate his meal – at least it felt that way to Kat's feet.

'Now remember,' Lauren instructed her, reaching over to straighten Kat's dragon pendant. 'Easy and breezy.'

'I'm not auditioning for a make-up ad.' Kat rolled her eyes.

'Just try and do all the things we talked about: you're looking for possible contacts, insider info, any job leads you can get. And be nice!'

'Relax, he'll help me out.' Kat was amused. All this strategy and planning, just to get some information from an old friend. She pushed the door open and made straight for his table, threading through the room full of fake red leather booths and retro Americana prints. Springsteen was playing, which was always a good sign, so although Lauren's plan was for Kat to 'accidentally' bump into him, feigning surprise, she cut the needless subterfuge and simply slid into the seat opposite.

'Hey you.'

Nate choked on his drink.

'Well, it's lovely to see you too,' Kat replied, reaching over to take a chip. She dunked it in the tiny dish of ketchup. 'How have you been?'

'Ah, good.' Nate recovered, wide-eyed behind his glasses. 'You look . . . different.'

'Thanks.' Kat decided to overlook the less-than-enthusiastic welcome. After all, she was wearing a vivid, cerulean-blue cropped blazer, and half a pound of shine serum in her hair. Her ridiculous, traffic-stopping hair. Such things could only be expected to prompt confusion and fear in the hearts of men. 'It was time for a change.'

'Huh.' Nate paused. The beard, she was surprised to see, had been trimmed back to mere German-philosopher length, but his shirt was still a thick check flannel despite the summer warmth. Kat wondered why he didn't just move to Vancouver and take up carpentry, but she supposed that if he did that, he wouldn't feel different or special at all.

'So, what's happening?' Kat prompted, keen to get all the details. 'Jessica's probably driven you mad with her incompetence, right? God, I still can't believe Mac's gave her a column.'

'Everything's . . . all right, I guess. Jessica's doing OK.'

'Sure she is,' Kat laughed, and took another chip. 'Come on, you don't need to be discreet. I want all the gossip.'

Nate just sat there. 'I don't know, things have been pretty quiet since you've been gone. No scandals, no lawsuits.' He managed a wry smile.

'And Mac is still ruling things with an iron fist?' Kat was undeterred. Despite her vague answers to Lauren, she had one very specific goal still in mind: winning her old job at *Think Louder* back.

'He's doing all right,' Nate shrugged. 'You know how it goes.'

Kat didn't. Nate was looking decidedly uncomfortable, and she began to wonder if she should be doing all the things

Lauren had insisted on, the neuro-linguistic programming, body language mirroring and something involving sub-conscious trigger words she still wasn't quite clear on.

'Were you meeting someone?' Nate asked, glancing around. Kat stumbled.

'No, I just saw you and thought . . . You know, that we could catch up. It's been a while.'

'Right.' There was a long pause. 'And we should.' Nate finally made a show of looking down at his watch. 'It's just, I've got this meeting and I'm running late, so . . .' He pulled out his wallet and made to get up.

'Oh, right, of course.' Kat blinked. This wasn't how it was supposed to go: they should be laughing over Jessica's idiotic scribblings or Mac's temper by now.

'It was, uh, great seeing you. Give me a call; I'll buy you a drink sometime.' Nate put a ten-pound note on the table and, with a final awkward grin, walked away.

'Great job,' Lauren sighed, sliding into the booth next to her.

'I tried.' Kat stared after him, still confused. 'He's just busy, I think.'

'Sure he is.'

The pair fell silent as Kat tried to ignore her faint sense of rejection and began to absently disassemble Nate's untouched burger. Splitting the bun, she neatly laid the bacon and cheese on one side, salad garnish on the other. Mayo on Lauren's half, ketchup on hers, chips on top of both. Same as they'd always had.

'So what are we going to do now?' Kat slid Lauren's half over to her and bit down on her own. The idea that Nate wouldn't help hadn't even occurred to her; she thought of that slim list of other allies and tried not to panic.

'I'll figure out something.' Lauren prodded the lone lettuce leaf with a look of suspicion. 'Come on, we'd better get back. Nina's probably plotting a royal coup as we speak.'

'But there's free food—' Kat didn't get a chance to finish; Lauren was already striding towards the exit. She sighed, and – shooting a final, longing look at the delicious array of grease, salt and saturated fat on the table – followed her out.

'I think I'm still overestimating your basic social skills,' Lauren pondered, when Kat caught up with her on the dusty pavement. 'I mean, couldn't you have flirted with him, even just a little?'

Kat paused. 'What?'

Lauren stared at her expectantly as they waited on the kerb for the lights to change. Traffic streamed past in a rush of midday noise and exhaust fumes, grimy and a world away from the leafy streets of Notting Hill. 'You know, flirting. That thing where you make a man feel necessary and worthwhile?' she asked. 'It tends to make them more . . . What's the word? Amenable – that's it – when you need a favour.'

'Wait a minute,' Kat spoke slowly. 'Are you my teacher or my pimp?'

Lauren gave a breezy laugh. 'Don't be so damn over-dramatic. It's called having people skills.'

'No,' Kat corrected her, lip curled in distaste. 'It's called being a whore.'

'Like I said,' Lauren's eyes narrowed, 'overdramatic. We'll have to do something about that, too.'

Kat tried to pull her initial outrage under some semblance of control. She waited until they had crossed the street and were out of range of moving vehicles before carefully asking, 'Are you seriously telling me you support that sort of thing – reducing yourself to be some sort of pathetic sexual object, just to get ahead?' She glared at Lauren. 'I should have guessed.'

Lauren took a sip of water from the bottle she kept in her bag. 'I support getting what I want, and if there's a man involved along the way . . . Well,' she gave a nonchalant gesture, keeping one eye on the road for a taxi, 'I've found they tend to be more receptive if there's some cleavage and a smile thrown in.'

Kat drew in a sharp breath. 'You know, it's women like you who make it so fucking hard for the rest of us! Some people are actually trying to get ahead on our merits, not our blow-jobs!' A man was passing by, his hair gelled into a tousled mess. He paused, studying them with interest. Kat glared at him. He moved on.

'I'm talking about charm and persuasion here, not prostitution.' Lauren seemed bored. 'In case you haven't noticed, the world runs on flattery. Is it any wonder you've got so little influence when you do nothing but judge and criticise?'

'Some things need criticising,' Kat shot back, 'because they're just wrong.'

'And I suppose making a man feel useful is a massive crime in your book.'

'If it means sacrificing my sexual integrity, then yes.'

'Sexual integrity?' Lauren burst into laugher. She abandoned her search for a taxi and looked at Kat with amusement. 'You're talking like I drop to my knees every time I want a new contract. Trust me, honey, I'd be asking a far higher price if I was.'

'God!' Kat exclaimed. 'It's not a joke. Don't you get it? As long as you're out, whoring yourself around for the next promotion, we'll never get anywhere. Things will never change!'

Something in Lauren seemed to snap. 'You want to keep

calling me a whore? Fine, do it.' She glared back, eyes fierce. 'But we're all whores, every one of us.'

'You—'

'No, you're the one who doesn't get it.' She stepped closer, until her face was only inches from Kat's. Her voice stayed low, but it rang with a bleak intensity as she continued, 'We're all selling something. Every relationship is a transaction. You get by as long as you've got the goods on offer; it doesn't matter if that's backstage access or beauty or a fucking awesome blow-job. Trust me, Kat,' she shook her head bitterly, 'it's all currency and we're all in the market.'

Kat just looked, anger fading as she took in Lauren's expression. This wasn't just manipulative cynicism, this was a hollow, soulless view of the world. It broke her heart a little to hear Lauren talk this way. 'Have you even listened to yourself?' she asked, still thrown. 'What is this crap?'

'The truth.' Lauren surveyed the traffic-clogged road and made a noise of frustration. She began walking again, towards a busy junction further up the street. 'I know you don't believe me yet,' she added, 'but you signed up for the Popularity Rules, so somewhere behind all that naivety, you must know I'm right.'

'I don't understand.' Kat kept pace, the balls of her feet now shot through with pain. Damn boots. 'The way you're talking, it's as if you believe everyone is just out for what they can get, like all our relationships are nothing but some cost-benefit calculation. You can't mean it.'

'Can't I?' Lauren replied, arching one eyebrow. She looked casual, smug even, but Kat thought she saw a flicker of something else behind the expression. Something regretful. She hoped it was more than her own wishful thinking. 'So Nate fell over himself to help you out back there – because of loyalty, and true friendship? And Whitney's been calling all the time to check how you are?' Lauren shook her head impatiently. 'You don't have value to them any more, Kat: no guest-list tickets or work camaraderie to offer, so they won't lift a finger for you. That's just how this works.'

'No.' Kat glared at her. 'Not everyone is so shallow.'

Lauren sighed, as if humouring a small child who still believed in Santa. 'OK, your friends are true and noble and just incredibly busy right now, et cetera. What about everyone else? Those are the people you've got to charm to get your career back on track, so what are you going to do?'

Kat could only stand there, confused, as a group of painfully hip young women in leggings and high-top Converse sneakers swarmed around her en route to the vintage record store. Ever since she'd embarked on the Popularity Rules project, Kat's centre of gravity had been thrown into a spin – she'd watched with numb resignation as Lauren matter-of-factly deconstructed every last one of her beliefs and behaviours. She'd signed up for change, but now it felt like she was fighting against every new lesson, trying in vain to cling to her old view of the world.

She shivered, trying not to let Lauren's hollow words settle in her mind. 'I don't know.'

'Well, I do.' Lauren finally flagged down a taxi and turned to Kat with a determined look. 'You'll get the hang of it, I know you will. Starting tonight.'

Speak their language.

All cliques and social circles revolve around superficial conversations, so to be a part of that world, you've got to be able to join in. It doesn't matter if it's music, celebrities, gossip or intellectual stuff – get a crash-course in their culture and research like hell to make sure you can hold your own. You may think it's stupid, but making small-talk with strangers is the start of every useful relationship.

Remember, you're not just chatting about your favorite TV character, you're actually validating their cultural choices. 'Did you see that show last night?' really just means, 'Are you like me?'

Your answer should always be yes.

Chapter Fifteen

'I still can't believe I let you talk me into this.' Kat leaned over the railings on the yacht's upper deck and watched the city reflect in the murky water below. The day had turned into a muggy, warm night that even the breeze from the river couldn't save; she would be better at home with air-conditioning and a tub of ice-cream. She would be better anywhere but here.

'Are you kidding?' Lauren's voice was full of enthusiasm. 'This is perfect. I don't know why I didn't think of it sooner.'

'Where did you get this equipment, anyway?' Kat fingered the tiny transmitter plugged into her ear. 'Or does your bookcase swivel around to reveal a secret-agent lair?'

Lauren giggled. 'It's amazing what you can find on the internet. Take my new contact, Yuri: he spent half his life in the KGB, and now he outfits Western executives with all the gadgets they need.'

'And I thought we only had to worry about overzealous government surveillance,' Kat noted. 'Honestly Lauren, I'm at a vapid launch party, not infiltrating the embassy for nuclear codes!' She wasn't surprised when people looked over at the sound of her voice; she was, after all, standing completely alone on the side of the boat.

'Shh!' Lauren reminded her, the voice coming through Kat's earpiece as clearly as if she was merely three feet away. 'It may be vapid, but half the freeloaders in town wanted to come tonight; I had to call in a favour to get you on the guest-list.

Anyway,' she pointed out, 'you should be glad I'm giving you back-up. Do you really want to have to network alone?'

'Or, I don't know, you could actually be here in person. It's revolutionary, I understand.' Kat angled her body so nobody could see her lips move. At worst, she would just look like a faintly demented person muttering to the water. Or a meth-head.

'This is the next step of the plan, your big debut.'

'Which still doesn't explain why you can't come too.' Kat knew she was complaining again, but she couldn't help it. Lauren was throwing her to the wolves after only two weeks of Popularity Rules training. The usual gestation period was apparently over two months!

'We both know you'd just stand there, feeling superior, while I did all the talking. No,' Lauren said firmly, 'this is best for everyone.'

'Perhaps I've moved on to an advanced stage of mental breakdown,' Kat mused, ignoring her. 'I am hearing voices in my head, after all – voices with strange instructions.'

Lauren made a noise of impatience, but Kat was warming to her theme. 'And now that I think about it, the whole affair is rather *Fight Club*: a top-secret project that reveals the nihilistic barbarism in contemporary society. So really, all I have to do is blow half my brains out to be free of you. Simple.' She ran her fingers back and forth along the narrow railing and considered the distance to the dock. It was just a pity she was such a bad swimmer.

'Are you done complaining?' Lauren finally spoke up. 'I was just checking emails.'

Kat sighed. 'I suppose.'

'Well, turn around. I want to take a look at the party.'

Bracing herself, Kat turned.

It was almost amusing, how somebody had taken Kat's vision of a personal hell and somehow conjured it to life. An inspired PR firm had decided that the obvious move to launch an MP3 player was co-branding with an amateur erotica website, thus Kat was both trapped in a confined space with the usual dregs of London's freeloading hipster elite, and surrounded by porn. Not the traditional 'bleached babes and bikers' stuff, because, obviously, that would be offensive and exploitative; instead, huge screens were set up in the main cabin, showing live webcam feeds from the bedrooms of several pale, tattooed women in various states of loud arousal. Meanwhile another legion of pierced burlesque pin-ups wandered through the overstyled crowd in bondage gear and garters, enticing patrons to test the high-tech gadgets on offer.

Kat couldn't even find the words.

'It looks like a great spread,' Lauren remarked. Kat decided it would be futile to respond. 'Plenty of photographers anyway, so you should get your picture in the fashion pages and blogs.'

'In this thing?' Kat snorted, looking down at her ridiculous confection of a dress. It was not only a truly horrifying shade of chartreuse, but ruffled with satin and blessed with a curiously asymmetrical neckline that was draped in a huge silver necklace consisting entirely of cogs – and a pin-point hidden camera.

'That thing, as you so disdainfully put it, is fresh from Proenza Shuler's latest collection. It's the perfect mix of high-fashion and hipster.'

'It's a perfect mess.'

'And you need to stop whining and start networking. This is your chance to show everyone the new Kat Elliot, remember, and you've got years of bad impressions to make up for.'

Kat tried to muster a little enthusiasm for her task. The secret-agent gadgets were a novelty, at least, and who knew – perhaps with Lauren talking her through this she could actually emerge unscathed, for once? For a moment, she allowed herself a fantasy of waltzing into the cliques and being greeted with something other than indifference. She could be charming and sociable, as if she really belonged . . .

She steeled herself. 'Just point me in the right direction.'

'Let's see . . .' Kat could just picture Lauren studying the visual relay on-screen, no doubt surrounded by strategy charts and planning. 'That dark-haired woman at four o'clock, she looks familiar.'

'Where?' Kat swivelled around.

'Four o'clock, Kat! The other way.'

'Oh.' She swivelled back, peering at the crowd. 'The one in the go-go boots? That's Lacey, a PR girl.' Kat sighed. 'She hates me.'

'All the more reason to start with her!'

Kat rolled her eyes at the upbeat tone. That was one advantage to the camera set-up: Lauren couldn't see her expression.

'Kat,' Lauren's voice was warning her, 'you'll never get back into the scene without people like her. You need access to bands, right? And gig tickets, and after-party info, and—'

Kat snagged a drink from a passing waif in a leather bustier and blocked out Lauren's monologue for a moment. Taking a long swallow of something fruity and alcoholic, she plastered a grin on her face. 'OK, I'm fortified.'

Lacey was clustered across the deck with a gaggle of dewy-faced, long-limbed girls, smoking with studied nonchalance what were no doubt imported French cigarettes, as the breeze whipped around their thin scarves and shiny fringes. Kat edged over, full of trepidation.

'Hi Lacey!' she began, trying to reach that effortless enthusiasm Lauren used so well, but her voice came out slightly strangled.

Lacey turned. There was a pause. 'Kat?' she said faintly, as if Kat was just a mirage.

'That's me.' Oh God, already she sounded awkward.

'Oh. Hi.' Lacey shot her an insincere smile and then angled her body away slightly, back to the group. The other girls looked bored, but utterly at ease as they blew streams of smoke into the air and murmured quietly amongst themselves. They weren't the inane groupie types that showed up to most gigs, no; they were too haughty for that. Probably assistants at artsy fashion magazines, or the lit student girlfriends of some underground DJ type, Kat decided, pleased for a moment that she could actually distinguish them now. She focused on Lacey and attempted to follow Lauren's instructions.

'How have you been?' Kat tried to casually lean on the railing, but the metal was cold and she felt strange, twisting her body at a difficult angle.

'You know . . .' Lacey shrugged, looking away. More silence.

'Any good new bands you're working with?' Kat persisted.

'A few.'

Kat swallowed. Designer dress or not, this really wasn't the glittering re-entry into scene society they'd planned.

One of the ingénues flicked her cigarette butt overboard and turned to the others. 'Let's go find Rafi.' They moved off in a shuffle of skinny denim and mod dresses, while Kat felt something in her shrink away. Even in her hipster costume, she didn't warrant a second glance from these people.

'Maybe we should try with some strangers,' Lauren said tactfully. 'Blank slate, you know?'

'Fine,' Kat agreed dully. The dream of charm and social ease

181

was already fading. She could tell that the whole outing was a lost cause.

A long, painful hour later, Kat hadn't revised her judgement.

'The woman by the buffet is Mimi Maher, a commissioning editor for *NYLON*,' Lauren instructed in her ear, her voice now fixed with a note of desperation. 'She's with a diary editor for *Metro*. Go talk to them.'

'Give me an in this time,' Kat whispered, hiding her mouth with a hand as she shuffled closer. All night she'd done nothing but stumble over awkward introductions and linger, unwanted on the edge of a crowd. She didn't know how much social humiliation she could take, but surely, it couldn't be any more.

'Wait for a break in conversation and then compliment her on that bag. It's a new Henrietta; she probably spent six months on the waiting list for it.'

She should be used to stalking a complete stranger, but Kat still felt foolish as she backed closer, pretending to be engrossed in the user manual of her freebie gadget until the music faded slightly and she could overhear their discussion.

'The spoilers say it's a total mislead.'

'But as long as they keep his shirt off, I don't care!'

Kat wasn't sure what they were talking about but plunged ahead anyway. 'Mimi?' she brushed the brunette woman's arm and tried to adopt a tone of surprise. 'Umm, how are you?'

Mimi turned and looked at her blankly, but, dressed in a similar vintage confection to Mimi's own, Kat evidently passed the style test: blankness soon gave way to a careful smile.

'Hi, hon! It's been ages, hasn't it? Since . . .' Mimi tailed off, tactfully waiting for Kat to jog her memory.

'The MIA launch,' Kat dutifully repeated every word Lauren was whispering. She felt trapped in an absurd piece of performance art, echoing everything the voice in her ear demanded. 'Oh my God, is that a Henrietta?' Mustering all her dramatic skills, Kat feigned a squeal of delight and stared at the boxy leather bag as if it were the Holy Grail.

'Yes, actually,' Mimi preened, swinging it around in casual triumph.

'I'm so jealous!' Was she really saying this?

'Thank you,' Mimi laughed, face glowing at the thought of her own exclusive status. Standing to the side, she ushered Kat into the circle. Kat tried not to blink in surprise; the tactics were actually working.

'Kat Elliot. It's lovely to meet you all.'

There was an awkward moment when a blonde woman to her right – resplendent in a huge grey Mickey Mouse T-shirt, wet-look black leggings and four-inch gold heels – leaned in before Kat remembered that she just wanted to exchange the perfunctory double air-kisses. She pressed her lips to the stranger's cheek and felt some last spark of hope in her begin to glow. Perhaps she could make it, after all.

'We were just talking about *Kudos*,' Mimi drew her back into the discussion, naming a recent cult TV hit. 'I think they're stuck in a space-time wormhole; such a metaphor for the feedback loop of modern culture.'

'Metaphor or not, I'm sick of the whole series,' the blonde woman beside her declared.

'I bet it's got something to do with that Lucille's father,' a slick, besuited man added, taking another drink from the tray proffered by a silent (and no doubt by now truly suicidal) girl. Kat nodded vaguely, trying to disguise her disappointment as they continued to argue. She could hold her own in many conversational arenas, but crappy TV wasn't one of them.

'Chances are they're just making it up as they go along. What do you think?' Mimi turned to her.

'I, ah, don't watch,' she mumbled. Lauren made an audible noise of frustration in her ear. They both knew there was a summary of every important TV show sitting, untouched, on Kat's bedside table.

'Oh. Well.' Mimi was taken aback, but quickly recovered. 'Did any of you see the sneaker ad Katya did?'

'It'll wreck their credibility,' the blonde said, with obvious satisfaction. 'They're supposed to be DJs, not branding projects.'

'What's next, Troika vodka, right?' the man snorted with laughter and turned to Kat for approval.

She made a noncommittal noise, busying herself with her drink and wondering when she might actually be able to offer a coherent word.

No time soon. Five minutes later and Kat was still stood in silent confusion. She was clueless about the hot blogger-beloved band of the week, lost in the debate over the latest show at the Tate and had no interest in whom Lily Larton was dating. She barely even recognised half the brand names Mimi and her friends bantered about with such all-knowing ease.

Kat felt as much an outsider as ever. Only this time, she was an outsider clad in ruffled chartreuse.

Mute, she finally looked around for an escape. 'I'll, umm, I'll see you around,' she ventured. The trio looked over briefly, deep in conversation about an Iranian rapper's politically charged new lyrics. Their eyes drifted past her.

'Sure,' Mimi nodded absently.

'Mmm,' the blonde agreed, before turning back. 'But this isn't just a free speech issue; we're talking about incitement here . . .'

Kat backed away, already forgotten.

'Where are you going?' Lauren's voice crackled to life in her ear.

'To find a toilet. Or is that not allowed?' Her head, feet and pride all ached. Kat wanted nothing more than a quiet corner and hide until they docked again.

'Good plan, then need to canvas a new location. Let me see . . .'

Kat interrupted. 'Can't you just admit I'm a lost cause?' She slipped through a pack of men, golden with a fake tan that glowed against their deep, V-necked T-shirts. 'I don't belong here and I never will!'

'Not if you mooch around looking all sullen and dejected. You've got to bring something to the interaction!'

There it was again: the aching reminder that Kat – just Kat – was never going to be enough.

The bar area was loud and raucous, packed so tightly with revellers in search of free alcohol that Kat had to push her way through with elbows and well-placed nudges. It certainly didn't help that her dress billowed out around her, adding another two feet to her circumference and making her the target of several eye-rolls and double-takes. High-fashion and hipster? She should have known better than to accept sartorial guidance from Gabi – the woman who could wear a jump-suit and still be effortlessly chic. She looked like a joke, but nobody even cared enough to laugh along.

At last she made it through the melee, slipping down a narrow staircase to the bowels of the yacht where plush cream carpeting stretched down a long corridor, lined with huge monochrome erotic prints. The loud thunder of electronic beats dulled to a low thump, and Kat found herself staring at an extreme close-up of a man's nipple, wiry dark hairs twisting like weeds.

'Listen, Kat, you need to pull yourself together,' Lauren told her firmly. 'You can't let anyone see you upset. It could ruin everything!'

'Right,' Kat said quietly. 'I forgot. No expression of human emotion allowed; isn't that what the Popularity Rules say?'

'It'll be OK, I promise.'

'Really?' Kat managed a tired laugh. 'Because you keep telling me that, and I keep looking like a fool.'

Lauren paused. 'It was always going to be a challenge. It'll get easier, it really will, but only if you put yourself out there and keep trying.'

'On with the show, huh?' Did she even have a choice? With a sigh, Kat stood up again. 'Well, can you give me some privacy in the toilet, at least?'

'It'll be my pleasure. I'll just get some more coffee.'

Kat's earpiece went silent, and she began to test each of the black lacquered doors. There was a bathroom upstairs, but fighting through a line of coke-snorting waifs wasn't high on her 'to-do' list right then. At last a door opened, and Kat reached around on the wall for the light switch.

'What the fuck?' a male voice slurred loudly as the room was flooded with light. Kat looked up in horror.

There, sprawled across the bed, was Devon Darsel.

Give them what they want.

If you want something, you don't get it by asking nicely – you make it so they want to help you out. The thing is, everyone has a picture of themselves in their head: as good, or powerful, or pretty – regardless of what they actually are in real life. The cheerleader may want to be thought of as smart, not shallow, men just want to be a heroic knight in shining armour, and even outcast geeks like to think of themselves as brainy in a cool way, rather than a total loser. So, exploit that any way you can. Make them feel like they really are that awesome, and they'll fall over themselves to lend a hand.

Whatever you do, never try a guilt-trip. You might get the job done this once, but they'll resent you for making them feel bad for a long, long time.

Chapter Sixteen

Kat took in the scene. Devon lay draped across the bed in the black and chrome master suite, his scrawny chest bare, a half-empty vodka bottle in his hand and a frighteningly thin girl draped over his lap, working her way down towards his crotch.

Of course. Kat had officially descended to the ninth circle of her personal hell.

She backed towards the door.

'Where you goin'?' Devon slurred at her, his face nothing but achingly pale skin and sharp angles under the too-bright lights. 'Come join the party.'

Kat paused, a curious calm descending over her. From the very start, the night had been an absurd piece of performance art: she had put on her costume, recited her lines and stumbled around on somebody else's set. She wasn't this person.

She didn't know this person.

Kat turned back to them, her gaze drifting over his bloodshot eyes and the girl's blank stare. The girl's very blank stare.

'Are you OK?' she asked. With rib-bones visible beneath her transparent slip and a tiny cassette tape tattooed on her wrist, the girl couldn't be older than sixteen.

The girl blinked back, mute. Her eyes shifted out of focus, liner smudged into hollow circles. She slipped lower on the bed.

'Apparently not,' Kat decided, striding forward and gently taking hold of one spindly arm. 'I think it's time to go.'

'Wha . . . ?'

'Come on,' Kat instructed, half-lifting her from the bed. At least her malnourished frame was easy to carry.

'Mhnmm,' the girl mumbled incoherently, but didn't offer any resistance as Kat guided her towards the cabin door.

'What you doin'?' Devon looked around in confusion, grabbing at Kat. 'We were jus' havin' some fun.'

'Sure you were,' she answered shortly. The poor girl couldn't even walk, let alone give meaningful consent!

'Hey, c'mon!'

Kat ignored him, carefully steering the girl down the hallway, testing doors until she found a slim galley kitchen at the other end of the boat.

'Don't feel . . . very well.' The girl lurched forwards, retching into the sink.

'Lovely,' Kat muttered as the girl curled up in the corner, groaning. Running the tap, Kat passed her a glass of water and pushed damp hair off her clammy forehead. She was completely out of it. What on earth was Devon thinking?

Nothing, as usual.

Kat felt anger building in her chest, a sharp relief from the rejection and insecurity that had been haunting her all night.

Devon Darsel.

That wasted pile of crap was the reason she was there in the first place, hovering on the edge of all the stupid cliques to make tedious small-talk instead of back in the magazine where she belonged. If it weren't for his messiah complex, she would never have been in trouble. Mackenzie wouldn't have fired her. Every other magazine wouldn't have turned her down. Because of his stupid ego, she was untouchable.

189

And here he was, wreaking havoc as usual, as if there were no consequences. There were always fucking consequences.

Kat stormed back to the cabin, flinging open the door with a crash. This rage was familiar; it was safe. She knew how to use this.

Devon was still lolled on the bed, oblivious to the statutory rape charge he'd narrowly avoided. 'You came back,' he blinked up at her, lips spreading into a lascivious smile. Journalists and fans alike had swooned over those 'plump, poetic pillows' but Kat couldn't be less impressed. 'Guess you wanna play, huh?'

'Play?' she spat, fire surging through her. 'This is all just a game to you, isn't it?'

'What?' Squinting, Devon lurched upright. 'Don . . . don't I know you?'

'I'm wounded you don't remember.' Her tone was ice.

Devon's eyes finally widened. 'You! You're the bitch from that magazine . . . whassis name? Noise or Play or—'

'*Think Louder*,' she enlightened him.

'Thas the one!' he frowned, as if trying to recall their beautiful friendship. 'You're the cunt who needs a good fuck.'

Kat watched him, now struggling to his feet. His polo T-shirt was rumpled, the fly on his jeans still unzipped. He looked like a wayward child, but unlike a child, Devon should know better.

'You're nothing,' Kat realised, speaking aloud as she surveyed the pathetic mess. Alone, away from paparazzi and adoring crowds, he was nothing but a gangly boy with bad fashion sense. No spotlights, no bodyguards: nothing but pale skin and bedraggled hair. Not so big any more.

Smiling dangerously, Kat closed the door behind her and

turned to Devon with a look of pure venom. She could do nothing about her social inadequacies, her loneliness, her failure these past months. But this? This she could handle.

'I think it's time we had a little talk.'

'Huh?' he stared at her blankly.

'Sit down.'

Disorientated, Devon tried to push past her.

'SIT DOWN!' Reeling back at the force of her words, Devon tripped and fell back onto the bed.

'Do you have a sister, Devon?' Kat asked him, almost conversationally as she leaned back against the wall and folded her arms. 'A mother? Niece?'

'Uh, sure. A sister, I mean.' Thrown off-guard by her sudden change in tone, Devon paused, frowning. 'And, like, there's my mum.'

'They're important to you, are they? Good women?'

'Um, I guess.' He shifted his eyes around the small cabin, completely baffled by her questioning.

'So if your sister was walking down the street, say, and a man walked up to her and told her she needed a good fuck, you wouldn't be happy, would you?' Kat's words were friendly, but the sheer rage building in her tone was unmistakeable.

'Who said that?' Devon demanded, belligerent. 'I'll fucking beat him up.'

'Relax,' Kat sighed, 'nobody said anything. I'm just pointing out, it's not a very respectful thing to say, is it?'

'No.' A long beat, and then he frowned. Aha!

'So when you say that to me, don't you think I might get offended by it?' Her jaw was clenched, but she fought to stay calm.

Another frown, but this time he was defensive. 'Why should I give a fuck what you think?'

191

That was it. Finally, something in Kat snapped. All night, all week, she'd played her part. She'd played nice. She couldn't take it any more.

'You should give a fuck, as you so eloquently put it, because talking like that is demeaning and offensive.' Kat shook her head in disgust. 'You think it's acceptable to reduce me to nothing but a pair of breasts and a cunt?' Slashing the air in angry quote marks, she mimicked his charming words.

'Or perhaps the reason you're such a dick all the time is that you can't get it up. Having problems in the bedroom? Not able to keep your groupies happy? Is that what's making you such a bastard?'

'Fuck you.' Even in his inebriated state, she could see he was shaken.

'I'm not done.' Kat laughed, feeling in her element for the first time in God knew how long. 'Look at you, fucking your way around town as if it doesn't matter, as if they don't matter.' She laughed in bitter disbelief. 'How on earth did you end up this way? You're a guitar and a dick and nothing else besides. Are you even happy?'

Devon looked shocked. He tried to get up, but she was standing so close he didn't even have room to move. Men like him made the world like this, just screwing and bombing and leaving, and fuck the wreckage they left behind.

'You aren't, are you? You can't be. Of course, the drinking and partying help you ignore what a fucking wasteland your life is, but then you sober up and look around and there's nothing, nobody.' Kat took a breath, shaking with adrenalin. 'There are consequences. There are always fucking consequences. I know, that girl will know tomorrow, but you?' She stared down at him. 'You're still the bastard who thinks he's God. Well, look around: you've got nobody!'

Kat turned to leave. 'I may be a cunt who needs a fuck, but you're alone. And you always will be.'

With that, she wrenched the door open and stalked away.

The fresh air upstairs was cool against her flushed skin, and without the overstyled cliques cluttering the deck, Kat could almost forget what a failure her night had been. No awkwardness, no exclusion – Kat just felt her heart pumping as she leaned over the railings and gazed at the skyline. Big Ben, Parliament, the London Eye; the city towered above her in a glorious panorama of light and colour, and for a moment, she felt like herself again.

She'd done it! She'd actually told him everything that had been burning in her for so long, and oh, the look on his face! Kat laughed out loud, still amazed by the whole thing.

'Sorry I was so long.' Her earpiece crackled to life again, and she could hear Lauren crunching on something. Probably a rice cake. 'Did I miss much?'

'Umm . . .' Kat's glow began to dissipate as quickly as it had arrived. If Lauren knew what she'd said to Devon . . . She made a quick decision. 'No, nothing much at all.'

'Well, the facts on the ground aren't great for you, so I think we need to change tactics for the rest of the night. No point chasing even more failure,' Lauren said, only faintly sympathetic. 'How about we just try to get you in as many photographs as possible? That way, we'll at least meet your exposure objective, and everyone who wasn't there will believe you were having a great time.'

'Are you sure I can't find some way off this thing?' Kat answered. Her perilous situation was only just beginning to sink in: she was trapped on the boat, and if Devon found her for a more public re-match . . .

'We're staging a tactical retreat, not quitting completely. I checked the press release, and Freddie Fitzgerald is supposed to be around somewhere.'

'I'm supposed to know who that is?'

'The photographer!' Lauren exclaimed. 'His website is the go-to place for hipster nightlife shots – haven't you been reading any of your research magazines?'

That she hadn't should be perfectly clear. 'Fine, whatever you want.'

She must have sounded defeated, because Lauren softened. 'There are only a few more hours, don't worry.'

A few more hours. Kat shivered. Trapped on the Boat of Doom with . . . She looked around, realising for the first time that the deck was almost empty. 'Why am I the only one out here?'

'I don't know.' Lauren's voice took on an edge of concern. 'Go and find out.'

Kat reluctantly peeled herself away from the solitary spot and edged towards the main cabin, where clusters of partiers were all trying to catch a glimpse of something inside. She strained to see what was happening, hoping fervently they hadn't decided to upgrade the porn to a live sex show.

'Did you see her dress?' a rockabilly-styled man asked his friend, a woman with perfect starlet red lipstick.

'I know! He couldn't tell what the hell was going on.'

Kat's view was blocked by the thick knot of bodies, so she edged deeper into the crowd.

'. . . Smack, I'll bet you,' two industry suits muttered as she elbowed her way between them.

'No, not with those pupils; it's crack for sure.'

'Well?' Lauren demanded.

'Calm down,' Kat whispered, coughing as she sucked in a breath of smoky air. 'It's probably just some tedious break-up drama.' Finally, she pushed through to the front of the room and looked up to see what the big attraction was.

Towering above her on every wall, her own face stared back.

Kat gasped.

'. . . The drinking and partying help you ignore what a fucking wasteland your life is, but then you sober up and look around and there's nothing, nobody!'

Her fight with Devon, down in the cabin – it was playing for everyone to see! But . . . how was this even possible?

Kat stayed frozen to the spot, watching herself on the huge screens until she stormed out, leaving Devon staring blankly on that bed.

And then the scene began to play, all over again.

Her insides contracted as, slowly, it began to make sense. The webcams. The sex shows on-screen from earlier must have been taking place downstairs: the cabins rigged with cameras and microphones to broadcast to the partygoers up above. Devon would have been too wasted to notice the set-up, but . . . Kat gulped. Her tirade had been streaming over the internet the whole time.

She didn't have to say a word. Lauren spoke for her.

'Oh God, Kat. What have you done?'

All around her was the buzz of gossip, people's faces twisted with glee. Kat felt a slow wash of humiliation fall over her. Bad enough to be insignificant, ignored, but a public joke? She couldn't breathe. They were all looking at her, she was sure – all laughing, ridiculing her. She backed away, breaking through the crowd and out onto the deck.

'How could you be so stupid?' The moment Kat was clear of

the crowd, Lauren exploded. 'What about all your training, our plans?!'

Kat wandered to the end of the boat as if in a daze. The gleeful chatter faded, until it was drowned out by the growl of the engine and the bustle in the city beyond.

'After everything we've done, you still can't just keep quiet and think about the game plan! Are you sabotaging this on purpose? Because if you are, I don't know if—'

Cutting off Lauren's wails, Kat plucked the small transmitter out of her ear and tucked it into her purse, along with the heavy necklace housing the hidden camera. She came to a bank of cabinets and sank down behind them, out of sight. There. Alone again. Taking a deep breath, Kat tried to resign herself to this, her latest failure.

And oh, what a failure.

She wasn't sure how long she stayed there, watching lights ripple off the inky water and replaying her doom, but it wasn't until a pair of spotless white sneakers came to a halt in front of her that Kat slipped back out of her reverie.

'That was quite a show you put on.'

Kat followed the shoes up to casually draped black denim, and then past a crumpled lightweight shirt to a smudge of stubble and that familiar boyish smile. Ash. The last time she'd seen him, she'd silently snuck out of his bed while he was still unconscious. In her world, that sort of cavalier behaviour would be met by avoidance and glares, but apparently to him, it merited some charm.

Despite herself, Kat felt relief. At least it wasn't a gossiping partygoer, or even Devon. Gathering herself, she mustered a shrug. 'Things were getting rather dull.'

Now that she had absorbed some of the Popularity Rules' wisdom, Kat could see that he was one of them – the fashionable in-crowd of this city. His clothing may not have been hipster-level ridiculous, but he had that nonchalance in his posture that meant he was utterly at ease in this circus. He was an insider, and now he knew she didn't belong.

But instead of disdain, Ash laughed, 'Well, you sure sorted that one out.' He looked down at her crumpled figure, his expression becoming slightly concerned. 'Are you OK? It was pretty brutal in there.'

'I'm fine,' Kat answered shortly. He blinked with surprise at her tone, and Kat was reminded suddenly of what the Popularity Rules had said about making a man feel useful. It was almost a waste, to start following the instructions now, but Kat had nothing else to offer. 'Actually,' with no small effort, she allowed herself to sound vulnerable, 'I'm not really all right. I wish I could just get away from here.'

The words almost stuck in her throat; Katherine Emmeline Elliot did not show weakness.

'C'mon.' Ash held his hand out and pulled her gently to her feet. 'I might just be able to help you with that.'

Within ten minutes, Kat was sitting in the back of a water taxi, speeding away from the Boat of Doom. If only she'd known it could be that simple: both the leaving of the party and the eliciting assistance from strange men. Lauren would be proud of her for one thing, at least.

Lauren. Kat traced the clasp of her clutch purse and thought of the gadgets – and Lauren's rage – contained within. She turned back to Ash.

'My hero,' she tried at last. His smile widened.

'Just call me your white knight.' He slipped an arm around her. 'Are you cold?'

Kat shook her head. She felt as if she was still burning with the humiliation of the video scene. 'So what sins did you commit in a past life to get sentenced to that hell?' she nodded back towards the yacht, before realising that he might actually enjoy those kinds of parties.

'What makes you think my sins weren't all in this life?' Ash made such an exaggerated lecherous expression that Kat laughed – sharp, real and full of relief. The faux-coy act didn't sit well with her.

'Don't try and play the bad-boy card now. You're forgetting I've already seen your *Gilmore Girls* DVDs.'

'They belonged to an ex!' he protested.

She nudged him lightly. 'Of course they do. Which is why the box was open right next to that ridiculous entertainment system of yours.'

'Ahem, no comment.' He grinned at her. 'What about you? Is harassing rock stars a hobby or something?'

Kat tried to look unconcerned, as if she hadn't just wrecked all her chances of a fresh start. 'Only on slow nights. Usually I stick to mere mortals.'

'Well, I can't say I didn't enjoy it,' Ash admitted, shifting his body slightly so that Kat was firmly tucked against his torso. 'I had the honour of working with him last year, and let me tell you, he's a nightmare in the studio.'

'The studio?'

'I'm a producer,' he explained, looking surprised. He obviously thought she should know who he was. Suddenly it all made perfect sense to Kat. The sprawling Hoxton flat filled with turntables and vinyl, the stacks of untouched graphic print T-shirts, his unerring confidence. Of course he slipped around the scene with ease; he was practically the poster-boy for hip young London things.

'Oh.' Kat realised her tone was less than appreciative, and

quickly continued, 'I'm a music journalist. Well, freelancing right now,' she admitted. Lauren was emphatic that she declare her profession like she was successful and sought-after, but Kat couldn't help the regretful note in her voice. As far as she was concerned, running around for a teen branding expert didn't count as music writing.

'Yes, the famous Kat Elliot.' Ash drummed a light rhythm on her shoulder. 'You know, if you'd mentioned your surname, you would have been easier to track down. But maybe that was the point?' he added.

Kat simply looked out at the dock ahead. 'We're here.'

Once they were back on solid ground, Ash turned to her. 'Do you have anywhere you need to be? Or . . .' The suggestion was clear in his eyes, and the soft trace of his thumb against the palm of her hand.

Kat paused. All she had waiting back in Notting Hill was Lauren's disapproval and the painful chronicle of her own failure. But Ash . . . She remembered the shock of a cold, white wall pressed against her bare back, the red pressure marks on her wrists that had lingered the morning after. She wanted to escape, and as she remembered, Ash was good for that, at least.

'Or,' she decided, meeting his gaze.

He chuckled, 'Whatever the lady wants.'

Lauren could wait.

Evolve or die.

You can plan and predict all you want, but the world is full of random events – something will always happen that you didn't see coming. Learn from third-grade science and the joys of evolution. Instead of panicking, adapt to whatever comes your way. The golden couple breaks up? Maybe that puts some cracks in her perfection, so help them along with well-placed whispers and see if he needs a shoulder to cry on. A former ally turns on you? That just means you've got another target – and insider info about how to bring them down.

Plans change, scenes move on, but the Popularity Rules stay the same.

Chapter Seventeen

At five a.m. Kat finally accepted the inevitable: she was never going to get to sleep.

Even after Ash had fallen unconscious, one arm draped heavily around her and the cool, navy sheets kicked away, Kat had lain awake, her bones hollow and overtired. She never slept soundly with someone else in the bed, but this was even worse; watching every hour flick past at an unbearably slow pace on his bedside digital clock. She couldn't relax, or drift into pleasant oblivion; she could only lie still, replaying the humiliation of the night before.

She'd ruined everything.

Kat stared blindly at the ceiling, tears pooling in the mascara debris still cluttering the edge of her eyes as she tried to quantify the damage she'd done. It had been so easy to ignore when Ash was awake, doing everything he could to distract her with hard kisses and the breathless sweat of their bodies, but now daylight was pale outside the windows and Kat couldn't mask the sick dread in her stomach with desire any more.

They had all been laughing at her. That fact alone would usually be enough to fill Kat with burning shame, but those people were industry players: editors, PR staff, journalists . . . Lauren had made it clear that they were the tastemakers, the trendsetters. They were the people who decided who and what qualified as cool. Without their support, Kat would struggle to secure even an entry-level admin job, let alone waltz back into her old, prestigious position.

Rolling out of bed, Kat stumbled over their discarded clothes towards the cool, dark marble sanctuary of a bathroom as the catalogue of her failings continued. She hadn't listened when Lauren told her to watch TV and keep up with the tabloid press; she'd thought it a waste of time to read *Cosmo* and *Entertainment Weekly* when there were political biographies and thick, new novels to concern herself with instead. Why bother suffering through the dregs of celebrity gossip, she'd thought, all that hateful misogyny and shallow consumerism?

If only she'd listened! Then Kat wouldn't have stood there, silent and awkward as the groups gossiped around her until they'd forgotten she even existed. All this time she'd been so disdainful about networking: she'd thought it the domain of shiny-haired girls and men with soap-opera smiles who masked their lack of talent and hard work with insincerity and old-school ties, but really, it was the very foundation of her industry. Kat let the shower jets beat into her tired skin, remembering how a nondescript brunette had spent ten minutes talking about *American Idol* to an older man before he suggested she pitch him a feature on the new reality TV winners. It turned out he was an editor-at-large for *Rolling Stone*! Kat's emails to them had gone unnoticed for months, but just a few minutes of chat and that woman had a lead.

And why, oh why had she raged at Devon?

He had deserved her wrath – he deserved so much more – but as much as it pained her to admit, Kat knew that her outburst had been the worst strike of all. Her 'difficult' record had already shut her out of the job at *Music Nation*, but there she was all over again, reminding people that they couldn't trust her to show some self-restraint. And even if it hadn't all been caught on camera . . . Kat wiped steam from the mirror and stared in resignation at her wet and bedraggled reflection. Even without the video streaming and live broadcast, she still would have been screwed. Devon would have told his bosses at the label, or mentioned it to another journalist. It was just as the Popularity Rules said: all that mattered was her reputation, and now Kat had destroyed hers for good.

The worst part was that she had nobody else to blame. It was all her fault.

The thought lingered as she plucked her underwear from the floor and quickly dressed, keeping one eye on Ash's motionless form. She couldn't bring herself to even touch the chartreuse horror, so she left it in a ruffled heap beside the couch and found a shirt of his instead, belting it over her leggings to create a look she hoped would pass as daywear – in this part of town, at least.

She paused in the doorway, checking her tiny bag for money and keys. Ash looked almost innocent, sprawled across the sheets, and for a moment Kat considered waking him or leaving a note, something more than the silent escape she was making. But what then – sweet nothings over Starbucks muffins, another round of sex? Kat's head was already back to that battered red Popularity Rules notebook, her thoughts far away from the unnecessary complications of men.

No, it was easier this way.

She let herself out without another hesitation. It was a glorious day, with clear skies and bright sun, but Kat barely noticed as she wandered towards the Tube station.

It was all. Her. Fault.

In a daze, she swiped her Oyster card, drifting down the empty escalators and onto the platform. That was what stung, what made the shame knot tightly in her stomach. Until now, she'd been blaming the world for the sorry state of her life, chalking her failures up to peculiar and unfortunate turns in circumstance, or other people's back-stabbing weakness. She was doing the best she could, and that was all.

But now? Now she knew differently. Now she knew it was her own short temper and sense of superiority that had been wrecking things all this time. Because even though Kat had accepted Lauren's proposal, had changed her clothes and hairstyle, and followed those Popularity Rules, she'd done it half-heartedly, with resentment and rolled eyes – and look where it had left her. Still outside. Still unwanted. She'd had a glistening chance to change her life and make it everything she ever dreamed, but somehow, she'd sabotaged everything.

If only she could take it back. Kat didn't notice the rattle of the deserted carriage or the drunk slumped on a far seat; she thought only of what could have been. If she did it all over again, she would take Lauren seriously, commit to the Popularity Rules, throw herself into every aspect of that book and work until she'd won her life back. She understood now the sacrifice it took to really make things change, but it was too late.

She was done.

Kat was already composing her new CV when she let herself back into Lauren's flat and slowly climbed the stairs for what she knew might be the last time. She could dredge up old work with feminist groups, she supposed, even accept that position transcribing human rights abuses. And move all her things up to her mother's house in Oxford . . . The future loomed, dull and lonely, and Kat felt that bleak hopelessness she knew so well return.

'You should let me know if you're going to stay out all night.' To Kat's surprise, Lauren was already awake, swathed in her silk dressing gown and sitting at the long dining table with a steaming mug and her laptop. 'I didn't know if you'd hurled yourself into the Thames.'

'Almost,' Kat replied, letting her bag fall to the floor with a clatter. She braced herself for Lauren's wrath, or worse yet, her disappointment. 'I'm sorry. I didn't know you would worry.'

'There's fresh coffee, if you want.' Her reply was even.

'You mean your liquid heart attack?' Kat tried to joke, crossing to the kitchen and pouring herself a cup of the terrifyingly strong brew. She was uneasy with Lauren's emotionless tone, waiting for a long lecture about public performance. Kat's stomach gurgled, reminding her she'd not eaten since the evening before. 'Are you hungry?' she asked. Lauren was still sitting at the table, tapping away at her keyboard. 'I could make us an omelette, or something.'

Lauren looked up at this, surprised either by Kat's contrite offer or the suggestion that she eat, Kat wasn't sure.

'No, I'm fine.'

Kat nodded, but her unease grew all the while as she found an apple and a handful of walnuts to munch on. By the time she slid into a chair opposite Lauren, she couldn't hold it in any longer.

'Will you just say something?' she burst. 'I fucked up; I know I did.'

Lauren raised an eyebrow, still cool. 'I didn't think what I said mattered.'

She deserved that. 'You're right, it didn't. But maybe I was wrong. No,' she corrected herself. If she was going to stop pretending to herself, she needed to be honest. 'I was wrong. I understand that now.'

'You do?' Lauren's face seemed to unfold.

'I'd have to be an idiot not to. I mean, last night was just one long disaster. The Popularity Rules, everything – I fucked them up, and now it's too late . . .' Kat swallowed, determined not to let the full extent of her misery show. 'It's too late to take it back.'

Lauren's eyes seemed to drill right into her, fixed and intense. 'Do you really mean that?'

Kat abandoned her apple. 'I do, but what does it even matter any more? It's all over now. I made sure of that last night.' She let out a long, regretful sigh. 'What are they saying, anyway?' She nodded to the computer. 'I may as well hear the worst.'

'Well,' Lauren began, 'they're saying that you're stylish, rebellious and, I quote, "so freaking cool".'

'What?' Kat stared back at her blankly.

And then Lauren smiled, wide and full of triumph. 'Your showdown with Devon Darsel is everywhere. People love you for it!'

'They love . . . me?'

'It's just one of those things,' Lauren laughed, her excitement now clear. 'You never know how something will get spun. But someone blogged live from the yacht, and then Ubergirl picked it up—'

'Who?'

'Ubergirl, the hipster star!' Lauren slid the computer around so Kat could see the blog, run by a sharp-haired girl with the requisite perfect eyeliner. 'Party, blah blah, DJ set . . . Here it is: "I hear the highlight was seeing DD ripped a new one by some mystery angel. Don't know her name, but we all owe her a drink or ten for that totally deserved rant. Rock on!"'

Kat didn't understand.

'She's the hottest scene blogger around right now,' Lauren

exclaimed, already taking the computer back to click through to other pages. '*Elle* loves her; she's modelled for Harry Sharp; even Perez Hilton reports on what she's doing. If she says you're in, you're *in*.'

'Charm the tastemakers . . .' Kat murmured, quoting from the rulebook. Could it really be so simple? One moment she was doomed to certain failure, and the next, everything was on-track again – better than before, even – and all because of the opinions of a few random strangers?

'Exactly! Mob mentality is a basic Popularity Rule. It's why I sent her the tip in the first place.'

'You what?'

'Now everyone's just repeating the same lines – that you're stylish and brave and the next hipster it-girl.' Lauren beamed. Kat couldn't remember ever having seen her so enthusiastic. 'We've established your brand literally overnight; I thought it would take weeks!'

Kat clutched her coffee mug, trying to take it all in.

'And look at this: the YouTube clip is most-viewed of the week and I only put it up a few hours ago!'

Kat almost choked. 'Lauren!'

'What? The footage was bound to leak eventually; I just figured we'd get it out now before the backlash. I had one of my tech guys intercept the feed and upload it. Don't worry,' Lauren added, noticing Kat's strangled expression, 'there's always a backlash. The important thing is that we shore up your key brand assets while this is still hot news.'

Kat watched her tapping merrily away – no doubt forwarding the video files to every major gossip player in the Western world – and tried to collect herself. This was what she'd wanted, wasn't it? The third and final chance she'd thought she'd never get. Somehow, things had switched around overnight, and now it was up to her to make it work. Evolve or die.

'So what's my next move?' Kat leaned forwards and waited for instructions. This time, she would actually follow them.

Lauren paused her typing and pushed a bullet-point list over to Kat. 'You lie low for a couple of days, let this story play itself out. Right now you're mysterious; that's good. People can speculate about you all weekend, and then come Monday, we start hitting them with selected appearances, maybe a gig or two. You need to keep everything coming back to music, remember.'

'Focus the brand,' Kat echoed, recalling some of Lauren's client files. 'So the message is coherent and simple.'

'Exactly!' Lauren agreed. She smiled across the table at Kat, a real, honest smile that was quieter than the wide grins she threw around so easily. 'You know that even if this had gone wrong – if they'd slammed you for what happened – I wouldn't have let you give up. I made you a promise, and I'm keeping it.'

The unspoken 'this time' lingered between them, but for what felt like the first time since laying eyes on Lauren in that bar, Kat didn't feel her old resentment return at the memory of past betrayals.

'We're going to win.' Lauren said it calmly, certainty in every syllable and Kat saw for a moment her sixteen-year-old self making that same promise: to never be left on the outside, to never feel not good enough, to never face such humiliation and pain. Something shifted in Kat as she sat there, under-standing, finally, what had driven Lauren to make those choices. Where for so long there had been only bitterness towards the Popularity Rules, she was surprised now to find something new – something she hadn't felt in such a long time.

She had faith.

Friendship is just a transaction.

No matter how cute and meaningful you think your friendships are, they're all a simple balance sheet in the end. He invites you out because you're entertaining, you stay in touch because she's got job contacts for you – it doesn't matter if they're your boyfriend or your boss, things will only stay smooth as long as the exchange keeps running.

So, decide what you have to give as your side of the bargain. Is it free therapy sessions? Contacts? Status by association? Make it clear to people what you can do for them and the relationship will be a breeze, but don't ever think they stick around because they genuinely like you. Affection is never enough.

Chapter Eighteen

It wasn't until they were out of London that the tension began to uncoil from Kat's body. She hadn't realised how much stress she'd been carrying: the fear of failure, the dull twist of resentment, the old sense she was selling out – it all somehow eased from her limbs the further they sped down the winding motorway away from the city.

'This was the perfect idea.' Kat put her seat back another notch and draped one arm outside the car window, feeling the cool air whip around her skin. 'I haven't been to Brighton in, God, so long.'

Lauren smiled, raising her voice to be heard over the roar of the wind. 'I figured it would do us both good to have a break . . . And I haven't been on a road-trip since college!'

'Wait, you have driven in England before, haven't you?' Kat bolted upright, panicking. Visions of drifting into oncoming traffic—

'Relax! Roads are roads,' Lauren replied with a shrug, adjusting her Wayfarer sunglasses in the rear-view mirror. 'Besides, you guys have nothing on asshole New York drivers.'

'I wouldn't count on it.' Kat shot another worried look at Lauren – one hand on the steering wheel, the other twisting her now-tangled hair back into a knot – and forced herself to relax. When had questioning Lauren's abilities ever paid off?

'You got any road-trip tunes?' Lauren asked, after they had driven in companionable silence for a little while. The roads were busy with weekend traffic, but since Lauren was using the overtaking lane as her personal highway, they were making good time.

'That I do.' Kat dug out her iPod and plugged it into the stereo jack. She scrolled through her substantial library, looking for that perfect playlist; indie and rock were fine for most of the time, but she felt like something different right now: something real and unpretentious and beloved . . . Selecting the track, she waited for Lauren's inevitable reaction.

'Country?' Lauren exclaimed, right on cue, as the steel guitars began to twang. 'You like country? Since when?'

Kat shrugged, a small smile on her lips as she listened to the familiar bluegrass beat and those lyrics about first loves and country fairs. 'Since ages. I even had a country show on the student radio station, back at Oxford. At least, I did until my anti-Valentine's Day programme; apparently songs about cheating and murder didn't go down too well with the five whole people listening that day.' She looked over at Lauren. 'What?' Kat protested.

'Nothing!' Lauren laughed. 'Hey, I'm not complaining; I love some Carrie Underwood. I just wouldn't have pegged you for a country girl, that's all. I mean, it's not exactly the home of enlightened feminism.'

'You'd be surprised.' Kat gave a wicked grin and scrolled through her iPod until she found the right track. Soon, the car was filled with the sound of a dulcet female voice describing how she planned to ambush her abusive ex with a rather large shotgun.

Kat sang along, while Lauren wove the rental car through gaps in traffic as if she was a frustrated Formula One driver. It was strangely liberating to be belting the songs out loud for a change, Kat had to admit. These days, she was more used to hiding her penchant for Taylor Swift and Tim McGraw: switching CD cases and filing the songs under unlabelled playlists to avoid anyone stumbling upon her secret love.

'If you like it so much, why don't you write about it?' Lauren asked, after the final gunshot had died away.

'Are you kidding?' Kat laughed. 'Country is officially the least cool genre in the world!'

'Less cool than goth metal?' Lauren teased. 'Geeky electronica? Emo?'

'By a mile! This isn't alt-country, or even classic bluegrass – they have a tiny amount of credibility at least – this is modern, red-state music. If I'd ever pitched this at *Think Louder*, they'd have crucified me!' Kat warmed to the theme, kicking off her shoes and propping her bare feet on the hot dashboard. 'Music critics are the ultimate poseurs. Even the ones who cover mainstream acts can only pretend to like Gwen and Britney in this cool, post-ironic way. I swear, unless you've got a closet full of Girl Talk B-sides or Santogold demos, you're not welcome.'

'You're exaggerating.'

'I'm not,' she swore, digging some sweets out of their bag of petrol-station provisions. 'Last year they found that one of the art designers, Kelvin, had a hard-drive full of Nickelback songs. They teased him about it for months until he quit.'

'That's completely crazy.'

'That's the music industry.' Kat passed her a twist of red liquorice. It had been their tuck-shop favourite back in school, affording a good twenty minutes of dedicated chewing over chocolate's more temporary pleasure. 'It's just another dick-stick thing.'

Lauren snorted. 'A what?'

'You know, another way for the boys to try and

212

out-do each other. "My twelve-inch vinyl LCD Soundsystem reissue is rarer than your limited-edition Ladytron down-load."' Kat curled her lip in disdain. She wasn't a fan of Britney and that parade of writhing, subjugated pop princesses preaching empowerment through glittering panties, but if you liked what you liked . . .

'And you put up with this?'

'It's the way it is.'

'Interesting.'

'What is?' Kat caught something in her tone.

'Well, it's just that you made such a fuss over that part of the Popularity Rules – as if you could never edit your public persona to get ahead. But really, you've been doing it all along.'

'That's different.' Kat was unsettled.

'How so?' Lauren challenged, biting off another stretch of liquorice. 'I know, it sounds trivial, but you've hidden a real part of your identity – an appreciation of big hair and cowboy boots – for the sake of image and professional advancement. I'm not saying it's a bad thing,' she quickly added, shooting a glance over at Kat. 'It's just if you're going to fight over the principle of selling out, well, that battle was already over the moment you disowned the Dixie Chicks.'

There was silence for a long while, nothing but the low roar of passing cars and the engine. 'I didn't think about it like that,' Kat said slowly. Her first instinct was to be defensive, but she carefully controlled the urge and tried to think clearly instead: rational, assessing, like Lauren seemed able to be. There was a gaping conceptual distance between concealing her love of country music and pretending to be someone else entirely, but somehow, Kat knew Lauren was right. It was the principle she'd objected so strongly to, but those principles hadn't stopped her standing silently by while Nate and Warren had joked about 'stupid red-necks' in rhinestones and American flags.

'Perhaps we're all compromising,' she wondered, watching the traffic outside stream past. 'Just some of us don't realise it yet.'

'Of course we are, but that's how you take the power back,' Lauren declared. 'When you finally wake up and choose which compromises to make, rather than blindly stumbling through life thinking you're above it all. Selling out is just an idea designed to keep you poor and anonymous for the sake of what – noble authenticity? Give me a break. Nothing's that black and white.'

Kat wondered if the old-school punks would see it that way, but she knew Lauren had a point. Selling out or not, things were different now; she was taking control. She would make those decisions for herself with eyes wide open.

They checked into a small but exquisitely hip hotel in the Lanes, a tiny paean to forties noir with old-fashioned dial telephones, deep scarlet walls and a concierge with a pinstripe suit and a thin worm of a moustache. Kat usually hated the overpriced boutique travel scene – why pay hundreds of pounds when you're going to be unconscious most of the time? – but there was something about the rich colours and tiny, jewel-like details that made her thrill like a wide-eyed traveller again: sampling the truffles laid out on the marshmallow-soft pillows, perusing the selection of l'Occitane lavender bath oils arranged around a bulb-lit vanity mirror, and throwing herself into the soft folds of the hunter-green bed covers.

'Oh, cute!' Lauren stuck her head around Kat's door and took in the walnut wood fixtures and rosy glow from the ornate Tiffany lamp. 'My room's done in a vampy red – very starlet.'

'You are keeping track of everything, aren't you?' Kat lifted her head – with some effort – from the folds of soft duvet. 'The clothes, the cost of this, even the rent. I want to be able to pay you back in the end.'

Lauren bounced gently on the end of the bed. 'Don't worry, I'm writing a nice long list of what you'll owe. I can even charge interest, if you want.'

'I think I'll live.' Kat bit into another piece of Turkish delight and wondered how long it would take Lauren to marshal them into a schedule. She was guessing in three . . . two . . . one . . .

'So, the plan,' Lauren started, getting out her iPhone.

Kat laughed. 'Of course, there has to be a plan!'

'Hey!' Lauren elbowed her lightly. 'Nothing crazy. I was thinking we stroll around, maybe do some shopping, spa treatments.'

'Throw in a pair of Manolos and a classic Madonna number and you've got yourself a chick-flick,' Kat noted.

'She says, sarcastically!' Lauren elbowed her again. 'You won't be so disdainful with a face full of cleansing mud and Lars working his magic on your back muscles.'

'No comment.' Kat busied herself with the confections. She was building to a nice sugar high at this rate.

'That's right, I forgot,' Lauren declared dramatically. 'Katherine Elliot is above such trivial things. She is a woman of substance and education!'

'No.' Kat tossed a mini pillow in her general direction. 'Katherine Elliot just wishes there were more constructive portrayals of women on-screen. I wouldn't have a problem with all the shiny consumer crap if we had real, meaningful parts too.'

'But honey, you're saying the ditsy shopaholic who trips over her own feet isn't real?' Lauren batted her eyelashes. 'What next? Dashing, commitment-phobic bachelors don't just need to find the right woman to settle down? Spunky inner-city kids won't triumph over adversity, after all?'

'Do you want me to launch into a lecture on the damage of negative cultural stereotyping?' Kat countered, but she couldn't keep a grin from her face at Lauren's dramatic gestures.

'Hmmm, maybe not.'

They lay in silence for a moment, the midday sun streaming in pale ribbons through the open window. Kat tried to relax, but she couldn't shake the persistent curiosity niggling away in the back of her mind.

'Say, you don't happen to have internet on your phone . . .'

'Yes, I do, and no, you are not checking,' Lauren cut her off. She rolled over and fixed Kat with a knowing look.

'But—'

'No.'

'If I could—'

'Nuh uh.'

'Argh!' Kat let out a small cry of frustration.

'I've seen it so many times before,' Lauren smirked. 'One minute you couldn't care less what people say about you, and then all it takes is one little blog post and suddenly you're refreshing for new comments twenty times a day.'

'Not even a peek?' Kat asked in a small voice. She shouldn't care, and ordinarily she wouldn't, but . . .

'Half of London is still drooling and hungover! I promise, we can find out what they're saying later. This is supposed to be an escape, remember?'

'Fine.' Kat sighed. She wished she didn't want to know what

216

some greasy DJ-slash-graphic-designer from Dalston thought about her, but now that video of her fight with Devon was out there, cluttering the news-feeds and gossip pages, she couldn't help but wonder. 'Let's go find some lunch.'

They ate fish and chips from greasy brown paper, staining their fingers with vinegar as they tramped along the stony beach. It was a hot, blue-skied day and all around them were pink-tinged crowds of sun-worshippers determined to make the most of the British seaside, despite the wind and faint clatter of arcade games drifting from the pier.

Kat munched on a chip. 'Enid Blyton was right: things always taste better out of doors.'

Lauren eyed the ketchup mess with a look of somebody calculating fat content, but she prodded her wooden fork into the crispy cod batter all the same. 'My nutritionist would kill me.'

'Not if I kill you first, for even having a nutritionist!' Kat laughed. 'What else, have you got a yoga instructor and dermatologist too?'

'Of course.' Lauren shrugged. 'You're forgetting I'm from New York; normal means something else altogether over there.'

'Right: crazy,' Kat agreed. 'You ever thought about moving to, I don't know, the middle of nowhere? That way you could be the most radiant woman in town without having to spend a bloody fortune on waxing.'

Lauren carefully speared another chip. 'But then what would I do? Means to an end, Kat; it's all just means to an end.'

Kat didn't need to ask what that end was. Only power, success and global domination.

They reached the big iron supports of the pier, a group

of teenage boys playing football in the shadows underneath.

'Remember when—' Lauren stopped, glancing cautiously at Kat.

'When we would come down here on exeat weekends?' Kat finished. 'Of course. I would spend all my money on second-hand books and you would always have to get a stick of that Brighton rock.'

'It was tradition!' Lauren protested.

'It was disgusting,' Kat corrected with a grin. 'You'd lose interest after half the thing and leave those sticky wrappings all over the bus.'

'Better than buying all those copies of Anaïs Nin and Erica Jong and then having to smuggle them back into the dorm,' Lauren countered. 'Didn't we end up wrapping them in Sweet Valley High covers?'

'God, you're right!' Kat gave a nostalgic sigh. She paused. 'Have you been back? To Park House, I mean? I got this letter last month . . .'

'About the reunion? Me too.' Lauren crumpled the cold food package into a plastic bag and pushed it aside as they found a free patch of shore to settle. 'Ten marvellous years away from that place!' They both gave a tense laugh. 'I'm not sure,' Lauren continued. 'I didn't keep in contact with anyone after graduating, and the only reason I'd go back is . . . Well, would be to see you again.'

Kat pulled her knees up to her chest and looked sideways at Lauren. She waited for the familiar swell of bitterness, but none came. 'Me too,' she answered slowly. 'Although, part of me does want to see what Lulu and Alison made of themselves.'

'Not much, I hope.'

'Who are we kidding?' Kat gave a short laugh. 'They'll be

elegantly groomed PR girls with shiny highlights and an investment banker boyfriend.'

'Named Chuck,' Lauren agreed. She began to pick up pebbles and toss them lazily towards the tide. 'You're nearly right: Lulu does PR for a beauty firm, and Alison recently married a man called Royston Medhurst the Third. I Googled them,' she explained.

'Did you ever look me up?' Kat asked, hesitant. She'd been tempted to search for Lauren from time to time, but had never allowed herself to make those keystrokes. It would have been admitting Lauren still mattered, during all those years when Kat was determined to forget she'd ever existed.

'Of course,' Lauren said quietly. 'You were easy to track with all those angry articles. And everyone bitching about your angry articles.'

Kat cracked a grin. 'Oh, the internet . . . What did mildly disaffected music fans do before thee?'

'Stalked their idols in real life?'

'See, technology has taken the effort out of everything.'

They sat watching the murky waves.

'I haven't written anything in six weeks,' Kat said quietly, thinking of the battered old Macs at the *Think Louder* office that would rebel at the slightest formatting demand. 'Not since I was fired. Am I really even still a writer, if I'm not actually writing?'

'Going all existential, are we?' Lauren must have sensed her wistfulness, because she quickly dropped the teasing note. 'Tell me about the magazine. It's more than just a job to you, isn't it?'

Kat stared at the horizon. It was strange to think of the gaps in their knowledge, the mystery decade that stretched in each of their lives. 'It started back in university,' she started slowly.

'They ran this big piece on women in rock, and it was just pathetic: patronising and shallow, so I wrote a letter to the editor. I hoped that maybe they'd print it, but Alan wrote me back. This was in the days he was still resisting email,' she added.

'Alan was the old editor, right?' Lauren frowned.

'My mentor,' Kat answered simply. 'He died last year. Heart attack; it was all pretty sudden.'

'Oh.' Lauren looked at her. 'I'm sorry.'

Kat shrugged, uncomfortable. 'Anyway, he told me that if I could do better than his writers, I should pitch him.' She watched the slow wash of the tide, remembering her determination and the hours she'd worked, crafting that perfect article. 'I spent ages on the piece. I was so sure he'd publish it, but then the next week, he sent it straight back, covered with red ink.'

'Put you in your place,' Lauren smiled softly.

'Exactly. We went back and forth for another month after that,' Kat recalled, 'until in the end, it was a completely different piece. But better, far better.'

'So he printed it?'

Kat nodded. 'I heard nothing for two months, and then I got a copy of the latest issue in the mail, before it hit newsstands. There was no note, just a post-it on the front saying, *Do it better next time*.'

Lauren laughed.

'So I ended up pitching articles for the rest of my last year at Oxford. He ran some of them, and said to get in touch after graduation, so I did. I started as his assistant on poverty-level pay.' Kat shook her head. 'I had to borrow from Mum, just to pay my bills, but I got to see everything: news, features, advertising. And when the editorial assistant quit, I moved up a little. And when a staff writer got sacked, I moved up some more.' She sighed. For years there had been a tight-knit staff, but over time, they had all drifted in different directions.

'But he was more than just a boss to you.' Lauren studied her intently. Kat nodded.

'I think he felt a little responsible for me,' she admitted. 'We settled into a great dynamic at the office, and I got on with his wife, Hélène, too.' She smiled. 'My first year, she heard that Susanne was over in Massachusetts for Christmas, so she insisted I spend it with them. It kind of became a tradition after that.' Kat paused. 'She moved back to France after he died.'

'I'm sorry.'

Kat shrugged again, awkward. 'It's fine.' She gave a rueful laugh. 'As much as I hate to admit it, Mum's probably right. He was like a father-figure to me. Which is why that job meant so much to me: it was all I had left of him. Making sure his legacy stayed true.'

'Then we've found our real goal,' Lauren said, her blue eyes set with a steely determination. 'We get you that job back.'

Kat looked at her hopefully. 'But I thought . . . You said that you could never go back.'

'This is different. This matters.'

Kat ran a smooth pebble through her fingers, trying not to let her hopes rise too high. 'We'll see,' she hedged. 'And after everything with Devon . . .'

Lauren reached over and linked her little finger through Kat's, just the way they'd always done. '*Especially* after everything with Devon. Trust me, now we've started spinning it, that fight might be the best thing you've ever done.'

Find some fans.

If you think popularity is about blending in and being one of the crowd, you're wrong; it's about leading them too. Trends change, allegiances shift all the time, and all it takes is a petty feud or jealous rival and you'll be out on your own again, so don't let that happen. Figure out who's weak and easily led, and use flattery and fear to make them your loyal followers – once you have an entourage, everyone else will think you have power and fall in line too.

Chapter Nineteen

'You know how I said this was an escape?'

'Yeees . . .' Kat turned to look at Lauren as she tapped away at her phone. They had spent the morning strolling through the cobbled back-streets, stopping occasionally to look in record stores and vintage clothing shops, slow with the relaxed warmth of a holiday. Now they were perched at a table on the front patio of a little restaurant, watching packs of goth teens and an assortment of Euro-shoppers bustle by.

'How would you feel about doing one little Popularity Rules thing?' Lauren asked with a sideways glance. 'One tiny status-building event. Barely even work; you might even have fun!'

'What is it?' Kat waited, sipping her glass of wine. Sunlight was falling through the trees and shrubbery lining the patio, burning through the edges of her sunglasses with a pleasant intensity. Even Lauren looked relaxed, her posture less stiff and purposeful as she lounged in her seat, both of them reluctant to start moving again.

It felt good to be out of the city.

Lauren's lips began to tug into a grin. 'A slow-dance prom.'

'A what?'

'It's this hipster party thing.' Lauren gestured vaguely. 'They dress up in retro outfits and go slow-dance to power ballads, but that's not the point.'

'I should hope not!'

'The point is, it's being hosted by Harry Sharp – that

designer I've been talking about. The Troika are DJing. It's going to be invite-only, full of hipster music types. In other words . . .'

'. . . I need to be there to network,' Kat finished. She thought of the debacle at the boat party, and swiftly gulped back the rest of her drink. It was inevitable, of course, that she'd have to wade out into the treacherous waters of public life again, but part of her had been hoping the respite would last longer than forty-eight whole, blissful hours. 'Oh, go on then.'

'Really?' Lauren seemed surprised by her acquiescence.

'If it's going to help me . . .' she shrugged. 'Let me see the invite.'

'Well . . .' Lauren paused. 'I don't exactly have one.'

'Lauren!'

'So we'll gatecrash, no big deal.' She gave Kat a conspiratorial grin. 'I do it all the time. How else are you supposed to meet the right people when you're not already part of their crowd?'

'But . . .' Kat bit her lip. 'Don't you feel awkward, like an impostor? I get insecure enough at these things even when I am on the list.'

'Not any more.' Lauren put her phone aside. 'I did at first, back in college. I would just show up to every event I figured was cool enough, even if I didn't know a single person in the room. I would say I was a friend of John's, or Katy's, and even if I was nervous and wretched inside, nobody even cared.' She gave a wry look. 'Of course, it helped that I was a skinny blonde in a tank top.'

'Naturally,' Kat agreed.

'But that's just the way it is.' Lauren shrugged. 'Pretty people always get a free pass.'

Kat leaned back on her chair and considered the strange and

224

uneven hierarchy of attractiveness. She wasn't sure how old she'd been when it first occurred to her how the world worked. It wasn't a blinding epiphany or dramatic revelation, just the gradual acknowledgement of that universal truth, so that by the time she was a teenager, the rules were set. 'They' were them, and she was her, and somehow the rules were different.

'Do you think they appreciate it? The pretty ones, I mean,' she wondered. 'The people who are popular without trying, without the rules or planning. Do you think they realise just how much easier their lives are?'

'Of course not.' Lauren's voice was matter-of-fact. 'They have their angst and their problems, like us all, but the real core of it – all the power and free rides? They take it for granted, they always do. They don't know what lies behind it, not like we do. Not like you will,' she added. 'That's the thing about the Popularity Rules: it's the ultimate revenge. They get to taste popularity for a few years, but we get it for life.'

Life . . .

Kat looked out across the winding street, past the people and storefronts to some distant future. She couldn't see it clearly yet, or even predict its contents, but she savoured her sense of reassurance nonetheless. Instead of the chilled fear or insecurity that the gaping, distant future usually brought, Kat felt calm inside. Perhaps this was what religion felt like to all those believers she'd never quite understood: a peaceful, sure knowledge that everything would be all right.

The waitress brought their bill, startling Kat out of her reverie.

'I'd better do some more shopping,' Lauren sighed. 'Fall collections are in-store, and I need to start building next season's looks.'

Kat made a noise of amusement: not only was it

hot, summer weather, but she'd seen the size of Lauren's wardrobe. New additions were completely unnecessary.

'Want to split up?' Lauren suggested. 'I could blitz it in no time on my own.'

'Meet you in Borders in an hour?'

'Perfect.'

Kat settled into an armchair overlooking the square with an armful of magazines and a large Frappuccino. It was just like the Saturdays she'd used to spend in London, only this time, instead of *New Republic* and *Billboard* magazine, she leafed through a stack of *Grazia* and *Heat* instead, dutifully noting who was screwing and suing whom in the rarefied world of modern celebrity. It was a challenge, of course, to flick past yet another 'Miracle Diet!' story where a star weighing all the hefty bulk of nine stone cooed over her life-changing transformation to a slimmer, more serene seven-and-a-half, but Kat was nothing if not dedicated to her cause, simply sending a silent plea to the feminist gods and continuing on her quest for meaningless small-talk fodder. The next time she was trapped in a confined space with someone longing to discuss the minutiae of Lily Larton's love life, she'd be ready.

After a pleasant few moments slurping her icy drink and despairing about mainstream media, Kat's senses began to prickle: somebody was watching her. She glanced up. A couple of tables away, a thin boy looked away quickly, studying the fair-trade coffee leaflet with surprising intensity. Kat surreptitiously sneaked out a compact mirror and checked her face: no lipstick smudges, no stray mascara smears. All clear.

She turned back to the riveting rumours of Chris Carmel's crack addiction, but the strange feeling didn't go away. She looked up again. He looked away again. Kat sighed.

'Can I help you?' she called over, looking at him more closely. He was nineteen or twenty, dressed in some sort of uniform of a black T-shirt and trousers, but his hair was something else altogether: a complicated mix of under-cut, faux-hawk and sweeping fringe, it started shaven and dark behind one pierced ear and somehow ended up platinum, hanging low over his other eye. Kat took brief comfort in the fact that there were people on this earth with more ridiculous hairstyles than her. 'Well?' she snapped, when the boy simply blinked at her. 'Did you want something in particular, or are you just going to sit there, staring at me?'

'It *is* you!' he breathed, leaping up. 'No. Fucking. Way!'

Now it was Kat's turn to blink, as the boy sat himself down opposite her and launched into a monologue, his voice arch and expressive. 'So, of course the alert came through when I was locked in the stock room, cataloguing Razorlight albums, of all things, but I promised Kurt I'd pick up some of his god-awful B&H fags if he let me take my break, and came right over. I wasn't sure, with the hair – my God, the hair! – but I *had* to see for myself, and they were right, it's you!' He finally paused for breath and surveyed her. 'Katherine Emmeline Elliot. In the flesh!'

Kat was thrown, and not just by the casual familiarity. He knew her middle name. Nobody knew her middle name. And why was he looking at her so expectantly? Reaching for her bag, Kat got up and slowly began to edge away.

'It's me!' The boy frowned, searching her with a sharp gaze. 'Oscar.'

She stared back, blank.

'Oscar!' he repeated, smile slipping slightly. Kat waited, wondering if the name was supposed to hold some great significance to—

Oh. *Oscar*. Her 'eccentric and possibly unstable' letter-writer from back at the magazine?

'Oscar!' she managed, trying to rouse whatever enthusiasm he obviously was waiting for. As her voice left her lips, she recognised the tone: the same one Lauren would employ when faced with vague acquaintances. 'Of course!'

Oscar clapped his hands together and launched himself at her, wrapping his bony limbs around her in a hug. 'God, it's about time someone gave you a freaking makeover. Before this, the only picture I could find of you online had you glowering like you were about to reach for Radiohead and slit your wrists.' The words tumbled quickly out of his mouth as Kat tried to detangle herself. 'And what are you even doing down here? No, forget that, first you have to tell me about Devon Darsel – I want all the dirty little details. He was a bastard, right? I knew it. So pretty, but so doomed.' He sighed, 'Kurt, River, Pete – they're all the same.'

Kat took a tiny step back and caught her breath as Oscar continued his meditation on the tragedies of modern genius, his hands fluttering along with every other syllable. 'Wait, slow down.' She shook her head. The chance of him discovering her in a city she rarely visited, in the middle of a crowded shopping centre, was non-existent. 'How did you find me? Nobody knows I'm here.'

Oscar laughed. 'Nobody and the entire internet, more like!' He brandished his mobile phone. 'Stalkerati sent out the tip half an hour ago.'

'Stalker-what?' Kat repeated.

'The website, silly.' He looked mildly confused. 'You know, people send in tips about who's where and when, and they post it to real-time maps. I have it set up to ping me alerts whenever any of my favourites are in town. You're one of them, obviously,' he added. Oscar glanced down at the screen again. 'Ugh, Kurt is probably dying of nicotine withdrawal by now. Oh well. Fuck him.' He shrugged. 'What's he going to do, fire me? I swear, unemployment would be better than enabling those morons to buy The Hoosiers and Scouting for Girls and *The View*.' On that last band, his lip curled into a magnificent sneer.

'Oh.' Kat could only answer faintly. After all those eloquent letters, Oscar was really no more than a camp hipster child?

'There you are.'

Kat turned with relief to find Lauren, crisp paper bags dangling from both arms. 'Lauren, finally. This is . . .'

'Oscar Lovato.' He thrust himself forwards and kissed Lauren on both cheeks. 'And you must be Katherine's makeover angel.'

Lauren shot a look at Kat.

'Oh, come on,' Oscar continued, his voice laced with a knowing edge. 'We both know she didn't just wake up one morning blessed with the ability to accessorise! For that, my dear, the world thanks you.'

'Oscar is a . . . fan of mine,' Kat explained faintly. 'From the magazine.'

'Oh.' Lauren brightened. 'Well, great to meet you.'

'But we have to get going,' Kat said quickly, trying to catch her eye. 'We've got all this planning. Our costumes. For the party.'

'Costumes?' Oscar asked, lounging against the magazine rack as if it was a bar. Kat half expected to see him pull out a cigarette holder and shrug on a smoking jacket. 'No wait, don't tell me, the Harry Sharp debacle.' His nonchalance slipped. 'God, half of Shoreditch has descended for that thing. I should have known you'd be going. Who are you wearing?'

'I was thinking classic Marc Jacobs,' Lauren mused, oblivious to Kat's tugging on her arm. 'And maybe something more aggressive for Kat?'

'Hmmm.' Oscar assessed Lauren swiftly. 'Sweetheart neckline, am I right? A deep blue, maybe some bright pinks . . .'

'That's right!' She looked at Oscar with a new hint of admiration.

'You Southern belles, always the same.' He sighed. 'Always so pretty-pretty, never the risks.'

'We call it classic style,' Lauren replied.

'Well, I call it dull.' Oscar shot back, and then gave a wink.

Kat witnessed the fashion debate with a growing sense of unease. Lauren was supposed to have whisked her away by now, far from the strange adoration of this boy, but instead, she was . . . smiling at him, with a strategic glint in her eyes.

'Why don't you come?' Lauren asked suddenly. Kat turned to her in protest, but she was quelled with a stare.

'To the prom?' Oscar gave an exaggerated shrug. 'Perhaps. I could see. If you want me to.' He looked back and forth between the women, obviously waiting for something.

'Yes, you should come,' Lauren announced, with a decisive nod. She elbowed Kat.

'Umm, sure. Come along.' Kat rubbed her side and wondered what on earth Lauren was playing at.

'Well, I suppose I could clear my schedule,' Oscar admitted. 'Can't leave you two ladies unescorted, can we?'

'Absolutely not.' Lauren rewarded him with a dazzling smile. 'Meet you there at eleven.'

Only when she had Oscar's mobile number tapped into her phone and had exchanged a round of air-kisses did she allow Kat to pull her towards the lifts.

'What did you have to do that for?' Kat hissed, the moment the doors closed.

'What do you mean?'

'Encourage him!' Kat was unnerved by the whole encounter. 'He basically stalked me here, and you went and invited him out with us, to an important event, no less.'

'Calm down.' Lauren patted her arm. 'He's harmless.'

'Yes but . . .' Kat tried to find the words for her profound discomfort. 'It's not right, is it? I mean, he reads all my articles, writes those long letters . . . Aren't teenage boys supposed to be worshipping Scarlett Johansson or, failing that, Jake Gyllenhaal?'

'He's a fan, get used to it!' Lauren laughed as they exited the shop and strolled out onto the square. 'And quit complaining; most people would kill to have someone hanging off their every word.'

'Then they're more than welcome to him.' Kat still felt uncomfortable, as if she needed to take a long shower to scrub away that devoted gleam in his eye.

'You won't be saying that later tonight,' Lauren predicted. 'I invited him along for a reason: you need an entourage, and two is better than one.'

Target the tastemakers.

Every scene has a secret leader. They may not be the prettiest or most popular kid, but they're the one who has the respect of the in-crowd and sets all the trends. This person is your short-cut to status: if you win them over, everyone else will start to follow.

Hunt them down and put everything you've got into winning their good opinion. Go where they go, know what they know and don't ever screw them over.

Chapter Twenty

Lauren was right, of course. Kat used to find her constant rightness irritating, but as they climbed out of their taxi at the front steps to the grand, sea-front hotel, she decided it was something of a relief. Perhaps after another few months – or years – with the Popularity Rules, she would know these things by instinct too: that wearing a bright blue dress with her hair may make her feel like a walking Union Jack, but gave the impression she was actually a confident fashionista; that four-inch heels may hurt like hell, but provided a certain twisted power knowing she could crush someone's windpipe with her footwear; and finally, that having even one person as back-up made her feel that little bit invincible as they waltzed past the line.

'I don't see Oscar . . .' Lauren quickly surveyed the crowd. 'Damn. He was supposed to meet us out front.'

'Do we wait?' Kat asked, hoping he wouldn't show at all.

'No,' Lauren decided. 'It'll look bad. Important people never wait.' And with that, she led them up the steps to the row of big, bald doormen.

'Name.' The first hulking man blocked their path. He was at least six foot three, wearing a black suit and brandishing a clipboard and a headset. Wannabe partiers were jostling behind the gold velvet rope, and there were even some photographers poised along the kerb. Kat felt a brief tremor of nerves. Gatecrashing a casual party or drinks event was one thing, but would they really be able to pull this off?

Lauren, on the other hand, didn't miss a beat.

'We were supposed to like, RSVP?' Twirling a glossy strand of hair, Lauren gazed at the man blankly. In an instant, she was the picture of vapid innocence, with her flouncy blue dress and tumbling curls.

'No name, no entry.'

Lauren squeezed Kat's hand gently. This was her cue. 'Kat Elliot?' she asked, with what she hoped was a brilliant smile.

'You're not down,' the man repeated, but this time with apology in his voice. At the sign of weakness, Lauren turned on the charm.

'Oh, I'm so sorry! I thought all this was fixed.' She flashed a sugar-sweet grin, her Southern drawl suddenly thicker. 'Cosmo said something about a list, and I just assumed he'd take care of it.' She giggled prettily. All it had taken was a quick internet search to learn the names of some key PR staff. The man began to soften.

'Well . . .' He wavered. Kat held her breath.

'What's the hold-up?' Suddenly a small, hard-eyed woman appeared. 'We're getting backed up here.'

'These ladies say Cosmo sorted—'

'If they're not on the list, they don't get in.' The woman glared at them impatiently. 'Get them out of here.'

Kat's first instinct was to slink away, but something other than Lauren's vice-like grip held her in place. She was done with slinking. Act like you belong, the Popularity Rules instructed; radiate entitlement. So, with what she hoped was a suitably radiant and snooty tone, Kat glared down at the woman. 'Ex-*cuse* me, but you need to go fetch Francis or Marie or someone who knows what the hell they're doing. I cut short my Paris trip for this!' Part of her hated acting like every guest-list blagger she loathed, but Kat had to admit, it was sort of fun.

The woman's eyes began to bulge. 'I said—'

'Ohmygod!' A familiar voice rose above the crowd. 'Kat? Kat Elliot? Ohmygod!'

Before any of them could react, Oscar rushed up the steps and grabbed Kat's arm as if he'd never met her before. 'I love you!' he shrieked, as Kat stared at him in amazement. 'Can I get an autograph? Can I get a photo? Can you call my friends and say "hi", so they'll believe it's you? Ohmygod!'

'Uh . . .'

'Aren't you *sweet*?' Lauren cried. 'Sure you can, right Kat? Come on!' Linking one arm through Oscar's and the other with Kat, Lauren beamed at the lady on the door. 'Fans! I don't know how she puts up with them. Can we get moving before she gets mobbed?'

To Kat's amazement, the immovable frown was moved. 'I'm sorry!' The woman hurried to move the rope aside, looking at Kat with new respect. 'Come right ahead.' Beckoning them in, she ushered them towards the doors, apologising as she went. 'Just a misunderstanding, I'm so sorry. I don't know how it happened.'

'No probs!' With that, Lauren waltzed inside, dragging a stunned Kat after her.

'Don't thank me all at once,' Oscar crowed, when they were out of earshot. 'You can just reward me with drinks and ooh, that's Natalia Revana. And Luke Bently!' He tried to keep up his jaded detachment as they entered the lobby, but excitement clearly won out: soon, he was giving a running commentary of all the various fashion and media sightings.

Kat couldn't help but be infected by his enthusiasm. The planners had clearly gone all-out in an effort to lend some exclusive credibility to whatever they were celebrating – the room was already buzzing with anticipation, full of people in vintage suits or prom dresses with tiny, net-edged hats sitting atop artfully retro styles. In the far corner a crowd of partiers was waiting to have their photos taken, a kaleidoscope of mirrored walls set up in lieu of a red carpet, so they could simultaneously check out their outfits and be immortalised in all their exquisite, fashionable glory.

'Should we . . . ?' Kat paused, remembering her goals. They may be in, but the hard work was all still ahead of her. Exposure, visibility, and above all, fearlessness were still waiting on her agenda.

'Later,' Lauren murmured, her eyes flicking over the scene. And it was certainly a scene. What was once a faded, elegant ballroom had been transformed into the uber-prom, distilling every American movie and TV setting into one vast array of shimmering retro decor. There was nothing so tacky as the limp crêpe paper or cardboard cut-out signs Kat remembered from the few school dances she'd ever seen; instead, gold and silver streamers drifted gently from the grand chandeliers, a constellation of mirror-balls flecked the ceiling with light, and an afro-haired man in a ringmaster's outfit presided from a spot-lit DJ booth on the stage.

'Fucking hipsters,' Oscar sighed affectionately. For someone wearing impossibly tight black skinny jeans and a dragon-patterned cravat, Kat didn't think he could claim the sartorial high ground, but then again, she was dressed the part too.

'So what's the plan of attack?' she asked, pushing back the curl of fringe that Lauren had styled to fall directly over her eye. It wasn't yet midnight, so the dance-floor was still empty. She guessed that meant the networking portion of the evening was about to get started. Kat felt a surreptitious squeeze on her elbow, and looked up. Of course, the Popularity Rules were a secret. 'I mean, alcohol, dancing, alcohol?' Kat added quickly.

'I'll go!' Oscar announced. He must have realised how eager he sounded, because he quickly covered with an arch drawl. 'I'm going to need an ocean of vodka to make it through the night without an aneurysm.' He looked out over the sea of glittering bodies towards the bar. 'I'll go hunt and gather something. If I don't make it back, look for me under the trample of confetti.' He held one hand dramatically to his forehead and looked so mournful that Kat couldn't help but smile.

The moment he'd been swallowed by the mass of taffeta and lace, Lauren pulled Kat closer and surveyed the room. 'Now, you're going to get some attention,' Lauren warned. 'You are, after all, an internet celebrity right now.'

'Lovely,' Kat replied faintly. She had pledged to do better this time, to try and be that confident, attention-worthy woman, but now she was there amongst the crowds and chatter, it wasn't so easy to shake off twenty-odd years of social discomfort. She could already sense people looking at her, bringing back memories of the boat party and all that laughter. A group of women in flouncy fifties dresses began to whisper gleefully, and for a moment, Kat's newfound resolve slipped. 'I don't know if I can—'

'You can, and you will.' Lauren linked an arm through hers. 'We've already switched the story about you to being rebellious and cool; now you just have to look glamorous and unconcerned, and the narrative will be set.'

'Where do you get this stuff?' Kat wondered, side-stepping to avoid a dangerous trail of sparkling streamers. 'I mean, the spinning, the narrative – they weren't in the original Rules, were they?'

'Think of it as bonus material.' Lauren was already looking

around for their first targets, but Kat cleared her throat and waited for a real answer.

'I did a dissertation on gossip and narrative constructions,' Lauren finally explained. They began to circle the edge of the dance-floor, their dresses rustling together as they walked. 'How people look to celebrity gossip as a kind of real-life fiction that gets told through TV and magazines and such. It seems to be human nature to want to push life into a recognisable structure – you know, with chapters and plot twists and villains.'

'Hence reality TV, and all that editing,' Kat realised, thinking of the endless parade of MTV shows about doe-eyed girls and their romantic failings.

'Exactly. So we're just using that to write our own narrative for you, via blogs and tabloids.' Lauren took in the attention from nearby partiers, obviously satisfied. 'Chapter one was your showdown with Devon, so now we need to create more material before anyone else hijacks the story or it fades away.'

Kat knew she should feel chilled at such a detached assessment of what was, in the end, her real life, but Lauren's logic was irrefutable. PR people stage-managed events; politicians created ideological fairy tales; and millions of people scoured the internet for the latest instalment of the Britney saga or the Angelina affair. Everyone wanted a story to follow, and now they were going to make her that tale: only instead of the plot summary reading 'obstructive, antagonistic feminist', she could write whatever she wanted.

'Two apple martinis.' Oscar materialised with their drinks. 'I decided you were beyond the *Cosmo* cliché.'

'Thanks, sweetie.' Lauren took the glass but didn't drink, instead holding it at a casual angle like just another prop. Kat carefully followed suit. Lowered inhibitions were the antithesis of the Popularity Rules: she needed to be utterly in control.

'So, here you have it: the Brighton scene,' Oscar announced, pushing back his flash of platinum fringe. 'Otherwise known as the London scene after sixty minutes on the train. Delightful, don't you think?'

'Totally,' Lauren laughed, clearly amused by him. Kat wasn't quite so easily charmed.

'Of course, we also get the art fags and bohemian bitches who made enough in property to fuck off out of the capital and open their organic tea rooms, or spas or whatever.' Oscar managed to lift the corner of his top lip in a magnificent sneer.

'So what brought you to town?' Lauren began her subtle interrogation, while Kat kept an eye on the crowd. The room was almost full by now, clusters of twenty-somethings in their very best dresses jostling for prime people-watching positions. It was clearly a 'see and be seen' affair; loud greetings and lashings of air-kisses at every turn.

'. . . and so I decided it was either leave or resign myself to stocking shelves in the local Co-op for ever more,' Oscar was saying. 'And trust me, these hands aren't made for manual labour, ugh.' He shuddered. 'So I slung my checked handkerchief over my shoulder, bid Lower Higgledown farewell and made for the bright lights and the big city. Not that Brighton's much better. I'm so over this place.'

'You'll end up in London eventually,' Kat warned him, turning back to the conversation. 'Everybody does.'

'I love this song!' Lauren suddenly exclaimed, as the familiar chords of Bon Jovi began play. She wasn't alone. At the first, epic notes, a sudden surge of hipsters filled the polished floor, evidently not as uber-cool or detached as they'd like to believe. 'Oscar, dance with me?'

'It would be a pleasure.' He held out his arm and Lauren slipped a net-gloved hand through it.

'But—' Kat protested, as they abandoned her by a trestle table of cupcakes.

'Go, circulate!' Lauren called back over her shoulder with a wink before Oscar twirled her away and they were swallowed into the joyful crowd.

Then Kat realised, this was a test. Lauren was cutting her loose to go seal her own fate, alone in a room full of strangers all over again.

Kat clutched her small, gold purse and automatically stepped back against the wall, activity swirling past her in a blur of party dresses, disco-ball lights and laughing, happy faces. She watched them all with faint detachment, replaying their youthful rites of passage with such excitement and nostalgia. Was this what her teenage years were supposed to have been like? She'd made it a rule to avoid school discos at Park House: sitting sullenly on the edge of the room with Lauren and then staying in the dorms, alone, when Lauren ascended to the popular clique. Her only nod to teen hi-jinx had been the huge party in the woods at the end of A-levels, where she'd got hideously drunk and woken up with 'bitch' and 'frigid cunt' scrawled across her face with a permanent marker – a humiliation that lingered far longer than the two weeks it took the ink to fade.

Joyful times indeed.

But she was older now. Older, wiser and armed with scarlet lipstick and a host of psychological tricks to evoke status and belonging. Allowing herself one more sigh, Kat straightened her posture, ruffled her hair, and launched herself casually towards the closest group of stylish spectators with what she hoped was the perfect superior-yet-friendly voice.

'That's such a cute dress – is it vintage?'

Stay cool.

The last thing you want during the Popularity Rules is to get attached. If you're swept up in romance or what you think is real friendship, you risk losing your edge and jeopardizing all your dreams. Would you rather turn into a simpering girlfriend or achieve those goals you've worked so hard for? Guys have a funny habit of sending even the most cool-headed girl crazy, so stay alert! Date your way up the social food-chain for sure, but steer clear of the boys who really affect you: they'll be nothing but trouble.

Chapter Twenty-one

After an hour of dancing, mingling and making mindless small-talk with various hipster types, Kat was exhausted. Mustering compliments and brushing off bitchy comments was tiring work; she now had a newfound respect for Lauren's stamina when it came to social niceties. And the conversation! Nothing but showbiz gossip and how profound the new MGMT album was. She felt *old*.

Escaping to the faded, gilt-edged bathroom, Kat kicked off her heels for a blissful moment and checked her reflection. An unfamiliar face stared back at her, the careful mask of someone far cooler and more fashionable than she really was. Kat studied herself curiously. The Popularity Rules were right: it was easier this way – to have a person on the outside, separate from her actual self. The networking and strategic social manoeuvring made less of a dent on her soul now that she could think of it all as a game her other half was playing.

'Katherine! Sweetie! There you are!'

Kat barely had time to register a syrupy voice before she was enveloped by a plump woman dressed all in black. She blinked, untangling herself. 'Umm, hi?' Remembering the mission, Kat added a smile, 'Great to meet you . . . ?'

'Annette Fallon,' the woman answered, her hair falling in a thick bob around large eyes and a small, pouting mouth.

'I'm—'

'Yes, Kat Elliot, I know.' Annette laughed, applying a layer of vamp red lipstick and shooting her a sideways look. 'I know *all* about you.'

'Oh?' Kat took a tiny step backwards, disconcerted by the sharp look in the woman's eyes.

'Devon must have been a handful, hmmm?' Annette lowered her voice conspiratorially. 'But of course, you know how to handle yourself. That's what I hear, anyway.'

Kat paused. She'd spent the better part of a week trying to understand how to establish a dominant power dynamic, but now it was clear. Annette was a stranger, but here she was, hinting at knowing Kat's deep, dark secrets to make herself seem more powerful. She wanted Kat to ask what she knew, to feel insecure and off-balance. It wouldn't work.

'Oh, I'm sure you know better than to believe all that gossip.' Kat pulled her shoes back on and forced herself to sound breezy. 'But thanks for saying hi; it's always fun to meet a fan.' She flashed another fake grin and headed back out into the crowded lobby.

Annette didn't let Kat get far. 'Say, didn't you work with Jessica Star?' She trotted to keep up with Kat. 'That must have been fun, I'll bet.'

Kat tried not to scowl. She had a bad feeling about this woman, and all her knowing insinuations. 'Oh, you know.' She looked around for escape. 'Jessica's a doll.'

'But you must be furious, with what she's saying about you,' Annette tried again, and despite herself, Kat couldn't help but waver.

'What do you mean—?'

'There you are!' Before she could finish her question, Oscar rushed over, linking his arm firmly through Kat's. He looked breathless, and his cravat was now in disarray. 'We were ready to send out a search team. You owe me at least one dance, and the cards say that "Total Eclipse of the Heart" is due soon.' As he chattered, Oscar angled his body to block Annette completely, practically dragging Kat away.

'Oww!' she protested, once they were clear across the lobby. 'Bonnie Tyler can wait!'

'Uh, not when you're talking to the bitchiest gossip columnist in town!'

'I what?' Kat glanced back. Annette was watching them, the syrupy smile now replaced with a calculating stare.

Oscar sighed, clearly unimpressed by her ignorance. 'She was one of the "3 a.m. Girls", until the high journalistic standards became too much. Now she just buzzes around, picking up what trashy details she can and hawks them to the highest bidder. Ooh, goodie bags.' He set upon the table of freebies with glee.

Kat turned back to him. 'Wait, how do you know this? I thought you shunned tabloid idiocy.'

Oscar rolled his eyes. 'Everybody knows Annette. They call her the Viper.'

'Charming.' Kat acted unconcerned, but she felt a definite chill. That had been close!

'So, do you actually want to dance?' Oscar looked reluctant, still picking through his bag. 'I was only saying that to get you out of there. I hate that fucking song.'

'You're off the hook,' Kat reassured him. 'I couldn't manage it anyway – not in these shoes.'

'Thank God, I—' Oscar's eyes widened, and then a pair of hands descended over her eyes.

'Kirsty McColl would be disappointed in you, Ms Elliot.'

The voice in her ear was low, and sent an involuntary shiver down Kat's spine as she recalled that same tone whispering unspeakable things as his bare flesh pressed against hers.

'Ash.' She recovered, greeting him quickly with a kiss on each stubbled cheek. He looked just as good as he had forty-eight hours earlier; better, in fact, in a sharply tailored navy suit and crisp white shirt that nonetheless had a faint rumple to them. Kat tried very hard not to remember how he looked without the clothes. 'What are you doing here?'

'Stalking you,' he said with a grin. 'No, I have a studio nearby, and a friend mentioned this event.'

Typical hipster clusterfuck.

'Well, hello.' Oscar inserted herself between them, sizing Ash up. 'And who might you be?'

'Ash Delaney,' he introduced himself courteously. 'A . . . friend of Kat's.'

Oscar turned to Kat and arched one eyebrow in question. Kat evaded his gaze.

'Now, I think you owe me a dance,' Ash decided, taking Kat's hand and backing away, his eyes never leaving hers. 'And I won't take high heels as an excuse.'

'Again with the talk of obligations,' she replied, but let herself be tugged towards the dance-floor all the same. For some reason, her feet weren't hurting quite so much.

Ash twirled her around, pulling her into his arms in one swift motion. 'Somebody's done this before,' Kat noted, feeling his arm firm at her waist and his fingers gently folded around her right hand.

'Ballroom classes, boarding school,' he explained, tilting his face so that his lips grazed against her cheek. 'If they'd just told us it was the fastest way to a woman's heart, we wouldn't have put up such a fight.'

Kat laughed, letting her body sink against his. 'We're going to have to work on this ego of yours.'

'Going to?' He twirled her away and then brought her back,

245

closer this time, so she could smell the faint hint of his cologne. Cinnamon and citrus: she remembered it from his immaculate bathroom cabinet. 'Katherine, you've made a run for it twice now without a word. A lesser man would have quit chasing you by now.'

'You're chasing?' She was dimly aware of the formality of their banter, as if the dancing was taking them back half a century.

'Ambling, perhaps,' he modified. 'Maybe even a brisk stroll.'

Kat laughed.

'So which one am I?' Ash asked, lightly squeezing her hand. 'Stupid or misguided?'

Kat waited before answering, enjoying the sway of their bodies and the glitter from the mirror-balls above. She hadn't allowed herself to think of the possibilities of this man; with the Popularity Rules and *Think Louder*, she'd had far too much else on to let herself be distracted by romantic entanglements with unsuitable men. But now, his body solid against hers, the idea began to blossom in her mind.

'Neither, perhaps.' She replied minutes later, shifting her hand in his so that her thumb stroked his palm, back and forth. The movement was almost imperceptible, but the way Ash's dancing slowed told Kat it hadn't gone unnoticed.

'Good,' he whispered. The music suddenly swelled to a climax and Kat found herself dipped, suspended only inches from the floor. She gasped for breath.

'Thanks for the dance.' Kat untangled herself from him the moment the last chords faded away. Possibilities were one thing, but slow-dances were a perilous sport. The spotlights, the false sense of intimacy . . . Another few twirls and dips, and who knew what Kat would do? 'Be a darling and find me a

246

drink? It's the least you can do,' she added, 'after wearing me out like this.'

'Whatever you want,' Ash agreed, mock-saluting and then backing away into the crowd.

Kat drifted to the side of the room and sank onto a chaise longue, waiting for her pulse to return to normal.

Lauren slipped onto the seat beside her. 'So who was that?'

Kat started. 'Is everyone here keeping track of my every move?'

'Nope,' Lauren grinned, biting into a cherry from her cocktail. 'Just Oscar and me. Plus half a dozen journalists. And you didn't answer my question.'

'He's from Friday night, after the boat party. And, another time too, before all this began.' Kat gazed after him, still spinning from their dance. And oh, that dip!

'Hey, it's OK.' Lauren snapped her fingers in front of Kat's face. She blinked. 'He's just like everyone else; you can handle him. Remember the Popularity Rules: casual detachment, charm, status.'

'Uh huh,' Kat murmured. The Rules, of course. She just needed to focus on the Rules.

'You shouldn't be hiding away in the corner here; let's go find somewhere more visible.'

'But Ash—'

'Ash can find you, if he wants.' Lauren looked mildly disapproving at the idea that Kat should sit, waiting for the man. 'Now, where's Oscar?'

'You mean, your new favourite person?'

'What? Oh, come on, Kat. He's like a freaking puppy – how can you not like him?'

'I don't know,' Kat shrugged. 'There's just something . . . sort of false about him, that's all. It's like he's swallowed the

247

safe media version of what it means to be a gay boy, without thinking for a moment if it means anything.'

'So the boy hasn't figured out who he is yet. Give him a break. It's not as if you have to be best friends with him.' She shot Kat a look. 'That's something else you'll need to learn: how to maintain a circle of loose acquaintances. You need a large group of people considering you a friend, not just the rare few who pass your impossible standards.'

'I'm going to choose to take that as a compliment,' Kat informed her, 'and a testament to my discerning taste.' Her energy was starting to return, the brief wooziness subsiding. The fact the DJ had replaced Backstreet Boys with 'Maps' by the Yeah Yeah Yeahs was also a bonus.

'Oh, there he is.' Kat spotted Oscar in a raised section of seating at the far end of the room. Set back from the main crowd, a black cord marked what had to be the VIP section – if the cluster of vaguely recognisable women with expensive dresses and heavy eyeliner was anything to go by. 'See, in the corner with that older guy.' He was lounging on an overstuffed couch, deep in conversation with a man wearing a white tuxedo jacket over a black T-shirt, his dark hair slicked back like the hero from a classic screwball comedy.

'Nice work, Oscar!' Lauren exclaimed. 'You know who that is, don't you?'

'Apparently not.'

'That's Freddie Fitzgerald.'

Kat searched the dark recesses of Lauren's name-dropping. 'The photographer?'

'Exactly! The highest-value target in the room, and Oscar's already got us an introduction. See, I told you he was adorable.' Lauren whisked them through the slow-dancing crowd, Kat tripping to keep up.

'There you girls are.' Oscar apparently didn't see the irony in calling them 'girls' when they were at least five years older than him. He took Kat's hand, looking supremely smug. 'This is the one I was telling you about,' he said, passing her to Freddie as if he owned her. 'The incorrigible Katherine Elliot.'

Kat decided not to hit him for that. Instead, she gave Freddie a cool smile and waited while he kissed her hand. 'Lovely to meet you,' she said with a now-practised blend of absent boredom. She glanced past him quickly, as if looking for somebody more important, before allowing her gaze to drift back to him. Then, finally, she smiled. It was truly an award-worthy performance, designed to make her look superior, important and oh so coolly detached – God forbid that she actually just shake the man's hand and offer a 'hi'.

'Charmed.' The man assessed her slowly and then matched her smile with his own. He was tanned and dark-eyed, with the bulky nose that hinted at a past spent playing all-boys contact sports, but despite the brutish look about him, he exuded a sort of sophistication that made Kat think of the covers of all those Harlequin romances her mother critiqued: *The Italian Tycoon's Secret Virgin Mistress*, perhaps. 'You've been causing quite a stir.'

Kat tried not to blush awkwardly. 'People are easily stirred,' she shrugged. The off-hand display won her an admiring look from Lauren.

'That they are – fucking vultures.' Freddie's smile broadened, just like all the others. It was the same every time, she'd found: the initial cautious assessment, and then acceptance once she'd given some droll comment or merely occupied her designer outfit well enough. 'Mind if I . . . ?' He dangled an expensive-looking camera from a wide, leather strap.

Jackpot.

Kat gave a little shrug, and let him direct her against one of the glittering back-cloths, draping her body in various nonchalant poses and lifting her head to glare at him. If she'd learned one thing from the galleries of hipsters in *I-D* and *NYLON* magazines, it was that smiling was forbidden; the more moody, pained and downright angry they looked, the better. Freddie began to shoot, his flash blazing in the dark corner as the fringed, eyelinered girls stopped to watch, and out of the corner of her eye, Kat saw Ash approach the edge of their group.

Calm detachment, she told herself. He's just like the rest of them.

'Thanks, sweetheart,' Freddie declared at last. Ash sauntered over and ceremoniously presented Kat with a glass.

'Jack Daniel's, on the rocks. Just how you like it.'

'Oh, thanks,' she said, trying not to be impressed. Remembering her order from the first night they met shouldn't win him any points. 'This is Lauren,' she gestured vaguely, 'and Freddie.'

'Sure, I know Freddie.' The men greeted each other with back-slapping and fist-bumps.

'You tell that fucking sister of yours to call me,' Freddie pointed at him. 'I've been trying to shoot that bitch for months.'

'Dana Delaney,' Lauren whispered in Kat's ear. 'His step-sister. She's some kind of indie movie starlet over in the States.'

'How do you . . . ?'

Lauren waved her phone. Of course; they were in the middle of a party and she'd taken a moment to research everyone online. Turning back to Ash, Lauren gave him a disarming smile. 'Great work on the Jared Jameson album,' she said, her voice striking that perfect mix of complimentary superiority Kat was still trying to achieve. 'What are you working on right now?'

'Too many things . . .' He seemed bashful. 'I'm doing a remix for the Polaroid Kids record, and working on some demos with a new pop group.'

'This place is fucking dead,' Freddie interrupted, apparently oblivious to the hundreds of hipster kids swirling around the dance-floor. 'Who's up for food, some beers?'

'I'm in,' Oscar said immediately, and Freddie gave him a slow grin that Kat wished she hadn't seen.

'Why not?' Ash agreed. 'How about it, Kat?'

'Hmmm?' She looked around to find that everyone was watching her expectantly. It was a new experience – being the one with the deciding vote, rather than tagging along at the end – and she paused to relish it. 'Oh, go on then,' she finally agreed. 'Any more of this Celine Dion and I swear I'll scream.'

'You and me both, sweetheart.' Freddie offered to help her up at the same moment that Ash held out his hand. Kat smiled at both of them but got up on her own, linking her arm through Lauren's and walking towards the main doors.

'You're doing great,' Lauren told her in a low voice. 'Keep this up and we'll have you some sure allies by the end of the night.'

So even though Kat was tired, she spun back, making her dress kick up around her thighs and her keeping her smile playful. 'Well?' she called back to the men, following a few paces behind. Freddie's camera flashed again, but she didn't show she'd even noticed. 'Where to now?'

Edit everything.

When it comes to controlling the way other people see you, less is always more. Don't babble about the most mundane details of your life, because you cheapen your own status with every word – mystery is good, occasional awe-inspiring details are better. With the internet, you have the power to create the perfect version of yourself, so for God's sake don't be one of those clueless girls blogging about every tiny drama or posting those bikini pics: you look cheap, indiscreet and powerless. Instead, craft the profiles that will fit you right inside your target group. By the time they actually meet you, they'll already think you're great.

Chapter Twenty-two

The photographs Freddie took of her, sullen and defiant, were on his website when Kat arrived back in London on Monday, and within a few more days, the rest of the images from that night had filtered through the network of style and magazine blogs until the sight of her – crushed between Lauren and Oscar and gazing at the camera with a lazy disdain – became the default illustration for any mention of Kat. And there were plenty. The online alert Lauren had started to keep them updated about any reference to her swelled from just a couple of articles before that infamous Devon debacle to dozens every day.

Just over three weeks into the Popularity Rules, and Kat was no longer invisible.

She was also no longer tucked safely in her old routine of office, commute and DVDs in the evening at home. With Lauren, every day brought a new, surreal sort of chaos.

'Hey Kat, can you try Gabi again?' Lauren called over from the fountain. They were shooting the autumn advertising campaign for Domina Jeans in a pretty corner of St James's Park, descending on a tranquil, leafy corner with a riot of lighting rigs, clothing and staff. For all the fuss and preparation, Lauren was still attempting to coax the clique of doe-eyed Russian models into something resembling enthusiasm. 'These tank tops are too *My So-Called Life*-ish. I need the *OC* singlets!'

'Sorry, but you're going to have to wait.' Kat reluctantly peeled herself away from a prized spot in the shade and made her way carefully through the tangle of cables and stray shoot assistants. 'I just checked in. She's stuck in traffic by Marble Arch. She'll be another fifteen minutes, at least.'

Lauren put her hands on her hips and took a long breath, her white shirt dress still crisp and neat despite the fact that everyone else was gleaming with sweat. 'Details,' she muttered to herself, 'just manage the details.' She clapped her hands together and turned to yell at the staff. 'OK people, take a break. Ten minutes to cool off!'

'Not working out?' Kat asked sympathetically, as Lauren gulped at her bottle of mineral water. It was one of the hottest days of the summer, and they were all wilting in the midday sun.

'What do you think?' Lauren jerked her head towards the laptop. Kat moved closer and clicked through the gallery of digital prints, wincing at some of the awkward shots.

'I think they look like a group of bored, hungry models.' The faces were smiling, but the eyes were all empty.

Lauren sighed. 'The whole campaign hinges on the images being fun, relatable, you know? I want teen girls to see the ad as achievable – like the models are just like them, only, you know, with better skin and half the body weight.'

'Why not use real girls then?' Kat asked the obvious.

Lauren snorted. 'Come on, I had to battle hard enough to get the client away from that awful American Apparel city-hooker look. Oh crap.' Kat turned to see the overtanned marketing guy bearing down on them, Ray-Ban sunglasses and a white vest displaying his prized body like an art exhibit.

'Klaus, I thought you were still in Stockholm.' Lauren intercepted him before he could reach the photos.

'I got back this morning. Figured I'd drop by, check how things are going.' He glanced around, lingering on the coterie of models.

'That's so great,' Lauren beamed, steering him a safe distance away from anything important. 'In fact, it's perfect timing. I need a second opinion on some of the locations, and I know you have an eye for that kind of thing . . .'

Kat watched with equal parts amusement and admiration as Lauren parked him in a folding chair directly in the hot sun, found an assistant to tend to his every need, and left him poring over a stack of completely superfluous scenery reports.

'Now, what am I going to do about the shoot?' Lauren returned, looking faintly frazzled. 'Could those girls be any more depressed?'

'I'd be depressed too, if I subsisted on nicotine and rice cakes,' Kat agreed, 'but they seem to be having fun now. Maybe it's just the heat.'

'What?' Lauren turned and saw the models splashing around in the water. With the spotlights off and crew ignoring them, the girls actually looked relaxed. 'Perfect!' Lauren cried. She hurried over to the photographer and whispered quickly. Soon, he was casually circling the fountain with his camera, the girls oblivious to his presence without the usual circus of lighting and assistants around. They happily shrieked and splashed in their expensive jeans and brightly coloured vests, the very picture of youthful enthusiasm, and within fifteen minutes Lauren was clicking through a new gallery of images, relief clear on her face.

Crisis averted, Kat retreated to their shady, makeshift camp, sprawling on a blanket to check her email again. Thanks to a well-placed wi-fi spot, she had no excuse not to forge ahead with her next Popularity Rules task. Unfortunately. She'd held out against social networking as long as possible while everyone else poked, tweeted, instant messaged, and generally otherwise degraded the quality of human communication, but now Kat had to admit, it was time to surrender. Controlling her image and status included the virtual one too, so now she had to create the 'online presence' that seemed to be vital for music journalists to promote their brilliance and stay in touch with the dizzying array of identikit guitar bands already littering her email in-box.

'Thank God, those shots should work great, even if they scowl the rest of the day.' Lauren sank down on the blanket next to her and kicked off her navy wedge heels. 'Sorry, I know we were supposed to strategise *Think Louder* stuff all day. I just get crazy when everyone decides to be so fucking incompetent.'

'Freddie's not here; you can drop the foul mouth,' Kat yawned, inching deeper into the shade. One of Lauren's little tricks seemed to be mirroring people's language. By the end of their night with Freddie, she'd been swearing with abandon.

Lauren grinned. 'You noticed, huh? I don't even realise I'm doing it any more.'

'It's a good move. I'll have to try it sometime.' Kat clicked through to her MySpace profile and stopped. 'Wow, they must really hate Devon. I've got another four hundred friends to confirm.'

'Hate to break it to you,' Lauren looked over the top of her sunglasses, 'but I don't think they're picking sides so much as piling on to the latest bandwagon.'

'And there I was thinking they loved and adored me.'

'Ah, disillusionment.' Lauren laughed. 'How are you coming with that blog?'

'Meh.' Kat grimaced. 'Do I have to? Aren't the profile pages enough?'

'Not for total internet domination.'

'Domination . . . ation . . . ation . . .' Kat echoed, quoting a genius example of early twenty-first-century cinema, also known as *Bring It On*. Lauren had forced her to watch it the other night, and she had to admit, it had its charm.

'So you do like teen movies!' Lauren swatted her with a stack of papers.

'It's . . . research,' Kat replied with a grin.

'Of course it is. Anyway, don't stress about the blogging side of things. As long as you update regularly with new song tips and a picture of you pouting in front of a DJ booth, you'll get readers. Less is more, remember?'

'Keeping the brand value through scarcity,' Kat recited. 'But . . .'

Lauren looked up.

'All this exposure . . .' Her gaze drifted back to the screen and that photograph. Shiny hair, darkly lined eyes. It was disconcerting. She wasn't used to seeing herself everywhere – or at least, the new approximation of herself. 'It's not what I thought we'd be doing, that's all. I never wanted to be, you know, famous.'

Lauren took out a small battery fan and began to blow sticky strands of hair from her forehead. 'I know. And maybe ten years ago, you wouldn't have to be. But this is the playing field, Kat; these are the rules of the game. First comes the profile, then the work: everything's been switched around now.'

'Yes, but . . .' she sighed, that niggle in the back of her mind returning. 'I don't know. The micro-celebrity thing is just so ridiculous – I mean, all these people wasting time reading and writing meaningless crap about what, the dress I wore? The fact I might be Freddie's new muse?' She collapsed backwards, her shoulders deep in the prickly grass. 'It would be one thing if they were talking about what I'd actually said, the misogyny in the rock scene—'

'Come on, you're expecting the internet to have a coherent political discussion?' Lauren laughed.

'Fine! Then at least . . .' Kat tried to find the words for this discomfort she felt, seeing herself up alongside all the minor scene non-celebrities she'd always viewed with such disdain. 'I'm a writer! Not a model, or an actress or anything.'

'Which means it's even more important for you to get this kind of public profile,' Lauren argued. 'Haven't you learned already that just being talented isn't enough? I mean, it was the reason you decided to follow the Popularity Rules in the first place.'

'Right,' Kat sighed, remembering that particularly painful epiphany.

'So, don't lose focus now. We're done with the hard part; now it's just building on all this hype and turning page-views into freelance work.'

'And a way back to *Think Louder*,' Kat added, still on her back, watching the tree branches above. 'I don't suppose you've had any flashes of blinding inspiration about that, have you?'

Lauren finished clicking through her digital organiser and lay down beside Kat. 'Nope.' She began ripping up blades of grass. 'See, usually there's an ally within the organisation to work with, or someone we can plant for insider info, but right now we've got . . .'

'Nothing.' Kat finished for her. 'Zilch, zippo, nada.'

'Pas de rien.'

'But do we really need an insider?' Kat tried. 'With all this status stuff I'm building, couldn't I find a way of getting my job back from the outside?'

Lauren sighed. 'It's just too risky. You've got to keep thinking of it like military strategy: how are we supposed to know who has power, what their weaknesses are? You can't keep hanging around, begging to be let in again; it's demeaning. You need to know exactly when they'd be open to you coming back.' She rolled over to look at Kat. 'You know, it would be a whole lot easier to get a job somewhere else – a better job, with more money and people who actually respect you.'

'You know why I need to be there,' Kat repeated stubbornly.

'Right, Alan, emotional obligation, et cetera. Then I guess we'll think of something.'

'Is that Lauren Anderville I see?' Gabi's voice carried over to them. 'Actually relaxing?' Buried under a stack of clothes in protective plastic bags, she staggered closer. Her sunglasses were heart-shaped in classic Lolita style, and matched with her petite frame, tiny denim cut-off shorts and pigtails, Kat wondered if her outfit was strictly legal.

'Me? Never!' Lauren stood up and brushed off her skirt. 'Just waiting around for my lazy stylist.'

'Love you too, bitch,' Gabi grinned, chewing gum. 'And hey to you, Miss Rock Star Destroyer.'

Kat laughed and got up to help Gabi unload the outfits onto portable racks. 'How have you been?'

'Geeking out,' Gabi replied, swiftly plucking a series of candy-coloured T-shirts from the stack. 'I spent the weekend re-watching two whole seasons of *Battlestar Galactica*, including the mini-series.'

'That's, umm, impressive?'

'And anti-social,' she agreed. 'But I met this girl, and she'd never seen them, can you believe it? Oh, I brought you something.' Kat must have visibly perked up because Gabi laughed, 'Don't get too excited – this one's for life, not just Christmas.' She nodded behind Kat, who turned to see a familiar skinny figure bearing down on them, almost hidden behind an armful of bags.

'Oscar?' Kat said faintly.

'I found him wandering the halls of *ChicK*,' Gabi said with a grin. 'He pestered me for ever, so I figured I'd better bring him along before they used him for a "Weird But Cute!" photostory.'

'Surprise!' Oscar planted himself in front of Kat and gave her an enthusiastic hug.

'It certainly is,' she replied, gingerly accepting the vast bouquet of roses he thrust at her chest. 'I thought you were in Brighton.'

'I was, until somebody complained about my customer service.' He rolled his eyes. 'It's not my fault Enya fans are, like, the least humorous people ever. I'm crashing with Freddie,' he added, with a significant look.

'Great,' Kat replied, refusing to consider that unlikely match. She examined the flowers dubiously, 'And these are . . .?'

'No idea. They were waiting for you at the office, so I decided I'd make myself useful and bring them over.' He paused, producing a Starbucks. 'You like caramel, right?'

'Oh, thanks.' Kat took the icy Frappuccino. What with the pink block print on his T-shirt and the slice of blond in his hair, she was almost dazzled by the riot of colour. She slurped at the drink. At least he had taste in refreshments.

'Who's the admirer then? Whoever they are, they looove you.' He peeked over, trying to take a look at the card on the flowers. Kat snatched it away.

'Coy. Whatever.' he sighed. 'Ooh, Lauren!' And with that, he bounded away.

'Why do I get the feeling I'm going to be seeing an awful lot more of that boy?' Kat asked, watching him launch into another round of air-kisses and adoration.

'Because he totally worships you,' Gabi called over her shoulder as she advanced on the models, wielding bikini tops and tiny T-shirts.

'And that's supposed to be a good thing?' Kat murmured to herself, absently sniffing the roses.

'Flowers! Let me see . . .' Lauren returned, having safely escorted Klaus into a taxi. She tore into the tiny envelope. '*My words/ Got left behind/ Your eyes/ Told me everything*.' What is this?'

'*My words got left behind*,' Kat muttered. 'It sounds familiar; is that a poem?' Suddenly, Lauren burst into laughter. 'What?' Kat asked. Lauren just kept laughing, her whole body shaking with mirth. 'Come on!' Kat complained. 'Tell me!'

'And you call yourself a music journalist,' Lauren said through her giggles.

'What do you mean?'

'Don't you recognise it?'

'Umm, no.' Kat scowled. 'That's the point.'

'You must have made some impression,' Lauren said in a sing-song voice.

Kat threw her empty water bottle at her in frustration. 'Stop teasing and tell me!'

Lauren passed her the note. 'It's been playing in the office all morning: The Alarm's new song. "Your Eyes".' She grinned at Kat. 'I guess Devon's sorry.'

'Devon Darsel?' Kat couldn't believe it.

'The one and only.' Lauren shook her head, idly running her fingers over the delicate petals. 'He's got taste, I'll give him that.'

'Are you kidding?' Kat scoffed. 'I bet all he did was call a bloody florist. Or had his assistant do it. In fact,' she added, pushing the flowers away, 'I doubt he had anything to do with it. It's probably just some PR person at his label trying to smooth things over.'

'Either way, it's a pretty great score,' Lauren noted. 'From a Popularity Rules perspective,' she quickly added, seeing Kat's stormy expression. 'He's still an asshole.'

'And always will be. Enough about him.' Kat tried to snap out of her sudden temper. 'Where did your bestest friend go?'

'I sent him to sort Polaroids – should keep him busy for a while.' Kat searched the knot of people until she saw Oscar, flipping through a stack of pictures with disdain clear even from thirty feet away as he discarded every image.

Slowly, Lauren's face split with a devious grin. 'Although . . .'

'Uh oh.' Kat sighed.

'What?'

'That look.' Kat studied her. 'That look means you have a plan, and I'm probably not going to like it.'

'I don't know what you mean!' Lauren couldn't keep her indignant face in place for long. 'Well . . .'

'Mmhmm.' Kat waited.

'What we were saying, about needing an insider . . .' She looked at Oscar again, and then back to Kat, raising her eyebrows in suggestion.

'Him?' Of all the covert operatives possible, the boy in orange skinny denim was not her first pick.

'Think about it,' Lauren brightened, obviously warming to her idea. 'We need a source for info inside the magazine, and you've got enough work to do with research and strategy and our trip to New York coming up, so why—'

'Wait, what trip?' Kat interrupted, confused.

Lauren looked evasive. 'Oh, didn't I say? I have to go over in a couple of weeks – Dee's wedding planning stuff. I thought you could come with me. Work the New York scene,' she added quickly.

'And you were planning on telling me when?' Kat exclaimed.

'When I'd exhausted all escape plans.' Lauren looked so grim, Kat had to laugh at her expression.

'I'm guessing your mother will be there too.'

'Yup.' Lauren practically shuddered. 'Anyway, we were talking about Oscar, not my peach of a family.'

'Oh. Right.' Kat sighed.

'Don't look like that; this is a good thing. He's bouncing around with nothing to do, and I'm sure Freddie can pull some strings, get him set up as an intern. Voilà – we'd have a source for all the office news and gossip.'

'I don't know.' Oscar seemed determined to fix himself to her side; this would only encourage him. 'Do you think we could even trust him with all the Popularity Rules stuff?'

'Hell no!' Lauren baulked. 'We wouldn't tell him anything; just drop a hint here and there about wanting to know what's going on, and he'd spill it all.'

Kat hesitated, still watching him. 'But isn't that sort of . . . manipulative?'

'And everything we've been doing so far isn't?' Lauren countered.

'I know, I know, but still . . .' she wavered. 'Setting him up like that – like some kind of pawn.'

Lauren seemed genuinely unconcerned. 'As far as I can see, we're doing him a favour. The boy's unemployed now, and clearly wants to be part of the music scene.' She shrugged. 'If it makes you feel any better, just think of him as your latest protégé. I bet he'd be overjoyed to know how much he's helping you out.'

The fact that Lauren had moved from 'would' to 'will' didn't pass Kat by un-noticed.

'But we don't tell him the truth?'

'Absolutely not.' Lauren was firm. 'Can you imagine? One after-hours booze-up and he'd be spilling everything to Jessica and Nate.'

Jessica Star. The mention of her replacement steeled something inside Kat. 'OK,' she admitted at last. 'We try it. But only if he really wants to.'

'He will.' Lauren nodded, satisfied.

Watch your back.

Popularity is a zero-sum game: for you to win it, somebody else has to be losing, and that means they'll be out for your blood. Avoid getting dragged into their petty dramas at all costs or you'll wind up a spectacle for all the wrong reasons. Any attacks you make should be private, subtle and distanced from you. A well-placed rumour can be way more destructive than a messy bitch-fight, and saves you stooping to their level. When a public put-down is necessary to save face, be swift, cutting and never show any weakness.

If you don't act like you're above them, nobody will think you are.

Chapter Twenty-three

'I love guest-lists.' Oscar declared the very next night, as the trio piled out of the taxi and surveyed the thick crowds still winding around the outside of Brixton Academy. 'Can't be done with all this waiting around.' He waved his hand happily at the mess of people as they waltzed straight past the noise and confusion towards the main doors. As Kat followed, she had to agree. Around them, T-shirt vendors hustled for attention, shady-looking touts edged closer to every passer-by and unwanted flyers fluttered across the dirty street.

'Perks of the industry,' Lauren agreed, shooting him a sideways look. 'Backstage passes, free CDs, access to all the best parties . . .'

'Slave wages and twelve-hour work days,' Kat added, before she received a swift elbow in the ribs. Of course, Lauren thought that they needed to paint a rose-tinted version of reality to lure Oscar to his intern position, but Kat wanted her conscience clear. 'What? It's true,' she protested. 'There's no point in pretending the job's perfect, but it's worth it in the end.' If it hadn't been, she would be safely ensconced in an NGO office, editing a charity newsletter by now, instead of spending half an hour deliberating the subliminal effects of a navy dress versus grey, black boots versus dark-red heels.

'But we're right where the action is,' Lauren added firmly. 'Or at least, Kat is now.'

That part was true, at least. A single call to the label and they had places for the sold-out show of a particularly hirsute band of American rockers; a mention of her name to the PR girl on the door, and they were whisked up to the VIP bar. Kat was no stranger to all-access, but this was different – edged with deference and widened eyes instead of a begrudging sigh. It was empty, she knew: nothing but shallow affection that deemed her far more worthy a person now – after some blog hype and a few photographs – than she was when a mere serious professional, but even Kat could see it made life far, far easier.

'Kat!'

They had barely edged into the crowded room when Kat was buried under an avalanche of air-kisses.

'Lacey?' she said, unable to hide her surprise.

'Oh my God, I haven't seen you in ages!' Lacey shrieked, her dark ringlets bouncing up around her face like those of a tiny cherub. The pack of waifish New Wave girls stood silently behind her, a thin pride of monochrome stripes and skinny denim. 'How *are* you?'

'Just fine,' Kat managed, recalling her last icy encounter with the woman. On the yacht, Lacey had barely said three words to her. 'And . . . you're good?'

'So good! Let me get you a drink. Hi, hi.' Evidently registering that Kat was not alone, Lacey turned her affections to Lauren and Oscar. 'Wine? Beer? Water?'

'Water's great,' Kat answered faintly.

'Fab! Don't go anywhere. I'll be back in a mo.'

Kat watched her duck through the noisy crowd towards the bar. 'Okaaay . . .'

'A friend?' Oscar asked, tugging his fringe into position.

'Try "complete stranger". In fact, I sort of think she hates me. Or rather, she used to.'

'Get used to it,' Lauren advised, leading them to a set of

uncomfortable leather cubes in the corner. 'Everyone you've ever met is going to come crawling out to pay tribute.'

'Lucky me.'

Lauren raised her eyebrows. 'You'd prefer to go back to endless networking, would you?'

'Good point.' Kat took a long breath, relishing the idea that her days of hanging on the edge of somebody else's crowd may be well and truly over.

For the next half-hour, she held court there under the dim neon lights. There was no other way of describing it, as every A&R guy and PR girl she'd even vaguely met came flocking to pay tribute. They gushed over her hair and clothes, offered up amusing anecdotes in an effort to keep her entertained and agreed, time and time again, that Devon Darsel was an arrogant wastrel and Kat was, like, soo brave to stand up to him. Kat should have been rolling her eyes with disdain, but she was taking a strange satisfaction from the whole spectacle; their transparent advances were almost a pleasure after so many years of relentless indifference.

'. . . And then he made out with the waitress, right in front of her!' Lacey squealed, her face flushed almost as pink as her vest. She'd stuck to Kat tightly, refusing to relinquish her precious leather cube even when her phone began to vibrate angrily every thirty seconds. 'You know,' she added, fixing Kat with an eager gaze across the low glass tabletop now littered with glasses, 'I think you'd love his new material. It's gone very retro nineties Brooklyn hip-hop, sort of Janet Jackson meets Wu-Tang – you'd love it. I can set up an interview with him, whatever you want.'

'Hmmm?' Kat tried not to laugh. At least Lacey had taken her time before angling for the sell: some of the other PR types swarming around had barely said 'hello' before pushing their latest act on her. 'Well, I'm scaling back my freelance work right now, trying to be more selective,' she improvised. 'But of course I'll keep you in mind. Why don't you send over your current roster and I'll see if anything fits my projects?'

'Fab!' Lacey exclaimed. 'That would be so great. I know you're like, so busy, but just say the word and you can have whatever access or interview time you want.'

'Uh huh . . .' Kat turned to look for some distraction, but Lauren was talking to some suited men by the bar and Oscar had been swallowed by a gaggle of overstyled fashion gays. There was nobody except the eager industry types around her: shiny-haired, sharp-eyed, and all determined to recruit her for their various self-serving causes.

And Jessica Star.

'Lacey! Sweets!' There was a blur of blonde hair and shining metallic jewellery as Jessica thrust herself into the middle of the group and embraced Lacey. 'I've been looking for you everywhere!'

Kat flinched as an elbow jabbed at her stomach. Jessica babbled on about a new denim store launch and Suki's 'like, amazing' new haircut, all the while with her body angled to keep her back to Kat and not a single acknowledgement that her arse was practically resting in Kat's lap.

Kat coughed pointedly and tried to push Jessica off her.

'Oh, Katy, I didn't see you there.' Jessica finally turned, her face perfectly even and sweet. 'Maybe you shouldn't wear all those dark clothes; you blend straight into the background. Doesn't she?' With a giggle, Jessica appealed to the crowd for confirmation. Kat was gratified to see them shoot uneasy looks around, as if they weren't sure where their loyalties should lie.

'Thanks.' Kat decided to act oblivious. 'And that's such a . . . daring dress you've chosen.' She stopped herself going any

269

further. Catfights were beneath her. Or rather, they should be.

'You know, I'm glad I found you.' Jessica wiggled around until Kat had no choice but to give up her prime position in the centre of the couch, instead now shoved against the end. 'I wanted to have a chat – some girl talk.'

Kat braced herself.

'It's about Devon.' Jessica's face slipped into an overly concerned expression. She laid one fuchsia-nailed hand on Kat's arm and leaned closer, until Kat could smell the faint traces of smoke on her breath. 'Now, I know it must be flattering for you, to have someone like Devon interested in you for the first time, but I feel like I should warn you.'

She hadn't, Kat noted, lowered her voice at all.

'I know he's a big star, and has all that fame and, God, I'm sure you know the rest.' Jessica nodded meaningfully, her eyes wide and calculating. 'And for someone like you, that's got to be attractive, especially after you got dumped from the magazine. But it's like, really important you have a better opinion of yourself,' Jessica continued, as Kat imagined all the ways she could murder her with nothing more than the contents of her purse. 'I mean, women like Emily Pankhurst didn't starve themselves so you could sleep with men for their money, you know? You've got to think of, like, the sisterhood.' She sat back, satisfied. 'Right guys?'

'Emmeline.' Kat said quietly, rage seething in her veins. 'Her name was Emmeline.' She would know; she'd been named after her.

Jessica shrugged, reaching for a drink. 'See? I knew you'd understand.'

Kat swallowed. She was holding onto her temper by the thinnest thread, but that thread was more than she would usually manage. Think, she ordered herself. They were in a group; there was status to be defended here: Jessica had just done everything she could to make Kat look like a desperate, pathetic star-fucker, while she remained sweet, concerned and superior. Lauren would probably give her a round of applause, but Kat wanted nothing more than to rip off every neon fingernail and then drag them across those bitchy blue eyeballs.

Think, Kat.

'You know, that's so sweet of you,' she began, taking a lip balm out of her clutch and slowly applying it, more to keep herself from throttling Jessica than out of an overwhelming need to touch up her raspberry stain. 'I really appreciate it, and especially after everything he put you through.' Kat nodded carefully, still wishing she could just say 'fuck you' and walk away. But there was work to be done, so she managed a light laugh. 'God, if I had a pound for every time you went home crying!'

She patted Jessica's Lycra-clad thigh as if they were comrades in arms. Jessica's lips began to press thinly, and Kat caught one of the women opposite grinning. 'But there's really no need. Devon's just got this silly little obsession; you know how men can be sometimes. Don't worry,' she added, with a reassuring grin. 'I'm not stupid enough to fall for it.' A pause, just to make sure the audience was with her, and then the sugar-coated finish. 'After all, it's like you said about sisterhood: we've got to learn from each other's mistakes!'

And then, as if some mobile phone god had heard her mental plea for an exit, Kat's phone buzzed with a text message. 'You won't mind if I just . . .' she gestured towards the door and brandished her mobile as some kind of evidence.

'Oh, no, not at all!' Lacey enthused. As Kat manoeuvred away, Jessica was silent, looking as if it took all of her energy just to keep smiling.

Game, set and match.

'*Assaulted any more rock stars yet? Actually, don't answer – I might get jealous.*' The text was from Ash – and complete sentences too. She couldn't help but grin.

'*Only the ones who asked nicely,*' she sent back, after much deliberation. It worked.

'*I'll remember that for next time.*'

The corridor outside echoed with babble and the distant echo of the supporting act. Kat wandered aimlessly past doors labelled with dire 'keep out' warnings and down the back staircase; she didn't care where she ended up, only that it was somewhere far from Jessica's veiled bitching and the blizzard of insincere flattery that was making her veins itch. Her tolerance levels may have risen exponentially these past weeks, but she still had her limit.

'You can't come through here.' A burly production man in ripped denim and a raggedy shirt tried to bar her way.

'Oh, I'm sorry.' Kat's first instinct was to apologise and retreat, but she caught herself, instead flashing the red laminate that swung from her waistband. The man took a closer look and then melted back.

'Sorry, love, go ahead.'

The backstage area wasn't much to speak of, just a black space cluttered with haphazard stacks of equipment, stressed-looking roadies and too many hangers-on, but Kat felt the familiar buzz of excitement return. She'd probably spent hundreds of hours waiting around dressing rooms and in the wings, but there was still some magic to it all. Out in front of those heavy black drapes, a band was doing its best to take the audience somewhere else; to send bass and beats rattling through their brains until the world receded and they were nothing more than in that moment, right there. Some of the best times in Kat's life had been at live shows, watching her idols unleash something wonderful up there on-stage, a vivid experience that would never be replicated. Oh, she could buy the concert DVDs and replay the live recordings, but to Kat, part of the glory of it all was that thud of bass shaking her ribcage from the inside, the hush that falls over a stunned audience, and the sweat and stick and singing in her heart that could only come from being in the centre of a crowd all strung out on the same invisible chords.

But there she was, backstage instead of out in that crowd, wearing heels instead of her crowd-friendly boots and a dress that was most certainly not designed to even think about sweating in. Realising the irony, Kat couldn't help but give a wry grin. This must be what Lauren meant with her constant refrain about means and ends.

'Hey, you got a light?'

She looked over. A group of men were loitering by the emergency exit. The door was wedged half-open and their expressions were anxious.

'N—actually, yes,' Kat corrected herself. She fished in her small clutch bag for the simple silver lighter Lauren had insisted she carry for just such encounters. Just because she refused to rot her lungs, it didn't mean she couldn't use the excuse to strike up conversations. 'Be my guests.'

'You fucking angel,' the first man groaned, grabbing it from her, lighting his cigarette and then sucking down a lungful of smoke in one smooth motion. His compatriots swiftly followed suit. Kat laughed.

'Getting desperate?'

'You've got no idea,' one of the other men answered fervently. She took a closer look at the collective, scruffy in battered, tight jeans, faded T-shirts and beards, and realised why they looked so familiar: this was the band whose name was up over the front entrance.

If Lauren was here, she would know what Kat should do; what move to make, the right things to say to turn this unexpected encounter into something useful. But Kat was alone amongst the bustle and low echoes backstage, and had nothing to guide her but the faint imprint of the Popularity Rules that lingered in her mind from last night's late reading.

It was enough.

'There's a good crowd tonight,' Kat remarked, gripped by a sudden determination. She strolled closer, ignoring the fact she felt naked without a notebook and dictaphone. 'Should be a fun show. Oh, thanks, but I'm fine.' She waved away the offer of a smoke and tried not to cough at the cloud now billowing around her. The alleyway outside was dark and smelled faintly of rotting food, but Kat carefully leaned back against the wall and struck what she hoped was a casual pose. 'Tour going well so far?'

'Pretty decent,' the lead singer shrugged. 'The crowd in Berlin was fucking unmovable, so hopefully you guys will be better.'

'Yes, but that's Berlin,' Kat cracked, glancing around for confirmation. 'Those guys are too cool to express real emotion.' The men smiled slightly, so Kat continued, 'I swear, the Beatles could resurrect on-stage and they'd all just be slouching around talking about post-modernism.' She took care to deliver the comment in a casual, lazy fashion – well aware that any hint that she was eager for their approval, and the star–fan dynamic would be set.

'They're not as bad as the Brooklyn crowds,' the long-haired man Kat recognised as the drummer pitched in. 'Remember that show at McCarren Pool, when that dude tried to pick a fight over that Smiths cover?'

'Aw, man, he fucked up my hand so bad.'

Kat was tempted to retreat before she looked like just another hanger-on, but she caught a glimpse of a photographer and journalist skulking towards them, eyes darting around as they murmured over the perfect backstage illustration. There. What had the rulebook said – that life only mattered from the outside in? Catching the photographer's eye, Kat smiled slightly, and then turned back to the band. Sure enough, from the corner of her vision she spied him moving closer, snapping frame after frame as Kat pretended to ignore the camera, laughing along with whatever the band said and hiding her sharp sense of victory.

'Guys, I need you over for miking.' A harassed-looking woman with a headset approached, her arms full of water bottles and hand-towels. The band moved slowly, taking final drags of smoke and unfolding themselves.

'Here we go, I guess,' the lead singer sighed, as if he was about to embark on eight hours in an office cubicle instead of playing a packed-out rock show to thousands of devoted fans.

'Good luck,' Kat shrugged, matching his nonchalance. 'And hey, at least it's not Berlin.'

'Ha.' As he passed her, he held out his fist. Kat matched it with her own, and in the moment their knuckles touched, she saw the dazzle of a flash. Another image to promote the new Katherine Elliot; she almost wanted to laugh. There had been whole generations before this who measured success as something other than a photograph on a glossy page, who hadn't constructed their lives as a series of picturesque snippets on a social-networking site. Or maybe Lauren was right, and it had always been thus, only instead of new media and blogging and gossip site updates, it was a single byline that counted as the ultimate achievement.

Oh, simpler times.

She was drifting back to the VIP suite the long way, through the main crowd, when she caught a glimpse of red hair, looped into a casual knot. 'Whitney?' she called in surprise, threading through the packs of teenage girls hovering around the merchandise tables.

'Kat! Hi,' Whitney cried, giving her a brief hug and then holding her at arm's length. 'God, I didn't recognise you.' Her eyes were wide as they swept her from head to toe. Of course – they hadn't managed to catch up in person since before Kat's makeover.

For the first time in days, Kat felt self-conscious of her new look. 'Umm, I decided it was time for a change. You know . . .'

'Oh, completely.' Whitney was bright. 'I just dashed here from work, so, well . . .' she laughed, gesturing at her grey trousers and pale silk blouse.

'How are things?' Kat couldn't believe it had been weeks since they'd even spoken. So much had changed, it felt like a lifetime.

'Good, great, hectic!' Whitney gave a rueful shrug. 'And you? Did you manage to find a new job? I asked around, of course,' she added quickly, 'but there really wasn't anything going to speak of.'

'No, it's fine,' Kat reassured her. 'Everything's worked out. Sort of. I'm helping an old friend with some consultancy work and freelancing on the side.' The details fell easily from her lips, but for the first time in their friendship, Kat was holding plenty back.

'Oh, super!' Whitney beamed, hitching her oversized purple bag up onto her shoulder. 'I knew you'd land on your feet.'

'Right.' Kat wouldn't have put her months of strife and toil quite like that, but it was still a relief to see Whitney again, some hint of her former life. 'We have to get together for something soon.'

'Definitely,' Whitney vowed. She began to rummage in her purse. 'I know I've got about a million different things on, but if I can just find . . .' After a moment, she gave up. 'Why don't you call and set something up when I've got my book on me? We'll have lunch, or drinks, or something. I want to hear all about your new job!'

Kat grinned. 'That would be great. Maybe next weekend?'

'Perfect,' Whitney agreed.

'There you are.' A man rushed over, out of breath. 'They were out of gin, but I managed the tonic.' He passed Whitney a bottle.

'Nate?' Kat exclaimed, staring at the beard and thick glasses. 'What are you . . .? I mean,' she looked back and forth between them as the truth dawned. 'Oh.'

'Hi Kat.' Nate gave her an awkward little wave, and even Whitney looked uncomfortable for a moment.

'No, I mean, this is great,' Kat added quickly. 'How long? I mean . . .' she fumbled. In all the time she'd known the both of them separately, she'd never seen this coming. Whitney, the super-efficient eco-woman, with her 'minimal effort' scruffy web-editor?

'Not long,' Whitney said, slipping her arm through Nate's.

'Well, it's great,' Kat repeated, shifting from the heel of one foot to the other. There was another pause.

'We'd better . . .' Whitney gestured vaguely towards the auditorium. 'But it was great to run into you!'

'Oh, of course.' Then Kat remembered. 'I know, why don't you both come upstairs for the show? I'm sure they have plenty of gin,' she added with a smile.

'The VIP lounge?' Whitney asked. 'You could do that?'

'Sure.' Kat grinned. 'I think this thing gives me unlimited everything,' she admitted, fingering the red laminate. 'I could probably wander out on-stage and they wouldn't mind. I mean, obviously the audience might . . .' she heard herself begin to babble, still thrown by the sight of Whitney intertwined with Nate. 'Anyway, come right up.'

Whitney looked at Nate with raised eyebrows. 'Sure,' he shrugged amiably. 'Sounds good to me.'

Kat led them back to the lounge, where she was promptly accosted by Oscar.

'I've been looking everywhere for you!' he beamed, gripping both her arms. 'I'm going to be an intern at *Think Louder* – isn't that a hoot?'

'Really?' Kat tried to sound surprised. Under two days flat – Lauren really had been working hard. 'That's great!' She turned. 'These are—' But Whitney and Nate were already edging towards the bar.

'Call me,' Whitney mouthed with a grin, waving farewell before they slipped away. It was probably just as well, Kat noted, as Oscar launched into a gleeful monologue about his future as the next great music critic. Some worlds were never meant to collide.

Be prepared for the backlash.

There's a reason you should ditch everyone in your old life to get ahead with the Popularity Rules: not only are they dragging you down and making you look pathetic by association, but they'll do everything they can to undermine you. All this time, you've been their companion in loserdom – making them feel better about their own passive choices and letting them take you for granted – and now, suddenly, you're trying to make something of yourself? Cue the jealous bitching.

Ignore them all. You don't need them any more, and besides, why would you want to stay around people who don't really want you to be awesome?

Chapter Twenty-four

Now that she'd been tipped as the music scene's hottest 'new' thing, Kat's schedule leapt from busy to hectic. Instead of fetching coffees and doing Lauren's bidding, she had her own project to run: from assembling profiles of all the major commissioning editors to ruthlessly tracking down invites to the most exclusive shows and parties (aka, networking opportunities), Kat began to see just how much preparation was behind Lauren's apparently effortless success. Freddie, as predicted, had called in some favours and installed Oscar at *Think Louder* (and, Kat suspected, in his bedroom), providing even more information for Kat's rapidly expanding file. It seemed like no sooner had she kicked off those killer heels after another night 'accidentally' bumping into key media taste-makers at a gig or after-show party, than she was flailing at her alarm clock and pulling on her workout clothes to start another busy day.

The Popularity Rules were certainly not for slackers.

'. . . Absolutely. No, I'll get it to you by next week.' Kat put down her phone with a whoop.

'What's up?' Lauren wandered back into their office at *ChicK*, looking mildly alarmed.

'My first freelance commission!' Kat spun around on her chair in triumph.

Lauren clapped her hands together. 'No, really? Who is it?'

'The *Observer* music pages,' Kat beamed. 'So I don't even

have to sell my soul! They want five hundred words on blogger bands and websites, and all that hot new breakthrough stuff.' She laughed. 'I don't know why they can't just get a staff writer to spend ten minutes on Pitchfork, but I won't complain!'

'Damn right you won't; that's awesome.' Flicking through some paperwork on her desk, Lauren frowned absently for a moment and then pushed everything aside, turning back to Kat with a grin. 'And the *Observer* – that's just the right kind of platform for you. It's a picture byline, right?'

'Of course. And they only wanted a basic list to start, but I told them I wouldn't bother unless I had space to actually talk about the artists. I even negotiated more than their initial rates,' Kat added proudly.

'You are learning,' Lauren congratulated her. 'See, what did I tell you? As soon as you get status, everything else follows.'

'All right, o wise one. You are, as ever, completely infallible.'

'And don't you forget it,' Lauren added with a wink, before they were interrupted by one of the effervescent *ChicK* interns, her usual bounce weighed down by the armful of flowers and gift-bags she was carrying.

'Flowers for you, Kat.' She struggled to unload them, sneezing three times in quick succession.

'Anna, your allergies!' Kat leapt up to take the bouquet. 'You shouldn't bring them when you're like this, I keep telling you.'

'No, no, I'm fine!' Anna smiled bravely. 'Really. I'll go get the rest.' She ducked away quickly, her sneezes fading down the hallway.

'More?' Lauren glanced at the card and raised her eyebrows. 'He's persistent, I'll give him that.'

Kat sighed, tossing the exquisite display of silk-soft roses towards the corner already stacked with exotic flowers. The deliveries had come from Devon all week; the office was long since out of vases, and while undeniably beautiful, the flowers were taking up far too much space. She'd tried to arrange them out in the main office space, but Nina had decided to make a small stand over her territory, and declared them to be a health hazard. 'What does this one say?'

'*My heart . . . your smile . . . our love . . .*' Lauren glanced at the card. 'The usual.'

'You know, if he really wanted to win some favour with me, he should be writing exceptionally large cheques to pro-choice charities and abuse shelters,' Kat noted, picking through a box of Godiva truffles for the gooey, caramel ones.

'Nice to know you've got your price.'

'Oh, I figure I'll just be a martyr for the cause,' she grinned. 'Doomed to tolerate wanker rock-star theatrics, all for the sake of the women of England.'

'So noble.'

'It's my middle name, remember?' She pushed the box towards Lauren, who wavered for a moment before taking a tiny truffle. They sat for a moment, enjoying a rare silence while chatter and music drifted in from outside, until Lauren finally began to muse.

'You know . . .'

'No.' Kat cut her off, reaching for a hazelnut fondant. She'd been wondering how long it would take for Lauren to start.

'Hey! You don't even know what I was going to say.'

'No, I do.' Kat gave her a look. 'You were going to say that as long as Devon is hanging around, I should find a way to make him useful. Am I right?'

Lauren paused. 'Well, actually—'

'See!' Kat began to laugh. 'Textbook, you really are.'

'More like "rulebook".' Lauren gave a grin. 'But it's true. I mean, he has status and influence, and—'

'A drug habit,' Kat began ticking off her own list of attributes, 'and a damaging attitude towards women, and—'

'OK, OK, I get it! But you're going to have to stop being so picky some time. Everyone can serve a purpose, fucked-up rock star or not.'

'Give me another few weeks with my honour, at least,' Kat joked.

'It's true. After all,' Lauren added, 'did you ever think Oscar could be such a great source?'

Kat paused. The kid had virtues, she had to admit: the chatty emails he sent at least three times a day babbled about everything from stories in the upcoming issues to the 'major drama' over switching coffee filter brands. 'Not for a moment.'

'Anything useful so far?'

'Not so much from him, more just building background details.'

Lauren paused. 'Nothing about . . . ? Never mind.'

'What?' Kat looked up, alarmed.

'Don't panic,' Lauren warned, 'but I'm hearing rumours there might be a takeover on the horizon.'

Kat's mouth fell open. 'Who? What?'

'I said don't panic! This kind of thing happens all the time, especially with print media right now,' Lauren reassured her. 'I'm finding out who the interested parties are, so don't even think about it until we know more.'

Kat swallowed. She could only imagine what a takeover would do to her precious magazine; it had been a lone beacon of quality in the music scene for so long, and even Rob's moves towards the lowest common denominator could never be as bad as a complete ownership change.

'I'm serious; put it out of your mind,' Lauren advised. 'Focus on that freelance career of yours.'

So Kat tried to ignore the possibility that all her work could be for nothing and focused on the positives instead. Like her commission. It was just one article, she knew, but as she hurried through Soho to meet Whitney for lunch, she couldn't help but feel a glow of satisfaction. The commission may be small, but it was a reminder of what she was doing this for; a validation that the Popularity Rules weren't just empty gestures leading her further away from her plans. She was a writer, she was supposed to be writing, and this was the first sign that all the changes she'd been making were actually paying off.

Spotting Whitney's slim frame at a table near the window, Kat ducked into the air-conditioned chill of the cafe. 'Hi!' she called, greeting her with the air-kisses that had become second nature. 'Oh great, you ordered already. I got stuck in an editorial meeting and couldn't leave until they'd argued the merits of punk versus preppy for the next issue.' Breathlessly, she slid into a chair and took a long swallow from her waiting glass of cool water. 'There, OK, now I feel human; this heat is killing me.'

Collecting herself, Kat looked across at Whitney, who was regarding her with bemusement. 'So, what's up?'

'What's up?' Whitney repeated with a faint smile. In a long, gauzy print dress and ropes of wooden beads, she looked like the earth mother polar opposite to Kat's high-waisted black city shorts and white, scoop-necked T.

'Oh, sorry.' Kat laughed self-consciously. 'I've been spending too much time with Americans,' she explained. 'My vocabulary is shot to pieces. As I should have said, how are you?'

'I'm well.' Whitney sipped her bilious-looking smoothie.

'What is that concoction?' Kat interrupted, peering over at the green drink, studded with flecks of brown and orange. 'It looks poisonous.'

'It's detoxifying, actually. A great blend of herbs and vegetable pulp.' Whitney smiled beatifically as she took another sip, but Kat caught her involuntary shudder nonetheless.

'You detoxify all you like then; I'm sticking to, hmmm, an iced tea I think, and the chicken salad, dressing on the side.' She passed her menu back to the pale, hovering waitress and relaxed back in her seat. 'So, tell me everything – it's been ages since we caught up properly. How's your promotion working out?'

'Good!' Tearing off a corner of bread, Whitney launched into a full run-down of her new responsibilities and all the stress that came along with them. 'I'm telling you, Kat,' she said, finally pausing for breath, 'part of me wishes I'd never taken the job!'

'Come on, I know you love it really,' Kat teased. 'Saving the world, one inefficient bureaucracy at a time – it's what you do best.'

Whitney smiled. 'I suppose so. My new manager can't believe the progress I've made already, but there aren't enough hours in the day.'

'Tell me about it,' Kat agreed. She'd been up until three a.m. watching old concert footage for a pitch she had in mind about her favourite reclusive singer.

'You're so lucky to be just freelancing,' Whitney sighed, pausing as their food arrived. 'And after that wonderful break you had so recently, too. I wish I could take a chunk of time off like that.'

'It wasn't exactly by choice,' Kat reminded her, smothering her salad with balsamic dressing.

'But still . . .' Whitney gazed into the distance, no doubt envisioning a holiday that had more to do with yoga retreats and meditation than Kat's old regime of pyjamas, daytime TV, and quiet desperation.

'Anyway,' Kat steered her away from those happy memories of unemployment and despair, 'I'm more interested in hearing about you and Nate. How did that even happen?'

Whitney shrugged delicately. 'It just . . . did.' Kat waited expectantly while she ate a mouthful of soup. 'He invited me to be his plus-one for some gigs,' she elaborated, 'after you left *Think Louder*, and things developed from there.'

'And it's working?' Kat asked curiously. 'I mean, he doesn't drive you insane with that wannabe-woodsman hipster thing?'

Whitney pressed her lips together. 'We have a lot in common, with our environmentalism. Nathaniel is a big fan of Whitman and Thoreau.'

Nathaniel? Kat kept her face even. Things must really be serious if he was letting her call him that. 'I'm glad,' she offered, meaning it. 'It's great, for both of you.'

'Yes.' Whitney seemed to relax. 'And I'm guessing I don't need to ask about your romantic life, or lack thereof,' she added with a laugh.

Kat tried to laugh it off, even though the comment stung. 'Oh, you know me . . .'

'Don't worry, you'll find somebody perfect soon,' Whitney insisted warmly. 'And it's probably a good thing to be single right now – you know, so you can focus on rebuilding your career. How is all that, by the way?'

'Really good!' Kat declared, but Whitney gave a kind of supportive smile and reached across the table to squeeze her hand.

'It's OK, I know things must be difficult. You don't need to pretend with me.'

'No, really,' Kat insisted. 'It's all going great. I'm busy with the consulting, and I just got a freelance commission from the *Observer*!'

'Oh? That's wonderful.' Whitney's eyes widened. 'Give it some time, and perhaps you won't even have to do all that mind-numbing teen stuff too. I don't know how you've stayed so motivated; I'm so impressed.'

Kat slowly chewed a slice of chicken breast. Was she being oversensitive, or was Whitney's tone just the tiniest bit . . . patronising? No, Kat quelled the cynical voice of the Popularity Rules, evidently still lingering in her mind. Whitney didn't play those undermining games; she was reading too much into it.

'And after that awful business with Devon . . .' Whitney continued, shaking her head. 'Nathaniel showed me the video clip. You must have been so humiliated!'

'God, it really was embarrassing,' Kat admitted. See, Whitney was just being supportive. 'But it didn't last long. Everyone wrote such amazing things online and in those magazines, it's really turned around. Back in May, I couldn't get anyone to even return my calls, and now they're falling over themselves to get me guest-list and promos and everything.'

'I'm so glad,' Whitney smiled, warm and genuine, and straight away, Kat felt guilty for thinking ill of her. 'I was really starting to worry about you.'

'No need.' Kat grinned. 'I've got everything under control.'

It rained during their lunch, and Kat walked back to the *ChicK* offices in the muggy after-mists of the short downpour, idling along the wet pavements and under dripping awnings. It had been good to see Whitney, of course, but Kat now felt slightly off-balance, reminded again of the widening space between the old and new versions of her life. All through the meal, she'd had to edit herself: holding back news about the Popularity Rules, skirting around the substance of her days now – not being completely honest with her old friend for what felt like the first time. She didn't talk about blogging, or backstage encounters; she didn't mention sociological theories of status or inclusion. They chatted about Whitney's work, her relationship, news and current political topics, and all along, Kat's life was full of things her friend would never know.

Was this how Lauren had felt back in school, hiding her thoughts from Kat, worried about the judgement she'd find if she ever did confide the reason for her transformation?

Whitney wouldn't understand the Popularity Rules. Kat skirted another puddle and tried to imagine her old friend's reaction if she ever revealed the truth. Whitney had always been direct and up-front – it was what had brought them together: cutting through the egos and endless rhetorical combat sessions that made up student politics. Kat had run for Women's Rep in her second year at university, while Whitney was up for Secretary; they'd bonded over flyers and campaign pledges, and while Kat lost the election to an effortlessly chatty girl who seemed to know everyone in college, their friendship had lasted.

But now Kat was lying to her. No, not lying, she reminded herself as she fished in her bag to retrieve her ringing mobile, just holding back certain details.

'I'm losing my mind.'

Kat paused. 'Who is this?'

There was a low chuckle. 'Who do you want it to be?'

'Somebody who doesn't fuck around and waste my time?' she answered sweetly. The sweet voice was very important, Kat

288

was discovering. She could say almost anything and not cause offence, as long as the barb was delivered in warm enough tones.

'Sorry, I didn't mean . . .' the man was chastened. 'It's Ash. Ash Delaney?'

Kat stopped in the middle of the pavement, pedestrians swerving around her. All thoughts of Whitney, half-truths and whole lies were forgotten as that spark of expectation lit up in her veins.

'Oh, Ash, I didn't recognise your voice!' she apologised lightly, stepping out of the flow of people and into a gap between buildings. 'Hi! How are you?'

'Hanging onto my sanity by a thread.' His voice was warm, and despite the noise and traffic around her, Kat could just picture his smile, those blue eyes. 'I'm working on some remixes that are due next week. I've almost forgotten what sunlight looks like.'

'Poor struggling artist,' she teased, leaning back against the wall. 'What toil and torment.'

'I knew you'd understand.'

'So what's going on? Besides the minor creative breakdown, of course.'

'Nothing as such. I just wondered how you were.'

Kat was surprised by the warmth she felt at his words. 'I'm good,' she answered. 'Busy though.' She quickly filled him in on the freelancing and latest work she was doing.

'Sounds like you need to celebrate,' Ash suggested. 'I may not have many skills in life, but I think I can muster something. How about you come down and drag me out of this studio?'

'Sounds fun, but I can't; I'm in New York this weekend.' Kat couldn't deny the satisfaction she felt at her breezy response. No 'I'm visiting my mum' or 'I'm busy doing taxes'; no, she was an international jet-setter now. Or rather, she would be. 'Maybe next week?'

Ash sighed dramatically. 'If I'm still alive by then.'

'Well, at least now you have something to live for,' she laughed.

'What are you doing over there?'

'Just some meetings and things,' she answered vaguely. Otherwise known as lending Lauren moral support while she suffered through her sister's wedding preparations.

'I'll email you some must-sees,' Ash promised. 'And we'll fix something up when you're back?'

'Sure. I'll be in touch.'

Kat hung up and made her way back onto the busy street, considerably more cheerful. A trip to New York, a freelance project and the possibilities of Ash . . . It was all working out perfectly.

Empathy is everything.

When you get right down to it, people are an emotional mess of insecurities, childhood traumas and subconscious desires. To figure them out, you need to play therapist and get inside their heads. Somewhere, there's a key to their whole personality, and once you understand why they act the way they do, you'll be able to talk to them properly, act like you're just the same and push those buttons to move them into place.

Chapter Twenty-five

For someone who insisted on providing detailed profiles of everyone Kat encountered – all the way down to the receptionists – Lauren had been surprisingly reluctant to talk about the current state of her family. As they neared their destination, Kat could feel her tension grow, until by the time they cleared customs at JFK, the breezy blonde who had secured them upgrades with nothing but charm and a substantial air-miles account had been replaced by a distracted, anxious woman who fumbled over her luggage and had to be led blindly towards the taxi rank.

'Is there anything you want to tell me before this lunch?' Kat asked, directing the cab driver to their hotel while Lauren stared blankly out of the window. 'It's been . . . a while since I've seen any of these people.'

'No, everything's fine,' Lauren answered absently.

'If things are fine, then why do you look as if we're heading to your execution?' Kat began to worry. 'What's going on?'

Lauren swallowed. 'Nothing, really. I just . . . I don't do too well with my family, that's all. You know I never have. And this wedding?' she sighed. 'Delilah's going to be impossible.'

'Ah yes, the great Delilah.' Kat was curious what the elder Anderville sister was like now. As with the rest of Lauren's family, Kat had only ever seen fleeting glimpses of her at prizegivings or parents' days, but it had been enough to catch the syrupy grin and air of entitlement. She was lovely, the teenage Lauren had insisted, with what Kat took to be a slightly wistful tone; lovely, and kind, and sweet to everyone – except Lauren.

'Hasn't she left it rather late to take her stroll down the aisle? After all,' she grinned, trying to cheer Lauren, 'she is thirty now.'

'Almost,' Lauren corrected her. 'Her birthday is in November. Why else do you think she's actually seeing this one through? Besides,' she added, 'two broken engagements is just about permissible, but three is really not the done thing.'

'Where's that written? Her debutante book of social training?'

'Yup, right after the chapter on catching yourself an investment banker and picking the perfect shade of blush pink for your bridesmaids.'

'See, it won't be so bad,' Kat joked. 'She could have chosen tangerine.'

Lauren smiled faintly, and by the time they reached the ultra-modern hotel overlooking Central Park, she was almost relaxed enough to walk in a straight line.

'Um, are you sure we're in the right place?' Kat asked, taking in the bare brick interior, shot through with neon Perspex and dark wood panelling. 'I thought Delilah was more the Ritz sort of bride.'

'She is.' Lauren strode towards the long front desk. 'The Saint Regis, to be exact, but I need at least a dozen city blocks between me and my family so they don't come knocking at my door demanding we go through floral samples.'

'Good plan,' Kat agreed. 'Perhaps now you'll be able to relax.'

Lauren shot her a dubious look.

'Well, at least *try* to relax.'

293

'You think I'm crazy.' Lauren shrugged, her skin pale under the harsh lights. 'But you'll see.'

They met Lauren's mother, Eleanor, and Delilah for lunch the next day in the gilt-edged restaurant of their uptown hotel. Lauren had fussed over her outfit for a full twenty minutes before deciding on an uncharacteristically demure poppy-print summer dress. Kat dutifully followed suit and squeezed into a borrowed linen skirt and summer blouse, her hair neatly pinned back and a sweet locket at her neck.

'Don't mention the Popularity Rules,' Lauren instructed her, as she trotted through the sprawling lobby, her heels tapping sharply on the cream marble floor. 'Or hipsters in general, or drug-addicted rock stars. Or feminism of *any* kind.'

Kat was amused, but when she saw the table of perfectly groomed blondes waiting for them in the corner, her laughter faded on her lips. Surrounded by extravagant displays of lilies, ornate columns and starched cream linens, the women looked like foreign creatures, polished and perfect.

'There you are.' A woman with chiselled bone structure embraced Lauren carefully, her ash blonde hair sculpted in a bob. 'I called your hotel to check if you were oversleeping. I don't understand why you couldn't just stay here with us.' She held Lauren away from her ice-blue tweed jacket and assessed her. 'You're looking . . . healthy.'

'Hi Mom, Dee,' Lauren added, turning to her sister, who was sipping champagne with a bored expression. They exchanged air-kisses but didn't touch, Delilah immediately smoothing down the front of her white embroidered top in case even the presence of her sister had put it out of place.

'I'm sorry if you were waiting,' Lauren apologised to the other guests. Her voice had become warmer at the edges, her

Southern accent already more defined. 'I thought we said two?' It was barely ten past.

'Yes, well never mind, you're here now.' Eleanor Anderville looked past her, settling on Kat. 'How do you do?' She held out a hand, her gaze sweeping from head to toe. Kat shook it and mustered her best manners.

'Lovely to see you again, Mrs Anderville.'

'Eleanor, please.' She smiled without a hint of recognition that Kat was the same girl who'd 'polluted' Lauren's mind all those years ago. 'And this is our maid of honour, Jennifer, and Carter's mother, Bitsy.' She gestured to a tanned brunette about their age with precise make-up and a navy dress, and another blonde matriarch in khaki trousers and heavy gold jewellery.

'This is Katherine, an old school-friend of mine,' Lauren introduced her quickly. 'She had some business in the city, so I invited her to join us.'

'Lovely.' They all beamed at Kat. That was a pass for the blouse and skirt then. Eleanor gestured for a waiter and within moments, an extra setting had been laid and they were all seated under the crystal chandelier, ordering lunch. Or rather, they were ordering an array of possibly edible vegetation. Kat looked longingly at the steak being served to the table next to them and decided on the Caesar salad – minus the dressing, croutons and chicken, of course. Something told her that this was not a group to look lightly on carbs.

'I've been thinking about tulips,' Delilah announced, once the waiter had retreated. 'Would the scent be overpowering, do you think? Should I go with something softer?'

Kat watched curiously as the whirl of wedding-related discussion spun around the table. Punctuated with news from back home about a scandalous divorce, fundraising for the new hospice and somebody's surprise elopement, it was a window on a foreign world. Only Lauren remained silent, sipping water from a heavy tumbler and avoiding almost all eye contact.

'Lauren, are you seeing anyone right now?' Eleanor pounced without warning. Kat saw Lauren stiffen.

'Not at the moment.' Lauren looked down at her untouched salad.

'But you will have a guest by the wedding, won't you honey?'

'It'll throw off the table placements if you come alone,' Delilah added, her forehead creasing with concern. It was, Kat noticed, the first time she'd so much as looked in Lauren's direction for the last twenty minutes.

'What made you decide to have the ceremony in New York?' Kat interrupted. Lauren shot her a grateful look. 'You all live down in North Carolina, don't you?'

'Carter is based here,' Delilah said, as if that was all that mattered. 'And anyway, I always dreamed of having my wedding in the city.'

'It's true,' Lauren added. 'She's been keeping a wedding planner scrapbook ever since junior high. I think there was a whole chart about the benefits of a roof garden over a formal ballroom.'

Lauren's comment had been slightly acerbic, but Bitsy and Jennifer fell about themselves cooing. 'Well, isn't that just darling?'

'I knew she was the one for him, from the very first day they met,' Bitsy beamed indulgently. 'It was at our summer barbecue last year, and she was wearing the prettiest white dress – looked like an angel.' Delilah smiled, as if she'd known just what a marriageable prospect she'd seemed. 'And they danced all afternoon, and after she'd gone, I said to him, I said, "Carter, I think you're going to marry that girl." And he turned to me and said, "Mama, you might just be right." '

'Oh, that's so romantic!' Jennifer squealed, with an equal mix of enthusiasm and envy. 'Carter is such a gem!'

'Yes he is.' His mother smiled, but Kat thought she detected a note of steel as she sized up her daughter-in-law-to-be.

'If you'll just excuse me . . .' While they were singing the rest of Carter's boundless praises, Kat took the opportunity to edge back her chair.

'Good idea.' Lauren leapt up. 'I think I need to freshen my lipstick.'

They retreated across the dining room to a vast, marble bathroom adorned with crystal chandeliers and a silent Mexican woman sitting by a table of beauty products.

'Carter sounds like a gem,' Kat teased.

'Carter Rutherford is an arrogant sleaze with a taste for hard liquor and fast cars,' Lauren said grimly, rinsing her hands under a pair of ornate golden taps. 'He'll cheat and she'll shop, and they'll be the perfect couple for repressed anger and middle-aged ennui.'

'Does she know?' Kat smoothed back stray strands of her fringe, already fighting to escape their neat clip.

'Of course,' Lauren laughed, a bitter sound. 'It's all part of the deal. She gets the Upper East Side apartment and a ring, and he has the right kind of wife to parade around the firm and make partner.'

'And I thought I was cynical when it came to love,' Kat murmured, taking in the ornate fixtures and all the trappings of wealth. They exchanged a rueful look.

'Mom keeps on at me about settling down, as if I'm rejecting the whole idea of love and a family because I'm not already married.' Lauren seemed tired, her usual perfect posture slipping by the hour. 'But I think I'm really the only one left who believes in any of that. Pretty ironic, that I'm the romantic one.' She laughed, but it was soft, and held no mirth at all.

After lunch, the wedding entourage headed to an exclusive Park Avenue bridal boutique. So exclusive, in fact, that the windows were tinted and the door manned by a moustachioed security guard in a brocade-trimmed uniform. God forbid any common, wayward brides should simply wander in off the street. Delilah's party was greeted by a duo of toothy, lacquered women and ushered into the hallowed, softly lit chamber where they were served with champagne, strawberries and a constant stream of flattery.

'No, I think I want the sleeves bigger,' Delilah mused, while Lauren stood silently in a hideous confection of lilac taffeta. Kat was perched on a pink, crushed-velvet pouf, watching a parade of dresses that seemed to be designed solely to show the bridesmaids in the least flattering light possible. 'Why don't you try that lemon-yellow one again?'

'Oh yes, the yellow was just darling!' Jennifer agreed, flicking through *Vogue*. Lauren shuffled back into the dressing room, shooting Kat a plaintive look as she went.

'Short or long veil; which do you think?' Delilah tried each style in turn, admiring herself slowly in front of a vast mirror.

'They're both great!' Jennifer cooed. 'I guess it depends on how you have your hair.'

'A modest, shorter veil is always a classic,' Bitsy Rutherford demurred, removing the longer one from Delilah's hands. 'Don't you think, Eleanor?'

Kat discreetly checked her phone for the time: still only five p.m.?

'Umm, Kat?' Lauren stuck her head around the curtain. 'Could you help me with the fastening on this?'

She leapt up. Any escape from the veil monologues. 'What do you need?' Kat asked, pulling the heavy folds of peach fabric closed behind her.

'Xanax,' Lauren answered, sinking down onto the chaise longue. 'Or a shotgun.' She had pale yellow silk bunched around her waist, the colour managing to wash her skin tone out completely.

'All I have are two aspirin and a nail file,' Kat offered.

'I'll take them.' Lauren's expression was one of utter defeat.

'You know, I'm surprised Delilah hasn't had all of this planned by now.' Kat idly ran her fingers across the long rail of dresses. 'I would have thought she'd have a composite photo of her ideal gown already designed.'

'She did, but then Carter happened to mention he thought off-the-shoulder was whorish and revealing, so she's back at square one,' Lauren replied gloomily. She hitched up the halter-neck straps and presented her back to Kat for zipping.

'Because obviously what he wants overrules everything. Breathe in,' Kat ordered, hoisting the catches closed. 'Wait, what size is this?'

'Zero.'

'What?!'

'Mom likes to be optimistic when it comes to these things. She says it gives us motivation.' Lauren looked at herself in the mirror, her shoulders slumped.

'Oh, Lauren.' Kat pulled her closer for a hug. 'A few more hours and it'll be over. Think, soon you'll have an ocean between you again!'

Lauren managed a weak smile. 'Until the wedding, you mean.'

'Are you ready yet?' Delilah's voice drifted back. 'Because I think I want to see the persimmon instead.'

Lauren and Kat turned to look at the dark orange gown hanging behind them.

'Only a few hours?' Lauren whispered, as they surveyed the horror of chiffon overlay and boned corseting.

'Remember, she's family,' Kat advised. 'If you kill her now, Thanksgiving dinner will be rather awkward.'

There was a faint beeping noise.

'Check my phone.' Lauren's voice was muffled as she struggled out of the lemon dress and into the orange. 'It might be something about *Think Louder*.'

'From Neale Jenkins?' Kat read.

'That's the one. What does he say?'

The missive was brief, but deadly. Kat gulped.

'What's wrong?' Lauren finally pulled the layers over her head and turned to Kat. 'Why are you looking like that?'

'ChannelCorp,' she whispered, taking Lauren's place on the couch. In the back of Kat's mind, she recalled the chaise longue being referred to as a ladies' fainting chair. How apt.

'Kat? Hello?' Lauren snapped her fingers in front of Kat's face. 'Stay with me.'

'Hmm?' Kat felt dizzy.

'Tell me what Neale said.'

'ChannelCorp,' Kat repeated. 'They might buy out the magazine.' It was worse than she'd ever imagined.

Delilah's voice called out again. 'Lauren, hon, the dress?'

'Did he send any names?' Lauren ignored her sister, already reaching for the phone.

'A couple. He says the new editor will either be Roger Altern, Michael Grant or Stevie Gold.' The names meant nothing to her.

'Excellent.'

'No it isn't!' Kat looked at Lauren in disbelief. 'How can you say that when—'

'Shhh!' Lauren hissed, glancing towards the showroom. 'I meant about the information, not the takeover. Although . . .' she paused, 'if it went through, it would probably be a good thing. For you,' she added quickly, seeing Kat's outraged expression. 'The Popularity Rules work best on empty corporate suits, and you'd have a total blank slate.'

'Lauren!' Delilah's sugary tone broke.

'Coming!' she called back. Lauren fastened the last hook and glanced at Kat. 'Do I need to confiscate those aspirin?'

Kat shook her head numbly, and then Lauren left and she was alone in the silk-draped boudoir to contemplate the unthinkable.

You can be good or you can win.

If you want to whine over right and wrong, this really isn't the book for you. When you get to college and take an intro to ethics class, maybe you'll realise that there's no such thing as morality, but for now, take our word for it: people do whatever they can to get what they want, and the only thing you need to worry about is getting caught. Instead of worrying about being 'bad', maybe you should be scared of living the rest of your life a pathetic failure.

Playing dirty isn't an option; it's a necessity.

Chapter Twenty-six

ChannelCorp.

Of all the companies, it had to be that one. A quasi-Christian behemoth, it straddled both sides of the Atlantic, the reach of its tentacles extending to anything remotely music-related. They owned stadiums and billboard contracts, record labels and radio networks, and now, apparently, they were getting into the publishing game.

'Don't get so stressed yet, Kat. These kinds of deals fall through all the time.'

'Then why are we here?' 'Here' was the street corner opposite ChannelCorp HQ. Or, as Kat preferred to think of it, their lair. She'd had hours to dwell on the terrible news – escaping the bridal boutique with the briefest of monosyllables and glowering all through dinner with Lauren – but she'd only managed to move from shock to fierce resentment.

'If the takeover goes ahead, we need to be prepared.' Lauren's gaze never left the revolving doors across the street. 'As long as we're in the same city as the editorial candidates, we should make the most of it and initiate contact.'

'I suppose . . .' Kat agreed reluctantly. She'd rather not even contemplate the fate of her beloved magazine, but some background research couldn't hurt. At least, this time, she was prepared for stake-out duty with flat shoes and snacks. 'Want a scone?' She offered Lauren the bag, not expecting her to accept, but to her surprise, Lauren took a pastry and began to nibble. Time with her family really had taken its toll.

'Wait, is that him?' Kat peered at the man emerging from the building, his jacket casually slung over one arm, the other already raised to hail a cab. She checked him against the printed photo Lauren had found online: tall, clean-shaven, blonde hair . . .

'That's him,' Lauren confirmed. They swept into action, flagging down their own taxi and directing the driver after the other car.

'This is why I don't like last-minute pursuits.' Lauren kept a worried watch on the yellow cab three cars in front. 'Too many unpredictable details.'

'You do this often?' Kat shouldn't be surprised by now, but some of Lauren's tactics gave her pause.

'The engineered meeting? Sure. Although these days I can usually find their schedule from a talkative secretary, or just hack their email. I did that for the other two,' she added casually, as if it wasn't a felony. 'They have plans for drinks and this rock show after-party. If we're lucky, we'll catch all three tonight.'

'Lauren!'

'What?' Lauren gave her a devious grin as they sped through the traffic. The covert action seemed to have revived her spirits, Kat noted. 'Once you've got copies of their diary and all their correspondence, it makes life so much easier.'

'Don't you ever feel you're going too far?' Kat asked, even as she was wishing they could do the same for this Stevie Gold. Think how simple it would be to find out about the *Think Louder* plans if she had full access to his every thought!

'I go as far as it takes.' Her voice was matter-of-fact. 'What's wrong about that?'

'Do you ever draw a line? I'm just curious.'

'I haven't had to yet.' Lauren shrugged, as Stevie's taxi came to a stop outside a busy bar. 'As long as nobody I care about gets hurt, it's fine. Now, tell me you don't live like that?'

They waited a respectable amount of time before following Stevie into what seemed to be the drinking spot of choice for young corporate types. Sandwiched between swanky, glass-fronted offices and a chic hotel, it spilled sharp-suited men and pencil-skirted women out onto the kerb, laughing in the summer breeze.

Lauren's mobile rang just as they slipped inside the dark glass doors. 'Hello? Oh, Mom.' Her face slipped. 'No, I can't, I'm out with Kat. We're at a bar uptown. No, Fermier, but we won't be out long and—' She sighed, agreeing meekly. 'Fine, they'll meet us here.'

Hanging up, Lauren turned to Kat. 'Dee and Jennifer are on their way.'

'Oh.' Kat couldn't disguise her lack of enthusiasm.

'It'll be fine.' Lauren sounded as if she was trying to convince herself. 'You only need quick chats with the prospective editors tonight, then if the magazine deal goes through . . . If,' she added pointedly, as if to stem Kat's whimper of protest. 'Then whoever they pick to run it will already have a great first impression of you.'

Kat made a quick sweep of the crowd as they edged towards the bar. Old-fashioned dark wood panelling, Wall Street suits and a smattering of glossy-haired women who swiftly sized up the newcomers and shifted slightly closer to their dates. 'What is it about New York women that's so terrifying?' Kat wondered, as they found a couple of stools by the long bar, carefully placed half a room away from Stevie. 'I feel like everyone in this city is a six-foot model with a law degree and a sideline as a DJ or artist or something.'

'It's because they probably are,' Lauren replied, matter-of-fact. She gestured a barman over and ordered them Martinis. 'Why do you think I have to work so hard? We're all fighting to seem like we're the best.'

'Hey.' Kat noticed the slight edge to her tone. 'We don't have to spend time with Delilah if you don't want. I can parade around a bit in front of Stevie and then we're out of here.'

Lauren let out a breath. 'It's OK. It'll probably make this easier. Dee always attracts a crowd,' she explained.

'Hmm.' Kat was liking Delilah less and less. She looked for a way to change the subject. 'Any feedback on the Domina campaign yet?

'Not yet.' Lauren didn't relax. 'I'm hearing rumours the brand director might take it in a different direction, so I just have to wait.'

'Don't worry, I'm sure they'll love it,' Kat comforted. She shot a glare at the two besuited men angling towards them; they promptly turned and went in search of more amenable companions. 'You're Lauren Amelia Anderville. I've never seen you lose anything before.'

Lauren managed a smile. 'See, now you're just tempting fate.'

'Fate?' Kat elbowed her lightly, 'Sure, and your star signs are out of synch too.'

They laughed. Fate and superstition were the reserve of woman without the Popularity Rules.

'Dee had her charts done for the wedding,' Lauren confided, stabbing the olive in her drink.

'Seriously?'

'Uh huh. A group of her old sorority sisters all took her, to celebrate the engagement.' Having spent all this time not uttering a single word about her family, Lauren finally began to unwind. 'And she's got her heart set on this particular arrangement of roses they're flying in from England, but Carter has this thing about being eco-friendly, so they're printing the invitations on recycled paper. As if that makes all the difference!'

'Is she quitting her job to move up here? Actually, wait.' Kat paused. 'Does she even have a job? I haven't heard her mention anything to do with work.'

'Oh yes, she's a consultant at an interior design firm down in Charlotte.' Lauren's face screwed up. 'She shops, professionally.' Then she checked herself. 'I shouldn't bitch about it. I try not to, I really do, but it would be different if she actually cared, if she'd worked for anything. But she just sails from lunches to spa treatments to cocktails without ever lifting one precious manicured finger.' She paused to gulp some of her drink. 'She lived at home until she was twenty-five. Twenty-five! Then Daddy moved her into an apartment downtown, because poor Dee can't possibly pay her own rent when there's shoes to buy.'

'You, uh, want to slow down?' Kat eyed the rapidly disappearing drink.

'They have lunch together three times a week. My mom and Dee, I mean.' Lauren slammed the glass down and gestured for the barman again. 'They go get their hair done together, and gossip while some Chinese woman soaks their feet. They even sit on the same charity boards. Did you know they host a fundraising dinner twice a year so they can look caring and thoughtful to all their friends – and her prospective husbands?'

Kat shook her head silently.

'Mom sends me the invites, and then acts hurt that I can't make it down. As if I can just drop everything to go admire their centrepieces and listen to a fucking jazz trio!' Lauren was slowly turning a rosy shade of pink. 'Like I'm the selfish one, when I send them big cheques every time. And you should see the holidays . . . I swear, I'm ready to inflict grievous bodily harm by the time Thanksgiving dinner's done. I'm skipping it this year, really I will. Christmas too, for the sake of my sanity. I'll go take a vacation in the Caribbean and lie out on a white, sandy beach while they're competitively under-eating in the formal dining room, and squawking over the fact Mindy Adams dared to play doubles at the club with a man who isn't her husband.' Lauren finally took a breath.

'Better now?' Kat asked, watching her with concern.

'Maybe,' Lauren answered in a small voice.

'Well, put the rest on hold for now,' Kat advised, spying Delilah strutting through the crowd in a very little black dress, her hair long and loose in soft waves. Jennifer followed, a respectful two steps behind. At least she knew her place, Kat thought wryly, before the women reached them.

'Katherine, look at you! I just love that dress; it makes you look so *wild*!' Delilah blinked her lovely eyes and kissed Kat affectionately. 'We missed you at dinner – it was such fun! I'll get a mint julep, honey,' she said to the bartender. 'To remind me of home.'

Again, she hadn't so much as looked at Lauren. Kat wondered if it had been this way always, or just since Lauren came back from camp that summer, finally competition for Delilah's golden crown.

'Let me guess: a Carolina girl?' Despite the women being clustered in a knot, a broad-shouldered man in a conservative blue shirt still managed to sidle up alongside Delilah. 'They always make the prettiest girls.'

'Oh, aren't you sweet?' Delilah beamed. 'And right on the money, too.'

'Let me,' he reached for his wallet. 'What about the rest of you ladies?'

Kat shook her head, Lauren sighed, and Jennifer accepted his offer.

'Another Southern belle?' The man flashed a grin. 'This is my lucky night.'

The pair of them laughed appreciatively and moved closer to Mr Generous, turning away from Kat and Lauren.

'Welcome to my world,' Lauren muttered. 'You should have seen her *before* she got the ring.'

Kat watched Delilah and Jennifer in action, flirting and syrupy sweet as they leaned against the polished bar and tilted their heads coquettishly, eyes sparkling under the soft spotlights. She could never understand women like that, willing to act like fluttering teenagers, and for what – a few moments of feminine validation? At least when she made the effort to charm someone now, it was for the sake of her career and not just a fifteen-dollar cocktail.

'Let's go to work.' She turned back to Lauren. 'I just need to strike up conversation, right?'

'Yes, but no mention of the magazine, or even what you do for a living,' Lauren warned, still watching her sister. 'He needs to think this is complete chance.'

Kat smiled. 'Just pure serendipity,' she agreed. 'All we did was stalk him halfway across town.'

Stevie was in a booth in the corner, surrounded by a pack of raucous men in designer suits and dapper ties. His top buttons were already loose, and there were half a dozen empty bottles on the table. Kat waited until he got up to go to the bar, and then, on Lauren's cue, made her way through the crowd towards him.

'Oh, I'm so sorry!' she exclaimed, 'accidentally' stumbling against him. A clichéd opener, she knew, but Lauren had assured her that the classics were always the best.

'No problem.' Stevie helped her up, his hand lingering on her arm for longer than entirely necessary. Kat looked into his bland, blue eyes and disliked him immediately.

'At least I got you before you made it to the bar!' Kat knew that an enthusiastic grin was beyond her given the circumstances, so she decided to work a mysterious half-smile instead.

'Right.' Stevie grinned widely, flashing her those teeth that they all seemed to be equipped with on this side of the Atlantic, the kind that could be used as an alternative light source. 'Then there really would be trouble.'

'That's quite a celebration you've got going.' Kat tried not to wince at the inane comments coming out of both their mouths. She nodded at his table, where a short, ruddy-cheeked man was now chugging a pint glass of something dark and foamy. 'Some good news?'

'Fifteen people in our office got fired today,' Stevie announced, still grinning. Kat raised her eyebrows. 'And we're not them!' he finished smugly.

'Oh. Lucky you!' Kat managed. Teamwork, nothing like it.

'Luck had nothing to do with it,' Stevie replied, and then, yes, to Kat's horror, he actually winked. Now she really did need a drink. He was just like those boys she'd known in university, who arrived as freshers sincerely preaching about going off to Africa with an NGO, but by the time their final

310

year rolled around had already signed their lives away to an investment bank. And he was on the shortlist to take over as editor of *Think Louder*.

Somewhere, on whatever celestial plane he inhabited, Alan was getting very, very drunk.

It took all of Kat's limited social training to accept Stevie's offer and maintain niceties, but for some reason, whatever bitterness she could feel radiating from her every pore seemed to be perceived as aloof charm.

'Maybe we could rendezvous later?' Stevie suggested, moving closer, after establishing that Kat was only in town for a brief stay. 'I could take your digits.'

'Oh, that's sweet,' Kat replied, 'but I should . . .' He looked away for a moment back to his table, and she took the opportunity to quickly slip into the crowd. It was so busy, she was able to wind her way swiftly back to their corner before he'd even said another word.

'Quick exit, kind of rude,' Lauren noted, hopping down off her stool. Delilah and Jennifer's crowd of adoring management consultants was swelling by the minute.

'I'm showing cleavage; he'll just mark it down as mysterious,' Kat replied, thankful for the first time for the wonderful double standards that let men overlook any bad behaviour as long as you were wearing lipstick and could be imagined into the femme fatale role. 'One possible future boss down, two to go.' She took a fortifying swallow of something fruity and bedecked with flowers. 'Should we say goodbye?' She gestured to where Delilah and Jennifer were still merrily flirting.

Lauren shrugged, already backing away through the crowd. 'If you think they'll care.'

*

Four bars, three cabs and two engineered encounters later, Kat and Lauren were wandering the West Village in search of a mystery piano joint.

'It's worth it, you'll see,' Lauren insisted, now a little unsteady on her feet.

'You're the boss!' Kat gripped her arm tighter. She'd had a few drinks herself – compliments of their stalking victims, as she liked to think of them. 'That last one wasn't so bad,' she mused, as they turned down a street with small boutique shop-fronts and cobbled stones underfoot. 'He wasn't wearing a suit, for starters. And he tapped his foot when that Hole song came on!'

'Is it . . . ?' Lauren peered across the road. 'No, wait, I think it's up here!' She picked up her pace, and Kat had no choice but to trot along next to her, breathless, until Lauren came to a triumphant halt under a nondescript red sign.

'Marie's Crisis?' Kat read aloud. Lauren's face was lit up.

'I come here whenever I need a fix. I've been waiting years to show it to you.' She dragged Kat down a narrow flight of stairs and into a small, wood-panelled room. Kat looked around dubiously. There were only a few occupied tables and a scruffy bar at the far end; hardly the slick bars or even fashionable dive spots they'd been racing between all night. This was the big surprise?

But then the piano at the side of the room struck up with a familiar tune, the entire room began to sing 'I Am Sixteen (Going On Seventeen)' and it all made perfect sense to Kat.

Musicals.

'See?' Lauren turned to her proudly. 'Oh, look, stools!' Before Kat could even make a sound, she was sat at the very side of the piano, watching a greying but undoubtedly dapper man lead them all in song. Lauren knew every word by heart.

And so did Kat.

'How did you find this place?' Kat asked, when the last voices faded away and their songmaster took a break for a glass of wine. As far as she could tell, it was the preserve of ageing Broadway queens and fresh-faced musical theatre boys.

'I stumbled on it by accident, back when I first moved to the city.' Lauren traced the etchings in the old wooden piano frame and paused for a second, as if she was deciding what to say next. Then she relaxed, confessing, 'I was staying home every night to watch musicals and weep anyway, so I figured I'd come here instead. At least then I wouldn't weep.'

'What happened?' Kat was careful not to sound too eager. Personal history was a rare thing with Lauren, admissions of vulnerability even rarer.

'There was a guy, at Yale.' Lauren's voice was soft. 'We were together for two years.'

'Oh.' Kat had never managed a relationship longer than a few months.

'And then he got accepted to Stanford, for law school,' she explained. 'I got in too, for my Masters. But Columbia wanted me too, and their programme was so much more prestigious.' She fell silent, still tracing those old pock-marks in the wood, but she didn't need to continue. Kat understood.

'I wanted to be the best,' Lauren said, as if she was still convincing herself.

'And now you are.' Kat tried to give her some comfort.

'I wonder sometimes . . .' Lauren's gaze drifted off. 'If I went back, would I pick differently? Not just with David, but before then. The Popularity Rules. You. Would I be happy being somebody else?'

'Are you happy now?'

Lauren looked back. 'Are you?'

They smiled: small, wry smiles laced with regrets and resignation.

'Have you ever thought about stopping – the Popularity Rules, I mean,' Kat asked quietly. 'Just quitting?'

Lauren looked at her, hard. 'It's been twelve years, Kat. It's in my head now; it's just how I think. This is what I am – I can't just turn it off.' She blinked, and for a moment, Kat saw what it must be like to live inside Lauren's world: those achingly cynical rules etched into her mind and no moment to let the planning, the performance slip away.

'Ooh, I know!' Lauren exclaimed suddenly, their piano man returning. Kat saw the serious moment slip away as Lauren leaned over and whispered enthusiastically in his ear. He laughed, rifled in his pile of sheet music for a moment and then plucked a page out with a flourish. After a few bars, Kat recognised the song: 'Anything You Can Do (I Can Do Better)'.

Love is a lie.

Boys are simple: they want sex. Men are just the same: they want sex and power.

Don't ever forget it or be charmed into thinking you're special, because they're putting on an act too, and you'll be the one left crying in the end. But if you know what they're after, then you can use it to your advantage, because a man will do almost anything if he thinks he's getting laid at the end of it. Contacts, invites, influence: nothing should be out of your reach if you learn to play him the right way, but be subtle, because it's your reputation on the line, not his.

Chapter Twenty-seven

Ash called the day after they returned to London.

'I know a great cure for jet-lag,' he promised. 'Come down to Brighton for the day.' Kat surreptitiously turned her body away from where Lauren, Gabi and Oscar were lounging, spending a lazy Saturday lunchtime on the balcony with the papers and coffee.

'I don't know . . .' Kat stretched her toes experimentally, but she couldn't stop herself having very pleasant flashbacks to Ash's previous cures for boredom, frustration and public humiliation.

'Come on.' She could hear the grin in his voice. 'I'll win you a stuffed animal; we'll eat candyfloss on the pier.'

'What is this, a music video you're setting up here? You're about ten years too late for that boyband stuff.'

Ash laughed. 'Well, if you can't make it . . .'

'No,' Kat decided suddenly. 'I can. It sounds like fun. I'll text you when I know what train I'm on.'

'Perfect. I'll see you later.'

Kat rolled back over to find three disapproving faces staring back at her.

'Tell me you didn't just agree to get on public transport and trek halfway across the country to meet him!' The disbelief in Lauren's voice was clear.

Kat kept the large sun-hat covering her eyes. 'It's not that far, and yes, I'll go see him.' She yawned, absently toying with the striped tie on her bikini top. 'What's so wrong with that?'

'Only that you're relinquishing all power to come running the moment he snaps his fingers!' Lauren exclaimed.

'And sending the message that you have nothing better to do but drop everything and make him a priority,' Gabi's drawl added from Kat's right-hand side.

'You might as well just present yourself to him, naked, with a fucking ribbon around your pussy.'

That last comment was Oscar's contribution, and prompted Kat to sit up, blinking at the bright light. 'People, please! Not that it's any of your business, but we're just going to hang out.'

They all began to laugh.

'I'm sorry, honey,' Gabi said, drinking beer from an ice-cold bottle. 'But that's bullshit and you know it.'

'Katherine's got a cru-ush,' Oscar hummed along.

She tried to glare at them as she levered herself off the lounger to grab her drink. Tiny lines criss-crossed her skin from a pleasant hour lying comatose. 'OK, so maybe I've slept with him a couple of times. But this is really just a casual thing – it's not even a date.'

'And that's the problem.' Lauren lazily swatted her with a magazine. 'Maybe in a few years you'll figure that out.'

'But I'm guessing that'll be too late.' Oscar propped his head on his elbows and assessed her shrewdly from over the top of his plastic eighties sunglasses. 'Since you're going down today, so to speak.'

'Who wants mimosas?' Kat leapt up.

'You didn't!' Lauren and Gabi wailed in unison.

'Kat, have we taught you nothing?'

'No? You're good? Time for a new jug anyway.' Making her escape into the cool flat, Kat slid her bare feet on the smooth floor and tried not to pay attention to their teasing. She and

317

Ash were adults, for God's sake – why all the need for power games and hard to get?

'This isn't just empty theory, hon.' Gabi trailed after her to fetch some ice-cubes from the freezer. 'People don't respect you if you jump on command.'

'And men don't buy the cow if they get the milk for free.' Kat rolled her eyes, splashing liberal amounts of champagne into a tall glass jug. 'Whoops, too late there. Let me guess, I should also only accept dates more than three days in advance, and always be the one to hang up first?' She shook her head, reaching past Gabi's small frame to get to the orange juice. 'Come on – I deconstructed those theories of feminine mating rituals for my bloody dissertation!'

Gabi's lips flicked into a grin. 'The poster-girl for tradition, am I? Can you go tell my mom, because I swear, the day she caught me making out with Lindsay Maranoto, I ceased to be a real woman.'

Kat shot her a sympathetic look. 'But surely you should be sticking up for me here! You know, ignoring all this old-fashioned etiquette crap.'

'That "old-fashioned crap", as you put it, doesn't disappear the minute you switch teams,' Gabi laughed. 'That girl I'm seeing, Mia, hasn't called me in three days and she's all I can think about. Hard to get works every time.'

'Well, perhaps I just don't want to be gotten,' Kat retorted, folding her arms.

'Sure you do.' Lauren joined them, pulling on a gauzy white cover-up. 'I know that look; it's the same one you'd get watching Christian Slater in *Heathers*. You want nothing more than for Ash to take you in his arms, stare deeply into your eyes and say, 'Katherine—'

'Darling,' Oscar added from the doorway.

318

'Darling Katherine,' Lauren continued, clasping her hands dramatically to her chest. 'You are a woman unlike any other. Be mine, always, in the non-co-dependent, gender-confine-free, mutually respecting relationship of your dreams.'

'Guys!' Kat couldn't stop herself snorting with laughter. 'You're being ridiculous.'

'And you are being naive,' Lauren warned. 'You already know he's charming, cute and good in bed. What's left to stop you falling for him?'

'Let's hope he has really bad BO,' Oscar agreed. 'Or a secret love for Conservative politics. Otherwise you are going to be totally screwed.'

Kat told herself that they were wrong for the duration of her train journey down. She didn't get crushes, she didn't fall giddily head over feet – and certainly not for a man who kept boxed rows of unworn designer trainers in the back of his spacious closet. But by the time they'd met at the station and wandered down to the pier, she couldn't deny that the tension between them was different from before. For the first time, they weren't in a dark club, with Jack Daniel's and slow-dancing to loosen their tongues. It was just the two of them, bright sunlight and a noisy sea-front scene.

'So what does Katherine Elliot like to do with herself, when she's not making amateur streaming videos, dancing to Meatloaf or making silent escapes the morning after?' Ash teased, leaning over the railings on the end of the pier and discarding pistachio shells into the murky water. 'I really don't know that much about you at all.'

'You know my love for Chinese takeaway at three a.m.,' Kat replied, tearing her gaze away from the tuft of dark hair sticking out over the back of his collar. She was struck by the sudden urge to smooth it down, but played with her necklace instead. 'And about my taste in underwear. I'd say you're doing pretty well so far.'

Ash sighed theatrically. 'God, it's like squeezing blood from a stone!'

'What do you want to know?' Kat laughed.

'Normal stuff.' He shrugged, shooting her a sidelong glance. 'Where you grew up, what got you into music journalism, how you ended up the scene queen you are today.'

He referred to that a few times, she noticed: her supposed status, the encounter with Devon Darsel. But then, he really didn't know anything more. 'I grew up in Wiltshire,' she answered. 'Academic mother, absent father. Some painful years at boarding school—'

'Sounds familiar.'

'And as for the light bulb moment with music writing . . . it was just always something I loved.' Kat felt the paint from the iron railings peeling under her fingertips. He didn't deserve the Alan story, not yet. 'What about you?'

Ash shrugged, both his hands now jammed in the front pockets of his black jeans, a familiar gesture. They began to stroll through the crowds of hyperactive children, the loud arcade ringing beside them. 'My mum's American. She was a model, and now she designs clothes, allegedly.' Kat raised an eyebrow. 'Tie-died hippy scraps,' he explained. 'This eco/ethical trend has her working overtime. And Dad was a manager for some rock bands, back in the day. They eloped to Ibiza and nearly gave her parents a heart attack.'

'So that's how you got into producing, through your dad?'

'Not really. There was always music around, when I grew up. And musicians,' he added with a loaded look. 'But I picked it up on my own, only a couple of years ago. A mate of mine was recording an album, so I started hanging out in the studio. It makes sense to me – the technology, how the sounds work . . .' he trailed off. 'I guess it's not something I can really describe.'

'Then I think we're doomed to an afternoon of awkward silence,' Kat quipped. He was quieter than he'd been before; a little more awkward, a little more endearing. She was, after all, highly suspicious of charm. On a whim, she reached up and kissed him, her lips cool on his. It wasn't a long embrace, but it was enough to send that shiver of anticipation through her chest – and remove the last tension that remained between them.

'I'd better shower you with lavish gifts then.' He slung his arm around her shoulder and surveyed the amusement stalls in front of them. 'How do you feel about stuffed animals?'

After seven pounds' worth of attempts, Ash finally shot enough skittles at a makeshift stall to win a hideous pink elephant.

'Be careful what you wish for.' He presented her with the toy, smirking as she held it at arm's length.

'I think the gesture was enough.' Kat looked into the elephant's dazed neon eyes. 'How about we set it free for some ADHD child to enjoy?'

They found a bench next to a stall selling taffy and popcorn, Kat placing it down with a furtive look in either direction. 'All clear,' Ash whispered dramatically.

'Come on,' she laughed, grabbing his hand as they raced away. She skidded to a stop only when they were out of sight of the offending beast, breathless. Ash pulled her closer, slipping his arms around her waist and landing small kisses on her cheeks before he finally found her mouth. Kat melted into him.

Oh God. They were right. She was already lost to this.

'What next?' she asked, detangling herself from him before she dissolved into a pile of hormones right there beside the amusement arcade.

'Maybe a change of scene?' Ash asked, his confidence now fully restored. 'My studio isn't far . . .' He linked his fingers through Kat's and slowly began walking backwards, the look in his eyes suggesting that it wasn't the mixing decks he wanted Kat to see.

'Let's do it,' she agreed simply, letting the pleasant rush of endorphins in her system propel her back to his car, and through the half-hour drive in the green countryside. One hand settled on her thigh as he drove. The scenery outside the window blurred at the edge of her vision, the music on the radio a sweet background song as Kat absently reflected on how much her life had changed since she'd started this Popularity Rules project – how much it had opened up.

'It doesn't look like much,' Ash warned, as he drove them down a winding country lane and slowed to a stop by a small bungalow.

'But it's your piece of home, right?' Kat looked curiously at the pebbledash and stone paving leading up to a red front door.

'More like my escape.' Ash let them in, flicking on the lights and moving straight to the phone to check for messages. The building had been completely gutted: soundproofed, she would guess, with most of the windows covered. It was all gleaming glass, silver and chrome again, a reproduction of Ash's warehouse loft that seemed entirely out of place in the idyllic setting.

'The main studio is through here,' Ash said, leading her past a small kitchen and lounge area to the black, hi-tech refuge.

Kat traced the mixing desk and its endless rows of dials and sliders. 'Don't!' Ash jerked her hand away. 'Sorry.' He apologised, kissing the hand he'd grabbed. 'I'm kind of midway through a mix – everything's set up.'

'Oh, sorry.' Kat blushed.

'No, it's fine!' he insisted. 'I just . . . There's a method to the madness, but it's just easy to lose track of everything.'

'Can I hear what you're working on?' she asked shyly. There was something very intimate about being alone in his workspace.

'Not this.' He seemed embarrassed. 'It's not ready yet. But wait, there was something I wanted you to listen to.' Crossing the room, he settled at the large flatscreen and clicked around. 'It's not my work; it's a new Max Martin cut, out of Sweden. It won't be released for another few months, but here, listen.'

He pulled up a large, leather work-chair and Kat settled into it obediently. A moment later, the room was flooded with sound, playing in every direction from what she guessed was a superbly expensive playback system.

Teen pop?

Kat was painfully aware of Ash's excitement – tapping the beat into the polished tabletop and watching her expectantly – but she couldn't believe all the enthusiasm was inspired by this, what sounded to her like a basic trashy rock-lite song.

'So?' Ash asked, the moment the female vocal faded away.

'Umm,' Kat wondered how to put it politely. 'It's . . . not exactly my thing.'

He laughed, leaning over to kiss her. 'I can tell. You should see your face!'

'Well, do you blame me?' Kat protested. 'Disney churns out half a dozen of those girls every year. I bet she has a TV show and a merchandising deal already contracted for the next ten years.'

'Listen to it again,' Ash insisted.

'Really?'

The music began to play again. 'Just focus on the bassline,' he told her, moving some of the sliders to quieten the other parts of the song. 'Hear how it flicks around, almost like an electric current or something? And then the way the beat falls out, just there.' His face was focused, frowning as he searched for the elements. 'It's new, completely new the way he does that.'

'He?' Kat tried not to roll her eyes.

'Max is an icon,' Ash said, almost reverently. 'Behind almost every new shift in pop production for the last ten years. Britney's debut, the Backstreet Boys, and then the rock sound with Kelly Clarkson – remember that? – and . . .'

Kat listened as he ran down the chronology of his craft. The names meant nothing to her, but the look on his face as he described their sounds and impact was something that stirred her: the clear intensity for his craft. That was what she wanted: a man with passions, direction. She rose from her seat and slid into his lap, letting her hand fall at the back of his neck where she could stroke that uneven hair above his collar. Ash gently traced along her forearms until she shivered, the song starting to play again.

'Hear how it dips, right before the bridge?' His words were a whisper now in her ear, and he drummed the beat onto her bare knee, his fingers slowly inching higher.

Kat nodded, light-headed.

'And that electronic note just behind the vocals . . .' His fingers were dancing on her thigh now, his other hand tracing over her shoulder and towards her chest. Her breath caught.

324

She could hear it, now: the strange alchemy the song produced. There was a pattern in the disparate threads, a way they wound themselves around the inside of her brain. As his fingers reached those last inches higher and Kat turned to straddle his lap, a corner of her mind admitted that maybe trashy teen pop had its redeeming qualities after all.

Never be too available.

People get bored of what they know, so you've got to keep some mystery going. Accepting invitations to every event that comes your way just screams that you're a loser with nothing better to do, so turn people down sometimes, even if it's just to stay in alone. They'll think you're in demand, and appreciate you even more when you are around. Be selective about what you choose to do – will it improve your image? Is it worth your effort? If not, blow them off for something better.

Chapter Twenty-eight

And so, despite every pledge to stay cool, calm and utterly collected, Kat found herself embarking on a breathless affair with Ash – of words, that was. Over the next week they shot emails back and forth across the ether, upgraded to ongoing instant message conversations and peppered their days with texts. But thanks to Ash's looming deadlines, he was still locked away down in Sussex, and the anticipation was driving Kat to distraction.

'That's him, isn't it?' Lauren cornered her in the gym changing rooms, as Kat grabbed for her vibrating mobile. 'You're texting again.'

'Maybe.' Wrapped in nothing but a towel and wet from the showers, Kat turned her body to shield the display. She quickly scanned the short missive.

'You were right – Joss Whedon is a god. What should I try next? Xx A.'

Kat felt herself begin to grin, that same smile that crept onto her face whenever some message came from him.

'Give that to me.' Lauren snatched the phone away and scrolled through her outbox. 'Five, ten messages a day? I thought we talked about this!'

'I don't see that it's any of your business,' Kat shot back defensively.

'Hey, calm down. I'm giving it back.' Lauren gently placed the offending item on the long bench. 'Stepping away from the cell phone . . .' She put her hands up as though surrendering.

'Sorry,' Kat caught herself. 'I didn't mean to snap.' She turned away towards the lockers and began to dry off. 'But you don't have to be so disapproving.'

'Or maybe you're so defensive because you know this is all wrong,' Lauren suggested.

Kat turned and gave Lauren a sharp look.

'OK, maybe not wrong,' Lauren backtracked, shaking her hair out of its tight workout bun. 'But you're not exactly going about this the right way.'

'Let me guess: I should be using the Popularity Rules on my romantic relationships too?' Kat pulled on her black, scoop-necked T-shirt and a high-waisted black pencil-skirt with braces, finishing the look with a huge unicorn pendant in twisted metal and an armful of cuffs. She had adjusted to her new wardrobe now, used to the vivid colours and strange cuts of the fashionable clothing that made up her new look: her basic jeans and comfy boots were long gone.

'Umm, yes.' Lauren looked as if she was stating the obvious. 'It's working great for your career, in case you've already forgotten that *Rolling Stone* commission you got this morning.'

'I haven't,' Kat said, allowing herself a smile at the thought. 'But this is different, can't you see? It's a relationship. Strategising and power games would just feel wrong.'

Lauren sighed, fastening her crisp shirt dress. She obviously didn't agree. 'Well, at the very least, find out how he really feels before you get too attached.' She caught Kat's eye and groaned. 'Oh no, it's too late for that, isn't it? You're already falling for him.'

'Maybe,' Kat said quietly. 'But is that such a bad thing?'

Lauren didn't answer.

They finished dressing in silence: smoothing down hair-styles, reapplying make-up and fastening the straps on their high-heeled shoes.

'Haven't you felt this way about anyone before? The first crush part of a relationship?' Kat tried again, making an appeal to Lauren's non-existent romantic side. 'You talk as if I could just step back and be clear and rational about everything. But I can't help it, Lauren. I really want this to be something real. Can't you understand that?'

Lauren made a show of sighing, as if she was begrudging Kat some Herculean effort, but Kat thought she saw something wistful in the other woman's face. 'You take leave of all your rational faculties and you want me to understand? Oh, OK then, if I have to . . .' Hoisting her bag onto her shoulder, Lauren led the way to the exit. 'Damage limitation,' she decided. 'We need to do some serious damage limitation, no question about it.'

Lauren's plan was, in essence, a slow fade. Kat couldn't just cut off all communication with Ash, since having established 'communicative norms', any sudden switch would apparently be a big deal. Instead, she had to redraw their boundaries slowly to be more in her favour, starting with leaving ten minutes before replying to each text or email, and gradually working up until whole hours passed without word. The next time they saw each other – for backstreet Thai food, a bad rock gig and at least four orgasms – he was the one to make the trip up to London, and as for the IM window always blinking in the corner of her screen, Kat began to ignore his messages: chatting only occasionally, briefly, and always being the one who had to leave the conversation first.

'Give him a chance to miss you,' Lauren advised. 'And give

yourself a chance to come down off all this frenzied dopamine in your system.'

There was something to the drugs comment, Kat realised over the next few days. With Lauren keeping careful watch (Kat drew the line at having her mobile phone confiscated), the state of constant expectation she'd been working herself into began to ease – not entirely, since her stomach still skipped like a teenager's at the sight of him – but enough that she could actually focus on her career again. Luckily, the Popularity Rules foundations laid by her high-profile partying and first few commissions proved to be solid; Kat's mind may have been scattered in a haze of distraction, but she snapped back to a reality full of freelance commissions, exclusive invites and a long, long list of unreturned, begging calls.

'I'm going to need a new number,' Kat announced, swinging her bag down ceremoniously onto a low tabletop already cluttered with bar debris. It was midnight, and the usual crowd was sprawled in the Shoreditch haunt that had quickly become their regular, thanks to the slick design, free drinks and control of the DJ booth that Freddie's business investment merited. 'Something private just for friends and actual colleagues, as opposed to every desperate PR person in the city – present company excluded, of course, Lacey,' she added as an afterthought.

'No problem!' Lacey leapt up, her tiny shorts revealing a long expanse of tanned flesh. 'Here, take my seat. I'm just heading to the bar.'

'Angel.' Kat collapsed on the vast velvet couch next to Gabi and her sweetly geeky new girlfriend, Mia, intertwined as usual. 'What do you think, guys? I swear I spent three hours today listening to marketing spiel.'

'Whatever. I'd play you the tiny violin of pity if it wasn't too hot for the effort.' Only Oscar's lips moved, his body stretched comatose on another couch. 'It's inhumane, I swear. Weather like this, I should be skinny-dipping in St Bart's or quaffing oysters in Sri Lanka, not melting in this fucking city.'

'So why aren't you?' Lauren interrupted, pushing his legs aside and taking the seat.

'Freddie needs to be in town for business: no long-haul flights.' Oscar pouted. Kat decided not to remind him that he could just as easily be cataloguing the folk music section back in Brighton as living a life of leisure in his sugar daddy's million-pound warehouse flat.

'Boo hoo.' Lauren had no such qualms. 'It's called having a job.'

'I do so have a job!' he protested. 'That slave-driver, Mackenzie, had me filing circulation figures for hours today; I got ink-stains all over me. See.' Oscar presented his almost-spotless hands for inspection.

'Poor dear,' Kat winked, reaching over to ruffle his hair. Oscar flinched away and immediately began smoothing it back into shape.

'I brought that mix I told you about, Kat,' a voice piped up from one of the tables around the central lounge area. Kat tried quickly to place her as the vaguely familiar woman passed her a CD. Their clique had expanded to feature a periphery of stylish friends-of-friends from parties and gigs, and Kat tried her best to keep track of them. Celia? Clara? Cara, that was it – with the severe Louise Brooks bob and a penchant for tiny, retro-print T-shirts.

'Thanks Cara,' she smiled warmly, taking the time to scan the track-listing before tucking it in her bag. 'The Chromeo remix is the killer one, didn't you say?'

'Right!' Cara beamed. 'It's a total change from their usual material, but . . .' She launched into an enthusiastic analysis of production techniques while Kat restrained herself from reaching for her mobile, currently vibrating in her pocket. After a respectable pause – by which point Cara and Mia were off on a tangent about festival line-ups – she slipped it out and read:

'This weekend's a no-go, I'm afraid. Too much work! Xxx'

'What's wrong?' Lauren must have caught her expression.

'Oh, nothing.' Kat tried to shake it off. It wasn't as if they'd made actual plans, she told herself. Ash had only suggested that 'maybe' they could meet up that weekend, so technically she hadn't been stood up. Still, Kat couldn't deny her disappointment.

'God, love, cheer up. You look like someone just crucified your fucking puppy.' Freddie strolled over, leaning down to kiss Oscar and then perching on the edge of the couch like a prince surveying his kingdom. A prince wearing a white linen suit and lilac shirt even in eighty-degree weather.

'No, I'm fine!' Kat started to insist, but then she stopped, struck by a sudden thought. 'Actually . . .' She let her tone become more melancholy, and sank back into the soft cushions with a limp movement.

'What?' Cara asked. 'Are you OK?'

Kat shrugged. 'Just some personal stuff.' She let out a listless sigh. 'I thought I could ignore it, but . . .' She caught Lauren's concerned gaze for a second, and then a look of understanding passed between them. This was part of Kat's plan.

'Is it the thing Annette was blogging?' Lacey asked.

'What thing?'

'Oh, no, don't worry,' Lacey quickly covered. 'And anyway, you shouldn't pay attention to that tabloid crap.'

Kat wanted to find out more, but she had a performance to maintain. She gave another sigh. 'I don't know. I just can't seem to get out of this mood.'

'We can't stand for that,' Freddie declared. 'What do you need: booze, pills, coke?'

'Nothing, thanks.' Kat looked around at the group of concerned faces. 'No, really guys,' she protested weakly. 'Don't worry. I'll be fine, honest.'

'Of course you will,' Freddie nodded, 'Because we're going to make sure of it. Now, what's happening tonight?'

'Silversmith are playing Metro,' Cara offered.

'Boring,' Freddie vetoed.

'They're doing a Lynch retrospective at the BFI,' Mia pitched in.

'She's already fucking depressed!'

'Take That's at G-A-Y, again,' Oscar added.

'People, come on. Where's your sense of imagination?'

'It's not our fault,' Gabi protested. 'Everyone's out of town. It's summer, remember?'

'Hmmm . . .' Freddie drummed his fingers on his thigh for a moment. 'They are, aren't they? So what the fuck are we still doing here?'

'You told me—' Oscar began to speak.

'That was a rhetorical question, love.' Freddie stood up. 'I'll be right back.'

He swaggered away, iPhone already out, and the rest of the group rushed to fill his void: cracking jokes, telling their best anecdotes, and generally doing everything possible to bring a smile to Kat's face. She sat quietly in the midst of it. Strategic displays of vulnerability would inspire affection, the Popularity Rules had said, but the rush of goodwill her small sadness had inspired was more than she'd ever expected.

'All right, it's sorted.' Freddie reappeared, looking smug. 'Car's on the way. I usually give the Secret Garden Party a miss – all those fucking hippy kids wafting around – but this girl needs something to cheer her up. What do you say to some fresh air in the countryside?'

Obligation takes two.

Despite what the world tries to teach us, you don't owe anything. The big secret is that social conventions only work if you decide to accept them: unless you agree to some unspoken obligation, it doesn't apply. So what if he bought you dinner? His mistake. She did you a favor? You don't have to repay it. These things are unspoken because they're awkward, so most people won't call you on it if you act oblivious to your end of the bargain.

You're a big girl – so make decisions for your own sake. Just realise that people will expect something in return for everything they do, and they'll be mad if you refuse to play along.

Chapter Twenty-nine

Speeding down a dark motorway in the back of a chauffeur-driven limo that night, Kat finally saw the temptations of insider access and ridiculous privilege, not just as a means to an end in getting her job back, or serving the Popularity Rules, but as a way of life. No crowded station platforms or endless front-gate lines, no scouring eBay for last-minute cheap tickets or spending hours cajoling a promo company for a precious press pass; Freddie simply made a few calls and voilà! Kat was curled up on the soft black leather between Oscar and Gabi, heading towards the deepest English countryside and a weekend of fun.

'None of that camping bullshit,' Freddie smirked, managing not to spill champagne as he poured glasses for them all. 'You think I own a sleeping bag?'

'He's right,' Lauren grinned, her usual nonchalance slipping just a little. Whether she was happy about their getaway or the fact that Freddie was clearly trying to impress, Kat wasn't sure. 'They've got a luxury zone full of furnished yurts, haute cuisine, even a spa.'

'You'll be under the stars, listening to some acoustic indie wanker by morning,' Oscar added, munching on a bag of nuts from the mini-bar.

'Then it sounds wonderful.' Kat managed to strike the right mix of dispirited gratitude. 'Thank you, Freddie.'

'No worries, love.' He looked supremely self-satisfied.

'Can't have you moping around now, can we?'

'But what about luggage?' Kat gasped suddenly. 'I don't have anything on me: no clothes, or a toothbrush—'

'Isn't she sweet?' Lauren interrupted with a quick laugh. Kat fell silent. Of course; a jaded scene star wouldn't get worked up over a clean change of underwear. She was supposed to be the kind of carefree party-girl who jetted off at a moment's notice. Luckily, no one seemed to notice her slip, and soon the chatter and gossip was whirling around her again, while Kat wondered what exactly she was supposed to wear tomorrow.

'Don't worry,' Lauren said later, when Freddie and Oscar were busy murmuring God knows what to each other and Gabi and Mia were sleeping, heads on each other's shoulders. It was almost dawn, and the sky was beginning to pale outside the tinted limo windows as they passed through small villages and fields. 'They'll have packs of toiletries and clothes and things waiting for us.'

'I just click my fingers and it all magically appears?' Kat yawned, liking this new way of doing things.

'Pretty much.' Lauren pulled a jacket around them.

'Life on the inside, huh?'

'Nothing like it.'

Kat woke later that morning tucked between crisp linens in a queen-sized bed, wooden decking on the ground, swathes of pale fabric rustling above her and only the scent of fresh flowers on her bedside cabinet hinting at the fact she was in the middle of a field, and not staying in a luxury hotel.

'Now this is my kind of festival.' She rolled over. Lauren was on the other side of the tall tent in her own comfortable bed, early-morning sunlight creeping through the gaps in their 'doorway'.

'Mhmmmhm.'

'I'm never getting buried in mud again. Or standing in line for half an hour to use the overflowing Portaloo. Or paying six pounds for a dodgy kebab.' Kat bounced out of bed, suddenly energised. 'Coming to check out the showers?'

'Mnnueh.' Lauren buried herself back in the pile of pillows. 'Maybe later.'

Pulling on her complimentary robe and flip-flops, Kat grabbed her bag and ventured out into the haven of a VIP area. In the valley below she could see a sprawl of tents, but around her, the strange canopied yurts were set up in small cul-de-sacs, with sheltered walkways leading through the neat grass to an array of spa areas, concessions and little cafes set up under brightly multi-coloured awnings. She took a deep breath of fresh, non-polluted air and couldn't help but smile.

Yes, VIP access could be a marvellous thing.

After making plentiful use of the counter-top full of products in the spotless, gleaming shower area, Kat stopped for a bacon sandwich; apparently it was locally raised, humanely slaughtered and no doubt trained to trot in formation, but Kat's growling stomach cared only that it was thick-cut and smothered in ketchup. She sat in blissful silence beneath the trees, peacefully contemplating nature, the unexpected joys of life, the curious—

'Fuck me, I'm famished.' Oscar collapsed next to her with a moan. He was wearing a neon-pink tank top and skinny jeans cut off above the ankle, looking far too bright and artificial for her idyllic pastoral scene.

Kat sighed, shifting over to avoid his bony limbs. 'So get some food then.'

Oscar sneered. 'Everything's so healthy, all alfalfa this and beansprout that.' Kat brandished her bacon sarnie as evidence to the contrary. 'Well yes,' he acknowledged, 'but think of the saturated fat! It'll play havoc on my pores.'

Kat took another bite and concentrated on chewing. She could tolerate Oscar's camp theatrics when they were diluted in a group setting, or if Lauren was around to pet and tend to him, but alone, he was just too much for her.

'I checked the line-up today,' he continued unawares. 'Nothing but wimpy acoustic dudes breathing softly into the mic, or whatever. And there's circus performances, can you imagine? I walked out of our yurt right into a troupe of clowning dwarves – thought I was still tripping off the pills I took last night. Should have paid more attention to what they were, I suppose, but they were the cutest little things printed with rainbows and—'

'Oscar!'

'What?' He pouted at her.

Kat let her breath hiss through her clenched teeth. 'Can you just dial it down for five minutes, please? Relax, enjoy the scenery, I don't care – just quit with the drama queen routine already.'

There was silence.

'OK.' Oscar shrugged, his voice suddenly at least two octaves lower. 'No need to get so hormonal; you should have said something earlier.'

Kat blinked at him. His outrageous gossiping tone was gone and instead he had a look of quiet contemplation on his face. It was the first time she could remember seeing his features still, not stretched in motion.

Oscar noticed her surprise. 'You don't think I get sick of it sometimes too?' His expression was wistful, the boy she thought she knew suddenly somebody else entirely. 'It's fucking exhausting.'

'So why do it?' Kat was baffled.

Oscar rolled his eyes. 'Come on, the "gay best friend" routine? It's the easiest way to get by. Like being the court jester or whatever.'

Kat started to protest, but the truth of it couldn't be denied. He was fun, an amusement – even she had thought of him as a puppy dog to keep around as entertainment. She hadn't thought for one second he was pretending as well. Pretending to be what he thought people wanted from him.

'Maybe you don't have to put on an act,' she suggested softly.

'Oh really, Ms "I adore wearing three ounces of product in my hair and hanging in the VIP section"?' Oscar surveyed her with amusement. She wondered for a minute if he had picked up something about the Popularity Rules. 'I knew you back in the olden days, remember – when you bitched your way through every article.'

'OK, so I'm hardly the one to talk,' she admitted, relieved her secret wasn't out. 'But there's a difference between changing the surface details and pretending to be someone else entirely!'

At least, she liked to think there was.

Oscar shrugged again. 'It's not so bad. Better than being stuck in Lower Higglebottom, anyways.'

Kat smiled. 'It's actually called that? I thought you were joking.'

'I never joke about that town. Well, village, to be precise.' Oscar darkened. 'Complete with one corner shop, half a garage and five pubs. And a broken-down bus-shelter to loiter around.'

'All the essential services then.'

'Exactly.'

'It's not an either-or thing, you know,' Kat tried again, licking a glob of ketchup from her fingers. 'We're not going to send you back there if you don't provide constant entertainment.'

'Oh really?' Oscar looked dubious. 'I never took you for the optimist.'

'Come on, you don't—'

'There you are, love!' Kat was interrupted as Freddie swaggered over with a clique of stylish strangers. 'Hiding away in the forest; we can't have that.' Lazily lifting his camera away from his body, Freddie shot away in quick succession. 'Hmmm,' he said, regarding the display. 'Not your best angle. We can delete those. So, what's happening?'

'Bugger all,' Oscar declared, his arch voice back. He leapt up and bestowed a kiss on Freddie's cheek. 'Which is why you're here, to save us from our dull selves. After all, you were the one who dragged us to this godforsaken hippie commune.'

Freddie chuckled, clearly charmed. 'And you, Kat?'

'Oh, I'm just seeing where the day takes me.' She made the effort to smile, despite the faint pang she felt watching Oscar bounce around in his jester role again.

Freddie held out his hand and pulled her to her feet. 'The day is taking you over to the artists' camp for some fun and frolics.'

'Fun *and* frolics?' Kat joked, as the group moved away. 'I usually settle for either.'

Kat had sworn off festivals for good after a particularly muddy, miserable weekend chasing metal acts around Reading, but she had to admit that getting a soft, cushioned night's sleep far away from Chaz and Mike from Essex and their all-night chug-a-thon gave her an entirely new perspective. The day was warm, the lush fields surrounded them with green, and the artists' compound was a relaxing mix of Pimm's, sun loungers and the occasional softly strummed guitar. Of course, the industrial quantities of dope being smoked might also have something to do with the chilled atmosphere, but Kat was determined to focus on the positives. Oscar was wrong: she could be an optimist. Sometimes.

'Pass the sunscreen,' she asked lazily, stretched on a vast red-and-white check picnic blanket with their group, a couple of unshaven rock stars, and the ubiquitous array of long-limbed models. 'Oh, come on!' she protested, as Gabi and Mia rolled over, squealing between kisses. They were both wearing tiny bikini tops and hotpants, and the rock stars were watching the show with blatant leers. 'Keep it clean!'

'Jealous!' Gabi retorted, sticking her tongue out.

'Am not!' Kat cried, but she found herself reaching for her mobile all the same. No messages from Ash. She tried not to be disappointed.

'Advertising, huh?' On the other side of the blanket, a messy-haired blond man was focused intently on Lauren, his stubble, crumpled woven shirt and string bracelets all broadcasting his hippie musician background as loudly as the guitar resting by his side. 'Don't you find that lifestyle just so numbing?'

'No.' Lauren ignored his obvious interest, sipping mineral water and checking her electronic organiser, for what Kat knew must be the tenth time.

'I used to be in that too, the whole corporate grind scene.' Undeterred, he began talking about his breakdown and rebirth as a new, holistic kind of man, but Lauren just rolled her eyes and started talking to Freddie about his new exhibit while the angelic hippie fell silent, looking on with barely disguised adoration.

'You should give him a chance,' Kat suggested, when – after four hours consuming only alcohol and cucumber slices – she dragged Lauren in search of food. 'He seems nice.'

'I'm sure he is.' Lauren's voice wasn't exactly enthusiastic.

'So . . . ?'

'So, nothing.' She began walking again, skirting around a puddle and cutting through a cluster of tour buses.

'You haven't seen anyone in the past couple of months,' Kat remarked, shooting her a sideways glance. 'Not even a single date.'

'I've been busy, remember?' Lauren's face remained impassive behind her shades. 'With that little thing called work, and oh yes: remaking your entire life.'

'All work and no play . . .'

'Makes me a wealthy professional success,' Lauren finished, more than a touch defensive. 'And what do you want – me to waste whole hours of my time? Women decide within four seconds whether they're sexually attracted to a man. I don't want to sleep with him, so that's the end of it.'

Kat sighed. 'Well, when you put it like that . . .'

Lauren paused. 'And I won't even start on the "pot calling kettle black" part of this conversation.'

'I have Ash!' she protested.

'But you don't. Have him, I mean,' Lauren corrected her gently. 'Do you?'

Kat crossed her arms and regretted starting the conversation at all. 'I'm just saying you should give people a chance sometimes.'

'Oh really?' Lauren was looking over Kat's shoulder with a satisfied smile.

'Yes, really,' Kat insisted. 'If that's one thing all this networking crap has taught me, it's that not everyone is as worthless as they first seem. Take Lacey: she's not entirely irritating after all. And I was talking to Oscar earlier, and he—'

There was a nervous cough behind her, and Lauren's smile spread into a full-on beam. Kat turned.

'Er, all right?'

Dishevelled black hair. Rock star dirty denim.

'Devon Darsel.'

Everyone has their uses.

———— ⊗⊗⊗ ————

Think of your conscience as being like a muscle: if you don't use it for long enough, eventually it'll waste away. This is a good thing. Years of training have probably made you squeamish about blatant manipulation and shamelessly exploiting people to suit your own ends, but keep working, and you'll soon get the hang of it.

Assess every new person you meet for possible benefits, and be sure to cultivate friendships with the ones who have the most to offer. You want people who throw the hottest parties, have the richest, best-connected families, and the cutest friends. But even if someone doesn't have all that, they can still be useful as a loyal lapdog, or someone to take the fall for you. It just needs a little imagination...

Chapter Thirty

It was inevitable, she thought, surveying her least favourite person in the world. Kat should have known that showering her office with flowers, candy and sappy lyrics wasn't enough for such an egomaniac: no, he had to follow her to the furthest corners of the earth. Or rather, Somerset.

Lauren greeted Devon with more enthusiasm. 'Hi, great to meet you, mwah mwah.' She kissed him on both cheeks, smiling brightly and altogether acting as if he wasn't the Antichrist.

'Hi Kat.' He looked at her with puppy-dog eyes, hands jammed awkwardly in his pockets and hair in his face.

Kat glared back.

'Uh, what's up?' He blinked back and forth between them.

'We were just finding Kat some food,' Lauren replied cheerfully. 'But I have to head . . . away, so why don't you join her instead?'

'Lauren!' Kat hissed.

'Don't mind her,' Lauren quickly reassured Devon. 'She gets super-cranky when her blood sugar's low.'

'Oh, right. Like withdrawal.' He nodded slowly.

'Just give us a minute!' Lauren grabbed Kat's arm and pulled her away, into the shade of a psychedelic grafittied minivan. A few feet away, a group of long-haired boys in leather trousers and not much else lazed in the sun, painting each other's bare torsos with glow-in-the-dark painted swirls.

'What the hell?' Kat exclaimed, shaking free from Lauren's vice-like grip. 'Have you completely lost your mind? You want me to have lunch with him – the statutory rapist drug addict!'

Lauren waved away her protest. 'You shouldn't exaggerate like that; libel laws in this country are ridiculous.'

'Bu—'

'You said it yourself,' Lauren continued. Her smile was edged with smug satisfaction: she was enjoying this, Kat could tell. 'Giving people second chances. Looking beyond the first impression.'

'I've known Devon for two years.'

'Then shouldn't you be on better terms by now?'

Kat couldn't even find the words.

'Think, Kat.' Lauren's voice dropped, and she looked back at Devon meaningfully. 'He's a rock star. *The* rock star. And you're a journalist, looking for that dynamite story that will get you back in at *Think Louder*.'

The Popularity Rules. Of course.

'But *him*?' Kat moaned. 'Don't you remember the last time I was alone with him? I'm more likely to snap and stab him with a tent pole than pick up anything useful.'

Lauren laughed, beginning to steer her back towards where Devon was waiting, signing some breathless teenager's buxom chest. 'You're the strongest person I know. You can handle this, I promise.'

'I'll handle a tent pole all right too,' Kat muttered darkly, but she managed to stretch a faint smile across her face when they reached Devon, now surrounded by a gaggle of teenage girls.

'So, are we doing this?' He finished scrawling his name with a flourish and turned back to Kat.

'Are you on something?' she asked bluntly. Lauren gasped.

'No!' He had the gall to look hurt. 'I've been clean for a month now. Well, except for that time in Tunbridge Wells, but really, can you blame me?' He shook his head, the Irish accent becoming more pronounced. 'Tunbridge fucking Wells!'

'Fine then,' Kat finally agreed, regretting the words even as they left her lips. 'You can buy me lunch. But only on one condition.'

'Anything,' he declared, eager.

'You don't bother me again after this, understand?' Kat tried to sound resolute. 'No flowers, no phone calls, not even those little truffle things.'

Devon seemed to deflate, looking at her plaintively from below those thick eyelashes. 'But—'

'Deal?' Kat interrupted. She'd had enough.

Devon blinked. Probably not used to the eyelash trick failing him, Kat decided. 'OK,' he sighed. 'Deal.'

'Right.' Kat pulled herself up to her full height, shot one final glare at Lauren, and attempted to think calm, non-violent thoughts. 'Let's get this over with.'

They found a cafe set up nearby with woven rugs, cushions and dangling bunches of herbs for the authentic tapas experience. To Kat's relief, the dining area was shady, secluded, and most importantly, free from any more breathless teenage girls ready to tear their shirts off in offering to their god. She collapsed to the ground under a tree and ordered them some sangria.

'Mineral water, cheers,' Devon corrected the waitress, who was visibly swooning. An autograph, photo and lingering hug later, they were finally left alone.

'So you're serious about being clean?' Kat asked dubiously. Plastic cutlery, she noted – that was good – and paper cups instead of smashable glass, but still, those cords keeping the herbs in place . . . She could do some damage with them if worst came to worst.

Devon was playing with the paper napkin, tearing it into precise strips. He looked vaguely healthier than when she'd seen him last, Kat had to admit. His skin was merely pale, not pallid, and his hair might even have been washed some time that week. Devon gave an awkward kind of shrug. 'I guess.'

'Well,' she managed. 'That's . . . something.'

Another shrug.

Kat tried not to roll her eyes, waiting for the devoted waitress to bring their drinks and take her food order before speaking again. That was one advantage to dining with rock stars: the service really was excellent. 'Well?' she asked. 'Don't you have anything to say? Wasn't the whole point of your stalker routine to actually talk to me?'

He avoided her eyes, almost bashful. 'I guess.'

'You guess?' Kat sighed impatiently. 'You've been hassling me for ages, and now after all that, you just sit there?' She was going to kill Lauren. Or at the very least, force her to sit through the entire series of *The West Wing*.

'It's not . . .' Devon mumbled. 'It's like, different, you know. Now you're actually here. Like, I don't know,' he continued eloquently, looking up to meet her eyes. 'I'm sorry. For what happened that time.'

Kat stared at him in disbelief, still shredding napkins like a minor-level OCD patient. This was absurd. Three letters, a hot-house worth of flowers and enough Godiva chocolates to make the *ChicK* intern gain five pounds, and the most he could muster was 'Like, I don't know'?

God, he really was just a petulant child, Kat realised, as a ray of sunlight fell through the leaves, like a light bulb switching on. Without his microphone and an armful of chemicals, he was nothing but an awkward, moody boy with no grasp of reality. All this time she'd been raging at him as if his choices were conscious – some kind of misogynistic ideology – when really . . .

Petulant. Pathetic. Child.

She took a gulp of her drink and studied him. Her mother would have a field day with this.

'So, you're sorry.' Kat was struck by an unfamiliar sense of charity. Or maybe that was just the sangria. 'What have you done about it?'

'What do you mean?' Devon seemed bemused. 'I've tried to tell you. Like, the flowers, and the song, and I've even been writing something for the next album—'

'Not for me,' Kat explained slowly. 'For the others. You know,' she continued, noting his blank expression, 'all the women you've treated badly. The groupies and the interns and everyone else.'

'Oh.' Devon blinked. 'Them.'

Kat took a deep breath. 'Yes, them,' she replied evenly. 'If you're really sorry about the way you behaved, then I'm not the only one you need to make it up to.'

'OK,' he nodded, breaking into a puppy-dog grin. His dark eyes fixed on her intently, and for a moment, Kat could almost see what Jessica and all those fluttering girls found so attractive: the nineteenth-century tragic poet look wasn't to be underestimated. Then he tore off a section of bread roll and talked with his mouth full, spraying crumbs all over the chequered tablecloth. The moment passed. 'I'll do it, I'll do whatever.'

'That's it?' Kat asked, her voice heavy with scepticism. 'Overnight you're a different person?'

'I can try.'

350

'Sure you can,' she agreed. 'But do you understand what I mean?' Kat appreciated for the first time what nursery teachers must suffer. 'About how you treat women.'

'I guess.' Devon sank a little lower into the cushions. 'I've been better though, since I've been clean.' He looked at her hopefully. 'I even went out with this girl from a show, instead of just . . .' He stopped. 'You know.'

She knew.

'That's . . . good.' Kat tried to put herself in the mindset where buying a girl dinner before fucking and forgetting her was an improvement. 'At least you're trying.'

'I am,' he answered plaintively, sitting back to let the waitress put down their plates. Kat breathed in and attempted to concentrate on what Devon was saying, but the to food made it difficult. 'It's hard to respect them, that's all. Like when you're on the road and they blow half the roadies just to get backstage.'

Kat sent an apologetic look at the waitress, but she was still gazing at him in awe. 'So don't hang around those sorts of people,' she suggested, taking a forkful of braised lamb and trying not to swoon at the taste. 'You can stay away from that scene.' Had anybody told him to just say no?

'I do, but the rest of the band are just as bad.' He scowled at the mention of them. 'Now I'm sober – well, trying – they're being complete arses.'

'Suddenly?'

'Maybe they were all along,' Devon admitted sheepishly. 'But now, like, I notice it.'

'Mhnm,' Kat mumbled through some sizzling prawns. He took that as encouragement and sat up a little straighter.

'They don't even put the practice time in any more. And Carl keeps skipping studio sessions, and Artie only wants to play stupid soft-rock.' He grabbed some bread and dunked it angrily in the bowl of olive oil. 'It's like they only care about the fame shit now.'

Kat looked over at the man who had made his entrance to the MTV awards flanked by ten models with negligees and matching 'DD' tattoos.

'What?' he glared at her. 'It's important. The demos for the new record sound piss-poor. The label keeps sending in these wanker producers with whinging songwriters; we're going to end up sounding like bloody Coldplay at this rate!' He stuck his bottom lip out petulantly. 'All the label shit is driving me mad. Stylists and PR chicks and audience bloody feedback managers. Fucking idiots!' Kat raised her eyebrows pointedly at the swearing. 'Sorry,' he muttered. 'It just winds me up, that's all. Fucking vultures.'

'Then do something about it.' Kat was unsympathetic.

'What do you mean?'

'If you don't like it, change.' She surveyed the crumpled figure in front of her. He really was hopeless. 'You're the lead singer, remember? They can't do anything without you.'

'Yeah, but you haven't seen what it's like.' He pouted again. 'The touring and promos and bloody chat-show smile marathons. I can't change it! Sometimes I feel like quitting altogether.'

'OK then.' Kat poured herself another glass of sangria. 'Quit.'

'But I can't!' He looked at her, horrified.

'So deal with it!' This time, she couldn't help but roll her eyes. 'It's your life. If you don't make it so that you get what you want, nobody else will.' She batted his fork away from her plate. 'Hands off; this is mine.'

'But what would I do?' he frowned. 'I've only ever done this.'

'Stick to songwriting, go solo, start a charity foundation promoting better attitudes to women in the music industry,' she suggested, rapidly approaching the limits of her tolerance. 'Move to New Zealand and start sheep farming, for all I care. It's not like you need to worry about money.'

'I guess I could . . .' Devon's eyes began to brighten. 'But would it work? I mean, what if I crashed?'

'Then you start again,' Kat told him simply, recalling her days of lonely unemployment. 'But don't sit here complaining if you won't get off your arse and actually do something about it.'

'Quit,' he repeated thoughtfully. 'Just like that?'

'Just like that.' She flagged down their waitress again, sensing her work there was done. 'Can I get some more of the prawns?'

Learn to read.

If you take the time to look around, it's totally obvious: people have no control over their bodies, so they can't help giving their game away. A blink, a flinch – watch every move they make and you'll soon know how they feel better than even they do. Don't be fooled by big gestures or anything they say, because it's the tiny details that matter. She may swear she's telling you the truth, but if her breathing gets quicker or she can't hold eye-contact, that girl is lying through her teeth.

Use these clues to get further. Put them at ease, make them feel good and take control of the situation.

Chapter Thirty-one

'She's doing it again!'

'Who's doing what to whom?' Lauren looked up from her screen. It was a week after the festival, and as promised, Devon's tide of gifts had come to an abrupt stop, meaning Kat could actually see across their *ChicK* office without a miniature rose garden obstructing her view.

'Jessica, planting all these lies online.' Kat swiftly emailed the links over. 'See? We've got to do something!'

'Hang on.' Lauren scanned the pages. 'But these are blind items; how do you know it's her?'

'Oh, I know.' Kat's sunny mood had disappeared at the first thought of that woman's dismissive sneer. 'Who else would bother putting time and energy into badmouthing me?'

Lauren grinned. 'Because there's no way you have any other enemies . . .'

'Lauren!'

'Relax, it's fine,' she insisted. 'I don't know why you're getting so wound up. Remember, never believe your own press.'

Kat took a few short breaths. Calming thoughts, calming thoughts. 'Can we post some things about her?' she suggested. Lauren just raised her eyebrows. 'I know, sinking to her level, et cetera,' Kat admitted, slumping back in her seat. 'She just gets me so angry. I don't know why!'

'She's your nemesis.' Lauren shrugged. 'We all have to have one.'

'So who's yours?' Kat looked around for the last remnants of a box of Turkish delight.

'Melinda Roberts,' Lauren answered immediately, a tense look drifting over her face. 'We started as associates together at my first job, only she got promoted to partner within two years instead of me.'

'What?' Kat said in mock-disbelief. 'Somebody beat you for something?'

Lauren's lips thinned. 'Turns out all the strategising in the world won't help you if you don't fuck the CEO.'

'Ouch.'

'So, I left and started up on my own. I've won the last three accounts they pitched for,' she added with a satisfied smile, 'and if I have my way on this next project, it'll be four.'

'Anything I can help with?'

Lauren shrugged. 'We'll see. I'm still in the planning stages. But my sources say that if she loses another one, she's history.'

'So you know what I mean then, with all my irrational loathing.' Kat's focus drifted back to the vicious rumours on her screen involving her, three grams of coke and all of the Polaroid Kids. With an underage Estonian foot model.

'I do,' Lauren reassured her. 'But this stuff is too crazy for anyone to believe. And besides, the underdog status is always a good thing.'

'I suppose . . .' Kat gathered all her willpower and navigated away from the gossip pages. 'Although—' She caught sight of Gabi walking down the corridor, her usually perky expression morose and, worse than that, wearing shapeless generic jeans and an oversize college jumper. 'Umm, Lauren?' She nodded through the plate glass as Gabi passed. Lauren's eyes widened.

'Come on.'

They found Gabi deep in the fashion closet, picking through returns bags with pale dejection.

'Honey, what's the matter?' Lauren navigated her way around piles of clothing. 'This place is . . . a mess.'

Something was definitely wrong, Kat could tell. Gabi may be haphazard about many things in life, but fashion was not one of them.

'I got my dream job, in New York, for when our contract's up here.'

'But that's great!' Lauren cried.

'Congratulations.' Kat hugged her. 'Isn't that a good thing?'

A tear trickled down Gabi's cheek. Apparently not. 'I broke up with Mia.'

'Oh.'

Gabi collapsed, cross-legged on the floor. Lauren and Kat gingerly slid down and joined her on either side. The office had emptied out for lunch; now there was only the distant hum of a radio and abandoned phones ringing.

'I thought things were going well with you guys,' Kat ventured. 'It's been, what, a month?'

'Five weeks.' Gabi picked at the fraying cuff on her jeans. She fell silent again.

'So . . . ?' Lauren gently prompted.

'So, I'm leaving at the end of summer,' she sighed. 'And what's the point of falling for her more if it's just going to get messy and brutal in the end?'

There was silence. It was true.

Kat rubbed Gabi's shoulder sympathetically, but she didn't try to offer platitudes. They all were realists. There was no point in saying comforting things about loving and losing, about it always being worth it. Because honestly, Kat didn't think it was. Why set yourself up for heartbreak if the end was already in sight? Why put yourself through that pain for just a month or two of happiness?

'You could make it work.'

Both Kat and Gabi turned to Lauren in surprise.

'It's just a flight away, in the end, and if you have real feelings for her, you should try.' Lauren spoke with surprising sincerity.

'Long-distance relationships never work, you know that,' Kat said, careful to keep her tone supportive. What was Lauren thinking? 'You've probably got a host of statistics and studies saying just that.'

Lauren picked at her clear nailpolish. 'Have you ever done it?'

'No,' Kat tried again, confused. 'Because I'd never put myself in that position. And because I've never dated anyone worth trying for.'

'Exactly.' Lauren nudged Gabi gently. 'If you think Mia is worth the effort, then why not hang on to her?'

Gabi sighed, slow and full of longing. 'But I know Kat's right – it's pointless dragging out something that's doomed to total failure.'

'Isn't it all?' Lauren said, tilting her head back against the wall and looking around. 'Doomed, I mean. Every relationship ends, sooner or later. What is it you used to say, Kat? About men . . .'

'They leave, or they cheat, or they die,' she recited. Her mother had said it early and often, and Kat had never forgotten. You don't forget such a simple truth.

'And the same goes for women, I guess,' Lauren continued. 'So really, the trying part is all we can do.'

There was another long silence.

'God, we're a depressing lot.' Gabi gave a wry grin.

'Come out with us tonight,' Kat suggested, trying to lighten the mood. 'There's that ridiculous hotel destruction party thing Freddie's been going on about.'

'I don't know . . .'

'It'll be fun,' Kat insisted. 'I mean, all of London's fashion whores tearing apart a building as some kind of design statement – doesn't that just scream good times to you?'

Gabi smiled. 'Well, when you put it like that . . .' She paused, looking down the hallway. 'Umm, guys?'

Two police officers were walking towards them: a stern-looking woman and a man with a shock of red hair. For a moment, Kat wondered what kind of double-act they'd be on television: the sceptical harridan and her jovial bumbler of a partner, perhaps.

'We're looking for Katherine Elliot,' the man asked, consulting his notebook. Kat scrambled to her feet.

'That's me.' She looked back and forth between them, suddenly sick. 'Oh God, did something happen to my mother?'

'No, no,' the woman reassured her, her features softening. Not the harridan type then. 'We wanted to ask you some questions about Devon Darsel.'

'Why?' Lauren placed herself in front of Kat. 'What's this about?'

The officers exchanged a look. 'Mr Darsel is missing,' the man finally answered. 'And according to eye-witnesses, Miss Elliot here was the last person to see him.'

After lengthy questioning (with Lauren's hastily summoned solicitor standing by), Kat finally managed to convince the Greater Metropolitan Police that she had not, in fact, lured Devon to a remote field and choked him with his trademark scarf. Apparently, Devon had dropped off the face of the earth, without notifying the dozen-odd assistants, record label execs or dealers who usually followed his every move. Kat was the last person to be seen with him, and so an hour of waiting, questions and paperwork ensued.

By the time she hopped out of a cab in the unfamiliar neighbourhood, she was running far behind schedule. It was a good thing punctuality only showed obedience and pack mentality, Kat thought grimly, clutching her tiny purse closer as the dense crowd shifted and swayed. The street was seething with the shouts and cries of hungry paparazzi, panicked invitees and hopeful wannabe-guests. She stumbled on the kerb.

'Somebody should sue the organisers of this debacle.' Freddie materialised at her side, his usually spotless linen suit faintly rumpled from the melee. 'Would it have killed them to keep things orderly?'

'No, but it would have denied them the "Riot at the Roxbury" headlines they obviously want,' Kat noted, realising that the chaos was actually the result of careful planning. Nothing like a few hundred frustrated hipsters storming the streets of Mayfair to generate some press attention.

Freddie took her hand firmly. 'Once more unto the breach, dear friend!' Kat laughed. 'But whatever you do, don't let go,' he warned. 'I may not make it back for you.'

'You shouldn't!' Kat joked, holding the back of her hand to her forehead. 'Go on alone; have a long and fruitful life!'

'Be brave for me!' Freddie declared, kissing her on both cheeks before pushing his way towards the front entrance. Kat braced herself and followed in his wake, whipping past the jostling pack of hipsters and trying to keep her expression vaguely attractive for the sake of the flashing cameras.

Once they made it to the front doors, the woefully

overworked bouncers swung into action, ushering them inside to where the noise dulled to a distant roar and a different sort of crowd bustled: this one made up of black-uniformed PR staff brandishing clipboards and whispering intently into futuristic headsets.

'So they're gutting the whole building then?' Kat asked, gazing up at the faded gilt wallpaper and dull chandeliers.

'Everything but the bricks and mortar,' Freddie nodded, shooing a list girl away with his 'Don't you know who I am?' stare. 'It's a shame; I wish people would start restoring the historical details instead of going for another bloody minimalist look, but what can you do?'

'Pick up a sledgehammer and join in.' Kat scribbled her signature at the bottom of a very long legal disclaimer form. She wasn't sure her plunging metallic blue dress and stacked heels were quite the attire for a demolition job, but she knew a good photo opportunity when she saw one. 'Where's Oscar, by the way? I wouldn't have thought he'd miss a spectacle like this.'

Freddie shrugged. 'He knew I'd be working, so . . . Harry!' He yelled across the room, greeting the slim man with back-slapping and manly enthusiasm. Kat smilingly made her introductions and then excused herself with promises to pose for Freddie later. 'I want you beating the shit out of a bathroom suite,' he insisted.

'It would be my pleasure.'

Lauren was still tied up with work, so Kat moved through the fashionable throngs alone, stopping to say hi to Cara (the MTV producer) or Nicolai (the T-shirt designer) and any of the other hip young scene things she knew from their ever-decreasing circles of cool. Some of the hotel rooms had been turned into art installations by hot young names, while others played host to noisy rock bands, happily fulfilling their childhood dreams of trashing a hotel, without facing a hefty clean-up bill. Every corridor was packed with the fashionista elite, brandishing digital cameras and demi-bottles of champagne, their T-shirts oversized, their leggings multi-coloured and their expressions a curious mix of careful nonchalance and insider glee.

Kat took some champagne from a far table as her prop for the night and reviewed her careful action plan. She'd called ahead for the early RSVP list, and thanks to a few moments sympathising with a harried intern, she'd had plenty of time to plot her attack. Three primary targets, a dozen minors to make contact with, and enough circulating to ensure mentions in any party reports and thus keep her profile high. Kat wanted at least two solid freelancing leads by the end of the night, if not an actual commission. Checking her reflection in a broken shard of mirror on the wall, she wiped away a smudge of harlot red lipstick and adopted the perfect casual stare.

She had work to do.

'. . . And don't say I told you, but I saw the preview tapes for the next episode, and Tyler does all kinds of things in the hot-tub with that Tasha girl!' An hour later, Kat was regaling her group with spoilers from a mindless faux-reality show. The appeal of the clique of vapid girls on-screen was entirely beyond her – as anything more than a cautionary tale about the effects of early exposure to *Cosmo* magazine, lax parenting and shocking amounts of disposable income, that was – but she faithfully watched the screener episodes at *ChicK* every week for just such small-talk material.

'Ohmygod! Shannon must have lost it!' A doe-eyed model in a wisp of chiffon looked delighted at news of the betrayal.

'Absolutely.' Kat grinned. 'You have to watch.'

'I don't know why they even call them "reality" shows any more,' a tall man interrupted, his black shirt powdered with a faint coating of concrete dust. 'Everyone knows they're all scripted and shot like real dramas.'

Kat recognised him as one of her editor targets in an instant – after assembling photos and detailed history files of all of them, how could she not? – but feigned a blank stare anyway. 'I see it as a natural evolution,' she suggested. 'We had the surge to old-style pure reality because we wanted to indulge our voyeurism, but all the boring *Big Brother* exploits made us long for the aspirational element of entertainment again, the escapism.'

'You mean it was *too* real?' He laughed.

'Exactly!' Kat focused on him with an arch smile. 'Watching drunk louts fight and fuck is fine if we want to feel superior to people, but at the end of the day, we long for pretty people and dramatic entanglements, to feel as if that version of reality is within our reach. Hence the synthesis of all these new semi-scripted docu-dramas.'

The man studied her for a moment. 'Kat Elliot, right? I saw your piece on the Disney music machine. I'm Eli Hirschman.' He pulled a card from his back pocket. Kat glanced casually at it.

'Great to meet you.' She paused, creasing her forehead as if she was remembering something. 'Wait, aren't you the man behind Screen Dazed? I love that blog!'

He looked surprised. 'I thought that was secret; I've been trying to keep it anonymous.'

Kat gave a light laugh. 'I have my sources. Don't worry; these lips? Sealed.' She mimed zipping her mouth. She lowered her voice and moved closer, creating a conspiratorial effect, as if they were already friends. 'But between us, I liked that piece you did on that Jeff Buckley song. It reminded me of an essay Mike Barthel wrote, a while ago. Have you seen his blog?'

'Yes, it's one of my favourites, but I haven't read that piece. I'll have to check it out.' He looked thoughtful. 'Why don't you email me the link – my address is on the card. And while you're at it, put a pitch together about the reality TV things you were saying.'

'Hmm.' Kat pretended to muse, as if the thought had never occurred to her. 'I might just do that.'

She left him with casual air-kisses, but as Kat drifted away, she could barely contain her delight. From start to finish, the entire encounter had been a textbook Popularity Rules success. The early planning and reconnaissance about her targets; the pop culture research to help her blend in and sustain small-talk; even the tiny tricks of the way she built an 'insider-only' rapport with Eli there, name-dropping the kind of writers she knew he admired the most and affirming all his best opinions of himself. It had worked perfectly.

'The Polaroid Kids are tearing up the back ballroom!' A breathless hipster girl grabbed her arm, pupils tellingly dilated under a sheaf of jet-black fringe. 'You've got to see it!'

Still giddy, Kat allowed herself to be hustled out into the corridor and through the noisy halls. If anything, it had become even more chaotic since she'd arrived, the constant swell of new guests pushing up the main staircase in waves of excitement, faces cast in shadows under the bare bulbs still left intact.

'Wait!' She tugged away from the girl, catching sight of a tall, dark-haired man outlined for a moment in a far doorway.

It couldn't be . . . ? 'You go ahead.' Kat was already backing away, weaving through the flow of people until she reached the room. It was empty. She spun, scanning the crowd until she saw the shock of messy hair towering above a cluster of Asian girls in monochrome outfits. He turned, face visible for a moment.

Ash.

Kat felt a now-familiar rush of excitement. She cut across the room and attacked him with glee. 'Hey!' she cried, reaching up to kiss him. 'You're alive! I was beginning to think that talk about death-by-mixing-table wasn't just an empty threat.'

'Uh, almost!' Ash detangled himself from her arms. He was wearing his basic uniform of black jeans and a jacket with his usual effortless flair, this time paired with a vintage Bon Jovi tour T-shirt. She'd have to borrow that, Kat decided, kissing him again. 'I thought you were giving this one a miss?'

'I was, but Freddie insisted, and Gabi needed cheering up . . . Although I don't even think she came.' Kat paused. 'We should stop by on our way back, just so I can drop in and check on her. It's in your neighbourhood.'

'I'm not sure . . .' Ash looked apologetic. 'I think I have to head back to the studio after this.'

'Oh. Well, let's do something tomorrow,' she suggested. 'I could come down . . .' Kat took his hand and wove her fingers through his.

'Sounds good to me.' He grinned down at her. 'Hey, I saw Lacey out by the main staircase; she was looking for you.'

Kat laughed. 'She's always looking for me. Don't worry.'

'She seemed pretty worked up over something.' Ash frowned. 'Maybe you should go check it out.'

'Oh, all right.' Kat made a show of sighing. 'But I'll come

find you. Keep your phone handy,' she added. 'This place is bedlam.'

She kissed him again, but as Kat pulled away, she saw his eyes were open, focused on something behind her in the crowd.

And Kat knew.

She could call it intuition, honed by years of wretched disappointment; she could call it her skill for always expecting the worst; either way, it only took that flicker of expression for Kat's insides to contract. She swallowed, but there was no time to brace herself. Ash took two small steps away from her and then a lithe woman with translucently pale skin appeared between them.

'Hi sweetie,' she said, reaching up – just as Kat had done only moments before – and planting a sure, relaxed kiss on his lips. 'I've been looking everywhere for you.'

There was silence as Ash carefully avoided Kat's gaze, and her throat began to tighten.

'Oh, I'm so sorry.' The woman turned to Kat and smiled prettily. 'I'm Charlotte, Ash's girlfriend.'

They'll always let you down.

Like it or not, you need the Popularity Rules because you're the only one you can depend on in the end. Family, friends and boys will let you down – especially boys. It's human nature: we all put ourselves first, so don't think for a second that when it comes down to you versus them they won't pick themselves, even if it hurts you. Loyalty, trust . . . they're nothing but a fairy tale, so deal with it and stop expecting any different.

The higher your expectations, the worse you'll be disappointed, so you only have yourself to blame.

Chapter Thirty-two

Girlfriend.

Kat was still reeling from that one, casual word as Ash awkwardly slipped his arm around this Charlotte, refusing to meet Kat's eyes. Girlfriend. He had a girlfriend. The words were there in her mind, but slipping and swimming around as if she couldn't quite find a grip.

It didn't make sense. All this time, all this time with her; their days spent together, her nights tangled up in those cool navy sheets. The way he'd pursued her, won her over with his energy and charm . . .

All this, and he'd been somebody else's?

Suddenly, there was a loud crashing noise, and everybody paused to watch a group of skinny boys in neon hoodies demolish a set of cabinets. While their backs were turned, Kat was tempted to disappear: just melt into the crowd and flee from this man and all her worthless hopes. But then Ash and the woman turned back to her, and she realised that the torment was only just beginning.

'You're Kat, right?' Charlotte smiled at her without a hint of malice. Her hair fell in loose, natural waves to just below her shoulder-blades, and she was dressed in a simple navy shift dress: unadorned but perfect. 'Ashley's told me about you. I loved that last piece you did about Devon Darsel, the groupie one. Remember?' She turned back to Ash.

'Yeah, that one was great.'

He didn't even look panicked, Kat found herself thinking, as if her mind were separate from this mess. No, he just seemed vaguely uncomfortable, as if she was a dull relative he had to endure, or an old school acquaintance. Not the woman he'd fucked just two days ago, hard on the pale wooden floor of his flat because they couldn't even make it to the bed.

But watching them intertwined – his hand on her shoulder, her head tilted to rest against his crisp, white shirt – some masochistic instinct in Kat made her ask. 'So, how long . . . ?'

'Have we been together?' Charlotte beamed. 'It's been, what, two months now?' She looked to Ash for confirmation. He nodded, still looking around for an escape.

Two months ago they'd had sex against his door, hungry and frantic. A month ago, he'd slow-danced with Kat, dipping her low to a gleaming floor as if they were the centrepiece couple in a classic musical. Yesterday, he'd texted her to find out which restaurant she'd wanted him to book for dinner. She should have known there were no romantic heroes left in the world.

'Congratulations!' Kat managed. It was all she could do to keep standing up, yet somehow, a smile stretched across her face and words emerged from her lips as if she actually meant them. This must be what the Popularity Rules were really for: training you to fake ease and comfort until the day came when your heart was aching and tears welled up in your chest, but you still smiled brightly and laughed like nothing was wrong.

'Charlie!' A group of girls in shimmering black dresses accosted her. 'You've got to come watch Sukie!'

Charlotte gave a quick look to Ash – as if for permission, Kat couldn't help but think. He nodded, kissing her forehead.

'Go ahead.'

'It was lovely to meet you!' Charlotte called as she was pulled away.

'Lovely,' Kat repeated faintly. And then Charlotte was gone and it was just Ash left, shifting uncomfortably in front of her.

'Look, Kat—' he began, but she cut him off.

'Girlfriend?' Her voice was choked. She should have seen this coming. She should have known it would end with an ache in her chest and tears biting at the corners of her eyes. It always did.

'I'm sorry,' Ash said, sincere, but still not quite meeting her eyes, 'if you got the wrong idea about us. I never said this was serious.'

Kat swallowed. 'No, you didn't, but—'

'And you were the one who kept disappearing on me, remember?'

'In the beginning!' Kat protested, but it didn't seem to make a difference. Ash looked at her, and for a second Kat thought she saw real regret in his face.

'I thought maybe it would work, with us,' he said slowly. 'That once we got to know each other, you'd, I don't know – open up more.' He gave an awkward shrug. 'I was going to finish things with Charlie. But then you just stayed so . . . defensive, and I figured . . .'

Oh, Kat knew what he figured. He figured he'd keep the girl with the sweet smile and perky, twenty-two-year-old breasts. 'So this is my fault?' she asked incredulously. 'You cheat and it's because I'm, what – careful about letting people in?' The irony would have been amusing if it didn't hurt so much.

'I'm not saying that.' Ash moved closer, and actually tried to put his hand on her arm, as if comforting her. Kat pulled away. 'But come on, Kat, you never need anyone; it's like you're completely self-sufficient. What was I supposed to do?'

370

She blinked. 'Be honest?' Kat clenched her nails into her palms and shook her head. 'You know what? I don't want to hear any more. I'm done. OK, enjoy the rest of . . . everything.' She backed away to leave, but then turned, looking him straight in the eyes with what little poise she had left. 'But maybe I've learned to be self-sufficient because every time I do trust somebody, they end up letting me down.'

Kat disappeared into the crowd, slipping through noisy hallways and half-shattered rooms with that same smile fixed to her face as she desperately looked for somewhere to hide. Lacey tried to waylay her by a paint-splattered staircase, but Kat shook her off, speeding until she was at a half-trot pace. Event workers, society photographers, hipsters and models – they blurred into a cacophony of stretched faces and high-pitched cries. She recognised faces from her target list, and Freddie intertwined with a blond boy in some dark corner, but Kat didn't slow as she tried to escape the chaos.

'Hey, slow down!' Lauren appeared in front of her, sharp in pinstripe tailoring and a chignon. She grabbed both Kat's arms to steady her, and the daze must have shown on Kat's face, because immediately Lauren pulled her aside into a half-empty room. 'What's happened? What's wrong?'

Kat found herself breathing in small gasps. 'Ash. And Charlotte. His girlfriend.' She felt tears come now, feeling so, so foolish. Why had she believed he would be different from the rest of them?

Lauren darkened. 'He's been cheating?' Kat nodded helplessly. 'That fucker!' Her jaw was set, she was steely-eyed, and for a moment Kat expected her to go charging through the crowds and inflict some terrible violence on the pair.

Then she softened. 'Come with me.'

Kat allowed herself to be led up another flight of stairs,

along another corridor, deeper into the maze of destruction. Lauren presented her to a staff member at a peeling set of double-doors, and then helped her pull a pair of thick, scratchy overalls on top of Kat's dress while she stood, in a daze.

'At least you're in the right place for this,' Lauren noted, struggling into her own overalls and pushing a pair of thick protective glasses onto Kat's nose. 'But still . . . God, what an asshole!' She gently pushed Kat inside the room and handed her one of the sledgehammers that lay waiting on a rack. 'Go on, do your worst.'

Kat just stood uselessly in the middle of the crumbling room. Faded paper was peeling from the walls, and cracks had already come through the plaster. It was broken and dirty, the way she felt right then.

'Kat, it's OK,' Lauren urged. 'Let it out.'

Kat just wanted to cry. 'Why would he do this?' She was disgusted with the plaintive note in her voice, so wretched, but couldn't stop herself asking all the same. 'Why would he lie like that?'

'I don't know, honey,' Lauren sighed.

'He's the one who chased me!' Kat exclaimed. 'He called, and he emailed, and he asked me out, every time!' She gave the sledgehammer an experimental swing. 'Wasn't he worried he'd get caught? That somebody would see us together?' She took a sharp breath and hit the far wall. Her blow was too soft; it did nothing but crack the plaster and send a light shiver of dust to the ground. Kat pulled back the hammer and tried again. 'I didn't even want a fucking relationship!'

This time, a whole chunk of wall was dislodged, tumbling to the ground with a thump. She swung again. 'He could have settled for casual sex!' Thump. 'But no, he had to be charming.' Thump. 'And sweet.' Thump. 'And win me over with all that *bullshit*!' Striking again and again with every new crime, Kat didn't pause for breath until half the wall was crumbled on the floor in front of her, electrical wires and support beams visible through the gaping hole.

She stood, the first wave of anger receding, leaving only that aching misery in its place. She felt so stupid. She felt like a fool.

'I didn't even ask,' she admitted, tears thick in her throat, 'if we were exclusive, if he was seeing anyone else. I didn't think I had to.'

'Oh, Kat.'

'But who does that?' she cried. 'Who lies like that? Is it really too much for people to be honest? To show some fucking emotional integrity?'

'Yes.' Lauren answered simply. 'Most of the time, it is.'

'Freddie's screwing around on Oscar, too,' Kat added after a moment.

'Really?'

She nodded. 'I saw him kissing some blond boy downstairs. God, everyone's doing it, so why do I always expect more?' Kat began to attack the bed frame abandoned in the corner, smashing at the solid wood until splinters flew up. There it was: her second wave, sharper this time, focused and furious. 'Why is it my standards seem to be so high when all I want is some honesty and fucking respect? Is this really what they're like, all of them?' The questions kept coming: fast, bitter, and fuelled by years of casually inadequate behaviour. Lauren stood quietly out of range of the debris and let her rage.

And rage she did.

'When did it get acceptable for these guys to stay so fucking immature?' Another wall, another chunk of plaster flying. 'Just burning through their casual hook-ups and no-strings affairs and God forbid we actually expect them to tell us the

373

truth about how they feel!' She was sweaty now inside her overalls, hair in her eyes and blood singing in her veins. 'I want to believe there are good ones, who like it that I have ambition, or worse than that, some independence; but the world seems set on proving me wrong, every fucking time!'

The wall fell to pieces under her weapon, but Kat's hurt and resentment still remained. 'Did I tell you about my last relationship?' Lauren shook her head, silent. 'He was a writer: one of those sad young literary men the *New York Times* likes to fawn over.' She lowered the sledgehammer for a moment to give her aching arms a rest. 'We spent at least four nights a week together, but the man wouldn't leave so much as a clean shirt at my flat. He brought a toothbrush with him in his jacket pocket, as if one extra brush in my bathroom cup was this unbearable symbol of commitment.' She swallowed, feeling the rejection afresh. 'And the one before that, he two-timed me with a second-year law student at UCL. And when I confronted him about it, he said I shouldn't be mad, because we were still "fluid" and "undefined"!'

Kat sank to the messy floor, exhausted. 'It's not even as if I go for the crappy ones on purpose. I veto almost everyone before I waste my time because they seem evasive or unreliable.' She thought of the long stretches she spent alone, in between the underwhelming mediocrity of her love life. 'Those were the good ones! Or rather, they seemed to be. And now this.' She gave a bitter laugh. 'I hold back because I'm scared they'll turn out to be bastards, and so they go off and cheat because I'm holding back.'

Lauren kicked some rubble aside and sat down next to her, surveying the wreckage. 'I haven't been in a serious relationship since David,' she confessed after a moment. 'Five years. Five whole years. I mean, I've dated,' she sighed. 'Lots of useless dates with men who recoil at the idea I run my own business and won't go down on them in the back of a cab after two drinks, but that's all.'

They listened to the cries and thumping bass from the party, just down the corridor.

'And then I settle,' Lauren continued, her voice resigned. 'After six months or so watching happy couples make out on street corners, I break and say yes to whatever guy asks me. I sit through boring dinners and have bad, detached sex and regret it all over again.'

'I didn't think it would be like this,' Kat said softly, tracing circles in the dust. 'It's not like I was raised on Disney princess crap or Mills and Boon, but I always thought I'd find someone. More than one man, even. Not because I needed him, but, you know . . .'

'To love,' Lauren finished.

'To love,' Kat repeated, full of regret.

They sat quietly in the empty room, high in a dilapidated hotel full of raucous partygoers in the centre of a city Kat found cold and lonely at moments like these. But she wasn't alone this time. Reaching over, Kat took Lauren's hand, linking their little fingers the way they always used to. 'Thank you, for being here,' she said quietly.

Lauren looked at her in surprise. 'Of course.' She squeezed Kat's hand in response. 'Always.'

Tiredness took hold of Kat, draining the last reserve of her rage away. 'Can we go home now?' she asked. 'Go collapse, and eat Dulce de Leche ice-cream, and watch *The Daily Show*?'

'Good idea.' Lauren pulled Kat to her feet. They peeled off their overalls and made their way back out into the din, with arms linked and weary hearts. 'At least Jon Stewart will never let us down.'

You can't go back.

The Popularity Rules aren't a cute outfit you can take off once the job's done – they're a way of life. If you do them right, they'll stay with you for ever: a voice in the back of your mind to stop you messing up every new opportunity that comes your way.

Like it or not, nothing stays the same, and neither should you. Don't let people make you feel bad for moving on; just ask yourself why they haven't done it themselves, then use that fear or insecurity to your advantage. Good things always end, but that just means the bad stuff will as well, so get Zen about it and appreciate everything new the Rules bring into your life.

Either way, you'll get nowhere clinging to the past.

Chapter Thirty-three

The visit for her mother's birthday had caught Kat unawares, creeping up without warning while her hurt over Ash hardened into a cold resentment. Trying not to dwell on his lies and half-hearted apology, she threw herself into another whirl of article pitches, career-building parties and two a.m. champagne-fuelled conversations with commissioning editors. Thankfully, Devon had been located by a rambling email sent from the Arizona desert, but that just meant Kat was now fielding questions about rehab and her supposedly redemptive influence on him. It wasn't until she stepped out of the station in Oxford and saw her mother's old Fiat loitering by the kerb – Susanne's head bent over a stack of papers balanced on the steering wheel – that she felt a hint of trepidation.

Just what would her mother make of the new Katherine Elliot?

'Hi, darling.' Susanne shoved the marking back in her battered leather satchel and flung it on the back seat. 'Get in; that parking attendant's been eyeing me for the last ten minutes and I can't be bothered with the hassle of another ticket.'

'Another?' Kat asked, sweeping biscuit wrappers and books off the passenger seat. She carefully edged into the car. The last time she'd clambered in without proper preparation, she'd smeared ginger-nut fondant filling over her jeans – and a poor first year's discussion of the limits of Rawlsian theories of justice.

'Sometimes I just don't have time to pay the meter.' Susanne shrugged, coaxing the car back to life and swerving out onto the main road. Her hair was fading to an elegant grey (having sworn off the 'eternal shackles' of dye, of course), and she was dressed, as always, in her academic uniform of mismatched tweed, a shapeless cardigan and sturdy work boots. 'So, how are you? You're looking well.'

'Oh, thanks.' Kat toyed with her hair, freshly touched up by the ever-amenable Giles. She'd convinced him to tone the colour down half a shade, but it was still vivid, straight and falling gently over one eye. 'I thought . . . a new look, you know?' She waited for her mother's verdict, but Susanne was focused on the kamikaze cyclist ahead. 'Well . . . happy birthday,' Kat offered. 'How's all your planning for the conference?'

'Don't even let me start,' her mother sighed, but she began relating the dramas of warring ideological factions and the fraught nature of speech scheduling all the same. '. . . And then of course Penny Kilton couldn't bear her slot after Margaret Banks, because of everything that happened with their last book . . .'

'Of course,' Kat murmured softly, watching as the city-centre sandstone towers gave way to the river and then the basic brick of Cowley Road. She almost wished she didn't have to be there at all: she had leads to follow up, articles to write, revenge to daydream . . . But she hadn't had more than a brief chat with her mother in months, and avoiding this visit would only prompt questions. Difficult questions, about what she'd been doing, and with whom.

Susanne drew up outside her red-brick, mid-terrace house, idling by the kerb with the engine still running. The paint around the door was peeling, but roses wound up the front trellis and Kat could already see the overflow from Susanne's library stacked up inside the windows. 'You've got your keys?'

Kat waved them as evidence.

'I have tutorials until one, I'm afraid, but after that I thought we could meet for lunch. That place you like, by the Rad Cam?'

'Sure, whatever you want.' Kat grabbed her bag and climbed out of the car. 'I'm fine just to wander, maybe go to the Botanical Gardens.'

'Wonderful.' Susanne smiled at her. 'I want to hear everything that's going on with you.'

Kat left her bag in the hallway between her mother's sturdy walking boots and a dusty stack of politics textbooks, meandering back across the bridge towards the gardens. It had been one of her favourite spots as a student, the domed glass hot-houses and lush green lawns offering a small oasis, away from crowds and – crucially – students. As she strolled by the river, watching boatloads of tourists punt by, Kat wondered how university might have been different if she'd come to Oxford equipped with the Popularity Rules, instead of just a second-hand laptop and delusions of academic grandeur. She would have had more fun, of that she was certain, instead of bristling at every new rejection and careening between cliques, trying to find her place. She would have known how to slip through each social circle, camouflaged and safe, and perhaps even have made more friends, without the divisions of class and culture she had found insurmountable.

She may not yet be an ideologue of Lauren's fervency, but the battered red rulebook had become Kat's constant companion. It was a surprising comfort to be able to pull out the slim book and re-read the phrases she now knew almost by heart: the chatty tone and Lauren's neat cursive script. It had answers; it made sense of her world. After all, she was close to finding a way back to *Think Louder*, she just knew it. Her status was steadily increasing, her contacts list was growing exponentially and soon, her old life would be hers once more. And this time, she would have the skills to make it better than ever.

Kat found Susanne waiting at a table in her favourite cafe. Mismatched tables were set up amongst the grass of a church courtyard, looking out over the bulbous dome of the Radcliffe Camera library, and groups of pensioners nibbled on shortbread biscuits and drank large cups of tea from flower-print china.

'Sorry I'm late,' Kat apologised breathlessly, hurrying over. 'I lost track of— Whitney?' Kat stopped in surprise. Whitney had been half-hidden by a hedge, but now she leaned forwards, pale in a draped floral dress and sunhat. 'Wow, what a coincidence. It's great to see you!' She gave her a quick hug and sat down opposite the two of them. 'You'll have to join us for lunch! What brought you up here?'

Susanne and Whitney exchanged a look.

'Actually, I invited her,' Susanne began, moving aside her teacup and reaching across the table for Kat's hand. 'We've been talking . . .'

'We're worried, Kat,' Whitney finished, taking Kat's other hand and gazing at her earnestly. 'We thought it was best to sit down and talk to you together.'

Kat stared at them, bemused. 'What is this, an intervention?' she joked.

They didn't smile.

'Seriously?' Kat snatched her hands away. She looked back

380

and forth between them, but all she saw was concern.

'Now Kat, don't get angry,' Susanne tried to placate her. 'Whitney called me because she's concerned about you, about all the changes you've been making.'

'I didn't realise a haircut and new wardrobe were cause to sound the alarm.' Kat tried to laugh it off. She had made some dramatic changes, after all, and they meant well, that was the important thing. It was almost sweet.

Almost.

'You know that's not the only thing,' Whitney chided her, the sunhat casting criss-crossed shadows over her face. 'You've been out partying all the time, offering yourself up for objectification for all those websites and magazine shoots.'

'And your writing,' Susanne continued, looking every inch the stern, tweed-clad tutor. 'It's just not like you: all this commercial material and media gossip. I know you took losing your job hard, and perhaps we haven't been supportive enough—' At this, Whitney nodded. '—But we're concerned about this path you're taking.'

'Anything else?' Kat carefully folded her arms, anger slowly building. They were serious! 'Perhaps you think I'm on drugs. Or in a destructive relationship. Or running with a bad crowd.'

There was another look.

'Whitney mentioned you were living with a woman named Lauren,' her mother started carefully, shifting her wrought-iron chair closer. 'Is this Lauren Anderville? From Park House school?'

'Yes.' Kat wondered just how long their little informant sessions had been going on. She'd barely heard from Whitney in at least a month, but evidently she'd been talking up a storm with Susanne on a regular basis. She sighed, explaining, 'We bumped into each other a few months ago. She had a room going spare; I needed a place to live. It's worked out fine. Great, actually.'

'But Kat, surely you remember what happened with her?' Susanne looked shocked. 'She hurt you so much, and—'

'Mum!' She couldn't believe this. What was she, twelve years old? 'I'm fine. It's good; I'm glad we met up again.' As she said the words, Kat realised they were true. The circumstances had been terrible, but imagine where she'd be now if Lauren hadn't stepped in to help?

'Darling, I know it must be nice to get nostalgic sometimes, but she's not exactly trustworthy. And is she the one behind this new image of yours? Because you were never concerned with conforming to superficial standards of beauty before.' Her mother regarded Kat with regret, as if she'd come home bearing multiple piercings and a bad tattoo rather than a pair of fitted jeans and a hundred-pound haircut.

Kat felt an illogical surge of resentment. Maybe if she hadn't spent her childhood dressed in baggy, gender-neutral clothing, she wouldn't be sitting there right now. Susanne had made Kat in her image from the start, rejecting any notion that a teenage girl should be chatting about make-up and boys as well as Proust and politics, but she hadn't been the one left reading alone in the corner of the dorms while the other girls giggled and painted their toenails.

When it became clear Kat wasn't going to justify such radical fashion choices, Whitney took over. 'This Lauren isn't exactly friendly.' She fixed Kat with a disappointed look. 'And I checked on the work her company does: it's really not a positive contribution, or the sort of thing I thought you'd ever associate yourself with.'

'She's my friend.' Kat glared at them.

'But really, Kat—'

'I don't think you should—'

'Just stop!' Kat held up her hands. 'Both of you. Have you listened to yourselves?'

'We only want to help,' Whitney insisted, looking hurt. 'This isn't like you.'

'You're right, it isn't,' Kat agreed bitterly. 'I'm getting what I want, and that's not like me at all.'

'That's not what I meant,' Whitney tried to interrupt, but Kat wouldn't let her.

'I'm interested in where all this friendly concern is coming from. You know,' Kat added, narrowing her eyes, 'since you've been more than happy to benefit from my "damaging party lifestyle" and unsavoury contacts with all those free tickets and guest-list spots for years now.' She thought of all the times Whitney had invited herself along as Kat's plus-one, enjoying the view from the press area and open bar. And now she had the nerve to judge Kat for the very same thing!

'Now, that's not fair.' Whitney's eyes clouded with dismay.

'Isn't it?' Kat regarded her coolly. 'It's funny, a couple of months ago I was at rock bottom: lonely and unemployed and desperate, but you didn't think that warranted any special intervention. But now I'm happy and successful, and suddenly you're so worried.'

'But this isn't you!'

'What is me?' Kat challenged. 'I mean, really, who am I? I'm twenty-eight years old; am I supposed to already be set in stone? I can't change at all without triggering the end of the world.'

'No, darling,' Susanne interjected, 'but you've always had such a strong value system.'

Yes, the one she'd accepted unquestioningly from her mother.

'Would you please stop overreacting? I'm not breaking any laws!' Kat exclaimed, finally losing patience. 'I'm not hurting myself, or anyone else. I'm not even fucking my way up the food chain like other girls do. I'm just playing smarter, that's all.'

'But playing what? The choices you make matter.' The sadness in her mother's tone made Kat pause for a moment.

Choices had consequences, of course they did. The wrong person could ruin your life – it had practically been a mantra in their household, growing up. Susanne would know.

'I understand that, Mum,' Kat sighed softly. 'Believe me, I do. But the choices I make also determine if I can pay rent, or win a commission, or even manage to relate to the world. Would you prefer I sat in alone every night, reading my copy of *The Beauty Myth* instead?'

There was no reply. Instead, Whitney leaned over to Susanne as if Kat wasn't even there. 'I said she'd be resistant.'

'Resistant!' The OAPs looked up from their sticky buns at Kat's cry, but she didn't care. 'You're sitting there, passing judgement as if you're better than me! What did you expect – that I'd crumple in tears, admit the error of my ways and beg for forgiveness for finally making something of my life?'

'This is what you count as success?' Susanne gaped, but Kat was past caring. 'Just look at what you're doing to yourself. This isn't how I raised you!'

'So, you're hurt because this reflects badly on you?' Kat shot back.

'That isn't what I meant.'

'I think it is.' Kat looked at them both, so caught up in their careful concern when she needed it least. 'You liked it when I was Kat Elliot, angry feminist writer; never mind if I was happy and secure that way, just as long as I was carrying on the good Elliot name. And you,' she turned to Whitney, before she could interrupt with another 'helpful' comment. 'You preferred it when I was just an attentive audience to all your dramas.' She got up, despite their protests. 'Did it ever occur to either of you to ask me how I feel, if I'm actually happy? Well, I am! I'm finally in control of my life, actually having fun.'

She stormed away before they could launch into another phase of their guilt-tripping arguments. An intervention! As if she was a drug addict, or a prostitute, instead of just somebody mentioned in a few gossip columns. What would they have done if she'd actually done something drastic? Held her captive for a deprogramming session? Kat found a taxi on the busy main street and directed it to her mother's to pick up her bag before heading to the station. She fumed all the way.

They didn't understand; that was the problem. They didn't know what she'd gone through, what it took to get ahead in her world. Susanne was safe up in her ivory towers, surrounded by theory and rhetoric that bore little relation to Kat's real life. And as for Whitney . . .

Kat boarded the next train to London and threw herself down in a window seat, angrier by the minute as she remembered Whitney's look of superior concern. All this time she'd assumed Whitney was a real friend, someone who would support her in hard times, and celebrate her success. That was what real friends did, wasn't it? But no! Instead, Whitney had brushed her off when she was unemployed and alone, and started conspiring with her mother the moment she was successful.

Kat gulped at her bottle of water, trying to reach that state of detachment that Lauren preached and that still eluded her. They were only acting from their own agendas; that's what the Popularity Rules would say. Whitney was looking for a way to cut her back down to supporting-character size, and her mother was confused that anyone would reject her belief system. As she sped further from the city and their disapproval, Kat finally felt her anger subside. It was simple, she decided, as simple as Ash hiding his weakness and passive nature behind bullshit about her defence issues, and Jessica spreading nasty lies to reassert her own position. Everyone had their own agenda. She just had to stop reacting emotionally: decipher the real motives for their behaviour without taking every word as a personal attack.

Her phone began to ring, and a quick glance at the caller ID gave Kat a small twinge of guilt.

Oscar.

'Hi sweets, what's going on?' she asked, dreading an out-pouring of betrayed sobs. She hadn't told him about Freddie's infidelity; it wasn't her place to get involved, especially when all their lives were presently so intertwined.

'*Think Louder*!' he exclaimed, obviously out of breath. 'Takeover. ChannelCorp. Mac's gone!'

'What? Slow down. Tell me everything.' Kat leaned forward, gripping her phone.

'ChannelCorp have bought out the magazine! They've fired Mac; they're bringing in a whole new editorial team; they're even changing the name.'

'To what?' Kat was already reaching for her notebook.

'Just *Louder*.' She could practically hear Oscar's eyes roll. 'Apparently, the kid on the street doesn't want to think. I mean, obviously.'

'So that's it?' she said, still trying to keep up. 'It's really happening. The magazine is done.'

'Well, they're not folding it – just a complete revamp. You should see the dummy issue they handed out. God, Kat, you'd

die! Top ten ringtone charts, groupie pin-up of the month . . .
It's like they shoved a spectrum up a cretinous eighteen-year-
old's nostril and just scraped out whatever detritus was rotting
in his brain.'

Kat winced. 'They're changing everything?'

'Pretty much. It's a good thing you got out when you did, I
swear; you'd turn homicidal!' He laughed, as if the destruction
of Alan's legacy were actually an amusement.

'Thanks, Oscar.' She sighed. 'Wait, do you know who
they're installing as editor?' Kat prayed it was the one who
drank draft beer and actually looked her in the eyes, instead of
her chest.

'This wanker called Stevie Gold.'

Kat stifled a groan. She should have guessed!

'You don't think he'll fire me, do you?' For a moment,
Oscar's voice was genuinely worried. 'No,' he recovered,
answering himself. 'It's not like I'm costing them anything.
Anyways, we're off to drink ourselves into oblivion. And place
bets on how long it takes Jessica to screw him! Laters!'

It was ironic, Kat realised, snapping her phone shut and
resting her head against the cool glass. The biggest obstacle to
getting her job back had always been Mac, and his
immovable ego, and now he was gone. A new editor was
easily swayed, particularly an arrogant asshole like Stevie
Gold: a man who cared more about status than past scandals
was exactly what Kat needed. A few Popularity Rules moves,
and she could have him wrapped around her little finger.

Kat paused, the idea beginning to take root. Stevie would be
easy to manipulate, to run rings around until he was obedient
and drooling.

So what was she waiting for?

Information is everything.

———— ∞∞∞ ————

That 'knowledge is power' cliché is a classic for one simple reason: it's so true. When you know somebody's dirty little secrets, you have complete power over them, so start digging and don't rest until you have enough leverage to get whatever you want. Old relationships, high-school humiliations, even credit records and transcripts – nothing is off-limits if you want to get ahead, so find private investigators or a new hacking program.

Don't get carried away, though; keep your powder dry. You only have one shot to use what you know, so bide your time for that perfect moment and make sure it's worth it.

Chapter Thirty-four

By the time Kat bounded up the stairs of Lauren's flat, determination was hot in her veins. This was the moment she'd been waiting for, when all her training and groundwork would finally pay off.

'I thought you were staying a couple of days.' Lauren was working in her office when Kat burst in, but immediately she closed her laptop and met Kat in the hall. 'Your mom called three times. Are you OK? You've heard about the takeover, right?'

Kat nodded. 'Oscar filled me in; everything's fine.'

'Really?' Lauren studied her, worried. 'Because I could leave this all until tomorrow. We could go get drunk and eat our body weight in take-out. Well,' she corrected herself, 'you could eat your body weight in take-out.'

'No, I'm fine,' Kat insisted, tossing her bag down and peeling off her jacket. 'This is a good thing; I'm not in limbo any more. I've got the names – we knew this was coming. Now I can actually *do* something!'

Lauren seemed unconvinced. 'I know you didn't want anything to do with ChannelCorp – and especially Stevie.' She gave Kat a sympathetic hug. 'I'm sorry it turned out this way.'

Kat stepped away. 'I'm not.' She was full of a fierce energy, but she couldn't stop in case it ebbed away, and then what would she be left with? Ash's betrayal, her mother's and Whitney's hypocrisy, the final death of Alan's legacy? No, she had to stay focused on the task at hand. 'It's like you've been telling me all along: the Popularity Rules work best on fresh subjects. Stevie is the ideal target. I already made that approach in New York; now I just have to find the perfect leverage, and I can force him to give me my job back.'

Lauren blinked. 'That's . . . great. So where do you want to start? I could get an investigator to look into Stevie's background, or—'

'I think I need to do this on my own.' Kat paused, hoping she wouldn't be offended. 'I want to see if I'm ready to use everything. You've been teaching me all this time . . .'

Lauren clapped her hands together. 'Your first solo mission? I'm so proud!' she smiled. 'This must be what it's like sending a kid off to pre-school.' Pretending to wipe a tear away, she regarded Kat with obvious emotion. 'You're ready, I know you are. But I'm at your disposal; don't even hesitate to ask. I'm pretty busy on the new pitch, but I have the number of a great hacker over here, and some new password decoding software for remote access—'

'You'll be the first one I call,' Kat promised. 'And if I need to hack somebody's iPhone, you'll be the *only* one I call.'

Leverage.

As far as Kat could tell, this mysterious power could come from any number of things: weakness, dirty secrets, some sort of personal ambition – the possibilities were endless, but she was certain she would find it. The inner world of Steven 'call me Stevie' Gold and the ChannelCorp hierarchy became Kat's new obsession; from the moment she woke up to the second she fell asleep (often dreaming of Stevie's shark's-tooth grin), she was poring over the Popularity Rules and searching for that one, perfect breakthrough.

'I need dirt,' Kat repeated to herself, staring at what she now thought of as her operations centre. This sort of digging was too sensitive for the *ChicK* office, so she'd taken over a corner of Lauren's living room, plastering the walls with printouts, photographs and flow-charts as she picked apart Stevie's life. A decade ago she would have been limited to browsing through old archives or slyly befriending the target's sister or masseuse; now she had the full powers of the internet and ex-secret service investigators at her disposal. From high-school transcripts to credit card bills, nothing was out of Kat's reach, but despite almost a week of constant research – ignoring freelance pitches, social events and even basic nutrition – the key to success still eluded her.

'I need dirt,' she chanted over the high-energy rock mix blasting through the flat. In sweatpants and a baggy T-shirt, she'd been working for ten hours straight, but she was close, she just knew it. Her phone rang at frequent intervals, but she just let it go to voicemail: it would only be breathless PR people begging her to interview—

Damn. Kat abandoned her notes and fished around in the couch cushions for the phone. She'd been so caught up in her stalk-a-thon, she'd forgotten she was waiting on a call from Eliza Monroe's people: the reclusive singer had deigned to *consider* a *possible* conversation, *perhaps*. It was the interview Kat had been dreaming of for fourteen years.

'You have twenty-one messages.' In two days? Bracing herself, Kat wandered over to the kitchen and fished in the fridge for some cold pizza as she clicked through, her handset wedged between her ear and shoulder.

'Hey? Kat? It's Lacey? I just—' Delete.

'Katherine, it's your mother—' Delete.

'God, Kat, this reclusive thing is *old*. Anyone would think you're ignor—' Delete.

'Katherine, don't you think you're being immature?' Delete.

'Oh my God, Kat—'

'This is your mother, Katherine. Again. The least you could do is let me know you're all right and—' Delete, delete, delete! Kat stabbed the keys in frustration. Finding Stevie Gold's fatal flaw may be occupying all her energy, but that didn't mean she could just forgive Susanne and Whitney for their oh-so-helpful intervention stunt. Not that Whitney even wanted forgiveness: aside from one decidedly non-apologetic email, Kat hadn't heard from her. Nor would she, until she 'stopped projecting' her 'obvious trust issues and insecurities' onto her selfless, morally superior friend.

'Still no luck?'

Kat jumped. Lauren had appeared without warning. 'No,' she replied, chewing cold pizza crust. 'This guy is Google-proof! Nothing but official press releases and biographical information. It's like he's managed to delete the cache of anything remotely revealing.'

'Maybe he has. Some people hire companies to do just that.' Lauren unloaded an armful of files on her desk, her usually neat hair a touch dishevelled. She'd been working long hours too, locked away in her office and taking meetings for the new pitch she was intent on winning.

'Then perhaps he's a more dangerous target than I thought.' Kat studied the walls again. 'I could go back further, I suppose: see if I can dig up any social networking sites from when he was in college. Drunken photos and forum posts.' She looked to Lauren for confirmation.

'I doubt it.' Lauren flicked through her BlackBerry distractedly. 'Only sixteen-year-olds and complete idiots post incriminating things out in the open.'

Kat sighed. That fire in her veins was cooling, but she

couldn't bring herself to think about anything but her goal. 'So what's left?'

Lauren glanced up, studying the wall of research for a long minute as she tracked Kat's progress. She nodded occasionally, as if ticking things off her personal stalking checklist, before asking, 'Have you found his anonymous accounts yet?'

'How would I do that?' Kat blinked. 'I mean, aren't they anonymous?'

'Ah, but you can still find them, if you look hard enough.' Lauren's eyes lit up with a dangerous gleam. 'What you want is some kind of overlap, where they've used a known email address to register an anonymous username,' she explained. 'People usually aren't smart enough to get an anonymous email until later on, but they keep the same usernames for years. If you can find that first overlap, you can track everything they didn't want somebody to read.'

Kat was impressed. Clearly, the CIA's loss had been corporate espionage's gain.

'You're getting there,' Lauren reassured her. 'I'm sure—' Her phone began to ring. 'Damn, I've got to get this. I'll see you later?'

Kat nodded. She'd fallen into a dysfunctional routine: stopping her Stevie-hunt only at midnight or two a.m. when Lauren finally finished work and the two of them collapsed, numb and exhausted in front of a couple of M&S microwaved meals. 'How's the super-secret pitch going?'

Lauren shrugged, tiredly. 'I think I've got it, but you can never tell. To be honest, I'll just be happy if Melinda doesn't.'

Kat nodded, already wandering back towards the kitchen, and the caffeine to be found therein. 'See you later.'

She was still deep in research hours later when her phone began to ring again. It was Freddie, but he refused to give up no matter how many times Kat declined his call. 'Yes?' she sighed, finally admitting defeat.

'Kat, love, where the fuck are you?'

'Freddie, I'm busy,' she told him apologetically, stifling a yawn. Her eyes burned from too many hours in front of the computer screen, and she had a funny taste left in her mouth from that pizza.

'No, you're not. You're special guest DJing my party.' Kat could hear the exasperation in his tone.

'I'm sorry, but—'

'I won't hear it! I've already sent a car for you, so get your pretty arse over here.' He hung up.

Kat considered bailing on him for a moment, but it would cause more trouble than she wanted. With a sigh, she dragged herself to take a quick shower and put on an appropriately stylish outfit. Freddie had become her scene godfather, of sorts, passing on interesting commission contacts and making sure she was on the list for the best events. In turn, his own profile had never been hotter: his work was set to be featured in a handful of magazines, and he'd even been asked to be a judge on a *Project Runway* episode. It was a mutually exploitive relationship, and Kat knew it was in her best interests to keep it alive.

'I knew you wouldn't let me down.' Freddie greeted her with air-kisses once she'd been ushered inside the club. Kat looked out at the sea of rowdy hipsters and tried to muster some enthusiasm.

'No problem,' she smiled vaguely. 'You always throw the best parties.'

'Now you just do your thing.' He began steering her towards the DJ booth, tucked under one of the stone arches in the cavernous room. 'I'll send some champagne up, and have Harry around to cater to your every whim.'

Harry, hmmm. Kat was seeing more of him and his blond, chiselled features around these days. 'Oscar's not around?' she asked carefully, wondering how much drama the night could hold.

Freddie rolled his eyes. 'He got fired from that internship today, so he's wallowing in some overdramatic heap. You know how he gets.'

Kat blinked at the flashes of neon swooping over their heads. The room was hot and packed with people, bass thumping so hard it sent the beat right through her body. Her headache finally began to emerge. 'I need some painkillers,' she stopped him before he could leave. 'Nothing hard,' she added quickly, remembering Freddie's wide-ranging pharmaceutical supplies.

'Been partying too much, have we?' he winked. 'Don't you worry, I'll sort something.'

Kat's DJ set passed quickly, fuelled by more caffeine, aspirin and sheer nerves. She was still baffled at how pressing 'play' on her iPod qualified as DJing; even more so by the fact that standing behind the turntable with large headphones on somehow lent credibility to her image as a music writer, but she bluffed her way through the set nonetheless, playing the repertoire of edgy, mediocre new acts she knew the crowd were expecting.

'Awesome set,' Lacey beamed, welcoming her to the VIP corner and handing her another glass of champagne. She began to chatter about a new release and the current Hollywood gossip while Kat sipped silently. She still knew nothing real about Lacey: not her background or feelings or opinions on anything other than the most surface of industry gossip – and Lacey had never made any effort to discover more about Kat either. Lacey, Cara, Nicolai, Adam . . . These were her scene acquaintances; accumulated through months of after-parties and carefully chronicled late-night hi-jinx, they lounged around her in a mass of artfully chic clothing and smoky eyeliner.

Kat took her place among them and let her mind drift back to Stevie Gold. Had she covered every angle yet? She was keeping track of the corporate side of things, watching the ChannelCorp share price and key investors, even checking what other high-profile writers were doing in case he wanted to bring a whole new team on board . . .

That was it: the one thing she'd been overlooking, Kat realised in a flash. If he was going to bring her *in*, then somebody would have to go *out*. Jessica, to be precise. There was only ever room for one scene queen to pout from the pages of the magazine, and if she wanted it to be her, then she had to be sure Jessica was falling out of favour.

Kat focused back on the conversation and waited for somebody to give her an opening. She didn't have to wait long; the ChannelCorp takeover was big news.

'I heard he's a finance guy,' Nicolai remarked, his disapproving expression speaking volumes. 'No wonder he's ready to shake things up.'

'They'll cut payroll, of course,' Lacey claimed. 'I wonder who will go?'

There it was. Kat reached for her purse. 'Bathroom break, Lacey?' She began walking towards the back stairs, confident that Lacey would follow. She did.

'You know, it's such a shame for poor Jessica,' she began, when they were both applying fresh lipstick and smoothing down their hair in front of the long bank of mirrors. A group of teenage girls in skinny jeans and heels were giggling in the corner, but they fell silent, watching Kat with awe. 'Oh, I think my necklace is tangled. Can you give me a hand?'

'What do you mean?' Lacey moved behind her and fiddled with the clasp. She met Kat's eyes in the mirror, obviously curious.

'You know, with Stevie Gold at *Louder* now.' Kat raised her eyebrows meaningfully. She felt a pang that she was resorting to the lowest form of girl-on-girl hate crime, but quickly pushed it aside. Jessica had been playing nothing but dirty from the start.

Lacey couldn't have known what she was talking about – after all, there was nothing to talk about – but nodded along nonetheless. 'Of course, that!'

Kat sighed. 'Then again, who knows what kind of insider info it took to engineer the takeover? For all we know, she could have planned it this way.' She turned back to Lacey. 'Thanks sweetie. And forget I said anything about Jessica. I mean, I only heard rumours; it might not even be true. I'm sure she wouldn't do that.'

'Right. Not at all,' Lacey agreed quickly, but the look they exchanged was anything but reassured. That was the thing about spreading rumours, Kat knew now. The best ones had an element of believability. You could smear anyone's reputation with a few well-placed comments, but for the whispers to stick, they had to seem credible. Thanks to her history when it came to fucking her way to the top, the idea that Jessica would screw her future editor – and perhaps even usher in the takeover to begin with – was no stretch at all.

'Are you going to get that?' Lacey asked, as Kat's phone kept ringing with the harsh electronic beats of a new Scandinavian pop act. She checked the display.

'They can wait.' She mustered a bright smile, tucking it away. Oscar was calling again, but she couldn't exactly offer comfort and reassurances in the middle of a noisy club. 'Let's get back to the others.'

Kat stayed another hour out of politeness and then collapsed into a taxi home, secure in the knowledge that it would only take Lacey a matter of days before every scene gossip and blog site knew about Jessica and Stevie. And, judging by his internet history of self-Googling, so too would Stevie himself.

Lauren was still out when she got back, so Kat took her meal for one and set about picking a path through the internet again in search of Stevie's anonymous account.

This time, she found it.

A single email reference led her to an obscure username, which led her to another, private email and membership of a random message-board community, all the while Kat's heart beating faster. And there, buried between inane ramblings about the last Batman movie and commentary on the upcoming elections, she found exactly what she'd been looking for.

Kat sat for a moment, staring at the screen. Her leverage, her goal, everything she'd spent these months working towards was there, wrapped up in the most unlikely of names. Searching through her email until she found a phone number, Kat appreciated the twisted irony that led her to be calling this particular person, for this particular reason.

'Devon?' she said, when he finally picked up. 'It's Kat. I need a favour . . .'

Be smart, not clever.

Never underestimate how stupid people think you can be (especially men). Everybody wants to feel superior and powerful, so play dumb sometimes and give them the pleasure of explaining things to you. Men are always happy to believe they're better than you, so let them think they've won and watch them do whatever you planned.

Acting naive can also trap people into revealing something they would otherwise keep secret, so practice your best 'I don't understand' and open smile.

Chapter Thirty-five

Kat barely slept that night with anticipation, running through possible scenarios in her mind until she knew every outcome by heart, but as her dangerous heels tap-tapped on the pavement outside the *Louder* office the next morning, her body was still tight with nerves.

This was it.

'You can't go up without an appointment!'

There was a new intern guarding the main lobby, boxes piled high in every corner, but Kat paid no heed to her protests as she strode through the doors and into the rickety old lift, calmly pulling the wrought-iron gate closed on a confused face. She was on her final mission: perfect lipstick in place and all-important folder in hand. She wasn't stopping for anyone.

'If we just run those . . . Kat?'

Pivoting out of the elevator and breezing past a shocked-looking Nate, Kat headed straight through the clutter for the corner office. She could sense people falling silent as she passed, her purple ankle boots tapping on the hardwood floor in synch with the Blondie track blasting from the stereo. How apt, she thought, absorbing the strength of the platinum rock goddess and her purring certainty. I'm gonna getcha getcha getcha all right.

Kat reached the far end of the long, open-plan space and took a breath as she knocked, her heart racing so loudly she wondered if it would betray her.

'Yeah?'

And there he was.

Blond hair mussed just so, one of those ridiculous sci-fi headsets over his ear and his feet propped on what had been Alan's scratched old desk. Stevie Gold.

His ice blue eyes were already narrowing in recognition, trying to place her, as Kat gave him a broad smile. 'Got a moment?'

'Uh, did we have something arranged?' He hit some buttons on the phone, but the look he gave her was mild annoyance, rather than outright irritation.

'No.' She smiled again, soft and unthreatening. 'But I know you'll be interested. I'm Kat Elliot, by the way. I think we've met before . . . ?' Kat's confidence wavered for a moment as she took in the perfectly cut designer suit and easy posture. Her future was in his hands, but there would be no second chances. Keep your powder dry, the Rules said, and they were right: either she won now, or she had to bid farewell to her magazine for ever.

Then Stevie's gaze slid lower, slowly tracing Kat's body in the tight, military-style dress she'd picked out for this very occasion, and suddenly, Kat felt calm again. He was predictable, if nothing else.

By the time Stevie managed to drag his eyes above her neckline, Kat was firmly back in control. 'Call them back,' she told him, her warm voice making it more of a suggestion than an order. 'Trust me, you'll want to hear this.'

Stevie began to smile. 'Something's come up. I'll call you later.' Pulling his headset away, he thoughtfully regarded her. 'Kat, it's great to see you again. I'm all yours.'

Kat sashayed over and took a seat, slowly crossing her ankles. He glanced at her legs again. God, men. 'You too.' She was sure to speak casually, as if she was completely nonchalant despite the high stakes of the meeting. 'How are things shaping up here?' Smiling, Kat made an effort to glance around the room. Boxes, stacks of paperwork and bare walls: hardly the home for a big shot like Stevie.

'It's a mess right now,' Stevie laughed, relaxed. 'We're moving operations over to the ChannelCorp building, near Oxford Street.'

'Good call,' Kat lied. 'You'll be much more central.'

'It's like I told the board: you can't find the musical pulse of the city buried out here. I don't know how you survived so long. No decent restaurants, for a start.' There it was, that infamous shark's-tooth grin. He was at ease now, Kat could see. He thought he was the one in control here.

There was a long pause, but for once, she relished it. She may be the one who wanted something, but that didn't mean she had to be eager, begging. Let him ask. Still smiling that pleasant, noncommittal smile, Kat waited.

It wasn't for long.

'Let's cut right to it.' Stevie leaned forwards slightly. 'What brings you here?'

Kat felt her pulse pick up slightly. 'I'll be brief,' she began, anticipation rising. 'Devon Darsel has left The Alarm.'

'I know.' Stevie couldn't resist a slight sneer, but Kat was unconcerned.

'So you also know he's refusing to do any press,' she continued. Devon had issued a brief statement first thing that morning at her urging, confirming the Arizona ramblings. He was out of the band, and it was splashed across every website and news report. Stevie nodded imperceptibly, so Kat continued. 'He'll do no interviews at all . . . Except with me.'

'What?' Kat watched Stevie blink, trying to figure out his

angle and the best strategy to take with her. Too late, she wanted to tell him smugly, this is a *fait accompli*.

'He'll only talk to me,' Kat repeated casually. 'No TV, no press, nothing else for at least a month after publication. A real exclusive.' She drummed her fingers lazily on her chair and mused, as if for the first time, 'So perhaps I should do an in-depth feature. A no-holds-barred portrait of the voice of a generation.' Kat gestured vaguely. 'You know the kind of thing. Intimate confessions, backstage tell-all.' She had to hide her amusement as Stevie's mouth gaped open slightly. 'Run over two or three issues. What do you think?'

He swallowed quickly and tried to recover his composure, but Kat knew Stevie was already seeing the cover line and promotion, the hype and media blitz. And the sales figures! In the age of media-whore bands and recycled copy, a true exclusive – with the icon *du jour* no less – was a rare and precious thing. And in the wake of the band's split . . .

It was a rare, precious thing that could well make Stevie Gold's career. As an editor, he would always have been salivating, but Stevie wasn't just an editor, as Kat's research had discovered. No, he was a fan as well. A genuine, swooning, write-long-defences-of-his-idol, breathlessly-hype-every-word-that-dropped-from-Devon's-lips sort of fan. The irrational kind.

A vein on his forehead quivered as Stevie tried his hardest to appear nonchalant. 'I might be interested in that.'

'I thought so.' Kat reached for her portfolio and withdrew a couple of sheets. She slid them across his desk and watched him try not to grab for them. 'Just some ideas for the rough shape of things. Devon was thinking I could perhaps start with the band tension and split, then work backwards through the feud with the Hard-Ons . . .' Stevie's eyes flashed eagerly,

'. . . his battle with addiction . . .' a lick of his lips, '. . . the affair with Lily Larton . . .' Stevie made a strangled noise that almost sounded like a moan. Kat tried her hardest not to laugh. 'So?'

'Maybe.' Stevie coughed, reaching for a bottle of mineral water.

'Well, I guess I'll just give Darren a call and see what *Rolling Stone* think,' Kat shrugged, gleeful inside. This was more fun than she'd ever imagined. 'Or maybe even *Vanity Fair*.' She reached for the pages. Stevie snatched them back.

'Now, wait a sec . . .'

'I wish I could.' Kat gave a dramatic sigh, as if nothing would bring her more joy. 'But I don't need to tell you I have to move quickly on this. I mean, right now, thousands – no, *millions* – of devoted fans are in a frenzy. They want answers, and they'll rush to buy whatever magazine gives them.' Kat smiled, her victory already secure. 'Did you know The Alarm sold over twelve million albums last year alone? Actual physical CDs? That's practically unheard of these days.'

Stevie stared across the desk at her. They both knew she'd won. With a story like that, Kat could name her price to any publication in the world, and they'd throw themselves at her feet to pay. She didn't need to be there, talking to him.

'So why not go, take it to them?'

Kat almost laughed. He was calling her bluff. So maybe it was time to call his.

'Let's say it's staff loyalty,' she replied merrily. 'You know I used to work here?' He nodded faintly. 'And, well,' lowering her voice, Kat took on a sympathetic tone, 'I've heard the rumours. I know this is something of a trial period for you, and I would hate to see this place fold. So this way, everyone wins: I see my work back in my beloved magazine, and you get a massive circulation boost for your relaunch issue.'

Stevie deflated. Kat waited patiently. And just in case, she sweetened the deal even more.

'We should probably liaise on the feature together,' she suggested. 'Devon gets picky about who's actually in the room during the interview part, but if you were around, making sure everything went smoothly . . .' She let that sink in. 'How about you review the raw tapes and footage to make sure I don't miss any good stories?'

His eyes became slightly glazed as he considered all that time spent sharing breathing space with his idol. Then they came, the little words she'd been longing to hear.

'What's the price?'

Kat slowly exhaled. Her nerves were alive with adrenalin; her heartbeat danced in her chest. This was it.

End game.

'Three pounds a word for a three-part feature,' she paused, relishing the moment. 'And a staff position.' Stevie stared at her in surprise. 'I want a contract, complete editorial freedom and triple my old pay.'

Kat looked at him, suddenly nervous. She thought she'd backed him into a corner, but still . . . There was always a possibility he'd laugh her out of the office.

'Staff position?' he frowned.

'Now there's new management, a new leadership vision, I think there's a great opportunity here.'

There was another long pause as Kat watched him run the figures in his mind. Let him. She was asking an absurd amount, but Kat had picked her terms carefully. This wasn't about the expense outlay; it was about whether Stevie could ever forgive himself if she took the exclusive elsewhere.

'I wouldn't mention I came to you first,' she added sweetly, 'if you're worried.' Stevie's poker face slipped as he imagined what would happen when the exclusive was published else-where and the ChannelCorp bosses found out he'd passed. His career would never recover.

'Two pounds a word,' he managed to say. 'And your old wage rate.'

'Make it two and two-point-five, and it's yours,' Kat replied. Her savings account was suddenly looking about fifteen thousand pounds richer.

At the minor win, Stevie recovered his posture. 'I can give you that,' he declared, magnanimous in apparent triumph. Kat tried not to smirk. She'd inflated her initial demands just to give him the pretence of negotiation. Always make your opponent feel like it's their victory, the Popularity Rules said.

'The next issue goes to press in a week?'

Stevie nodded.

'Then you'd better hurry.' Kat stood suddenly and gathered her things. 'When my contract's signed, I'll set something up with Devon. We'll work around the clock and schedule a cover shoot.' Stevie hurried to the other side of the desk to show her out but Kat ignored his gesture.

'Whatever you need,' Stevie nodded. Kat paused in the doorway. Should she try and get Oscar back in too – demand a personal assistant, or hand-picked intern or something? No. She had other priorities to take care of.

'That Jessica girl,' Kat mused, as if it was an afterthought. She looked out across the office to where the star herself was idling with her feet up on the desk, chatting into her mobile. Kat turned back to Stevie and gave him a meaningful smile. 'I don't think we'll work that well together.'

Stevie blinked. 'No, right. Well, you don't need to worry about that.'

'I don't?'

Dropping his voice, Stevie held his finger to his lips. 'I was planning on letting her go anyway – not the best reflection of our brand, you know. But it's all hush hush for now.'

'My lips are sealed.' Kat could barely contain her glee. A rush of elation swept through her, strong enough to even make her lean over to air-kiss him. 'It's been a pleasure.'

With a twirl, she glided out of his office and all but floated back to the hallway.

She'd won.

Kat's breath shook as she waited for the elevator, oblivious to the noise and chatter around her as she ran over the meeting in her mind. She'd actually done it! All the strategy, all the planning; she'd used every status tool and power tactic the Popularity Rules had ever taught her, and it had worked. Her mother and Whitney were wrong: it had all been worth it in the end. Kat wanted to yell out a victory cry – anything to express the fierce joy inside – but she made sure not to let her feelings show. She had a reputation to uphold.

She was a *Louder* staffer once more! The office may be different, the name may have changed, but she was back where she belonged.

'Lauren!' Kat burst into their office at *ChicK*, full of excitement. 'I did it!'

'Did what?'

Kat laughed, 'Didn't you get my messages? I left you like, a dozen! *Louder*, Stevie – I did it. I got my job back!' Breathlessly, she relayed every detail of the meeting. 'You should have seen his face,' she grinned. 'Oh, it was perfect, like he knew he had no way out.'

'That's amazing!' Lauren exclaimed, pushing her paperwork

aside. 'I knew you could do it!' They hugged, Kat unable to resist jumping up and down in tiny leaps.

They were interrupted by a brisk knock on the doorframe. 'When you've got a minute . . .' Nina regarded them coolly, her fringe razor-sharp above a slim silk shift dress. 'Lauren, we need to confirm the final ad schedule.'

'Absolutely.' Lauren switched back into business mode with a brisk nod, but Nina had already marched away. Lauren turned back to Kat. 'You should go find Gabi. I'll only be ten minutes, and then we can celebrate. You know she's back with Mia, right? I'm thinking dim sum . . .'

'Hurry,' Kat pushed her out of the room, 'before I start brainstorming all the features I'll get to write with my *complete editorial freedom*!'

Lauren was barely gone before her phone began to ring. 'Lauren Anderville's office,' Kat reached across the desk to answer, idly leafing through the next month's issue.

'This is Buckley, Porter Buckley with Pure PACT.' The voice was American and gravelly.

'Can I take a message?' She paused on the music page layout; it had turned out exactly how she wanted, mixing pop girl acts with harder rock fare. She could do the same at *Louder* if she wanted; she could do *anything* at *Louder*.

'Sure, we just wanted to cross the Ts on the final contract. We're excited to see what Miss Anderville can come up with to launch our little campaign.'

'Ms,' Kat automatically corrected. She scrabbled around for a pen. 'Webb, you said, with . . . ?'

'Pure PACT. Promoting Abstinence and Chastity in Teens,' he announced proudly.

Kat paused, exhaling in a whoosh. 'And the contracts are . . . ?'

'Everything's ready to be signed, I just wanted a chat with *Ms* Anderville.'

'All right,' Kat replied faintly. 'I'll pass that along.'

She replaced the handset, her elation fading with every passing second. Purity? Abstinence? Cautiously, she reached for a stack of files on the side of Lauren's desk, the ones she'd pushed aside so quickly when Kat had entered the room. And there, hidden under a *ChicK* print schedule, was the confidential client fact-sheet that explained it all.

Pure PACT: bringing together Christian evangelical groups, political conservatives and even some Catholic subsidiaries, united in what they saw as the epic, noble quest to shame teenage girls into protecting their precious virtue. Because, apparently, a confident young woman making informed choices about her sexuality was nothing but filth and sin – they just needed some strategic brand repositioning so that the teen girls of today would swallow the message too.

Kat scanned the pages with dread. 'Purity' was mentioned twelve times; saving your 'gift' for your husband another three. She felt a shudder of revulsion just reading it.

'I found Gabi!' Lauren's voice echoed down the hallway as she rushed in. Kat stood, frozen by the desk. 'You coming?' Lauren asked, grabbing her bag and quickly twisting her hair up into a messy knot.

'Right, of course.' Kat recovered. 'I just . . .' she swallowed, holding out the booklet. 'I saw this.' She waited, watching Lauren's face as she recognised the print.

'Oh, that.' Lauren didn't flinch. She gave a laugh, taking it from Kat's outstretched hand and then flicking through it absently. 'I thought you'd want to see it. We get sent that stuff all the time.'

Kat blinked. 'So it was just a random mailing?'

'Sure.' Lauren tossed the booklet carelessly onto her desk and quickly applied a layer of lipstick. 'So, are you ready?' she asked brightly. 'The first round of cocktails are on me!'

'You're on,' Kat managed to reply, trailing silently down the hall after her.

Lauren was lying. Lauren was lying *to her*. That man from Pure PACT had said it himself: the contracts were signed! But something in Kat stopped her from interrupting Gabi's chatter as they all breezed out of the building onto the busy Soho street; something stopped Kat demanding the truth as they met Mia, laughing over the spread of cocktails and tiny nibbles.

She couldn't bear to know.

Not right then, not after everything had finally come together the way Lauren had promised. All that training and strategy, all those nights of networking and research; and every time, Lauren had been right there at her side. After all they'd been through those past months, Kat couldn't help but feel a faint sense of hope as she looked across the table at her friend. Lauren wouldn't do something like this; she wouldn't betray her values so completely.

Would she?

Pick your battles.

Social scenes are a weird mix of denial and amnesia. If you make a scene every time someone stabs you in the back, you'll become the number one drama queen, so stay cool. She may have spread mean rumours, and he might have cheated on you, but if you have a fit over it, you'll just split the scene apart in a messy war. Unless it keeps you looking powerful and in control, don't even say a word.

Just ask yourself: is telling someone what you really think of them worth ruining all your hard work and plans? Didn't think so. Find a way to pay them back later, when they can't trace it back to you.

Chapter Thirty-six

'Camilla, I asked for Hilary Duff clippings.' Kat flipped through the meagre file in front of her and sighed. It had been only ten days since her glorious showdown with Stevie, but already she was losing patience with the new *Louder* set-up: three website printouts and a tabloid photocopy did not background coverage make. She almost wished she'd demanded Oscar stick around: the boy was exhausting, but at least he was competent.

'And?' The intern rolled her heavily lined eyes impatiently. Jessica may be gone, but another mini-skirted girl had sprung up in her place, equally reluctant to do any sort of work at all other than scan the internet for her next band of dishevelled hipster conquests.

'These are about Haylie Duff.'

'Like there's a difference.'

Kat took a breath and reminded herself to stay calm. 'Sure,' she forced a pleasant tone, 'we know that, but I need the Hilary stuff too. Just stupid fact-checking.' She stretched her lips into a conspiratorial smile. 'You know what Stevie's like.'

At the mention of their boss, Camilla relented. 'Fine, I'll do it. He's in such a mood today.'

'Oh, I know!' Kat recognised a potential weak spot and gave her a sympathetic look. 'He was talking about getting the file storage unpacked.' Camilla blanched. 'I know.' Kat made sure to look thoughtful. 'Why don't you just hide away in the archive room during the staff meeting. I've got some more research I need, and that way I can tell him you're busy.'

'Really?' Camilla looked eager. 'You'd be saving my life! Filing makes me, like, die of boredom.'

'No problem,' Kat smiled through gritted teeth. She had spent months doing nothing but filing back when she was lucky enough to intern. 'Here's my list.' She passed across the page of requests that under any other circumstances would have the intern whining for hours.

'You're an angel,' Camilla beamed. 'Want me to run out for coffee first?'

'That would be lovely!'

There.

Kat sank back in relief as Camilla flounced away. Thanks to the Popularity Rules and a great deal of self-control, she could now make her interns work, rather than gossip idly all day. It may be a constant battle to keep her sarcasm in check, but it had to be worth it to get the job done.

'*See you at the gallery at eight?*' A chat message from Lauren appeared on her screen.

Kat paused. She had a phone interview lined up with an American singer that would keep her in the office until nine at least.

'*OK*,' she wrote at last. '*See you then.*'

Lauren could wait.

'Uh, hey Kat.' Nate stopped her as she passed, a lone familiar face in the revamped office. 'Got a minute?'

'Of course!' She detoured over to the 'web zone', closeted off from the rest of the floor behind a chest-high frosted glass partition. 'What's up? I've been meaning to come and say hi. This new floor plan makes it feel like we're miles apart!'

'You're settling in then?' he asked, rummaging in his drawer

413

for something. For a change, his desk was sparkling and clear. 'Back in, I mean.'

'Adjusting a little,' Kat admitted, drumming her fingers on the glass. 'But it's going well so far.'

'Cool . . .' he nodded, a little awkward. Kat wondered if he was still with Whitney, and what she'd said – if anything – about Kat. 'Anyway, I wanted to return some stuff – CDs and things you loaned me, ages ago.' He passed her an assortment of promo items.

'Oh, thanks, I'd forgotten about them.' Kat glanced through the pile. 'But there's no hurry, if you want to hang on to anything.'

Nate gave an awkward grin. 'Yeah, that's the thing. I'm, uh, leaving.'

Kat stared at him in surprise. 'What? When?'

'Now, pretty much.' Nate looked around and shrugged. 'I handed in my notice that day we found out about ChannelCorp. They wanted me to serve notice, to train up some new guys, but now that's done, I'm off.'

'But where will you go?' Kat felt a pang. Nate had been working there for years, one of the few people around she actually liked. 'I could check with some contacts if you want,' she offered. 'See if there's anything going.'

'No, it's cool. I'm actually taking a break from web stuff for a while. We're moving to Devon. Whitney and me,' he added, in case she didn't remember. 'She sold her flat, and we've found a cottage. We're going to try sustainable living for a while. Grow our own food, cut down our carbon footprint.' His expression lit up as he considered the rural idyll that awaited them. 'Anyway, she's waiting in the car downstairs. I just needed to clear some last things out. And say goodbye,' he added, hurriedly.

'Well, bye . . .' Kat hugged him, still processing the news. 'Good luck down there.' She paused. 'Whitney's downstairs, you said? She didn't want to come up?'

Nate looked incredibly awkward. 'Uh, no. She had to mind the car,' he explained, but she could tell from the way he avoided her eyes that he was lying.

'Oh. OK.' Kat swallowed. Despite the fact she hadn't reached out to contact Whitney either, the snub stung a little. 'Tell her . . . I wish you guys all the best.'

'I will.' Hoisting a small box of CDs, Nate took a look around and then gave her a mock-salute. 'Take care.' He walked towards the lifts, already striding like a man who chopped kindling and kept small livestock. His woodsman future awaited after all.

Kat stayed by his empty desk. For a moment she was tempted to follow him down and see Whitney for herself, to at least send her off with good wishes before they disappeared for ever into deepest Devon. But the urge quickly drifted away. Something was gone; whatever bond had kept them together through university and the last years in London had unravelled, and maybe it had happened even before Kat upended the status quo of their dynamic. She hadn't spoken to Whitney in over a month, but she hadn't wanted to, either. It was done.

Shaking off the past, Kat gathered her notes and made her way towards the gleaming new conference room for what would be her first staff meeting.

'Kat! Come in, come in.' Stevie smiled broadly and ushered her to a seat. Being Devon's preferred spokeswoman obviously afforded her a luxurious leather chair. 'How's my favourite staff writer?'

'Great!' Kat switched into her sparkly ChannelCorp mode

and gave a wide smile, resisting the urge to slap away the hand he placed on her back. Her lower back. Instead, she slipped out of reach and took her seat, sneaking a look around the table. For a moment, her shiny facade slipped.

There were so many new faces! So far, most of her time had been spent locked away interviewing Devon (with Stevie eagerly hovering nearby) and working fifteen-hour days to get her feature written, so Kat had barely had time to charm her interns into submission, let alone spend much time with the fresh crop of co-workers Stevie had stolen from other magazines. Kat swallowed, searching out any of the old team. Stevie had set about restaffing with swift and mercenary vigour, tempting the flashiest writers away from other publications with salary increases and a promise of the full use of ChannelCorp's perk package.

She was sitting at a table of strangers. Of strange men, Kat realised, taking another look. She was the only woman there.

'So what's everyone planning for October?' Stevie sat back and crossed his arms, and as the other staff began to pitch ideas, Kat tried to pull herself together. What would the Popularity Rules say? This was an opportunity, not a problem. Kat had been worried how her old co-workers would treat her – well, now she didn't have to. These new staffers would accept Kat as the scene queen everyone thought she was. Blank slate. And maybe being the only woman could work to her advantage.

'. . . plus we could have a new feature, a bling-o-meter: compare who's got the most ice!' A guy with fiercely side-swiped hair drummed the table with enthusiasm.

'Could work.' Stevie nodded slowly. Kat's mouth slipped open.

'Roll it out with a sponsor,' the writer continued eagerly.

'Bring in one of the jewellers, get some cross-branding going on.' Stevie began to smile.

'Get on it,' he instructed. 'Let's have more of this, guys; think about multi-platforms, user-generated content!'

'Dudes, I've got something.' The man across from Kat smoothed the sharp edges of his Mohawk. He paused, a slow smile creeping on his face. 'A groupie sex column.' There was a pause. All around Kat, the men began to nod. 'We get a panel of groupies, maybe some porn stars, strippers,' the man continued. 'Send it out online as well, let registered users post their own responses.'

'I like it,' Stevie decided, and although Kat knew she should just keep quiet, she couldn't help but lean forwards.

'It's an . . . interesting idea, but wouldn't it alienate our female readers?' The Mohawked guy stared back blankly. 'They might find it offensive,' Kat explained.

'No way, man,' he shrugged. 'The chicks who read *Louder* are like, totally liberated.'

'Right,' Stevie agreed. 'They'll understand how empowering it is, don't worry.'

'Oh.' Kat sat back, carefully biting the inside of her cheek until she tasted blood.

'What about you, Kat?' Stevie turned to her. 'What have you got lined up for us now? More exclusive material?'

'I'm working on a piece for next month on teen pop.'

'Hit me.'

'Well, I thought I'd look at some of the power structures and how those male-dominated fields use the teen girl as—' She caught herself, seeing Stevie's face pale slightly. 'What I mean is, I thought I'd focus on something mainstream instead of all those white indie bands. Demi, Miley, Taylor – they're all delivering big numbers right now, very hot.'

'Go on.' Stevie had recovered his tanned sheen, obviously relieved.

'Fresh, sexy faces in music,' Kat continued lightly, trying to hide her disdain. 'Movie synergy, tween dollars, going behind the machine.'

'A big photo-spread.' Stevie's eyes lit up.

'Yeah,' Mohawk man agreed. 'Maybe like a slumber-party theme? The girls singing into hairbrushes, pillow fighting?'

'Hot!' The table snickered.

'I suppose,' Kat agreed, her voice strained.

'I like it,' Stevie nodded, clicking his ballpoint rhythmically as he no doubt envisioned the barely legal lovelies frolicking. 'Now, where are we with reviews?'

Back at her desk, Kat stared idly at her mess of notes and tried to shake a faint sense of self-loathing. If her mother had been in that meeting . . . But it wasn't an issue, she reminded herself. She was writing the power structure piece, regardless of what Stevie thought. Technically, she didn't even need to play along with their macho games. Her contract was clear: complete, unfettered editorial freedom. But Kat knew that her life would be far simpler if she talked the corporate talk, even if the issue went to press with whatever she wanted. The circulation jump from the Devon Darsel exclusive would protect her for a long time, but she had to deal with the staff every day; setting herself up as the angry feminist again would hardly win them over.

'Hey Kat, we've got the Sony presentation at two,' a newbie features girl stopped by to remind her.

'Thanks, Ruby.' Ruby was nineteen and the daughter of Stevie's tennis club buddy. She had also 'lost' Kat's clippings pack every day until Kat mentioned she could put her on the guest-list for Devon's secret shows. 'I love that sweater, by the way.'

'Oh this? I've had it for ever,' Ruby sighed modestly, but she left with a smile. Kat would get her clippings that week.

It was just easier this way.

By the time Kat reached the gallery after work, she had talked herself into feeling marginally better about *Louder*'s complete transformation. The new offices were more central, and didn't pose a health hazard just reaching her desk, and so what if Stevie was steering them away from substance and meaningful debate? That was why the magazine needed her so much. In amongst the babes and bling, her voice of sanity would be that much more important. If anything, her presence mattered more than ever.

'I got held up,' she explained, finding Lauren trapped in a far corner between a vast video screen playing a loop of bouncing balls and a group of snooty twenty-something hipsters wearing an array of leggings and dishevelled mini-dresses. She didn't look impressed. 'But good news,' Kat continued. '*Louder* cut me my cheque, so I've started the search for a flat to move into.'

'There's no rush,' Lauren insisted, looking surprised. 'Really, you can stay as long as you want.'

'I know.' Kat shrugged, beginning to head back through the crowd towards the free bar. She spoke over her shoulder at Lauren, following behind. 'But I've been taking advantage of your hospitality for too long. It's about time I found my own space.'

'Do you want me to help?' Lauren squeezed in next to her and took a glass of cheap wine. 'I could ask some of my contacts if they know anywhere. I'm sure—'

'No, I've got it covered.' Kat paused, the chatter around them loud. 'What about you – anything new happening?'

'Nope, just work, the usual,' Lauren said vaguely, studying the exhibition leaflet.

'Really? How is work?' Kat tried to keep the edge from her tone. It had been over a week, and Lauren still hadn't mentioned anything about the Pure PACT group. Kat's hope that it was just a misunderstanding – a ploy for some larger plan – was fading fast. She hinted again, 'Did you find out about that new contract?'

'Oh, I meant to tell you: I got that job.'

'That's amazing!' Kat exclaimed, relieved. 'I want to hear all about it!'

But instead of explaining everything, Lauren stayed nonchalant, her gaze drifting over the crowd. 'It's nothing big – just some rebranding, market positioning, that kind of thing.'

'Oh.' Kat felt hollow inside, but couldn't bring herself to confront Lauren with the truth. 'Still, that's really good news,' she recovered, swallowing back her disappointment. 'You must be thrilled.'

'Oh, yes,' Lauren said, seeming anything but. 'What about you, at *Louder* – is it going OK?'

'Great,' Kat answered shortly. 'Really good.'

'It must be hard adjusting to all the changes,' Lauren said, her smile sympathetic. 'All those little things can add up. It mustn't even seem like the same magazine any more.'

'Oh no, it's fine.' Kat gulped down the rest of her drink and reached for another glass of wine. 'I mean, it's different, of course, but that's life, right? Things change. But it's a good opportunity; it's what I wanted.'

'That's good,' Lauren echoed, looking away. They fell silent until Gabi and Mia arrived, looking far too happy in matching jeans and cute printed T-shirts.

'So it's working out?' Kat asked quietly, when Mia and Lauren were caught up chatting to some others. 'You've decided to try long-distance?'

Gabi nodded, watching Mia with clear affection. 'I know it might not work, but I've got to try. I'll regret it if I don't.' She looked nervous but excited. 'We've worked out a schedule for visits, and she's got friends over there. We're nauseating, I know,' she added, 'but I'm just so happy!'

'I'm glad,' Kat smiled, even as she felt a stir of envy. She shouldn't hold it against Gabi for being brave, but something in her still smarted at Ash's betrayal.

'Darlings.' Freddie inserted himself between them, his navy suit marking the coming of autumn. 'What is this bullshit? Balls? Spirals of colour? They could have just photographed some puppies shitting rainbows for all the inane artistry around.'

'Lovely to see you too.' Kat made the effort to laugh and kiss him on the cheek.

'I quite like it,' Oscar said somewhat petulantly, almost hidden behind him. Or perhaps it was the tightness of his orange jeans squeezing all humour out of him. 'Hello, stranger.' He greeted Kat with a wounded look, reminding her just how unavailable she'd been.

'Hey sweetie,' she answered breezily, as if she hadn't forgotten to call him back all week. The handful of messages he'd left were full of job-hunting woe and romantic insecurity; Kat wasn't ready to face the full Oscar meltdown just yet, not when she had Devon and Stevie to babysit too. 'What's up?'

'Sweeping judgements about art, it seems.'

'You didn't have to come,' Freddie said, bored.

'But you made it sound so exciting.' Oscar's sarcasm was thick, and Lauren and Kat exchanged a quick look. The Oscar/Freddie break-up was looming any day now, and neither of them wanted to be caught in the crossfire.

'I heard you were doing a *Harpers* shoot next month,' Lauren interrupted quickly. 'And after swearing you wouldn't even touch that magazine again.'

Freddie laughed, relaxing against the bar with the look of a man about to launch into a scandalous story, but Oscar beat him to it.

'They threw money at him until he said yes. We all have our price.'

Freddie's jovial smile slipped. Oscar rolled his eyes. 'What? Did I steal your line?' He turned to Kat. 'Come look at the rest of the show. I haven't seen you in *ages*.'

'Maybe in a minute,' Kat replied, acutely aware of Freddie's eyes on her. 'You go on ahead.'

Oscar pouted, but he quickly recovered, drifting off into the crowd with Mia and Gabi. Freddie laughed awkwardly. 'Kids!' he joked. Kat and Lauren laughed along. 'Actually,' he turned to Kat, 'I was meaning to ask if you would do the shoot with me.'

'What? You mean, model?' Kat raised an eyebrow. 'Thanks, but that's really not my thing.'

'Of course it is.' Freddie dismissed her protest. 'We'll go to Iceland, make a trip of it. What do you say, Lauren? Are you in?'

'I'll have to check my schedule, but you should do it, Kat.'

'Really, no.' Kat imagined pictures of herself draped over icy rocks, dead-eyed, mannequin-like and layered with hideously expensive consumer goods. She shook her head firmly. 'I don't want to be objectified like that.'

Freddie laughed, as if her refusal was meaningless. 'Sure you do. What do you think you've been doing for the last couple of months, fucking astrophysics? I'll even tell the stylist to throw some leather Cavalli in there, keep your image intact, how about that?'

Kat bit back another objection. She'd find a way out later. 'Cavalli?' she said instead. 'You'll have to drag it out of Oscar's dead hands first.'

There was a pause. 'Yeah, I don't know if Oscar will be along for this one.' Freddie met her eyes with a long stare.

The subtext was clear, but Kat knew she couldn't just announce she was staying out of their mess. Instead, she looked away and replied casually, 'That's a shame. Still, I'm sure we'll have fun without him.'

Freddie relaxed. 'That's what I like to hear. See, you're already looking forward to it.' He swiftly changed the subject, launching into an anecdote about a celebrity child and her security blanket. Kat laughed along, relieved to be in less contentious conversational bounds. Then she caught sight of somebody across the room and all her humour disappeared.

Charlotte.

She was talking to another woman by the front window, ethereal in a gauzy blue dress and bare rope sandals. Her hair fell around her shoulders, long and simple, and she looked as if she wasn't wearing an ounce of make-up. Kat felt her whole body seize up with resentment. Ash was nowhere in sight, but he didn't have to be: Charlotte was glowing with serene happiness, every smile announcing that she was completely in love. She finished talking to her friend, moving towards the back of the room. As if on autopilot, Kat followed.

She found her in the small, white-tiled ladies bathroom, applying clear lip balm in the mirror. 'Kat!' she smiled, recognising her. 'How have you been? That dress is so cute, by the way.'

'Thanks.' Kat wished for a moment that Charlotte were a complete bitch. She would feel so much more justified in her anger if the 'other woman' was mean or possessive. Instead, she felt like she was hating Bambi. 'I'm good. How are things with you?'

'Hectic,' Charlotte grinned, closing her tiny beaded purse with a snap. 'My final coursework is due, so I'm trying to avoid a complete meltdown. Trying, and failing,' she confided.

'You're at uni?' Kat felt another hot spike of resentment.

'Studying fashion at St Martin's,' Charlotte confirmed. It was no wonder her skin looked so dewy; she was practically a teenager.

Oh, Ash.

'I'll let Ash know I ran into you,' she continued, as if reading Kat's mind. 'He told me you got your old job back. I'm so glad – we were both rooting for you.'

That was it. Something in Kat snapped. The thought of the two of them discussing her life, her dreams over some cosy Sunday brunch, or even sprawled in bed . . . She couldn't bear it any more.

'I wasn't going to say anything,' Kat began, careful to keep her expression supportive, warm even. 'But you seem like such a sweet girl. There's something I think you should know.' Charlotte blinked, her smile slipping a little. She wasn't stupid; Kat could see she had an inkling of what was coming. 'Ash and me . . . We were together. He's been cheating on you, I'm afraid.'

Charlotte swallowed. Her hands folded into small fists at her sides, but she kept calm. 'How long?'

'We started before he even met you.' For some perverse

reason, Kat found herself enjoying Charlotte's obvious distress. Why should she be the only one feeling insecure, inadequate? Why should she be the only one to hurt? 'I only found out about you when we met at that party. If I hadn't been there, he would have kept fucking around.'

Charlotte's lower lip began to tremble.

'Dump him,' Kat advised coolly, moving to reapply her own lipstick. 'He's nothing but a piece of shit.'

Charlotte made as if to leave but then turned back. 'Why did you tell me this?' Her voice cracked on the last word. 'Why now?'

Kat shrugged, still focused on her reflection. 'I thought you deserved to know.'

'Right. I'm sure this was all out of the kindness of your fucking heart.'

Kat turned at that. 'Oh, you're one of *those* girls, are you? Well, for your information, I'm not the evil seductress here; this isn't my fault. If you want to get angry, get angry at the bastard who was betraying you. And I'd get tested, if I were you,' she added, as an extra blow. 'I checked – I'm clean, but who knows where else he's been sticking it?'

Charlotte made a small sobbing noise and then fled. Kat turned back to smooth her hair into place, satisfied she wouldn't be faced with quite so much blissful happiness any more.

You can never win an argument.

Seriously.

Even if they're a dumbass, even if it's obvious, you'll never really win because the person you beat will always resent you for it. Until your popularity is secure, you can't risk backlash from anyone, so just accept defeat with a smile and know you'll prove your point some other way. Or, even better, avoid arguments in the first place; you'll end up looking like a bitch instead of the great person everyone should think you are.

Chapter Thirty-seven

After the angst, all-nighters and energy it took to get back in at *Louder*, Kat thought she'd have a chance to relax now her mission was complete. She was wrong. What with navigating Stevie Gold's new ChannelCorp vision of mediocrity, handling her uncooperative interns and keeping up her late-night party networking schedule – not to mention her actual journalistic duties – Kat's days became more stressful, not less. By the time the office emptied out for lunch after another delightful staff meeting, her cheeks ached from fake smiles, she had a headache taking root behind her eyeballs and there were what felt like permanent bite marks now indented on her tongue. Kat was ready to lock herself in the archive room and stay there until the end of the week.

But she still had work to do.

With a groan of resignation Kat put her sandwich aside, pulling her keyboard closer and letting her fingers rest on the keyboard for a moment as she steeled herself for the task ahead. She'd been avoiding this for too long. At last, Kat clicked in the search box and typed those two little words that could make her life so much more complicated.

Pure PACT.

She was being a coward, Kat knew: she should have confronted Lauren about that call weeks ago. If she'd just told her what the man had said, Lauren would have explained; they could have cleared everything up, out in the open with no room for Kat's whispering doubts and growing sense of betrayal. But she couldn't. Every time Kat even came close to bringing it up, something in her froze. Suppose there was no good explanation; suppose it wasn't just some part of a bigger master-plan. What if Lauren really was selling out, so completely?

It would ruin everything.

She'd never been one for denial before, Kat reminded herself as she finally forced herself to read the first page of Pure PACT misogyny and misdeeds. She'd always been one to pick the cold, brutal truth over self-deception, so why was it different this time?

Because it was Lauren.

A harsh, painful shard of fear and resentment had been building in her ever since discovering about the contract, and it was becoming harder to ignore. Kat couldn't bear to be proven right, all over again, but as she read on through page after page of reactionary sabre-rattling and cruel, spiteful sermons, it seemed impossible not to take Lauren's choices as a personal betrayal.

When her work phone rang, she picked it up without thinking.

'Katherine? Don't hang up again,' Susanne quickly added, her voice plaintive. 'It took me ages to track down this number.'

'Mum, hi.' Kat swallowed. She turned away from her computer screen and took a long breath, trying to ease some of her tension. The office was almost empty, only a lone web guy at his desk across the room eating a microwaved meal, and a staff writer on the phone – apparently Stevie's shiny new staff didn't need a work ethic.

'How are you? I've been worried.'

'I'm . . . fine.' Kat was surprised to find the sound of

Susanne's voice a comfort; she could just imagine her, sitting in her dim study at the college between tutorials. 'What have you been doing?'

'Oh, nothing new.' Her mum sounded surprised to find a normal question instead of more spitting acrimony. 'The conference went well.'

'I forgot about that,' Kat said quietly. 'Did your presentation work all right?'

'Yes, I think it was rather well-received. Not the way Julie Baxton's was, of course, but she always goes for crowd-pleasing over the content side of things.'

'I'm sure people appreciated your approach,' Kat reassured her. 'Sometimes the simple way is the best.'

'Does this mean you've had a chance to think about what we said?' Susanne asked gently. 'Because—'

'Mum, please.' Kat didn't want to fight. 'Not again.'

Susanne sighed. 'I just worry, that's all.'

'I know.' Kat swallowed, twisting the phone cord around her finger.

'Have you spoken to Whitney?'

'No. She hasn't been in touch. It's a shame,' Kat added, faltering. 'Not how it turned out in the end, but, well, I thought we were . . . *more* than that. I suppose you never know what people want you for, how they see your relationship.' She wondered briefly if she didn't prefer her pre-Popularity Rules outlook, when she couldn't assess someone's motives and ambition with quite the same cutting accuracy.

'That is a shame, sweetie.' Susanne paused, but then couldn't resist asking, 'And Lauren? How is she?'

Kat felt that shard of resentment again, glancing back at the Pure PACT website. She clicked to close it. 'It's . . . fine. It's all fine.'

429

Her mother must have heard something in her voice, because she waited, not saying a word. Kat kept twisting the cord, watching as the tip of her finger slowly turned a violent shade of maroon.

'Can you ever really forgive someone?' she asked, finally unwrapping the cord.

Her mother gave a soft laugh. 'Start with an easy one, why don't you?'

Kat exhaled. 'I just . . . I don't know. I thought things could be different. With Lauren. That it could be like before.' It sounded foolish even coming from her lips.

'Katherine,' Susanne urged her. 'Don't you remember what happened? You were devastated when she abandoned you. You barely spoke to a soul at that place for years; I was so worried.'

'I know, Mum, but it was a long time ago.' Kat didn't know whether she was justifying Lauren's actions or her own. 'I'm just wondering, how long can you hold someone responsible for what they did when they were a teenager?'

There was a pause. 'Perhaps you're right,' Susanne answered cautiously. 'If she really is sorry for what happened, then it could be time to let the past go. People can change, sometimes, so I suppose if she's a different person from the one who let you down . . .'

Kat felt the shard cut deeper. 'Right,' she said quietly. 'Anyway Mum, I have to go. I have so much work to do.'

'Of course. I just wanted to check in, make sure you were taking care of yourself.'

'I am, thank you. I think I'll have a quiet weekend,' Kat promised, already thinking of the long bath and the remainder of her *Veronica Mars* box-set that awaited her back home. 'You take care.'

'Love you.'

She was just settling in with the first episodes, wrapped in a fluffy dressing gown and clutching a mug of hot tea, when Lauren returned, more buoyant than she had been all week.

'I've got a surprise for you!' Lauren beamed. She kicked one patent leather heel towards the coffee table, the other at the TV, and planted herself in front of Kat with both hands behind her back. 'Pick one.'

Kat mustered some enthusiasm. 'That one.' She nodded to the left.

'Ta da!' Lauren sung out, presenting her with a ticket. 'We're going to Paris!'

Kat's heart sank. 'When?'

'Now!' Lauren waved another ticket around. 'I know you've been exhausted with the *Louder* switch, but we've hardly seen each other for weeks, so I planned the perfect getaway. Shopping, spa, fabulous food . . . We leave tonight.' She twirled around, obviously proud.

'That's . . . great.' Kat pulled herself upright and stared at the ticket. 'Wow, Paris. That'll be fun.' She sounded as if she was trying to convince herself.

'Oh,' Lauren's smile faded, 'I just thought—'

'No, really, this is lovely,' Kat insisted quickly, giving her a real grin. 'I'm just tired, that's all. I'm sure this is exactly what we need.'

'I figured Eurostar would be less hassle than fighting our way through Heathrow.' Lauren followed Kat to her bedroom. 'And this way you'll be able to relax on the train. Come Monday, you'll be back fresh and revitalised.'

'Like an expensive shower gel,' Kat agreed. Maybe this was the moment Lauren had been waiting for, when she would sit Kat down over a café au lait and some macaroons and explain what she was playing at with the Pure PACT project. Kat brightened. 'How long do I have to pack?'

'Not long. I made reservations for dinner before our train. I wouldn't try making you travel on an empty stomach,' Lauren added.

'Good plan.' Kat opened her wardrobe and stared at it blankly. 'Well . . . I'll meet you out front in ten minutes?'

'Perfect.' Lauren clapped her hands together in a familiar gesture of glee. 'This is going to be awesome, I just know it.'

Kat napped through most of the train journey, letting Lauren whisk them through station concourses and in and out of taxis. The lights of Paris blurred outside her window as she attempted to murmur suitable responses to Lauren's chatter. Three painkillers had reduced her headache to a groggy shadow, lacing her system with enough codeine that coherent conversation was beyond her. Declining midnight drinks, she drifted through check-in and tumbled into bed with only a faint impression of the gleaming marble splendour of her surroundings.

Until the next morning, that was.

Heavy brocade drapes and dark wooden headboards; bathroom taps that glimmered under intricate light fixtures – Kat felt as if she was sullying the gleaming splendour just cleaning her teeth. She discarded her planned outfit of jeans with a sigh, reaching instead for a jersey silk dress that would at least not get her politely removed by hotel security. So much for relaxing.

Unfortunately, her bedroom was the least of it. By the time Kat met Lauren in the lobby as planned, she was blinking from the reflections of the glossy chequerboard marble floors and curving balustrades. 'Umm, Lauren?'

'Morning!' Lauren hugged her hello. She perched on the edge

of an ornate antique chair, her golden colouring matching the gilt edging on what seemed like every surface. 'Did you sleep OK? You were so wiped out, we almost had to carry you up!'

Kat didn't reply, still gazing around the vast lobby.

'Isn't it gorgeous?' Lauren surveyed it with a sigh. 'I've been wanting to stay at the Crillon for ever, and luckily, I know a man who runs the marketing for the group.'

'Lucky,' Kat repeated. That was one way of putting it, but places like this – dripping with wealth and privilege – made her feel nothing but uncomfortable. Out of the corner of her eye she could see employees in crisp uniforms gliding past, waiting to serve every whim of their guests. She resigned herself to a weekend of effort and inadequacy.

'Come on.' Lauren bounced up. 'I know a great little bistro for brunch, and then there's shopping. I've got everything planned out.'

When Lauren made plans, she was serious about them. Kat spent the day whisked through a demanding schedule of boutiques, beauty treatments and sightseeing. They sipped *citron pressé* in St Germain, received artfully subtle manicures in the Marais district, and even found time to nibble tiny pastries under the gaze of Rodin statues in his garden.

And all the while, Kat's desire to act as if everything was fine between then gradually ebbed away.

Her resentment – until then smothered under exhaustion and deference to the effort that Lauren was clearly making – began to return, winding around her insides in a hot grip as the day passed, until by the time they set out for midnight drinks at the latest chic bar, Kat found herself answering with monosyllabic replies and snapping irritably at Lauren's every suggestion. Yet still Lauren acted like she was oblivious to

Kat's mood, chatting away as if everything was all right. In any ordinary person, Kat could have written it off as utter cluelessness; in a woman who had spent the past decade reading body language, tone and non-verbal cues from even the most fleeting stranger, the avoidance was even more infuriating.

'It's too loud in here.' No sooner had they been ushered to a purple velvet banquette than Kat wanted to leave. The club was low-ceilinged and dim, with pools of golden light cast across the black lacquered bar and plenty of dark corners that people were taking full advantage of. She sighed, restless and still itching with a hot spark of anger.

'We'll just have one drink and then go, OK?' Lauren ordered for both of them with the leggy waitress.

'I'm not a child; you don't have to bargain with me,' Kat retorted. Lauren's face became strained, but she did nothing but quietly sit and play with her charm bracelet.

'Aren't you going to ask if I'm all right?' Kat challenged, with mock-surprise. 'Or maybe you've been ignoring it all the time because you don't want to ask, because you don't want to hear it if I say no?'

Lauren's gaze shifted to the side as she checked to see if they had any witnesses. 'Kat . . .'

'And now you don't want me fighting in public.' Kat took an angry swallow of her drink, her civil act finally slipping completely. 'Because God forbid the Popularity Rules get broken.' The cocktail was cool in her mouth and hot burning down the back of her throat. She should get drunk. This would be easier drunk.

Lauren began to look anxious. She reached across and put one hand on Kat's arm. 'Calm down. Whatever this is, we can talk about it.'

'See.' Kat pulled back and folded her arms. 'You're still not asking. "What's wrong, Kat?" "What are you so mad about, Kat?"' she mimicked Lauren's drawl. 'It's not that hard.'

'Fine.' Lauren's voice was low. 'Since you seem to want me to ask, what the hell is going on with you?'

'I could ask you the same thing.'

Lauren sighed. 'Now you're just going around in circles,' she said. The waitress delivered another tray of drinks to the table. 'We didn't order these.' Lauren tried to dismiss her.

'*Non*, but the gentlemen over there wish to send their regards.' Her accent was thick as she pointed out the men; they lounged by the bar with expensive suits and artful facial hair.

'Thank you, but no,' Lauren insisted, not looking away from Kat.

'That's OK,' Kat replied at the same time, picking up the fresh cocktail and raising it in the men's direction. 'After all, aren't we always supposed to accept what someone offers with grace and dignity?'

Prompted, the men began to move over to their table. Kat gave them a wide, fake beam, but Lauren pulled her out of her seat. 'I'm sorry, we have to dash!' she told them, already propelling Kat towards the exit. 'Thanks so much!'

When they emerged onto the pavement outside, Kat angrily pulled away. 'That was rude,' she drawled, thick with sarcasm. 'No Popularity Rules points for you!'

'God Kat, what the fuck is going on?' Lauren finally exploded, just the way Kat had been waiting for.

'I don't know, Lauren,' she shot back, feeling her anger ignite. A strange euphoria was coming over her: this was it, no more excuses. 'Maybe there's something you want to tell me. About work,' she added, when Lauren still didn't say a word.

435

'About a wonderful new contract with those folks back at Pure PACT.'

Lauren breathed in sharply. 'Is that what this is about?'

'What do you think?' Kat began striding angrily across the street. Behind them, the Arc de Triomphe was lit up against a clear night's sky, and ahead, the Champs-Élysées stretched quiet and neat all the way to their hotel, but all Kat could see was a foreign city and the fucking distance still between them.

'Why didn't you say something? How did you find out?' Lauren trotted after her, heels clicking on the hard paving slabs.

'I answered your phone by mistake.' Kat kept her pace up, pulling her thin cardigan closer against the late-night breeze. 'And believe me, it was a mistake.' She wheeled around, stopping dead in the middle of the wide pavement to face Lauren. 'How *could* you?' Kat was shocked to find her voice cracking; she was on the verge of tears. 'How could you do this, after everything? What they stand for, what they believe in – it's awful, Lauren, you know that!'

'Kat—'

'If there's one thing you always believed in, it's empowerment!' Kat cried. 'To make informed choices, to have control over our own bodies. This is going against everything – everything!' Kat's fingernails were digging into her palms and her entire body was stiff with rage, but all she could feel was the awful ache of betrayal. 'It's not even like you're standing by and letting it happen; this is your pitch, your campaign. You planned every fucking part of it!'

Lauren clutched her evening bag. 'It's just a job, Kat. You're overreacting.'

'I'm over . . .' Kat blinked, disbelieving. In all the scenarios she'd imagined, there was never any self-righteous justification. 'Are you even listening to yourself? If it was just a job, you wouldn't have hidden it from me, like some dirty little secret.'

'I didn't tell you because I knew you'd blow it out of proportion!' Lauren cried. She took a breath and looked around, but they were alone on the pavement with traffic speeding by. 'Look, it's been a long day. Let's just go back to the hotel and talk about it in the morning.'

'I don't want to talk about it!' Kat screamed. 'I wish I didn't have to! But this is it, isn't it? This is who you are.'

All her insecurities, all the little voices she'd been suppressing for months now became a chorus in her head. She'd ignored the past, she'd tried to move on with their friendship, but it had been a false foundation between them all along.

Some people never change.

Kat shook her head slowly, the anger giving way to a grief that clawed inside her. 'I thought this would be different,' she whispered, backing away. 'I actually thought we could be friends, like before. But it's all still the same. You'd sell anything out if the price was high enough. Anyone.'

Lauren's expression hardened. 'It's just a job, Kat. Don't be so immature.'

'Maybe I am the immature one,' Kat shrugged, an awful gesture of defeat. Her throat was tight and she could feel tears stinging her eyes. 'To think that principles actually mean something any more, that you would draw the line somewhere. You said so yourself, in New York, remember? God, Lauren, what are you thinking?' she implored her. 'Is that what you want your contribution to the world to be? Is that who you are, in the end?'

'You know it isn't.' Lauren's reply was defensive, her lips set in a thin line. 'And God forbid I ruin this self-righteous indignation thing you have going on, but did it ever occur to you that maybe me taking this campaign is a good thing? Isn't it better I run it than someone who'll do something truly tasteless and damaging?'

'Lauren Amelia Anderville, the lesser of two evils.' Kat began to slow-clap her, bitter and fuming. 'I'm curious; what counts as tasteful when it comes to calling teenage girls sluts? Writing it on a T-shirt instead of scrawling it into their foreheads the way they did to me back at Park House?' Lauren flinched. 'Oh, you remember that, do you? Not exactly one for the yearbook, but I didn't have anyone looking out for me, did I?' Kat swallowed back angry tears.

'You don't know what you're talking about.' Lauren's eyes widened. She stepped back.

'I know you sold me out then, and you've done it all over again!' It felt as if her heart was breaking, but it was her own fault this time. Thinking for one second she could trust Lauren . . .

'I didn't sell you out at that party. I did it to protect you.'

'Did what?' Kat looked at her in confusion, and then the truth dawned. 'It was you?' she gasped. 'You did that to me?'

And to her horror, Lauren slowly nodded.

Chapter Thirty-eight

Kat reeled away in disbelief. Around her, ornate wrought-iron gates marked the entrances to great embassies, lights strung prettily on every tree branch, but Kat didn't notice the pale sweep of spotlights or the chill on her bare legs. In her mind she was eighteen again, tearfully scrubbing her skin raw in an empty dormitory bathroom.

Lauren grabbed her arm and held fast. 'Listen, I did it to protect you.'

'How can you—?' Kat could hardly find the words. 'Do you know what it felt like to be so humiliated?' She looked at Lauren as if she was a stranger. 'I couldn't even go to my own graduation!' All this time, she'd told herself Lauren's betrayal was a passive thing; that she may have chosen popularity, but she'd never meant to directly hurt Kat.

She'd been wrong.

'Trust me, it was nothing.' Lauren's voice was bitter. 'If you knew what they wanted . . .'

'But you did that to me, *you*!' Kat cried. 'How could anything be worse?'

A harsh smile appeared on Lauren's lips. 'You really don't get it, do you? There's always something worse. There's always a greater evil.' She dropped Kat's arm, and when she spoke again, there was an ugly edge to her words. 'You were drunk, Kat, so drunk you could barely even stand. Lulu and the rest – they wanted to lock you in a room with Patrick and see how far he could go. So yes, unless you count some permanent marker as a fate worse than rape, I'd say I protected you just fine!'

Kat shook her head, trying to keep away from the brutal reality of those words. 'But it wasn't just either/or. You could have told them to go screw themselves and helped get me back to the dorms, but you didn't.' She found her anger again, grasping for a sure hold. 'You took the easy way out to protect your fucking popularity – anything not to risk standing out.'

'I made the best compromise!' Lauren cried.

'That's just it.' Kat was tired of this. The arguments wouldn't change a thing; there was no taking any of it back. 'You can defend yourself all you want, but what you let them do to me, what you're doing with PACT – it's already too late; it should never have got that far!'

The Popularity Rules were one thing: chasing asshole executives across the city and negotiating your way to the top – even she'd smudged her moral boundaries and played along with that. But there had to be a point you said 'no further'; there just had to be. Kat shivered. 'Some things shouldn't be negotiable.'

They stood, silent on the wide footpath as the city hummed around them.

'You'll never forgive me,' Lauren finally said. She looked at Kat as if she'd only just realised the truth. 'I thought . . . Maybe, now we could—' She stopped herself. 'But you won't ever move on, will you? You can't ever let it go.' Lauren's expression slipped, breaking apart in front of her, but Kat was unmoved. This woman had done nothing but let her down.

'How can I move on, when you just do the same thing over and over? You never said you were sorry,' Kat flung back. 'Not for anything.'

'Sorry? That's what you wanted from me?' Lauren laughed suddenly, a forced, painful sound. 'Apologies don't mean

440

anything, Kat, or haven't you been reading the Rules? They're just words; they don't change a thing. You think it would have been different if I'd said it? That you'd have forgiven me and hugged it out and moved on? Being sorry is about actions, not words. It's about doing something to show you mean it, that you care.' She gasped for air, face flushed. 'So don't talk to me about apologies, because this has all been my apology!'

'Actions, not words,' Kat repeated pointedly, ignoring the rest of her weak excuses. 'And you still think the Pure PACT contract doesn't mean anything? You're a fucking hypocrite.'

'And you're not?' Lauren's voice rose. Her eyes were teary, hair tangling in the breeze. 'Don't make out like you're up on some moral high ground. You're doing it just the same as me, with *Louder* and Freddie and Devon; we all compromise to make it, so don't you dare think you're any better than me!'

'You know what? Screw all your moral relativity crap!' Kat yelled back. A pair of tourists taking a midnight stroll hurried past them, averting their eyes, but she didn't care. 'You crossed a line and you know it; you can't bring yourself to admit the truth because maybe then you'd have to think about what you've made of your life.' She paused for breath. 'Do you even have any friends? Real ones, whom you're not just working as part of a big strategy?'

'I could ask you the same thing,' Lauren shot back fiercely. 'You like to think we can all be perfect and principled, but look how that worked out for you. Before I came along, you were unemployed and alone!'

'So I'm supposed to be grateful; is that how this works?' Kat could feel the bitterness like venom in her veins. 'And not ever question a single one of your magnificent choices?'

'That's not what I meant.' Lauren began to backtrack. She looked stricken, cheeks mottled with an uneven flush and a smudge of mascara under one eye. 'Kat, this has gone too far. Can't we just calm down before—?'

Kat's phone began to ring, the sudden noise loud and insistent. She ignored it and started walking again, back towards the hotel and Lauren's literal guilt-trip.

'Kat!' Lauren hurried after her. 'You don't understand. You're making out like the Pure PACT thing is personal – it's not about you!'

'I'm a woman, aren't I?' Kat couldn't resist rising to the bait. 'I have a fucking uterus. How is this not personal?' She gave a bitter laugh. 'What's next, rebranding the abortion debate?' Her phone rang again, and she angrily turned it off. 'And you're right, this has gone too far. I'm done, OK? I'll move out as soon as we get back; give you more space for all that chastity brainstorming you've got coming up.'

'I don't want you to go!' But Lauren's plaintive appeal meant nothing to Kat – she still wasn't apologising, or even admitting for one moment she was in the wrong. 'Please, Kat, just listen!' Now Lauren's mobile began to ring. She paused, fumbling for it in her tiny bag, and Kat felt another stab of resentment. Even their fight wasn't important enough to make a priority.

'Gabi, what is it?' Lauren turned away slightly and listened. 'Is he—? No, OK, we'll get back as soon as possible.' She snapped the mobile shut and paused a moment, her breathing slowing as she visibly pulled herself back together. Then she looked at Kat, her face blank in an expression Kat knew well: the autopilot Lauren was back. 'Oscar overdosed; he's in hospital. They've been trying to reach us.'

Kat stopped. 'He . . . On purpose?'

Lauren shrugged thinly. 'I don't know. Come on, we have to go.'

Kat had no choice but to follow her into a taxi and back to

the hotel. Just like that, the fight was done, even though nothing was settled and anger still seethed in her system.

'Did they reach his parents?' she asked, wondering – treacherously – why they'd been called.

'I think so.' Lauren looked away from her, already reaching for her purse and sliding out a few crisp notes.

'Then why . . . ?' Kat let the question drop before she'd even finished, but Lauren turned back with a tight expression.

'I guess we're all he has.'

After that, they barely said another word. Lauren checked them out of the hotel, hailed a taxi to take them to the station and then negotiated with the ticket office until two seats on the next train to London had been procured. Kat let her do all the talking. She was wrapped in the fierce aftermath of the fight – everything said and unsaid still buzzing in her body. She wasn't an automaton like Lauren: she couldn't just switch it all off.

'Cookie?' Lauren offered her a biscuit from the small pack she'd bought at the snack cart. Kat silently shook her head. Lauren must have been worried about Oscar to consume carbs with such nonchalance.

'Kat, are we—?' Lauren swallowed, trying to find her words.

'I meant what I said,' Kat answered for her, quiet but determined. 'I'll move out as soon as possible, and write you a cheque for back rent.'

'I don't want your money.' Lauren looked pale, exhausted, but Kat tried not to care.

'I'll write you a cheque,' she repeated. 'Let me know what I owe for rent, and all the clothes.' Kat pulled out her iPod and fixed her earbuds into place, turning to gaze out of the windows that showed nothing but pitch black. Lauren was still watching her, still waiting, but Kat turned the volume up and let the first slicing guitar chords wash over her; sharp and aggressive, they crashed and spun in the way she longed to right then, sitting still and tense as the miles rushed by.

It was six a.m. by the time they reached the hospital. Lauren stayed at the front desk, trying to find somebody who knew much about anything, but Kat pushed through a set of double doors and wandered the faded yellow hallways until she found Gabi, stretched out on a row of plastic chairs in an empty hallway, a paper coffee cup by her side.

'He's still unconscious,' she said, eyes bloodshot and tired. 'They pumped his stomach, put him on an IV and gave him . . . I don't know, something to balance whatever chemicals he took.'

'What was it?' Kat sat down next to her and gazed at the wall opposite, where a row of old health posters curled at the edges.

Gabi shrugged. 'Coke,' she replied, pulling her hood up over tangled hair. She looked tiny. 'A lot of it. Ecstasy too, some roofies.'

'Fucking idiot.' Kat said it quietly, but it still felt like sacrilege under the flickering strip lighting. 'Were you there?'

'Nope. Freddie found him at the flat. Put him in an ambulance and then called around until he got me.'

'Freddie's not here.' Kat looked around. It wasn't a question.

'Nope.'

'And his parents?'

'They're not coming.'

'Fuck.' Kat exhaled. She tilted her head back against the cold wall. 'You should go home, get some sleep.'

444

Gabi nodded, already reaching for her bag. 'Did you guys have fun in Paris?'

Kat sighed. 'Not at all.'

He finally woke up after seven, when weak light flooded through the high strip windows. There were five other beds in the room, filled with sleeping bodies hooked up to any number of machines and drip feeds, but Oscar was the only one who looked like a child. She forgot sometimes he was a child, Kat thought as she stood over the bed. Nothing more than a selfish, stupid child.

'Here, don't try and talk.' Lauren waited for the nurse to pull out his tube and then offered a cup of water. Oscar coughed, raising his head high enough to take the straw between his lips. 'You gave us all a pretty good scare.' Lauren smoothed his hair down, the way he liked it to go.

There was silence. Oscar flopped back onto the pillows and stared at the ceiling.

'I'm going to go see about getting you discharged.' Lauren shot a look at Kat over his body. He shrugged. 'You can stay with us, while you figure out . . .' she trailed off. Freddie's absence was glaring.

'He can take my room,' Kat said, studying the jagged lines on his monitor. 'It won't take me long to pack.' Lauren's eyes flashed, but she didn't object. The Champs-Élysées and their fight seemed an age ago, not just a matter of hours.

'Is there anything I can get you?' Lauren asked him gently. 'No? I won't be long.'

The room was silent again, save for the reassuring beeps and rushes of air from the machines around them.

'So . . .' Kat began. She didn't feel anything, looking down at him: no shock or concern. All her emotions had already been spent. 'Were you trying to kill yourself, or did this just get out of hand?'

'The famous Elliot tact.' Oscar announced the words as if he were reading a script. 'I'm surprised you came.'

'They called.'

'I've been calling you all month.'

Kat felt her guilt return, but then she stopped. 'I've been busy.'

'With your shiny new job.'

'Right.' Kat was thrown. She'd expected him to be embarrassed, even contrite, but instead, bitterness radiated from every word. 'You didn't answer my question.'

Oscar turned his head away. There were dark shadows under his eyes and his lips looked painfully dry. She wished for a moment she had balm or moisturiser in her bag, but then he gave a casual little shrug, as if he hadn't snorted half a coca plantation and landed himself in hospital. 'Does it matter?'

'Well, actually yes.' Kat didn't know how to get through to him. 'One would mean you're monumentally stupid, and the other would mean you're monumentally fucked up.'

'You don't need to worry,' he finally said. 'It won't happen again.'

'So it was on purpose? Jesus, Oscar.'

'No, I didn't mean to . . .' For a moment, he was almost vulnerable under the harsh fluorescent light. 'I just wanted an escape.'

'All the way to the ER. Good call.'

'Did you know?' He turned back to her suddenly, fixing Kat with a sharp stare.

'About what?' Kat replied, but she knew exactly what he was talking about. It must have shown, because he made a noise of disdain.

'You did, I can tell. How long?'

446

'I really—' Kat looked away. 'It's none of my business.'

'How long?'

Reluctantly, she told him. 'A few weeks. A month, maybe.'

Oscar just looked at her. 'And you didn't think to, I don't know, mention it to me?'

'Like I said, it's none of my business.' Kat didn't like where this was going. 'Your personal relationships have nothing to do with me.'

'Right.' Oscar's voice was dripping with sarcasm. 'Because that's not what friends are for.'

Kat was silent. Right now, Oscar wasn't so much a friend as an unnecessary burden.

'I thought so,' he said quietly. 'Why don't you just leave?'

'You're acting as if this is my fault,' Kat couldn't resist protesting.

'It isn't?'

She got up angrily. 'I'm not your keeper, Oscar, and neither was Freddie. You should think about taking responsibility for your own life some time.'

'Thanks for dropping by,' he called after her. 'I appreciate it *so* much.'

She hadn't slept in twenty-five hours, but Kat refused to rest until she was out of Lauren's flat. The majority of her things were still boxed from her last move, so Kat threw the rest into a jumble of black bags and boxes and piled them into a taxi. It felt like a small betrayal to go from Oscar's bedside to Freddie's doorstep, but Kat pushed the faint tremor of guilt aside. She only needed a place to crash for a couple of days, and she could hardly put Gabi in the middle of things.

'*Mi casa es su casa.*' Freddie greeted her with open arms. 'You look bloody exhausted. Here, let me take those.'

The converted warehouse was vast, full of steel pillars and bare brick. Kat followed wordlessly to the blood-red guest-room and dropped her armful of baggage.

'I really appreciate this, thank you.'

'Don't even think about it, love.' Freddie paused. 'And, uh, Oscar's all right?'

'Oh. Yes. He'll be fine.' Kat looked for something in her bag to avoid his guilty look. 'So you're off to New York?' she asked brightly.

'Yes,' Freddie looked incredibly relieved she wasn't pressing him about Oscar. 'To shoot a bunch of spoiled socialites for some magazine that will probably go bankrupt before it hits the stands.'

'Oh, the trials . . .' She managed to smile.

'I'll leave you to sleep, love.' Freddie winked. 'Keys are by the front door. I'll be back next week.'

She nodded. Minutes later the door slammed and Kat was left alone.

Completely.

For a second, Kat remembered when she'd last felt so isolated: back at the start of summer, when she'd been desperate enough to embark on the whole Popularity Rules project in the first place. Had she really come so short a distance so as to be back at square one again?

No, she told herself, rolling under the cover. She wasn't the pathetic shadow of herself she'd been back then. She had her job at *Louder*, a list of invitations and a contacts book packed with people who would drop everything to have lunch or drinks with her. Lauren had betrayed her, and it may ache to accept that right now, but Kat had always been the strong one. She would be fine without her.

She would be just fine.

Stay on top.

Don't give it up. Even when you've achieved your goals, you can't afford to let your game slide. When you stop playing by the rules, your status will fall again – you'll slip back into your old miserable world before you even realise what's happening. Keep up to date with the scene and stay on top of who's hot, because the new kids coming through will all be looking to take you down.

Chapter Thirty-nine

The trick about guilt, Kat soon realised, was not to think about it. Over the next weeks, she drifted between her new Clapham rental to the *Louder* offices, to a noisy crowded party and then back again, all the time focusing on the small, manageable things: organising her notes for a new story, chasing down a guest-pass, the choice between crayfish and rocket or roast beef in her lunch sandwich. It was surprising how quickly time could pass with a careful schedule of trivial decisions, and wrapping herself in a soundtrack of insistent rock chords every moment of the day, Kat could almost drown out the ache of loneliness and those tremors of regret. But they would pass, she was sure; she just needed not to think about it, and it would all pass.

Lauren hadn't called.

'I can't believe she hooked up with Adam!'

'I know! He only split with Mena yesterday. Does she have, like, a radar or something?'

'Probably. It's in her bag with the knee-pads and blow.'

Kat braced herself, making sure to smile before she re-emerged into the viper's nest of the women's bathroom. Ruby and Camilla barely looked over as they carefully touched up their make-up, but Kat didn't mind. After all, it took some concentration to juggle lip-gloss and character assassination with the same breath.

'And you know she only fucked Craig for the Arcade Fire tickets.'

'God yeah. You would have thought she'd hold out for a laminate.'

'Are you kidding me? That slut gives it up for two Miller Lights and cab fare.'

Kat rinsed her hands and tried to think happy thoughts. Calming, pleasant thoughts that didn't involve a bare room and the forceful indoctrination of the feminist canon. At first she'd just ignored it, but weeks of bitchy comments were wearing her down. These girls were toxic.

'Did you hear about this?' Ruby turned, a gleam in her dark eyes.

'Hmm? No,' Kat tried to be pleasant. 'I must have missed it.'

'Paula in the art department,' Camilla added, running her fingers through her long hair, never once taking her eyes off her own reflection. 'She's like, such a whore.'

'Really?' Kat scrunched a paper towel into a ball and tossed it neatly into the bin. Happy thoughts. Happy fucking thoughts.

'You know, if management found out about what happened with Adam, they'd probably fire her,' Ruby mused, a mean little smile on her cherry lips. 'Technically, it was office property they fucked on.'

'Oh my God, you have to tell!' Camilla squealed, spinning round.

'Maybe.' Ruby glanced back at Kat. 'What do you think I should do?'

Kat carefully pulled out her lipstick and applied a neat layer before replying. She didn't like the direction this was going. In fact, she didn't like much about Ruby at all.

'It depends,' she shrugged, feigning boredom. 'It sounds pretty trivial to me. Do you think it's worth your time?'

There.

Ruby's eyes flashed slightly at the put-down. 'I guess,' she agreed, momentarily defeated.

Camilla finished preening. 'Are you coming out later?'

'The ChannelCorp thing?' Kat tried not to sigh at the thought of it. 'Yes.'

'See you there then!'

Not that she wanted to. Kat headed back to her desk with resignation. As if spending eight hours a day in the same building as the staff wasn't exhausting enough, now she had to put on a happy face and party with them too, all in the name of corporate pandering.

The toxic green post-it on her screen didn't help to lift her mood.

'Not again!' Kat ripped it away and marched straight to the corner office. These chats were practically becoming a regular part of her routine: 1. Write interesting, provocative article, 2. Get yelled at by Stevie. Repeat, until hell froze over or she beat him unconscious with that framed photo of himself with Bono he loved so much.

'I'm not changing it!' Kat warned, with barely a high heel over the threshold. 'And you can't make me.'

'But Kat,' Stevie leapt to his feet. 'You've outed him!'

'I think he outed himself,' she told him firmly, 'when he went trawling for gay sex on the internet.'

'This guy is our biggest Christian breakthrough act!' Stevie ran both hands through that careful hairstyle in panic. 'We can't run this.'

'No, he's ChannelCorp subsidiary, MegaBeat Records' biggest act!' Kat couldn't even muster the effort to charm and cajole. Basic civility was about all she could manage today. 'And outing him wasn't the point of the article.'

'Then enlighten me!'

452

Kat rolled her eyes. 'Did you even read it before having a fit? It's about hypocrisy and the whitewash of alternative sexualities in music. He's barely even mentioned!'

'Then you can pull the reference.' Stevie looked relieved.

'No, I can't.' Kat sighed. 'That's kind of the whole point. Again, did you even read it?'

Stevie glared back. 'Are you trying to screw this company?'

'I'm trying to write something useful,' she explained calmly. 'Expose some industry truths. You know, inform, entertain, challenge. Or have you forgotten what those things mean?'

'Fucking hell, Kat!' Stevie hurled a file across the office. 'Every piece is the same. Gender crap, feminist bullshit—'

'And it will be, according to my contract,' Kat finished sweetly. Stevie seethed as she turned to go. 'So I'd better go check that the subs didn't accidentally omit anything from my copy. See you later.'

Kat returned to her desk with some measure of pride. She hadn't sworn, thrown things, or given in to the temptation to inflict bodily harm. Technically, she should have followed the Popularity Rules and manipulated him into thinking a subversive exposé was just what *Louder* needed, but really, it was all Kat could manage not to scream. In her eyes, that qualified it as a particularly successful encounter.

Of course, the problem with doing battle with her editor was that the war never ended. He hadn't liked her last story, and he wouldn't like her next either. And every time it was the same: he ranted, she smiled patiently, and the copy was filed regardless. But Kat was finding it increasingly hard to muster that patient smile. Recently, it was resembling more of a grimace. Constant tension and endless fights: her days at *Louder* now seemed to stretch into a never-ending performance, always holding back and keeping her true feelings in check.

It wasn't even as if her stories were inaccessible any more – the training peddling feminism in *ChicK's* clothing was inadvertently paying off and now Kat made sure to mask the political venom with a few well-placed quips and gentle disdain, drawing the reader in with mainstream topics before delivering those cutting conclusions. Not that Stevie would ever notice. Kat sometimes thought he only scanned her work for the dreaded watch-words: homosexuality, feminism, power, system, male-dominated . . . She remembered her threat to him and clicked through the internal network to review the final page layouts, carefully reading her article for any changes. None? Good, she wouldn't have to fight him again for at least another week.

Oh, the luxury.

Kat was the last to leave the office that night. Everyone else disappeared early to attack the free bar over at the party venue, but she wasn't quite so enthusiastic. A ChannelCorp event to reward their advertisers, showcase their latest acts and ply every major shareholder with crates of champagne? It was nothing but one great big conflict of interest, and it made Kat ill to even think about. Besides, she liked it best when the office was empty: when there was no bitching or petty egos to spoil the clean design and opaque glass decor. Without having to worry about power struggles and status, she could actually think.

Not that thinking was a good idea.

With a sigh she reapplied her eyeliner, pulling on her coat to stroll the two streets over to where Stevie's members-only club had been temporarily invaded by ChannelCorp's nearest and dearest. This was part of the deal, she reminded herself, hurrying as a light drizzle of rain began to fall. Making nice with these people was a necessary evil, and besides, it was a good thing she had the chance to network with the corporate side of things. Should Stevie ever find himself out of the job, she wanted to be certain of her own security. By the time she reached the venue and made her way down the elaborate staircase to their den of iniquity, Kat had nearly dragged herself out of the bad mood. Then she caught her reflection in one of the mirrored wall panels. Dark glare, angry scowl. That just wouldn't do. Intimidating and stylish was one thing, unapproachable bitch another, so with painstaking self-control, Kat let out a slow breath and reassembled her reflection until there was nothing but a warm smile and welcoming expression staring back at her. She could fake it for a few more hours, Kat decided, before retreating to her DVD box-sets and take-out.

'You made it!' A high-pitched cry came from behind her.

'I did!' she echoed, mirroring Camilla's insincere tone and air-kisses. Beneath her black chiffon Victoriana blouse, Camilla's neon pink bra was clearly visible, perfectly matching her lipstick.

'Oh my God, Cami!' Ruby raced into the cloakroom. Her fringe cut across her eyes in an aggressive stripe, the hem of her black Lycra dress clinging to the very top of her thighs. 'You have to come look. The burlesque demonstration is starting!'

Burlesque?

Kat's heart sank as Camilla grabbed her hand and pulled her into the main room. She would have thought the Dita von Teese aesthetic would be 'like, so 2007', but the room was already packed with people, long red velvet curtains covering the walls and art deco furniture lining the floor. There were chandeliers, a glittering mirrored bar and waitresses with 1920s-style cigarette-girl uniforms. And lining up on-stage, half a dozen negligee-clad dancers were urging the revellers to learn some hip-thrusting, chest-jiggling moves.

'Let's do it!' Ruby grinned, downing her drink in a final gulp.

'I've taken stripper-cise classes.' Camilla looked at the stage nervously. 'You think this is the same?'

'Sure,' Ruby reassured her, eyes gleaming dangerously. 'Less grinding, more kicking. Coming, Kat?'

'I'll pass.' That was an understatement.

'Come on, aren't you supposed to be the liberated one?' Ruby's glossed lips twisted into a sneer. Kat looked back at the stage. Dolores from advertising was peeling off her blouse as her co-workers whooped from the front row. Liberation indeed.

'Maybe after a drink or two.' Kat forced another smile. 'You two go show them how it's done.'

Camilla and Ruby didn't hesitate, making a beeline for centre-stage and the harsh glare of the spotlight. Kat retreated to the bar.

'Rum and Coke, please. Double,' she added bleakly.

'Getting into the party spirit; now that's what I like to see.' She'd barely taken a single sip before Stevie appeared beside her with a grin that made Kat's skin crawl. He'd taken time to change since the office, and was now wearing black jeans and a black T-shirt scrawled with The Alarm's old logo. A nice way of reminding everyone of his editorial success, Kat noted, trying to edge away.

'Awesome party.' A group of men accosted Stevie, slapping him on the shoulder and jostling Kat from her stool. 'Bet you had fun auditioning the girls!'

'Someone had to do it!'

'Ha!' They laughed and clinked beer bottles before crowding closer to get a better view.

'You going to have a go?' Stevie gestured towards the stage, his eyes drifting down Kat's body.

'After you,' she replied sweetly. Throwing her drink at him would be a waste of good alcohol. And God, did she need alcohol right now.

'Funny,' he grinned at her. 'But I'm more of the spectator sort.'

'I kind of guessed.' Kat looked around for an escape.

'What about you?' Stevie edged closer. 'You like to watch?'

Kat took another gulp of her drink to refrain from hitting him. Luckily, a blonde woman came to the bar and Stevie paused, momentarily distracted by the cleavage displayed by her plunging, bustier-style top. Kat thought she recognised her, but the opportunity to get away was too good to miss.

'Oh, I see . . .' She gestured vaguely past him and backed into the crowd. 'Catch up with you later!'

For the next hour Kat kept to rum, Cokes and a disciplined networking plan. She circulated, smiled and even ignored the pole-dancers who had tastefully replaced the burlesque act as the evening's entertainment. The room was packed with ChannelCorp execs, and she was on a mission to cement her status as the jewel in the *Louder* crown.

'The user-generated content campaign had such amazing feedback,' she smiled at the anonymous suit beside her. He was VP of European operations, Stevie's immediate superior and thus worthy of a few platitudes. 'Were you involved with that?'

'Well,' he tilted his head modestly, 'we had a great team, but yeah, I guided that one.'

'Good work!' That was the great thing about alcohol, Kat decided as she drew some more suits into the conversation. It made statements like that sound almost sincere. Not to

457

mention the way it slowly smoothed over the sharp edges pressing painfully in her chest, almost letting her forget herself.

'Can you believe they actually ran it?' A man with a thick tie knotted at his throat was exclaiming, his cheeks flushed. 'Fucking brand suicide.'

'Whoever that ad company is, they're screwed,' another guy agreed, flicking through the pages of a magazine.

'I wouldn't have taken you for a *Teen Vogue* sort of man,' Kat commented with a smile, knowing better than to reveal her ignorance with a direct question.

'You seen this?' The man waved the magazine. 'Advertising standards people are having a field day.' They seemed thrilled at whatever the scandal was. 'Whoever made the call to launch has got to be the dumbest fuck around. Even the *Daily Mail* is baying for blood!'

Kat took the magazine. One page showed a typical teen magazine feature on back-to-school style, but opposite was a full-page advertisement. It showed two girls: one radiant, with a sweet, demure blouse and an athletic-looking boy gazing at her in adoration, the other, tired and hard-eyed, her mini-skirt hiked high, messy hair and a clique of girls in the background whispering with mean looks. 'Slut' was scrawled on her forehead, 'Virgin' on the other girl's, and above them, the text read, *What do you want them to say?*

Pure PACT.

'Seriously, what the fuck were they thinking?' The men were still laughing, but Kat just stared at the ad in confusion. It was appalling. Not just tasteless and insulting, but phenomenally bad from a strategic perspective – instead of rebranding abstinence as something cool and modern, the campaign revealed the ugly truth behind all the rhetoric, showing the message as something narrow-minded and misogynistic.

Kat didn't understand it. Lauren knew better than this – Lauren knew everything when it came to image and messages. She had to have seen how the ads would be received, that there would be complaints and outcry and . . .

Of course.

Kat gasped, the truth suddenly descending. Lauren had done this *on purpose*. She'd followed Kat's sarcastic suggestion, writing Pure PACT's subtext right on the models' faces so that nobody could be in any doubt what they really meant. Far from promoting her clients' cause, she'd used their money and name to smear them in the boldest, most obvious way. The men were right: this was sheer career suicide!

Blinking at the page, Kat ignored their chortling and the grinding dancers on-stage. She sank down into a nearby booth and tried to think of another explanation, but there was none: when the dust settled, PACT would be a laughing stock. After something like this, they'd probably have to disband and put their plans for a pure, chaste teenage population on hold for a while. But Lauren? Her professional reputation would be ruined for years to come. Why would she do something like that?

Because it was right.

'Hey, here's the talent!'

Kat jolted back to the party. The finance guys had drifted away, already forgetting about the PACT scandal, and Stevie was shifting over for a new group to join them. 'Guys, kick back, make yourself at home. I'll go find you some drinks.'

'NP – no problems, dawg.'

Kat almost choked, looking up in horror to find the pale, pimply faces of G-Link sliding into the circular booth, their baggy denim now accessorised with the bling a multi-platinum album provides. In the months since she'd last had the pleasure of their company, they'd achieved every bit of the success she'd feared; now a couple of bodyguards loomed over them, glaring menacingly at anyone nearby, and a matching pair of giggling twins snuggled between the boys, their truly impressive breasts straining at clinging white mini-dresses.

'Hey girl, I know you.' One of the skinny white guys tugged on his massive G pendant and winked at her.

'Anthony,' Kat answered faintly, her mind racing to think of the right tactic. Reminding him of their last, pepper-spray-filled encounter might not be the best move, so she opted for a blank look instead. 'I don't think we've met.'

Anthony, or rather, Triple A, squinted at her through the dim light for a moment before leering. 'Nah girl, you so fly I'd sho' remember you!'

Kat silently thanked her makeover and tried to edge further away from the men, but that only pressed her up against the solid muscle of their bodyguard: P-Dog, she thought his name was.

'An' then, he was all like, up in my grill but I was all like "hell no!"' Daryl B gestured wildly to the girls. They giggled admiringly. Or maybe they were just high.

'So I leap in all up to start somethin',' Flava continued, 'but the fuzz bust in and . . .'

Kat sipped her drink quietly as the bragging continued. The execs around her were lapping it up, despite probably being raised on meaner streets than these middle-class poseurs, and the blonde woman from the bar took a seat too, nearly lost under the shadow of their baseball caps. Even Camilla was hanging eagerly on the edge of their crowd, trying to get close to the rappers.

'Niggaz gots to represent!' Daryl finished with a fist-pumping yelp. The blonde woman couldn't help but laugh, quickly covering it with a cough. Kat looked at her with new interest, still trying to decide where she knew her from. The record label, perhaps, or maybe a PR firm? Kat was glazing over more at each new party or club night, and forgot too many names.

'Hi,' she began, leaning over with a conspiratorial tone. 'You drew the short straw then, huh?'

'What do you mean?' The woman was older, in her thirties perhaps, her hair cut in a complicated layered style, and the plunging neckline of her corset top lined with a handful of thick chain necklaces.

'Babysitting the band,' Kat explained. The woman gave a faint smile.

'I don't actually work for them, thank God.'

'So, what do you—?'

'Ladies! You've already met, fantastic.' Stevie returned, liberally splashing champagne over every glass. 'Eliza, this is the chick I was telling you about. Maybe you can hook up for an exclusive, huh? Mark your return to the spotlight!'

Eliza?

Kat blinked, and then the woman's features rearranged into something familiar. If she ignored the hair-dye, heavy make-up and surgical enhancing, she could almost see the woman whose honest, raw music had been soundtracking Kat's life for years.

'Eliza Monroe?' Kat gaped in disbelief. 'What are you . . . ?' She couldn't find the words, watching as one of the rappers casually threw an arm over Eliza's shoulder. The last press photo she'd seen had shown Eliza barefoot and brunette, painting abstract oil pictures in her Portland studio.

'The guys here are sampling one of my songs,' she explained, obviously pleased.

'Word!' Flava whooped. Eliza bumped her fist to his.

461

'The label think it could be huge,' she continued, surreptitiously hitching up her bustier. 'Like Dido and Eminem. It's great timing, because I'm relaunching this year with a new album – some awesome producers, a whole pop-rock thing.'

'Oh,' Kat managed. 'That's . . . great.'

'So, girlie.' Triple A leaned closer and drawled in Kat's ear. 'Wha's' up?'

Beneath the table, a hand gripped her knee.

Kat took refuge in her drink and ran through her options. 'Nothing much,' she replied at last, removing his hand and smiling absently at the table. Eliza sent her a sympathetic look, but she didn't say a word.

'Aww, c'mon.' The boy moved his hand back, higher this time, and draped an arm around her. 'Don't play like that.'

Kat's heart began to beat a little faster.

She glanced around for an easy escape, but there was none. Crammed in the back of the booth, Kat had no way of extracting herself save climbing over the table, and that would cause the kind of scene she didn't want, not in front of ChannelCorp's collected royalty. The group burst into laughter again at another hilarious anecdote and the music blared a little louder.

So Kat sat perfectly still and let the conversation flow around her, resigned to Triple A's arm weighing on her shoulders and his hand, heavy on her leg. Retreating into herself, she waited patiently for somebody to move or give her a reason to leave; another dance routine, a fire, nuclear apocalypse. She wasn't fussy.

And then the hand began to inch higher.

Popularity has a price.

Like everything worth a damn in the world, you'll have to pay to get what you want. It might be time, money or all the effort you put in, but something will be sacrificed to get ahead. Don't be a baby about it and focus on all the compromises you've made – just be grateful you had the choice at all. Other girls would give up everything for these secrets, so just remember what life was like for you before and focus on the prize.

It's all worth it.

Chapter Forty

Kat froze.

'Don't do that,' she managed at last, pushing away from him.

'You got a problem with me?' Triple A's voice was loud, and immediately the rest of the group fell silent and turned to stare at her. Kat swallowed, remembering what had happened the last time – the pepper spray, her probation, the start of this whole mess.

'I said, you got a problem, bitch?' Gripping her arm painfully, the rapper glared at her with icy eyes. Eliza looked away, but the rest of the group waited expectantly. Stevie shot her a warning stare.

'No.' Kat forced a trembling smile. Just don't think about it, she told herself.

'The hos are here!' Daryl whooped suddenly, breaking the tension as a pair of the strippers flocked towards the table. In a moment, the conversation was flowing again and Kat was forgotten, Triple A's arm still locked around her shoulders.

A calm detachment settled over Kat as she watched her co-workers laugh and joke: their painted faces and loud cries of insincerity almost lurid in the dim lights – the same detachment she'd wrapped herself in for days now. The painful irony wasn't lost on her. After everything she'd screamed to Lauren about principles and beliefs, Lauren had gone down in flames for the feminist cause while she was the one left with a sweaty hand creeping up her thigh and her mouth clenched shut so she wouldn't jeopardise her precious career.

Was this really who she was now?

Kat slipped back into reality, as if pulling herself from sleep. Her bag was on the floor beside her feet; she unzipped it without looking and reached inside. Side pocket, second compartment – she threw it in every night without even a thought. Some things, summer hadn't changed.

Kat closed her fingers around the small metal canister and turned to Triple A with a fierce glare. Eliza must have caught her expression, because she rose, already slipping out of the booth.

'Get your fucking hands off me.'

Kat's voice was harsh, and carried despite the cheap hip-hop beats thundering around them. Heads snapped around to stare in her direction, but Kat didn't care. She pushed away from his embrace and stood, adrenalin surging through her as she stared at the pathetic excuse for a man in front of her.

He snorted, arrogant until the end. 'Whatcha gonna do, bitch?'

Kat smiled, the familiar weight of the canister in her hand. 'Only what you deserve.'

Triple A was already screaming by the time Kat lowered the pepper spray and quickly climbed up onto the table, kicking bottles and stray fingers aside. She looked down at the rapper with satisfaction as he clawed his face through the bitter mist. Sobbing and pathetic. Good. Another G-Link member and a random ChannelCorp exec had been caught in the spray and flailed helplessly in their seats. The rest of the group stared at her, aghast.

'Milk will soothe their throats,' Kat suggested, picking her way through the glasses and hopping down on the other side of the table. 'But they'll need a trip to the ER. And Stevie?' Kat turned to him; his face was frozen. 'Consider this my resignation.'

Kat was halfway up the main staircase when a hand caught her arm. She spun around angrily.

'Woah, it's OK. It's just me.' Eliza reeled back. 'You left this.' She handed Kat her bag.

'Oh.' Kat felt her pulse slow. 'Thanks.'

'No,' Eliza said with a small smile. 'Thank *you*.' She turned to go back down.

'Wait, you're not coming?' Kat called after her.

She looked up Kat and slowly shook her head, her earrings rattling with the movement.

'But how can you? Go back in there, I mean.' Kat's disapproval must have shown, because a defensive expression slipped over Eliza's face.

'You think I'm selling out, don't you? With the pop songs and—'

'You're wrong.' Kat cut her off, hurrying down the stairs until they were on the same level. 'It's not about the music. You should make whatever kind of album you want; it's your art. But the rest of it . . . ?' She looked at Eliza, at the corset and the cleavage and the shadow of the icon she'd adored for so long, and despite their differences, for a moment, it was like looking in the mirror.

'It might not be worth it,' Kat told her, her voice choking slightly. 'The price you pay . . . it might not be worth it in the end. And you can't take it all back.'

She wanted Eliza to hear her, to really understand what she was saying, but the other woman's gaze flicked back to the main hall, and the scandalised chatter spilling out. She wouldn't listen.

'Good luck,' Kat told her softly, and then she walked away. This time, nobody followed.

What had she just done?

Kat felt giddy, her entire body suddenly shot through with endorphins as she hurried down the neon-lit street. What had she done? The question repeated as she played it all back. Not the pepper spray part, or causing that scene with G-Link, but all the rest of it: months of smiling vaguely through bullshit conversations, tolerating bitchiness and venom without a single word. Abandoning Oscar, pushing Lauren away. And for what – status that wasn't real? A magazine that was barely a shadow of the publication she'd loved? Alan would never have wanted this for her.

Kat could hardly believe what she'd become.

It had been so easy; that was what scared her the most. The lines she'd crossed hadn't been marked out with bright flashing letters and warning signs: she'd glided over them, fixing her mind on other things and carefully pretending that the small shiver of conscience she felt didn't matter at all. She'd wanted so hard to succeed, to be undeniable, that each tiny price had been so simply justified. We all make compromises, she'd told herself, while accusing Lauren of that very same thing.

Kat strode towards the main road with new purpose, waving down a taxi and directing it to Notting Hill. After all these years, she finally understood the choices Lauren had made: to be popular and accepted, to play along for the sake of the bigger prize. They both had burned to be recognised, respected, to make all those people who had ignored them clamour for attention and, thanks to the Popularity Rules, they'd succeeded. But for what? The Popularity Rules weren't an answer in themselves; they simply showed the world at its worst, and instructed how to play by its harsh rules. What they chose their lives to be, that was down to them. Down to her. And what a mess she'd made.

Kat paid the driver and climbed nervously out of the car. The momentum that had carried her there seemed to disappear completely. The things she'd said . . . What if it was too late to make things right?

It took her a full minute, wavering on the doorstep, before she could reach out and press the buzzer. There was a pause, and then Oscar's voice rang out.

'Yup?'

'I . . . it's me, Kat.' She swallowed. 'Can I come up?'

The wait stretched for another minute, until Kat deliberated ringing again. Then, finally, she heard the door click.

Oscar was lounging on the couch, flicking through a magazine as if he hadn't moved in hours – even though Kat knew that the buzzer was on the other side of the room. He didn't look up.

'Hi,' she started, awkward. He looked healthier now, but even the sight of him made her think of the hospital, and how coldly she'd behaved. 'Are you . . . Are you doing all right?'

'Am I about to go slash my wrists, you mean?' Oscar asked, turning a page. 'No, thank you for your concern.'

Kat swallowed. 'Is Lauren here?'

'She's in Sussex, a school reunion thing.'

'Oh.' Of course, the big Park House alumni event was tomorrow. Kat cleared her throat and considered all the ways she could try to apologise. She could beg, and plead over her transgressions, or appeal to his sense of loyalty. Or she could be real. Walking over, Kat threw herself down on the couch next to him and sighed. 'I really fucked things up, huh?'

Oscar almost smiled, but she could tell he was trying to maintain indifference.

'I'm sorry,' Kat told him simply. It was sort of liberating, having nothing to lose. He surely couldn't hate her any more than he already did. 'I was a complete bitch to you.'

His eyebrow flickered. 'Go on . . .'

'It's just . . .' she sighed. 'You made me feel as if you were my responsibility. The way you followed me up to London and attached yourself. I'm not saying it justifies how I treated you,' Kat added quickly, 'but do you see where I was coming from?'

'I only did it because I was like, your biggest fan. *Was*,' Oscar emphasised.

'I know. I suppose I don't deal too well with the whole fan dynamic.' Curling her legs up under her, Kat reached for her favourite throw.

'You seem like you're handling it pretty well, what with Lacey and Cara and Freddie—'

'That's different,' she cut him off. 'They're just in it because I'm the latest scene star. You practically worshipped me when you had nothing but my articles to go by.'

Oscar shifted. 'Maybe I did go kind of OTT,' he admitted, looking up at her for the first time. 'But you should have told me about Freddie. How would you feel if I'd known about Ash and that art school girl and—'

'I know, I know!' Kat apologised again. 'I was wrong about that; I get that. Really, I'm sorry.' Their eyes met for a moment and Kat tried to convey all her sincerity. Oscar nodded slightly, and when he spoke again his voice had lost some of the bitter edge.

'How sorry?'

'Sorry enough to sit through *Centre Stage* with you,' Kat offered, spotting the DVD cover under a pile of celebrity magazines.

'And the sequel?'

'See, now you're just pushing it.'

Oscar waited while she set up the movie. 'We're not OK just because you came and said the right things. You know that, right?'

'I do.' Kat reached over and squeezed his hand. 'But it's a start, isn't it?'

He sighed. 'I suppose.'

'Then I'll take what I can get.'

Oscar fell asleep before the final performance, but Kat wasn't so lucky; she spent the rest of the night out on the balcony, wrapped in a thin blanket and thinking over everything about Lauren and the Popularity Rules. Despite it all Kat had told herself for the last ten years, she was coming to realise that she hadn't let go of that teenage betrayal; she hadn't moved on at all. For some reason, the wound had been deep enough to shadow her all this time, those traces of insecurity hardening her against the world until she wrote everyone off before they'd even had a chance to let her down. It wasn't that she'd been wrong – about the shallow scene or all those weak, passive men – but Kat had felt something different these past months: an ease with people that helped her expect a little less, and appreciate a little more. The Popularity Rules painted such a bleak picture of humanity that every genuine connection or moment had taken Kat by surprise. She'd relaxed. She'd been having fun.

She'd been with Lauren.

As pale dawn light spilled across the sky, she knew what she had to do. Or, to be precise, where she had to go.

> 'True popularity isn't about being liked. It means people are too jealous of you to be a real friend, and scared enough that they pretend they are. If you want real friendship, go someplace else.'
>
> Anon, cabin log – 1989

470

Chapter Forty-one

It took three different trains to get her to the middle of the countryside, and a place Kat liked to call hell, but by the time she arrived at the wrought-iron gates, the traumatic schoolday flashbacks were in full force. From the itchy second-hand blazer she'd been forced to wear to the indignity of gasping her way through swimming lap relays, it all flooded back.

'Here is fine,' Kat told the taxi driver at the end of the winding drive, feeling as if she'd regressed ten years in a matter of hours. She climbed out slowly and took in the tall red-brick buildings, neat playing fields and the crested flag rippling lazily from the North Tower.

Park House Preparatory School.

With a sigh, Kat began the slow walk on the gravel road towards her doom. Cars passed her on the way, no doubt filled with old classmates eager to relive their happy adolescence. She hadn't been the only one miserable there – hindsight had taught her that – but Kat was sure she was the only outcast foolish enough to go back for this, the ultimate popularity contest.

'Hello!' She was greeted on the front lawn by a polished woman in a pale blue dress, standing guard over a table of nametags. 'And you are . . . ?'

'Katherine, umm, Katherine Elliot.' She was ashamed to find herself tongue-tied. Perhaps jeans and a Liz Phair T-shirt hadn't been the best choice of attire, but she hadn't wanted to wear a costume for this.

'You're not on my list.' The woman frowned. Kat squinted at her nametag.

'No, Penelope, I didn't RSVP.'

Penelope's lips tightened. 'Well, here, take one of my spare ones. And just write your name there. Would you like to pledge a donation to the fund, or buy some raffle tickets?'

'No, I think I'll just go . . .' Kat gestured towards the main hall. She was struck by a vague memory of Penelope as a perky, obedient girl hanging on the edge of Alison and Lulu's crowd.

'Lunch is a buffet on the back lawn,' Penelope called after her. 'Followed by the alumni cricket match!'

It was incredible how little had changed in ten long years. The classrooms were still dark, wood-panelled and musty, and the dining hall smelled faintly of macaroni cheese. The only nod to change was a shiny new technology centre and security cameras nestled in strategic corners. Kat checked each room in turn for Lauren, but there was no sign of her, just a frozen shrine to the worst years of her life.

'Oh my God, is that you, Kat?' A familiar squeal echoed in the hallway, sending a shiver down Kat's spine. Alison. Kat caught a glimpse of dyed blonde hair and expensive jewellery before she waved vaguely in her direction and then slipped through a side door. She hurried down a flight of stone steps and automatically cut through the courtyard, taking a well-worn path into the woods.

Kat didn't have any reason to expect it, but she knew before she even reached the reservoir that she'd find Lauren there. It was their spot, the place they would sneak off to after curfew, not to smoke or drink the way the other students would, but to lie on the banks of the water and listen to old cassette tapes, planning the great adventures they'd share. But despite her certainty, it still filled Kat with relief to see Lauren, shoulders hunched as she plucked pebbles from the ground and tossed them gently into the water.

Kat walked closer, lowering herself next to Lauren without a word. They sat for a moment, watching the murky water.

'I saw the PACT ads,' Kat finally offered. 'What will you do now?'

Lauren shrugged. 'I don't know. Maybe go into the non-profit sector.' She shot a sidelong glance at Kat. 'Those crazy feminist groups are the only ones who'll have me now, anyway.'

'Us crazy feminists are good like that.' Kat kicked off her Converses and lay back until she could see the sky. It was still the most beautiful thing about this place, the way the sky stretched boundless over the patchwork countryside. 'It sounds like a plan. We'd be doing something worthwhile, at least.'

'We?'

'Us,' Kat agreed, the tension she'd been carrying for weeks – years, even – finally melting away. Forgiveness, always such a remote concept to her, was suddenly as simple as the calm she felt lying beside her oldest friend: a choice, to be happy, or not. 'Now that I quit *Louder*, I'll have time to spare between freelance assignments.' She pulled out her iPod and handed Lauren an earpiece, dialling through her library until she found a song they both knew by heart.

They were going to be all right.

'But all this is just a stop-gap until you find a way to rule the world, right?' she added, only half-joking.

Lauren smiled, quiet and real. 'Absolutely.'

They lay there together, the water lapping at their feet, until the final chords had drifted away. And then Kat played another.

Acknowledgements

Thanks first must go to my wonderful agent, Jonny Geller; Alice Lutyens, and everyone at Curtis Brown. To my editor, Emma Rose, who believed in the book from the very beginning, and the rest of the amazing team at Arrow. Thanks to my father and sister for their enthusiasm, and to the friends who read every draft and supported me through the (many) years: Elisabeth Donnelly, Narmada Thiranagama, Veronique Watt, and Dom Passantino.

For the Poptext years: William B. Swygart, Matthew 'Fluxblog' Perpetua, Sean 'Said the Gramophone' Michaels, and Tom 'ILM' Ewing. And for general inspiration and distraction, thanks to Amy Sherman-Palladino, Emma Forrest, Rosie Thomas, Joss Whedon, Rob Thomas, Max Martin, Baz Lurhmann, and Aaron Sorkin.